JOEL RIVER

AND THE

ZOMBIE CHEERLEADERS

An Acadia Academy Novel

ASH MANNING

KANNON

Published by KANNON
Sydney, New South Wales, Australia

First published in 2025

National Library of Australia Cataloguing-in-Publication entry:

Manning, Ash. 1968–
Joel River and the Zombie Cheerleaders/ Ash Manning.
978-0-6458571-9-1 (pbk.)
Speculative fiction--Young adult fiction.
Paranormal romance--Young adult fiction.

Cover and interior design by JUJU QUEEN

ISBN: 978-0-6458571-9-1

DEDICATION

For Truman Capote, Harper Lee, Eudora Welty, Carson McCullers, and Anne Rice: Thank you for teaching me that the South is a haunted place, a holy place, and a place worth writing about. Your stories carved paths through shadow and light, and I've done my best to follow them with reverence and wonder. Each page of this book bears the trace of your influence and the echo of your strange, beautiful worlds. And to Martin, my dearest friend, partner, and unwavering emotional support: This book is also for you. ♥

CONTENTS

ACKNOWLEDGMENTS

It is true that it takes a village to create a book. Therefore, I want to acknowledge the input of the team at Stein & Wilde, who believed in this story and gave it a home. To the incredible editorial team: your insight, care, and patience is much appreciated. I'm especially grateful to the early readers who offered encouragement, clarity, and the gentle truth on rough drafts. Your thoughtful feedback was a great help through the writing process.

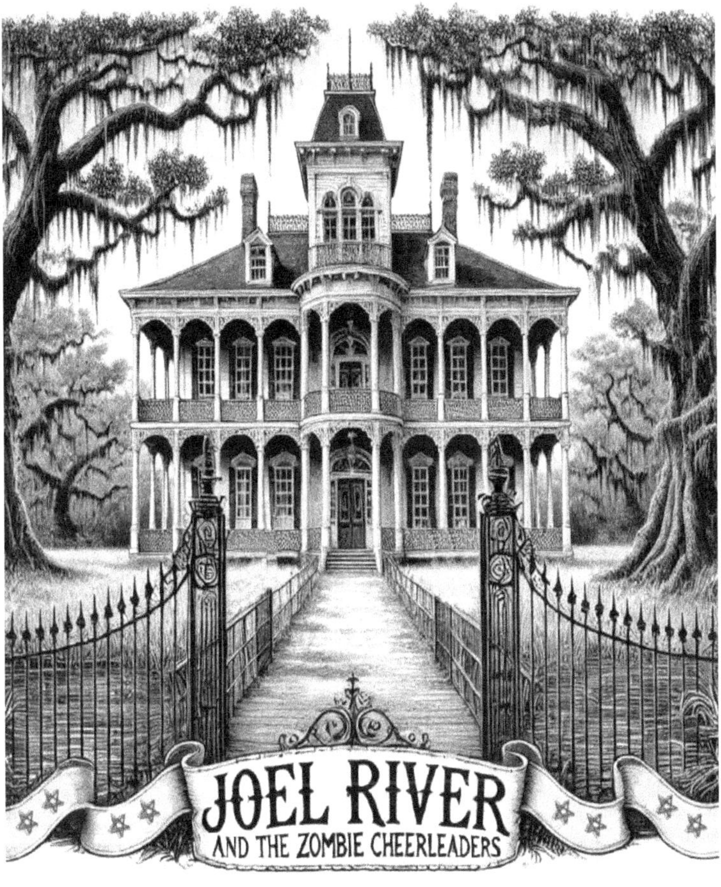

JOEL RIVER
AND THE ZOMBIE CHEERLEADERS

KANNON

PROLOGUE

Joel was trying desperately to explain, about the rumors that had caused the problem between them, and about the awful thing that had happened to him the year before they met, before he'd come to America to be a junior at Acadia Academy. The awful thing that had nearly broken him; that had woken his strange ability, his dreams of the future. Most of all he was trying to explain his feelings for the guy standing before him – his Louisiana prince.

It had taken so long for him to work his feelings out, not the least because of the zombies, vampires, and ghosts and such. Everything that happened since he'd arrived in Louisiana had been overwhelming and unbelievable, and crazy, but magical and wonderful too. Before he could explain any of it properly, he had arms around him. Strong arms holding him firmly but also carefully, gently. Joel thought of the first time those arms had held him that way. He felt the same rush of helplessness now, but this time the wave of emotion that hit him was not frightening but thrilling, though it still left him as limp as it had that first time.

As he leaned into that feeling, the memory of that embarrassing first day faded to nothing, replaced by the intensity of this new moment. Then those strong arms held Joel still as their lips suddenly met, so softly at first,

1

then more urgently. The delight of it made Joel dizzy; a delicious light-headedness. He clung to his prince's arms, fearful of falling to the ground like a dead weight. The kiss was sending tremors through his whole body, lighting up nerve endings Joel didn't know he had. It was as if a fire had been lit inside him. He was kissing his Louisiana prince with his whole being. It's what he'd hoped for – for so, so long. His first kiss with a guy. His first kiss ever. His first kiss with the guy who had so completely stolen his heart from the first moment they'd met.

THE SUMMER

MEET (NOT) CUTE

The walk from the bus stop in Acadiaville's town center to his new school was taking longer than Joel thought it would. When he'd mapped it on his phone it'd said it was a fifteen minute walk. Well, that must've been based on the pace of an Olympic athlete. An athlete with very long legs and exceptional lung capacity, travelling at a full sprint. Joel's natural pace was less Olympic athlete and more awkward sloth. With the full backpack he had slung over his shoulders, and the large suitcase with one broken wheel he was dragging along behind him, like an unwilling R2D2, his pace was even less impressive. He'd already been walking twenty minutes when the male voice in the GPS on his phone announced in a bored Southern accent that he'd only just reached the halfway point.

'You've got to be kidding!' Joel shook the phone, as though that would make the GPS come to its senses. 'You said fifteen minutes!'

He stopped beneath the shade of a massive live-oak tree festooned with Spanish moss, shrugged off the backpack and sat down on his suitcase, needing to rest for a while and catch his breath. This was his third rest break in twenty minutes. Full of stamina he was not. Full of jetlag and exhaustion, oh yes, he sure was.

As far as roadside, middle of nowhere places to rest went, it was a pretty good one. He looked up through the gnarled branches of the tree to the cloudless blue sky above. The shade was a relief from the sun, cool on his shoulders where the backpack straps had cut in and made him sweat. A slight breeze slinked through the shade, making the Spanish moss quiver, and taking the heat out of his face and hands, the only part of him not covered by dark clothing.

It had probably been a mistake to wear black jeans and a black long-sleeve t-shirt on the luggage-laden walk from the bus stop to Acadia Academy. He really should have changed into cooler clothes when he got off the bus. In his defense, he thought it would only be a brief stroll and hadn't expected it to be so humid, not having ever been to Louisiana before. He also couldn't have known that the roller on his suitcase would break. It'd jammed just minutes into the walk, just as he passed the town boundary sign that read: 'Acadiaville, The artistic heart of Cajun Country, population 3000'. Joel figured "artistic" referred to the dozen or so boujee stores gathered around the town's central square. From what he saw the stores didn't sell anything practical. It was all art and craft supplies, books, patchwork quilts, crystals, and oat-milk lattes. Not a bag of Cheetos or can of soda in sight.

Once he was sitting down he realized how overheated he was. He used his fingers to comb his shaggy brown hair out of his eyes. His scalp was hot and his hair damp from sweat. He bet his face was flushed red as well. Not a good look. Not quite a hot mess, but an over-heated mess, definitely. He lifted his t-shirt to fan his face, looking around to make sure he was completely alone, that no-one was watching. Tall swamp cypress trees crowded the water on both sides of the road here. He looked behind him, where the road curved sharply to the left, and ahead where it curved to the right. This short stretch of road was hidden from view on all sides. No-one could see him here. He knew he was being ridiculous, because he was miles from anything, but after what had happened to him last year he'd been super shy about his body. To the point of never wanting anyone to see any part of it, not even his belly button. Thus the neck to ankle black clothes. The breeze tickled the skin of his exposed stomach but otherwise the t-shirt made a poor fan and didn't help him cool down much. It was seriously humid, literally swampy.

Now that he was sure he couldn't be seen, he opened his backpack to check that his most valued, most secret possession was still there. He slipped his hand inside, brushing his fingers against the familiar softness hidden there. The instant he felt it, some tight part of him loosened, like a breath he hadn't realized he was holding. It was still safe, still there. A small voice inside him chastised him for needing this for comfort. But lots of people had ways to give themselves emotional support, right? It wasn't *that* weird. He zipped the backpack closed quickly. Some things were too important—and too easy to make fun of—to risk leaving out in the open.

To his left, to his right, ahead of him and behind him were miles of swamp, with the narrow road snaking its way through on the only dry ground – like a long, dusty bridge. The unhelpful GPS voice had called the swamp "Bayou Jeanne". When Joel Googled it on his first rest break he'd learned that Bayou Jeanne was one of the largest swamps in Louisiana, and the most pristine and untouched. Acadia Academy, his new school, was somewhere in the middle of it.

A bird sang far off in the swamp. It was a song unlike any he'd ever heard before. The birds back home in Australia didn't sound like that, kind of light and joyful.

And he would know. After what happened last year he'd spent months alone in his bedroom, causing his parents to say he needed a hobby. Something to get him outside in the fresh air, and preferably doing some form of exercise. They'd suggested tennis, soccer or basketball. He'd chosen bird watching. He chose it because, for the last year, every time he fainted he heard birdsong. Sometimes he even had dreams of birds when he was passed out. Well, just one bird actually. Always the same bird. A bird he'd never seen before. At first he only did the birdwatching ironically, and to annoy his folks, but after a while he kind of got into it. Part of him hoped that one day the birdwatching would help him figure out why he was hearing birdsong and having dreams of birds whenever he fainted.

Now would be a good time to explain the fainting thing. Joel's doctor had explained it to his parents like this:

> Joel has something called NMH which basically means his blood pressure can suddenly drop due to certain triggers, like when he's too stressed. That drop in blood pressure makes him feel dizzy or lightheaded, and sometimes he will even faint. It isn't dangerous if he lies down and lets the blood flow return to normal, but it can be scary and unpredictable.

When Joel had to explain it to anybody he just said "I'm a bit fainty". He hated how it made him feel fragile, like his own body was a traitor. The breeze picked up a little and he closed his eyes to listen to the strange joyful bird song, using it to settle himself in this unfamiliar place with its swamps, oak trees and Spanish moss. He'd been in Louisiana less than twenty-four hours, flying in to Louis Armstrong International Airport from Australia in the early hours of the morning. He then spent five hours in an uncomfortable seat in the airport arrival lounge forcing himself to stay awake while he waited, first for dawn to come and then for the time his aunt Penn was supposed to pick him up. But that time came and went. He tried to call his aunt but the call wouldn't go through. After another two hours waiting she still hadn't turned up so he did an online search and found a bus from the airport to Acadiaville.

Of course, right in line with his luck on the trip so far, the bus was leaving a little under a half hour from then, on the far side of the airport. He'd rushed from one end of the airport to the other, at an extreme pace for him, then across a huge carpark to where the bus was just about to pull out. After some frantic waiving of hands and shouting he was allowed to board. Then he was finally on his way, heading to a new life in a new school. He allowed himself to doze on the bus. That had been a mistake. He'd had another one of the strange, hyper-real dreams he'd been having ever since the terrible thing that'd happened to him the year before.

*** ***

He'd dreamt of a school bus crashed on its side in a swamp, half-swallowed by black water, its yellow paint faded to the color of old bones. In the water near the wreck, a few sad pom-poms floated like clumps of swamp grass. The bus's windshield was cracked, spider-webbed with a thousand tiny fractures, and beyond it in the murky, dark interior of the bus, something moved. A rustling, a stirring, a sound like dry leaves whispering together. The doors, twisted and broken, gaped open, and from the darkness within, something was emerging. Skeleton thin, bedraggled, two teenage girls were crawling out of the bus, moving like spiders. Pale, rotten things, streaked with mud and moss, they were clearly dead, and yet they moved. Those two girls emerged first, then three more, and yet more were crawling out behind them, all dressed exactly the same, in cheerleader uniforms.

Joel's breath caught and his dream-heart pounded. The girls dragged themselves out of the bus, their skirts torn, their smiles frozen and empty. Their hair hung in wet ropes, glistening in the dark moonlight. One of them twisted her head too far to one side, bones popping in a slow, deliberate motion. Another opened her mouth as if to speak, but no sound came out, only a foul gurgle of water.

Beyond the crashed bus and the dead cheerleaders, on a scrap of land barely above the water, a priest stood in the shadow of a ruined, partially-flooded church. His hooded cassock clung to his frame, heavy with damp. His hands were outstretched, his fingers twitching, as if pulling invisible strings; threads of magic that were attached to the dead girls. His eyes burned red in the dark, twin embers set deep in the sockets of a face too pale, too smooth, too still.

The cheerleaders turned in unison, following the direction of the priest's fingers, their bodies lurching into motion like puppets on unseen threads. The water around the bus rippled as more shapes stirred beneath the surface. Joel tried to move, to run, but the mud had swallowed his feet. The air smelled of rot and rust and something sharp, something electric. He shouted to wake himself up, and the cheerleaders all turned in his direction, their eyes gleaming like dull, wet coins. Joel lurched backward, falling into the slimy water. As he hit the surface with a splash, he was jolted awake, finding himself safe on the bus as it crossed a long bridge on the outskirts of New Orleans.

***   ***

As Joel sat under the live-oak tree on the road to Acadia Academy, he barely remembered the dream. What memory remained he shook off as he listened to the birdsong and enjoyed the breeze. He did feel that these surroundings were helping to ground him. Sitting still and quietly gave him a sense that the first part of the journey was nearly over, that after close to 24 hours travel he had arrived somewhere. This place would be his home now, at least for the next two years while he finished high school. He refused to think about why he was there, why he'd had to leave his home in Australia behind. The awful stuff that had happened at his old school. The stuff with Patrick, a boy he thought liked him but then betrayed him. The stuff that led to the onset of his fainting condition – NMH. Then the weird visions of birds, and of things that hadn't happened yet and then did. He pushed all thoughts of that stuff out of his mind. It wasn't good for him to dwell on all of that.

A splash in the water nearby made his heart jump. His eyes shot open and he bolted to his feet. 'That better not be an alligator!' Talking to himself again, something he did embarrassingly often. He hoped it was just an energetic fish but judging by how things were going for him it probably *was* an alligator, and not some run-of-the-mill alligator either. It would be a truck-sized homicidal reptile with a taste for human flesh. Not just any old human flesh, but boy-flesh – small, lean, perfectly bite-sized sixteen year-old boy flesh. Joel flesh. Another splash sent him staggering back so that he tripped over his suitcase and landed on his butt in the dirt. He scrambled to his feet and bolted to the other side of the road, his heart pounding in his ears. He positioned himself as far away from the murky part of the swamp where the splash had been as possible. He spun on the spot, realizing he was completely surrounded by swamp, possibly truck-sized alligator infested swamp.

'Calm down, calm down, don't freak out'. He repeated this to himself a few times as a kind of reassuring chant. It didn't work. He started to freak out. A wave of hot nausea and dizziness hit him and his knees went weak. The faint sound of birdsong echoed in his ears. He began the breathing exercise his therapist taught him to cope with anxiety. He couldn't panic. Not here. Not in the middle of nowhere. When he panicked it triggered his condition, NMH, which caused him to black out when stressed or overwhelmed. He couldn't let that happen. He couldn't pass out, not with possibly hundreds of boy-eating alligators lurking nearby. An image flashed in his mind of him passed out on the dirt road, a massive alligator dragging his unconscious boy-body by the ankles into the murky water.

Not. Helping. At. All. Dumb brain and its dumb imagination!

He focused on the breathing exercises. He had to stay conscious. He had to stay on his feet. Bending over, he hung his head low enough so that gravity increased blood flow to his brain, which would help him stay conscious. He grabbed hold of his calves to steady himself and kept a wary eye on the water. He breathed in slowly through his nose, then more slowly out through his mouth. The trick was to make the outbreath a little longer each time, without forcing it too much. His therapist had jokingly called this exercise "the tranquilizer" because it was so good at calming people down. People, yes; awkward, fainty boys, no. Besides, his therapist hadn't accounted for the truly mountainous anxiety levels triggered by murderous swamp alligators with a hankering for boy-flesh. Joel doubted slow breathing was going to cut it for this particular situation.

But what else could he do? He had to stop himself from passing out. He had to. So he hung his head a little lower and concentrated even harder on his breathing. Slowly in, more slowly out. Slowly in, more slowly out. Eyes always on the water.

As the breathing exercise started to work, Joel continued scanning the murky water for signs of alligators, and jolted with alarm every time he saw anything vaguely "gator-like" – a floating branch, a clump of Spanish moss drifting along the surface of the water, a twist of vine snagged on some underwater hazard. He'd half convinced himself he'd imagined the splash when he spotted something. About a hundred yards out on the swamp, in a patch of dark water in the shadow of a massive swamp cypress, two eyes were staring at him. He staggered back, because those were not alligator eyes. They were human. Joel peered into the shadow, unconvinced about what he was seeing. A black man, mostly submerged in the murky water except for his eyes and the top of his head. A man staring right at him. But the man didn't look right. He seemed barely there, sort of hollow and see-through. Like a ghost. Joel's heart stopped in terror and started up again in a frantic beat.

Joel blinked, wiped his eyes, then closed and opened them again to get them to refocus. He peered into the shadow, hoping he'd been seeing things, that it was a trick of the light. But there he was, staring right back at Joel. They locked eyes. A feeling of sorrow passed over Joel, and then the man faded into the shadow, dissolving like a lump of sugar dropped into warm water. Joel blinked again. Wiped his eyes again. The man was gone, but now there was something else in the water, gliding soundlessly toward him. A massive alligator! It opened its jaws and hiss-growled at Joel. Joel leapt back, stumbled, and landed on his butt in the dirt again. The gator veered away just before it reached the road and headed in the opposite direction, then dove and disappeared into the swampy water.

What. The. Dickens. Was. That.

Was all that a hallucination? Was he losing his mind? Joel's heart was really racing now. He could feel the pulse of it thumping in his ears. He focused on the breathing exercises again, desperate to stay conscious. He bent over and grabbed hold of his calves to steady himself again, hanging his head low enough so that gravity increased blood flow to his brain.

The sound of tires on the road reached him just as a long, black limousine came around the bend behind him. It pulled to a stop as he straightened up, less anxious and dizzy now thanks to the breathing but still a little dazed and shaky. Was he imagining this? Had a ritzy black limo just pulled to a stop beside him in the middle of the swamp? Or was this some kind of hallucination triggered by his panic? He'd never hallucinated before, that was not a symptom of his condition. But Joel thought anything was possible right now. His mental health was not exactly stellar. He reached out and touched the black window with a dusty finger. Real. Then the window slowly rolled down, revealing a concerned looking middle-aged woman with blonde hair and sapphire blue eyes.

'This is a strange place for yoga, sugar. You alright?'

Joel blinked. Yoga? What? Oh, the bending over and holding onto the calves thing. The woman was still looking at him with concerned eyes, waiting to know if he was alright. She was elegant, fortyish and intimidatingly rich-looking. Joel replied by nodding a yes, which was not exactly true and also a mistake because the movement of his head triggered a tremor of dizziness.

Feeling wobbly, he placed his sweaty hand on the window frame of the sleek limo to steady himself until the dizziness passed.

'Oh, sugar, I don't think you are alright.' The woman's accent was rich and unusual. Joel knew from his internet searches about Louisiana that this was Creole English, full of French sounds and inflections. She spoke to someone in the front seat.

'Doreen, collect the young man's luggage would you, we're going to give him a ride to the academy.' Joel didn't want to get in this limo with a total stranger but couldn't speak to protest. Too wobbly. The woman turned back to Joel. 'Doreen's our driver,' she explained.

A muscular and immaculately dressed African-American woman got out of the driver's seat and picked up his luggage, as though it were no heavier than two bags of potato crisps and not the leaden weights he'd needed all his strength to lug this far. Once his bags were sealed in the limo's trunk, Doreen opened the door for him, and the sapphire-eyed woman slid over to let Joel in. He hesitated a moment. She didn't look like a serial killer who preyed on slightly wobbly teenage boys, nor did Doreen the driver for that matter, but looks can be very deceiving when it comes to serial killers. Wasn't that their whole modus operandi – looking charming and harmless in order to lure their unsuspecting victims into their evil lairs/windowless white vans? But this was a limo not a windowless white van. Besides, his luggage was already locked in the trunk. He could hardly ask Doreen to haul it all out again. Another loud splash nearby made the decision for him. He scooted into the limo without another thought about being serial murdered.

*** ***

As soon as Joel was inside the limo he discovered the elegant blonde woman was not alone. Before he had time to register the other people in the car, Doreen the driver shut the door behind him with a near silent snap. The limo continued on its way again and Joel took in the other passengers. In the seat opposite was a man, also in his forties, with dark, silver-shot hair. Tall and solidly built, he was wearing a very expensive-looking suit. He smiled at Joel but the smile didn't reach his eyes. He was emanating tension.

Sitting next to the suited man was the most unbelievably handsome boy Joel had ever seen. He had his face turned away, staring unblinkingly out the window. His eyes were the same sapphire blue as the woman, his mother obviously, but his hair was a warm chestnut color. Unlike his mother's pale complexion, the boy's was olive, like a mid-summer tan. About sixteen years old, the boy was tall and strong-looking like the man beside him, his father obviously. Like his father, he emanated the same tension, a seething but bottled up irritation that threatened to erupt at any moment. He was wearing the Acadia Academy uniform with the gold neck tie that only the seniors wore. So, one of Joel's new schoolmates. Joel supposed there was a red junior tie waiting for him at his Aunt Penn's place. She was the principal of the academy and had organized his enrolment.

The atmosphere in the limo was so uncomfortable that Joel wished he'd taken his chances with the boy-hungry alligators. He started to feel anxious and panicky again.

'What's the matter, sugar?' the woman with the lovely accent said, sounding worried. 'You don't look at all well.'

The handsome boy's blue eyes darted towards Joel, just for a second, before going back to gazing out the window. That brief glance was enough to set Joel's heart racing. It should be against the law for a kid to be so breathtakingly handsome. The intimidatingly rich parents stared at him, partly concerned, partly curious. It must seem strange to find an awkward, breathless boy doing what they thought was yoga in the middle of a swamp. Joel felt he had to explain.

'Oh, I'm … um … fine, I'm … um … sloth!' He waved his arms about his person indicating he was talking about himself. 'Um … splash … fell over … alligators!'

He'd shouted "alligators" so loudly that they all jumped, including himself. The tall boy's lips quirked at the corners. What was that? The beginning of a smile or a sneer? Probably a sneer. What reason would a stunningly good-looking boy have to smile at an awkward Australian kid yelling "alligators" in the back of a limo? A sneer then. Now it was Joel's turn to be irritated. Great. Just great. First impression with new schoolmate thoroughly wrecked. Good one, Joel. He tried to salvage the situation by waving his hands around and stuttering some more.

'Sorry,' he said breathlessly. 'Not normally like this. Fell over … alligator!'

This. Was. Not. Going. Well.

Internally, Joel cursed the alligator. If that reptile hadn't made its presence known by splashing about in the murky water, Joel would never have panicked and would not have been in the middle of the road doing his breathing exercises when the limo came along. He also wouldn't be so breathless and out of sorts now. Yes, it was all the alligator's fault. That wretched alligator had conspired against him. He started his breathing exercise again to try to calm down. Slowly in through the nose, more slowly out through the mouth.

The handsome kid turned sharply in his seat and practically shouted at him.

'Do you need an inhaler or something?' His voice was deep for a kid. Joel's spine tingled with the low vibration of it.

'No, no,' Joel stuttered.

'Don't scare the boy,' the man shot at his son in a thick Creole accent. 'He's obviously skittish.'

Skittish? A word that described anxious kittens and hamsters. Could this moment get any worse?

'But seriously, kid,' the man said, looking Joel over as if scanning for an injury, 'are you asthmatic? Do you have medication to … sort *all that* out?' He made a gesture in Joel's general direction, as though Joel's whole being were some disorder that needed fixing. So, yes, the moment could be worse. It was.

'Christophe,' the woman half-whispered to her (probably) husband, as if Joel weren't sitting right there in the limo beside her and couldn't hear. 'You're making it worse'. She turned to Joel. 'What's your name, sugar, let's get properly introduced.'

'Joel River.'

'Pleasure to meet you, Joel, I'm Angeline Dumaine.'

Joel smiled a bit weakly as she gestured at the man opposite.

'That fellow there is my husband, Christophe Dumaine, and the beautiful boy staring out the window, pretending that none of us exist, is our son, Royal.'

'Don't call me beautiful,' Royal hissed, still facing the window, his breath fogging the dark glass. 'I'm not a girl.'

'No doubt about that,' Mr. Dumaine said. 'If you were a girl you might have some manners.'

'Well I'm not, so I don't.' Royal rolled his eyes.

Mrs. Dumaine sighed. 'But honey, boys can be beautiful too, can't they Joel?'

Oh god. Mrs. Dumaine's eyes encouraged Joel to agree with her. She had such kind eyes that Joel couldn't resist.

'Yeah, sure,' he said. Please let that be the end of it.

'And Royal is beautiful, isn't he?'

Oh, no, god no. He clamped his mouth shut to prevent it from betraying him again.

'Isn't he, Joel?' Her blue eyes were begging him again, but he resisted, closed his lips tighter. 'Come on now, Joel,' she coaxed, 'tell Royal he's beautiful. It might lift his sour mood.'

Joel's heart pounded in his chest. His palms were sweating.

After a seemingly long silence that was probably less than a billionth of a second, a nano-second, she pressed, 'Well?'

'Let it go, Angeline,' Mr. Dumaine said. 'The kid doesn't have to say anything. He's unlikely to have the same grand opinion of our son that you do.'

'Oh, no, I do,' Joel blurted out, shocking even himself. 'Agree, I mean.' Oh. God. No. Damn it, you dumb traitor mouth!

Mr. and Mrs. Dumaine looked at him, one smiling victoriously (Mrs.), one partly confused, partly amused (Mr.). The other Dumaine in the limo, Royal Dumaine, silent when not shouting about inhalers, turned away from the window and looked straight at Joel. Those blue eyes pierced Joel like lasers; or like the blue rays of twin supernovas, two brilliant stars. Joel couldn't breathe.

Royal stared at him for way longer than a billionth of a second, maybe three or four full seconds, before looking away again without saying a word.

What. Was. That?

The silence in the limo was deafening. If Joel had been alone he would have smacked himself in the forehead for ever having been so foolish to say out loud that he found a boy he'd only just met beautiful – in front of the boy's parents! What kind of person did that? Joel River, that's who. He contemplated leaping out of the moving car.

LIGHT AS A CUCKOO FEATHER

As if in answer to his prayer that this torturous limo ride be over, like ten minutes ago, the screen between the passenger seats and the driver slid down and chauffeur Doreen announced that they had arrived at Acadia Academy.

'Just coming up to the bridge now,' she said.

Still stinging with embarrassment, Joel looked out the window as the limo crossed an old wooden bridge and passed through large, ornate iron gates and onto a long driveway that was flanked on both sides by an avenue of huge live-oaks, all draped with Spanish moss like gothic Christmas trees. At the end of the driveway was a building that resembled something out of *Gone with the Wind*, a plantation house with colonnades at the front and verandas wrapping all the way around its two levels.

This was where Joel was going to live and go to school for the next two years. He could never have afforded it without the scholarship place he got because his aunt was the principal. Acadia Academy was a private high school for kids with 'exceptional talent in the creative arts'. When Joel had read that on the school website he'd felt anxious. He was grateful his aunt had got him in at the last minute, but his only exceptional talents were fainting and being a bit awkward. He

21

doubted these were the kind of talents they meant. He was joining the creative writing program, something he had a passion for but doubted he was any good at. He'd emailed his portfolio of short stories to his aunt never expecting they'd be good enough to get him in, but his aunt must have pulled some strings as principal. He'd never let anyone read his stories before, not even Patrick, the boy he thought might one day want him as a boyfriend. Until the terrible thing happened that ruined everything. The thing he travelled half way across the planet to get away from. The thing Joel pushed out of his mind so that he didn't start shaking uncontrollably in a limo full of strangers.

He turned his mind to wondering what Royal's exceptional talent was – being silent and excruciatingly handsome most likely. Or maybe he was a genius on the kazoo. Joel smirked at the image that summoned. No boy, no matter how handsome, was intimidating while playing a kazoo.

The limo pulled up in front of the old plantation house and Joel opened the door and shot out before Doreen had even turned the motor off, which startled all three of the Dumaines. The unnaturally beautiful family exited the car with a lot more grace than Joel had and looked everywhere but at him while Doreen unloaded the luggage. Terrible first impression well and truly cemented then.

Joel huffed, annoyed more than embarrassed now, and collected his bags from where Doreen had unloaded them. He looked around, not sure where to go. Beyond the plantation house he could see a number of other buildings arranged around a park-like quad. All of those buildings looked just as boujee as the main one. There were no signs pointing to an admin office, no signs at all.

'Joel, sugar,' Mrs. Dumaine said tentatively, 'I assume you're a boarder? Judging by your accent you're not from around here. Students sign in at Acadia House.' She gestured to the colonnaded mansion in front of them. 'They'll tell you where your room is, but most of the boys are in Nottoway House, over there.' She gestured to another grand-looking building over-looking the quad behind Acadia House.

'No, I mean, yes, I mean, I'm not a boarder but I'm not from here. I'm Australian.'

'Australia,' Mr. Dumaine said, 'I'd love to visit the Alps one day. Great ski resorts there, and world class strudel too.'

Joel didn't have the heart to tell him that was Austria, in Europe, not Australia in the Southern Hemisphere. He'd had to explain it to the bus driver already: Australia as in kangaroos and koalas not Austria as in strudel and *The Sound of Music*. Right on cue Mrs. Dumaine jumped in:

'Oh, yes, I just love Julie Andrews!'

The corner of Royal's lips quirked again, this time more a scoff. He rolled his perfectly blue eyes.

Right, Joel thought, hostile to me and my country as well. Got it.

'Okay, well, thanks for the ride.' Joel waved goodbye, heaved his backpack onto his shoulders and headed for the front steps of Acadia House, dragging his wonky R2D2 suitcase behind him. He was relieved to find that he was steady on his feet again and the dizziness had almost completely passed. After entering the open front door of Acadia House, Joel stopped dead in his tracks, causing the Dumaines to pile up behind him. The entrance hall was like a dream or something out of a movie. It looked to Joel like a palace, with its polished floorboards, oriental rugs and rich furnishings. The ornate staircase up to the second floor curved around a massive chandelier that glittered like a cascade of diamonds and glowed with the light of at least a hundred bulbs. Joel nearly whistled at it, it was that gorgeous.

Mr. Dumaine coughed behind him, impatient to get inside.

'Oh, sorry, just …' he waived his arms about, gesturing at the staircase and chandelier, 'pretty!'

All the Dumaines blinked at him in unison, synchronized surprise. He hurried on, turning at the sound of keyboard clacking to his left. He entered a room that was clearly an office, with a reception desk. Sitting behind the desk was a pretty African–American girl of about Joel's age wearing a badge that read 'Student Ambassador'. Her hair was a beautiful dark brown in long braids and her eyes were a bright amber. On the desk was a newspaper, *The Acadiaville Chronicle*, with the rather unsettling headline: "Disappearance: Second Woman Reported Missing". Joel wondered if he'd moved across the globe to escape trauma at home just to end up in a serial killer's hunting ground, but he put that thought away when the Student Ambassador addressed him.

'Can I help you?'

'Hi,' Joel said, clearing his throat a little feebly. 'I'm Joel River. I'm starting as a junior this year.'

'You're Joel River?' The girl looked alarmed.

'Yes.'

'This is a disaster,' she said as she looked over to a clock on the wall.

'A disaster? I don't understand.' He felt the Dumaines watching him from behind. His throat tightened. Maybe he'd misread his aunt's email. Maybe there wasn't a place for him here after all? Maybe that was why she hadn't met him at the airport? He'd known it was all too good to be true. He would have to face the ruin that was his life back home in Australia after all.

'You're supposed to be in New Orleans,' the girl said, her voice confused.

Wait. What?

'New Orleans?'

'Yes. You're aunt just left to pick you up from Louis Armstrong airport, where you are supposed to be in about three hours. Why are you here now and not there then?'

Joel blinked, translating what the pretty girl had said. 'Well, my connecting flight from Dallas was cancelled so they put me on a much earlier one.'

'An earlier flight?' She seemed to think this was all rather incredible.

'Yeah, so I got in early this morning. I texted Aunt Penn, err, Principal Stacey, to tell her the new time, but I guess she didn't get my text. I tried to call her too but the call wouldn't go through.'

'Foreign cell phones don't work here,' Mr. Dumaine said behind him. 'You need a new SIM card.'

'Right, I didn't know that, okay. Anyway, when my aunt Penn didn't turn up I kind of fully freaked out and so got a bus. Which is why I'm here, now, and not still waiting at the airport in New Orleans.'

'You kind of fully freaked out and got a bus?' She still sounded as though this was all completely unbelievable. Her amber eyes stared at Joel.

Joel nodded. It was all too believable for him. The whole trip so far had been tiring, stressful and humiliating.

'Alright, okay, so,' the girl began, 'would you mind hanging out on the porch while I call Principal Stacey? Then she can tell me what to do.'

'What to do?'

'With you and your things. You can't just hang out in the office for hours until she gets back, you look exhausted.'

Joel nodded. He was so exhausted it was a struggle to think, talk and act like a real human boy.

Mr. Dumaine stepped forward, tired of waiting for his turn. The girl turned her attention to him.

'Oh, hi, you must be Mr. and Mrs. Dumaine?'

'Yes, we're here to check in our son, Royal Dumaine. He's starting as a senior.'

'Yes,' the girl said. 'Principal Stacy asked me to check Royal in because you were coming a day early.'

'We're early because we have matters to attend to in Savannah,' Mr Dumaine said.

'A custody hearing, he means,' Royal muttered bitterly from behind them. 'About me.'

Mr. Dumaine gave Royal a quelling look. Mrs. Dumaine looked uncomfortable and upset. Maybe Royal's parents were getting divorced? Joel didn't think they seemed like two people about to end a relationship. Despite the tension in the limo the look they shared when their eyes met now spoke volumes. They loved each other. Yet sometimes love was not enough to keep people together. Joel knew that too well. He felt he was intruding on a family moment and so rolled his suitcase out to the porch.

He dropped his backpack on a bench and slumped down into it himself. How long would he have to sit here? The trip to New Orleans was about two hours each way. Surely he wouldn't have to sit on the bench the whole four hours? He yawned. He needed to sleep. It would be dark well before his aunt got back. He couldn't sleep there on the bench, not out in the open. He was tired enough to sleep anywhere, sure, but the thought of falling asleep unprotected, vulnerable, where anyone could come by, made his whole body tremble. No, he would stay awake until his aunt returned. No matter how long that took.

*** ***

From the bench on the front porch of Acadia House Joel looked out to the horizon. Dark clouds were rolling in. Great, Joel thought, the outside world was mirroring his interior world. A growl of thunder made him jump. A few minutes later the elder Dumaines came out to leave, Royal reluctantly following them onto the porch. When Royal's mother hugged him, he was like a statue, unresponsive. His father put a hand on his broad shoulder.

'See you at Thanksgiving break, son.' He paced down the steps, stopping at the bottom where his wife waited. 'It's for the best, Royal, you'll see.'

'Tell that to William, my *dad*.' He spat out the word 'dad' like a poison dart. He meant it to hurt, as a rejection of the man in front of him. Joel was really confused now. Maybe Mr. Dumaine was Royal's step dad? But they looked so alike. Like twins born forty years apart. He stared at his shoes trying to be inconspicuous.

'You know,' Royal continued, 'your partner of twenty years who you abandoned to hook up with my *surrogate*.' He shot a cold look at his mother.

Okay, Joel thought, I get it now. Royal had two dads and a surrogate mum. His dads were going through a break up because one had left the other for Royal's mum. And there was a custody battle. Joel felt a pang of sympathy for Royal. No matter how cold he acted even the toughest kid would be messed up by all that complication. The tension in the limo now made sense.

'She's your *mother*, Royal,' Mr. Dumaine hissed, his voice hard, 'your mother!'

Royal shrugged, unapologetic. Mr. Dumaine steered his wife to the limo. When she looked up to her son to wave farewell her eyes were brimming with tears. Royal stared into the distance, letting them get into the limo and roll out of sight without showing a hint of emotion.

Whoa. That was a level of intense Joel had not expected on his first day in a new country at his new fancy boarding school. Was that how rich American people behaved all the time? Like snakes hissing at each other twenty-four-seven? He put a great deal of effort into not looking at Royal. He wished the statuesque boy would just go somewhere else already.

The sky was completely blanketed by dark clouds now. Thunder rumbled close by. A flash of sheet lightning made Joel jump. He didn't like storms. Royal looked over at him, looking like he might say something. Just then the student ambassador came out onto the porch.

'I haven't been able to reach Principal Stacy … sorry, your aunt, Joel. She must have her cell off while she's driving. She probably won't check it until she gets to the airport. She won't make it back here until it's late, so I've made a grown up type decision. I'm going to put you in a dorm room for the night. You can move over to your aunt's place in the morning.'

'Can't you just let me into my aunt's place now? Her house is here on the grounds, isn't it?'

"Um, well, actually, no, I can't do that. It's … complicated.'

Complicated? What?

Joel sighed but was too tired to ask anything more about it. He stood up, dragging his backpack up with him.

'Where do I go?' It came out as a half-croak. He was barely able to speak.

'The only available bed is in the same room as Royal,' she nodded in the handsome boy's direction. 'That's over in Nottoway House. I'm sure he won't mind.' She smiled at Royal who looked like he definitely did mind but said nothing.

Joel shook his head, not believing what was happening. He was being put in a room with Royal, who was a total stranger and easily twice as big as him and likely ten times stronger. Joel couldn't accept that. He couldn't be alone with someone like Royal, not after what had happened back home. He would never sleep. He'd be constantly on edge and anxious. And what if Royal …

'No. No, I can't, I …' He started shaking, his whole body convulsing with panic. A bolt of lightning hit swamp water very close by with a boom and a hiss of steam. Joel flinched with his whole being. He lost hold of his backpack. The thud when it hit the floor was barely audible over the ringing in his ears and the storm. That familiar yet dreadful wave of nausea and dizziness hit him. He broke out in a sweat. His ears were full of birdsong. He could hear the girl say his name, asking if he was alright, but he couldn't respond. His head spun and his vision went dark. It started to rain heavily. That's when he went down.

How long he was out he didn't know, a few minutes, maybe more. That's how it normally was. The rain was pelting down, the sound nearly deafening. He couldn't open his eyes yet, overcome by the crushing weakness that always enveloped him whenever he had one of these episodes. Slowly he became aware that he was being held. His head was resting in the crook of someone's arm, and that someone was cradling Joel, holding him firmly. Joel squirmed to get free but it was a feeble effort. The person holding him tightened their grip a little, keeping him in place. It didn't feel threatening though, that grip, it felt protective. He allowed himself to relax into it, to just stay still until the strength returned to open his eyes and sit up. He heard the girl's voice then, somewhere above him. She sounded freaked out.

'Oh my god, is he dead? I'm on the phone with the paramedics, just hold onto him.'

Joel managed a few words. 'No paramedics … not dead … just fainted.'

He heard her come closer. 'You fainted, Joel, is that right?'

'Yes.'

'I still think we should get the paramedics to check you out.'

'No, I do it all the time, I have NMH, it's a fainting condition. Not life threatening. Not going to be dead. I'm just a bit fainty.'

'Just a bit fainty? Joel, you went down like a ton of bricks.' Her voice was much closer to him now. Then she was speaking on the phone to the paramedics. She was more shouting than speaking in order to be heard over the rain. 'Hi, my name is Starr Davis, I'm a student at Acadia Academy …'

She told them he'd fainted—"Pure blacked out" was how she put it—and that he had NMH. There was a pause while the person on the other end of the line looked up what NMH was. It's pretty rare. Then Starr was speaking to Joel again.

'I don't like it but the paramedics agree with you. You're in no danger. They said you just have to remain supine, which is just lying down, I googled it, and rest until you fully regain your senses … but we can't leave you out here on the porch for the raccoons and storm to get you.'

Fist alligators, now raccoons and a storm. Great. Why was nature out to get him today?

'I'll carry him over to Nottoway House.'

Joel recognized the voice of Royal Dumaine and realized it was the tall boy's muscled arms that held him protectively. He squirmed again, trying to escape.

'Joel, stop wriggling,' Starr said in a worried voice. She didn't understand. She didn't know that being in this vulnerable situation with this boy twice as big as him and much stronger was precisely his worst nightmare.

'Open your eyes, look at me.' Royal's Creole accented voice again. Deep and firm, but calm.

Joel struggled to open his eyes. When he did Royal was right there, so close, his blue eyes looking at Joel not with their usual stoniness but with concern. So much concern that his eyes seemed changed. Had they turned a deeper blue? Was that possible? Did some people's eyes change color with their feelings, like mood stones? Whatever the case, Joel responded to the concern in those eyes. He stopped struggling against Royal's hold and lay still.

'I'm sorry, I …' Joel felt ashamed. Ashamed that he'd fainted. Ashamed that he'd resisted help.

'Don't say sorry. It's not your fault.' Royal's voice had changed too. It was not the cold, clipped voice he'd used with his parents. It was warm, gentle even. 'If you let me, I'm going to carry you over to the room.' He dropped his voice and checked that Starr the student ambassador couldn't hear. 'I don't know for sure what you're frightened of, but I got the impression it was being alone with me. The shaking and fainting kind of gave it away.' His lips quirked at the corners again. 'You can have the room all to yourself. I can stay somewhere else. No-one needs to know.'

Joel's whole body un-tensed with a rush of relief. Royal must have felt it happen.

'Does that mean I can carry you over?' he asked.

After a pause that was many seconds long Joel nodded, closed his eyes and let it happen. Royal, strong as he was, lifted him effortlessly. Once he had Joel securely in his arms he whispered in his ear.

'I want you to know that I would never, ever do anything to hurt you, I promise.'

Joel wanted to believe him, and part of him did, but the other part, the part that was stuck in that awful night a year ago, just couldn't believe him, maybe never would. Royal carried him down the front stairs of Acadia House and across the quad, with Starr following along holding an umbrella to shield Joel from the rain. A few minutes later they went up some stairs, and through a door that Starr opened. They must be in Nottoway house now. Then Royal carried him up even more stairs. He did all this as though lugging a sixteen year old boy up a flight of stairs was no more strenuous than watching television. Joel's head was against Royal's chest. He could feel the bigger boy's heartbeat against his cheek. It stayed perfectly even. Starr followed behind them making the odd anxious sigh.

At the top of the stairs Joel opened his eyes as Royal turned down a long hallway with numbered doors on each side. At the end of the hall they came to a room with the number nineteen on it. Starr opened the door and ushered them in. Royal had to juggle Joel in his arms to get through the door. Joel grumbled with displeasure.

'Sorry,' Royal said, 'but your weight is tiring out my arms.'

Joel glared at Royal with an expression that said "How dare you! I weigh next to nothing!" At least that's what he intended the glare to express.

'Sorry,' Royal said again, smirking. 'I meant to say that you're as a light as a cuckoo feather, totally weightless, and I'm just a clumsy klutz.'

Joel accepted that with a weak smirk. He glanced around the room they'd entered. It had two beds on opposite walls. A window looked out to the park-like quad and the cloud-covered sky. The rain was easing off. Royal deposited Joel gently on one of the beds and stepped back, now breathing a little heavily. The movement of Royal's chest up and down was like a hypnotic lure to Joel's attention, so he looked away and tried to sit up.

'No you don't,' Starr scolded, pushing him back down.

'I'm fine, not at all dead.' Joel said, in no way in his right mind.

'Even so, you are to remain *supine* and rest. When your aunt calls back I'll tell her what happened and she'll come straight back to look after you. You don't need to worry. You'll be alright.'

She hesitated a moment, apparently unsure what to do, then turned and walked out of the room, shutting the door behind her, leaving Joel totally alone with Royal. The panic must've shown in Joel's eyes because Royal took a step back and raised his hands, palms facing Joel, as if to say "Wait, don't freak out". Then he said it out loud.

'Don't freak out. I'm not staying. I'll bring your bags up and then I'll get out of your hair.'

'Okay,' Joel mumbled, too weak to say much else.

Royal turned and opened the door, pausing with his hand on the doorknob.

'Your hair smells nice, by the way, like apples.'

Joel's brain struggled to comprehend what Royal had just said let alone respond with words other than: Huh? What? Apples? So he stayed quiet.

It was Royal's turn to mutter incoherently. 'Sorry. That was weird. Shouldn't have said … never mind, just, ah, resume what you were doing, ah, only without the fainting and freaking out bit. So, ah, yeah, I'll go get your bags now.' He walked out and shut the door, leaving Joel's head whirling.

He closed his eyes and sank down into the mattress. He couldn't have kept his eyes open a second longer. The fatigue was dragging on him like a weight, pulling him down into sleep. He tried to rouse himself— the door wasn't locked and that boy was coming back— but his eyes felt glued shut and the darkness was all encompassing. The rain was now nothing more than a gentle patter on the roof, kind of comforting. He was aware of breathing in and out once, twice, maybe a third time. His breath sounded just as feeble as he felt, but it was slowing, deepening. That was good. The last thing he heard before he fell into an exhausted sleep was an echo of Royal's voice in his mind:

'I would never, ever do anything to hurt you, I promise.'

ZOMBIE DREAM

A full moon shone over the still waters of the bayou, where its reflection gleamed so clearly that it was hard to tell which moon was the real one, which way was up. Stars twinkled above, and twinkled just as brightly below; the only difference being the occasional ripple that passed over the surface of the water, making the moon and stars undulate in a strange, shimmery dance.

Joel felt the rippling water gently rock the mattress beneath him, which was floating in the middle of the bayou. It didn't strike him as strange that he was floating on a mattress under the moon, that he was no longer in Royal's dorm room in Acadia House. His mind was on the twinkling stars above, and on the long tendrils of Spanish moss that dangled in the water, swaying to and fro in the breeze like fingers playing with the water. He reached out his hand and mirrored the movement, swirling the cold water with his fingertips.

The mattress drifted beneath the boughs of a swamp cypress, festooned in so much hanging moss that it looked like some kind of giant swamp creature, its many shaggy arms frozen in twisted positions, its buttressed trunk, deep in the water, like a single, gnarled leg. Joel shivered and closed his eyes, allowing the drifting motion of the mattress on the slow moving water to soothe him.

A strange, far off rustling sound caught his attention. He cocked his ear and listened. It was coming from the shore, from the forest of live-oaks that surrounded the bayou. The sound made him think of someone shuffling through fallen leaves. As he focused on it, the sound multiplied. Where before there had been just one pair of feet shuffling along, now it was three or four. Soon, it was as if a dozen people were shuffling towards him. He sat up and looked around.

On the muddy bank there was vague movement among the trees. Something or someone was creeping just out of sight. He stared into the shadows between the trees. At first, he couldn't see anything, just the refracted glimmer of moonlight shimmering on the tree trunks, but then he caught sight of a shape moving in the distance. The shadow of a person shuffling slowly towards him, moving with a weird jerky rhythm. It shuffled into a patch of moonlight and Joel saw it clearly for the first time. A teenage girl with hollow eyes, pallid skin and dirty, matted hair. A dead girl. Before Joel fully registered what he was seeing more shapes emerged from the shadows into the moonlight. More dead girls. All wearing the same outfit – a cheerleader's uniform. All shuffling menacingly towards him, their eyes gleaming like dull, wet coins. Joel freaked out. He stood up on the mattress. It tipped. He fell. As he splashed into the water the dream vanished, like a wisp of smoke blown away by a sudden gust of cold wind.

APPLES AND STARRS AND PIZZA

As Joel slowly woke he realized that he'd had a dream like that before. A dream with zombie cheerleaders. Why was he having that dream? His therapist would probably say it had something to do with the terrible thing that had happened to him last year. But what did zombie cheerleaders represent to his traumatized subconscious? He had no idea. He thought about it a while as he fully woke up, but then forgot about it when he heard that bird again, the one from the swamp with the light, joyful song. It gave him that same feeling he'd had yesterday – that his journey was over, that he had arrived at his new home. He kept his eyes closed, partially to avoid facing the bright sunlight that was already glowing on the other side of his closed eyelids, partly to listen to that song again. As he listened a strange thing happened. The birdsong seemed to shift from outside the room to inside his body. It was as if the bird were singing inside his heart, as though his heart itself was a bird; light and joyous, soaring in the sky, unfettered and free. A knock on the door brought him back to earth. The birdsong in his heart stopped.

What. Was. That?

He'd heard birds when he was fainting before, and sometimes saw them in visions when he passed out. But that was something new. And scary. Had he hit his head when he'd fainted yesterday? Did he have concussion or a contusion or something else awful starting with c-o-n? Confusion, contagion, consumption, conjunctivitis? His heart wasn't joyful and free. His heart was heavy and full of shame and fear over what had happened to him last year with Patrick and the group of boys from his old school. His heart was a dead weight inside him as heavy as a supergiant star. The knocking resumed, a soft rap, and was then joined by a voice.

'Joel, it's Penn, your aunt Penn.'

He slowly sat up, still a bit weak from the trials of the day before. He sealed the dream of the undead cheerleaders away, determined not to think of it again, stashing it in the part of his mind where he hid all of his weird dreams. He shut the door on it. He wiped his eyes and looked around. His backpack and suitcase were by his bed. True to his word, Royal Dumaine had brought them up and then left the room to him. The knocking was a little more insistent now.

'Come in, Aunt Penn.'

Penn opened the door and hesitantly peeked in. On seeing Joel her hesitancy dissolved and she rushed in.

'Joel! Look at you! You've grown so much!' She gesticulated wildly at him.

'It's too early for all the gesticulation, Aunt Penn, chill.' He said it smiling. His aunt Pen was an excitable sort of person and he loved that about her. She crossed the room in seconds and looked him over.

'You've grown into a proper boy!'

'Yep, that's me, real human boy.' He knocked on his knee. 'See, flesh and bone, not wood, and my nose stays the same size whether I lie or not. Watch: Aunt Penn, those open-toed shoes are a treat for everyone. You have such dainty foot-digits. Now, am I lying or not?' He moved his head left and right so Penn could see if his nose was growing.

'Same impish sense of humor, I see,' she said, eyebrows arched, before scooting him over and sitting on the end of his bed. 'What I meant was you're not a little kid anymore, but a proper human.'

'Well, you left Australia when I was ten, forever ago. I was bound to get a little taller.'

'So much taller! And now you're sixteen and a junior. I can't believe it.'

'Getting taller isn't magic, Penn, it's just human growth hormone.'

'Aww, look at you using your growing human brain. Definitely not an ankle-biter anymore.' She tussled his hair, smiling. He tussled it back to the way it was.

'You'd better not let anyone hear you calling me an "ankle-biter", Penn. These Americans won't know it's slang for a little kid. They'll probably think I'm a cannibal as well as a fainty, awkward weirdo.'

'Starr told me what happened yesterday. The fainting. Was it awful?'

'I passed out and was carried to bed by some rich kid I don't know at all. Just an average Sunday really.' His aunt patted his knee reassuringly and gave him one of her patented "I love you and I'm here for you" looks. That was enough for him to drop his defenses. 'Yes, it was awful. And humiliating.'

'You have nothing to feel humiliated about. It's a medical condition. You can't control it.'

'I know, but I hate it when it happens in front of people I don't know and don't trust.'

'I understand, especially after what happened last year—'

'I don't want to talk about that.' He regretted his harsh tone immediately. 'Sorry, I just—'

'Want a new start, and you deserve one. You also deserve a hug. May I?'

Joel nodded and opened his arms so that Penn could pull him into a tight embrace. It felt nice, so he let her hang on longer than he normally would have.

She squeezed a little tighter as she said: 'And I meant what I said before. You really are a proper human now, so tall and cool-looking. What are you, six foot?'

'I'm only five feet, eight inches, Penn.'

'Well, that's pretty tall. Taller than me.'

'Oompa Loompas are taller than you.'

She chuckled and let go, looking into his eyes. 'I'm so proud of you, Joel. It takes guts to leave home and travel half way across the planet to start fresh. New country, new home, new school. It's a lot; but if anyone can do it, you can.'

He smiled. Penn had always been his biggest fan. It was great to be in the same room with her again. For years they'd only talked by phone or online, except for the odd Christmas holidays when she'd come home to visit, carrying her new American accent and an armful of gifts.

'Come on then, Joel, let's get you and your stuff over to my place before this mansion is swarming with kids and parents. Today is first day back for the boarders. Besides, Royal Dumaine will be wanting his room back.'

Joel had a flash of memory, of being carried upstairs in Royal's arms. His stomach tightened with embarrassment. He put it out of his mind and got his stuff together to leave while Penn waited in the hallway. It took a bit to maneuver his wobbly suitcase into the hall, the roller was fully jammed now. After he pulled the door to room nineteen shut Penn took the suitcase, leaving him with the backpack, which he slung over his shoulders one last time. Next stop, Aunt Penn's cottage, where he'd have his own room and a brand new start.

'I can't wait to put my old life and yesterday and Royal Dumaine behind me,' he said, heading down the hallway.

'Don't write off Royal so quickly,' Penn whispered as she half dragged, half rolled the suitcase behind her.

'Why? He's just another rich kid isn't he?'

'You should know better than to judge someone by how much money their parents have or don't have.'

'You're right, I'm sorry. I'm just …'

'Embarrassed he saw you in a vulnerable state.'

'Yeah,'

'And probably even more embarrassed because he's a rich, handsome, popular type.'

Joel blushed but said nothing. She was right. They reached the stairs and headed down. A group of boys raced up past them, all talking loudly.

'Freshmen,' Penn said. 'They're quite rushy and loud at that age. It'll be a full house this year. We have a few more boys boarding than normal. We've only just managed to squeeze them all in here at Nottoway House.'

Joel thought about how the student ambassador, Starr, had said the bed in Royal's room was the only available one.

'Where did Royal end up last night, if all the rooms were allocated?'

'On a chair outside his room. I don't think he slept much. He was there when I peeked in on you when I got back from New Orleans last night and was still there this morning. He only headed down to breakfast after I turned up just now. He wanted to make sure you were alright and to be there if you needed something through the night.'

Penn watched him out of the corner of her eye, a knowing smile on her face. Joel pointedly looked at everything but her. Chandelier, ceiling, railings, lint on his t-shirt. Gorgeous Royal Dumaine had watched over him through the night. Before that he had carried Joel upstairs, then went back down to get his bags. After all that, he spent an uncomfortable night in a chair outside his own room so that Joel could be alone and have the space he needed to rest. He'd stayed in that chair right up until Penn had arrived that morning, just in case Joel needed something. This was not the surly kid he'd met on that uncomfortable limo ride. He didn't quite believe it, but a part of his heart did believe it, and that part was singing. A light and joyful song like a Louisiana swamp bird.

When they reached the bottom of the stairs they walked across the entrance hall and out the front door. Once in the quad they had to wend their way around two girls kissing. Two actual live girls actually full-on kissing. Joel couldn't believe his eyes, nor believe that no-one else seemed to notice or care. He looked to his aunt, the surprised look on his face making her chuckle.

'It's a school for the creative arts, Joel. Our student body is very … diverse.'

At that exact moment two older boys, seniors judging by their gold neckties, came strolling along, holding hands. Again, it was only Joel who paid them any attention. He'd actually stopped in his tracks, his eyes wide, and a goofy smile on his face. In unison the hand-holding boys said, 'Hi Principal Stacy.' Aunt Penn smiled at them like hand-holding boys was a perfectly normal thing to see at a high school.

'A *very* diverse student body,' Penn said, taking Joel by the hand and dragging him away. 'Now stop gawking.'

'At my old school girls didn't kiss each other.' He felt like a time traveler explaining to someone from the distant future what things were like in the medieval dark ages. 'And boys definitely didn't hold hands.'

'I'm sure they did, Joel, just not openly. Acadia Academy is different. On these grounds every student is free to be themselves.'

The bird in his heart started singing again. They turned down a path leading between two buildings on the quad. Penn pointed to the mansion closest to them.

'Female boarders are here in Rosedawn House, heavily guarded by Miss Dill, our girl's boarding house master. Miss Dill is very proud of the fact that not a single boy has breached her defenses and entered Rosedawn in her twenty years at the school.'

'Miss Dill will not have any trouble from me.'

'No, and for that reason I'm sure Miss Dill will love you.'

Joel had told his aunt he was gay when the plan to move him to America had formed a few months back. He'd told his parents some time before that and assumed they had let Penn know but he'd wanted everything to be open and cool between them so he'd told her himself. She'd acted like a champ, said she loved him no matter what before he'd even got the words fully out.

They cut across the quad and out onto some playing fields behind a large redbrick building that Penn said was the library. Penn gestured to the other edge of the playing fields where a white cottage sat in the shade of large oak trees. It looked like a postcard of the perfect Southern cottage.

'That's Oakshade Cottage, your new home.'

'Cute but, like, how far is that?' Joel whined.

'Not as close as it looks,' Penn teased.

She led him along a shady path that circled the playing fields. Some of the trees here were very old, with long tendrils of Spanish moss almost touching the ground. Once they'd got about half way along the path

Joel spotted a boy sitting in the shade of a tree, his back propped up against it, his school blazer rolled up and used as a makeshift pillow. Royal Dumaine. His sapphire blue eyes were closed. Was he asleep? He certainly looked very relaxed. His tie was loosened and his top three buttons undone. His sleeves were rolled half way up his forearm, which made his arms look even bigger. His hands were in his lap, one holding a half-eaten apple. Yes, he was asleep. Worn out by his overnight vigil.

How. Sweet. Is. That.

As Joel and Penn got closer the noise made by R2D2's rollers dragging in the dirt woke Royal. He looked up and saw Joel and leapt to his feet, his blazer falling in the grass, from where he quickly retrieved it. Joel stopped at the sudden movement, unsure what to do. His face must have looked odd because Royal raised his hand in that "It's okay, don't freak out" gesture again and backed off a little, as if to give Joel more space to pass by.

'Thanks, Royal,' Penn said as she took Joel's hand and got him walking again. Royal smiled, not just a quirk of the lips or a smirk but a proper smile. It was beautiful. A memory from the night before rose in Joel's mind: 'Your hair smells nice, by the way, like apples.' Joel looked at the apple in Royal's hand and blushed. His hand went involuntarily to his hair.

'Apples,' he said, as though to the air. Then Royal blushed too. Was it a flush of embarrassment or something else? Aunt Penn looked from one blushing boy to the other, confused, then dragged both Joel and the suitcase away, both seemingly unwilling to move. Royal smiled at them again, blushing even redder now. Joel waved goodbye, a coy half-wave that died before it really got started.

With Royal a few yards behind them Penn said

with a concerned voice, 'Once we've got you settled in your new room, I think you should rest some more. I don't think you've bounced back from yesterday. You still seem … addled.'

Joel nodded. He knew he should say something, agree with Penn that he needed more rest, but the bird in his heart had turned into a flock, all twittering and flapping and excited. All he could say, in a dazed voice, was, 'Pretty … pretty, Royal.'

Aunt Penn stifled a laugh and squeezed his hand, steering him towards his new home.

***   ***

When they finally reached the cottage, which Joel thought had taken a million eons, Penn stopped at the gate and stepped closer to him, speaking quietly.

'Before we go inside, I need to let you know that there's another student who'll be staying with us for the school year.'

Joel stiffened. Penn knew he didn't do well with strangers, especially not strange boys. His aunt noticed the increase in tension in his body and gently placed a hand on his shoulder.

'She's a lovely girl, incredibly smart. She's staying with us because the student accommodation isn't … well, isn't suitable for her needs. You both have a lot in common. I wouldn't have agreed to this if I didn't think you'd get along. You don't need to worry.'

A girl. Okay, maybe that would be alright. Joel did trust Penn's judgement. He knew she'd never do anything to make him uncomfortable. He pushed out a long breath and released the tension from his body. He nodded to let his aunt know he was ready to go in. She opened the gate and led him up onto the porch, puffing with the effort of lugging R2D2 up the stairs. She opened the door and let him go in first. The entrance way opened onto a light-filled and cozy-looking sitting room with a fireplace stacked with pinecones. Curled up in an armchair by a large window was a girl reading a book. Serious looking. The book not the girl. Joel recognized the girl immediately. Starr Davis, the student ambassador with beautiful brown braids and amber eyes that seemed to have a light behind them. The girl he'd passed out in front of. Great. Just great. She looked up and smiled.

'Hi, Joel, great to see you are still not dead.'

'Yeah, err, thanks. Sorry about yesterday.'

'Me too,' she said. "I'm so sorry that happened to you. And I'm sorry if I made it worse by being in your face. I was just desperate to help.'

Desperate to help. That made Joel feel better. It meant she probably wasn't going to use what happened to embarrass him in front of his schoolmates.

'It's fine. You did help. Thanks.'

'I was really worried I'd done all the wrong things. The badge says "student ambassador" but I'm just a kid.' She hopped up out of the chair. 'I'm sorry I didn't bring you straight here yesterday. Remember I said it was complicated? Well, the complication is my grandmother. She' very strict about me never being alone in a house with boys she doesn't know. Your aunt hadn't had a chance to tell her that we would both be staying here.'

'Perfectly understandable,' Penn added. 'That's all sorted now. I gave her a call and assured her that Joel is completely harmless.'

Joel flinched a little at being called completely harmless. What was he, a hamster? And why did people keep describing him as though he was a small, furry creature? He knew it was irrational but he would like to be thought of as at least a bit dangerous. Not dangerous like a lion, but definitely not a hamster. More a streetwise alley cat. He almost did a terrifying alley cat yowl but remembered at the last minute he was with company.

'Shall we unpack your things and talk about Bell Hooks?' Starr wiggled the cover of the serious looking book in his face.

'Sure, but, err, I don't even know what a bell hook is.'

'Bell Hooks is a *who* not a what. She's a black feminist philosopher.'

'Oh, okay, sorry, I didn't mean to be—'

'Don't be sorry, I love it when people have never heard of Bell Hooks. It means I get to tell them all about her. Why don't you unpack and I'll give you a full account of Bell Hooks's life and legacy?'

Penn intervened: 'How about we put off the presentation on Bell Hooks until after Joel has rested a bit?'

'Okay, sure' Starr said not daunted in the least. 'I'll take him to his room.' She took Joel's suitcase from Penn and led him down the hall. At the back of the house were three bedrooms. One was clearly Penn's (framed pictures of sunflowers), one Starr's (cool posters, lots of clothes on racks, and a shelf of vintage Barbie dolls), and the last undecorated one at the very back of the house was his.

'There used to be a painting of a horse on this wall,' Starr pointed to a spot by the one window, 'but it was an awful toothy horse so I made your aunt take it away.'

'Thanks, horses are fine enough but I don't want one staring toothily at me while I'm sleeping.'

'I know, right, me neither. Horses are a bit judgmental if you ask me. Too naturally beautiful for their own good.'

Joel smiled. He liked the way this girl's mind worked. She plopped down on the bed as Joel unpacked his clothes. He could rest later. He liked Starr and wanted to get to know her. He felt a little uncomfortable when he unpacked and put away his underwear, but Starr was in full flow explaining who Bell Hooks was, so he didn't think she saw anything. He doubted she could even tell if he was a boxers or briefs kind of guy. It's both, by the way, depending on mood and situation. When it came to unpacking his most valued, most secret possession, he kept his back turned to the room, pretending to fuss with a stubborn zipper on his backpack. When he was sure Starr was distracted, he slipped it onto a closet shelf, careful to keep it shielded with his back. He pushed it just far enough in that no one would notice it unless they were looking. Just knowing it was safely tucked away—out of sight but close enough if he needed it—settled something uneasy inside him. It wasn't a big deal, he told himself. Everyone had their little ways of feeling okay. Some just had to be kept private.

Most of what Starr said about Bell Hooks and feminism went over Joel's head, but some of it he understood and thought was cool. When he'd finished putting his things away he sat on the chair by the window and looked out. Through the trees he could see water, a quiet corner of the bayou.

'It's pretty, isn't it,' Starr said.

'It really is. Have you been here since grade nine, I mean, freshman year?'

'No, this is my first year here. We're both newbies. I'm a junior too.'

Joel was glad he wasn't going to be the only new kid in his class. He would still be the only one with an Australian accent and the only one who had dramatically fainted on the porch of Acadia House.

'Don't worry,' she said, spotting the worried look on his face. 'I did some summer classes here over the break and everyone was really nice.'

He wondered why a clearly brilliant girl who read college level books needed to do summer school but didn't want to make her feel uncomfortable by asking. The conversation paused and they sat quietly for a few minutes.

'It's good of you not to ask,' she said, 'about summer school, but I don't mind.'

He shrugged. She could tell him if she wanted to but he wouldn't press.

'I missed a lot of school last year,' she said quietly, 'because of my transition. I'm trans. It wasn't fun for me at Acadiaville High, the local high school. I got bullied a lot, which is why I'm here taking advantage of your aunt's hospitality.'

The thought of anyone bullying Starr made Joel instantly angry. He knew how damaging being bullied could be. He'd been through it himself. Starr was smart and beautiful and funny. How could anyone be cruel to her just because she was trans?

'You're not taking advantage,' he said firmly. 'I'm sure Penn's glad you're here. She's good like that, Penn, really welcoming and kind. It's why I'm here … Did, did she tell you what happened to me?'

Starr shook her head.

'No, but I can see in your eyes it was bad. You don't have to tell me, not now, not ever, but if you do decide to tell me I'm all ears, like literally; I've got some big ol' ears over here.'

Joel snorted.

'You do not. Your ears are perfectly in proportion with your,' he waved his hands to indicate her face and whole look, 'other features. You're really rather stunningly beautiful.'

She beamed.

'Thanks, Joel, you're the first person other than my

grandmother to compliment my appearance since I transitioned. It means a lot.'

'You're welcome, but don't get any ideas. All this,' he indicated his dark clothing covered body, 'is reserved for boys only.'

'Oh, Joel, honey,' she laughed, 'the cat is out of the bag on that little truth. As my gran says, that is as plain as the sun in the sky.'

'What gave me away? The rainbow wrist band? The rainbow Chuck Taylors?'

'The whole rainbow package. Besides, your aunt told me.'

"She did? What a dobber.'

"A what now?'

'A dobber, it's Australian slang for a tattle-tale or snitch.'

'Tattle-tale? What are we back in the Victorian era?'

He chuckled, feeling sincerely light-hearted and relaxed for the first time since Patrick had — He pushed those memories out of his mind. He wouldn't think about that. He wouldn't allow the past to overshadow this moment with Starr, who he felt might turn out to be a great friend. And a great friend was something he really needed right now.

SUPER SWOL BOYS

Joel put Patrick and the trauma of the previous year out of his mind and asked Starr to brief him on what he should expect when classes started in the morning.

'It depends what program you're in,' she said before launching into a discussion of what an average day at Acadia Academy was like. Every student had a major program and a minor, like college. Students in all four years, from freshman to seniors, attended program specific studios together. Everyone worked as one big class towards the end of semester showcases, one around Christmas and one during Mardi Gras, which were like mini festivals with a concert, play and art exhibition. Joel's major program was creative writing. Starr's was theater. She wanted to be a director and bring great feminist plays to the masses one day. Joel didn't think the masses would thank her for that, the masses are for the most part ignorant jerks, but admired her enthusiasm. Starr's minor program was costume design, which she said was basically fashion design but with more frills and lace. Joel admitted he hadn't signed up for a minor yet, and Starr reassured him that most kids did that on their first day.

'Do you know what program Royal is in?' Why did he ask that? He barely knew Royal. He knew that he was a confusing person – surly one day and sweet the next. He also knew he had two dads and a very stylish mum, and was rich. And was hot. He was really, really hot. Okay, so Joel did know a fair bit about him after all.

'You mean Royal Dumaine? From yesterday?'

'Yeah.' Joel pretended to find the view outside his window very interesting.

'He's actually a costume design major, so he and I will be in the costume studio classes together.'

'Really?' Royal didn't look like he was into fashion or clothes. He looked more like a sport and fitness kind of guy.

'Yeah, but he's only in that program because it was the last spot left in the whole school. His parents only enrolled him last week. Very last minute. His minor is music. He's in the Blues stream. That's his real passion.'

'Are you friends?'

'No. I only know about his Blues passion because he told me yesterday when he was handing over his paperwork. I'd never met him before. His family are Louisiana elite: really rich, connected to all the right people, and from the Garden District in New Orleans. *Very* fancy. My family are the opposite: poor and from here, swampy backwoods Acadiaville I mean. His family are also really old. Like they got here in the 1760s old. That matters in Louisiana. It makes them Creole royalty. He seemed nice though, for a one percenter.'

'Wow, so Royal's family are older than my country. That's intense.'

Starr looked at him curiously.

'Can I ask you something?' she said.

That sounded a bit serious.

'Um, yes.'

'Yesterday, when you had that episode, I didn't realize it then but after thinking about it overnight I thought what triggered it was having to share a room with Royal.'

Joel nodded and she went on.

'You don't need to explain that to me, but just now when you were asking about Royal it seemed like you wouldn't mind spending some alone time with him. Is that right?'

Joel thought about that before he answered.

'When I first met Royal I thought he hated me. Then I find out from Penn he was really kind after I fainted. He confuses me … but there is something about him. I still wouldn't want to be left alone with him, or any boy I don't know really well, but he does seem different to other boys. I think he has a soft side to him. He's interesting and, um—'

'Hot.'

'Yes, super hot!' He was glad Starr had lightened the mood.

'When you fainted, he moved so fast! He caught you before you hit the floor and then held you and wouldn't let you go. He was really concerned. He practically growled at me when he thought I was getting too close.'

'Seriously?'

'I may be exaggerating a little, but not much. He was very—'

'Protective.'

'Yes, exactly. It was kind of adorable.'

'He said my hair smells like apples.'

'He didn't!'

'He did. Then this morning he was eating an apple.'

'Really? That's all very—'

'Gay?'

'I was going to say romantic, but it's kind of gay too, yes.'

The room spun, and suddenly Joel was in a vivid memory, but so much more life-like than a memory. He was in Royal's arms as the beautiful Cajun boy carried him down a long hallway with numbered doors on each side. At the end of the hall they came to the room with the number nineteen on it. Starr opened the door and ushered them in. Royal had to juggle Joel in his arms to get through the door. Joel grumbled with displeasure.

'Sorry,' Royal said, as real as the first time he'd said it, 'but your weight is tiring out my arms.'

Joel glared at Royal with an expression that said "How dare you! I weigh next to nothing!"

'Sorry,' Royal said again, smirking. 'I meant to say that you're as a light as a cuckoo feather, totally weightless, and I'm just a clumsy klutz.'

Joel glanced around the room they'd entered. Trying to figure out how he was here again. Did he have a concussion? Had he hit his head when he'd fainted? The dorm room had two beds on opposite walls. A window looked out to the park-like quad and the cloud-covered sky. The rain was easing off. Just as it had the day before. The very same raindrops were coursing down the window pane. Royal deposited Joel gently on one of the beds and stepped back, now breathing a little heavily. The movement of Royal's chest up and down was like a hypnotic lure to Joel's attention, so he looked away and sat up. The room spun and Joel was back in his bedroom with Starr.

What. Was. That?

Joel had experienced flashbacks before. He'd had many flashbacks of the awful thing that happened to him last year. His therapist said flashbacks were a part of post-traumatic stress disorder, which he also had. Yay, more disorders. But he'd never experienced anything like that. That was more vivid than even real life. Starr was watching him curiously, wondering why the conversation had suddenly paused. Before it got too awkward and weird he said something.

'Don't tell anyone this, Starr, especially not Penn, I'd never hear the end of it from her, but I think I might have a proper crush on Royal Dumaine. So much so it's messing up my head'

Starr's eyes lit up and she started jigging in place on the bed. She could barely contain her excitement.

'Our junior year is going to be the best!'

Joel hoped she was right. He really needed a good year. They both did. They'd both been through a lot at their old schools. To stop Starr from wearing out his mattress springs Joel asked her a few more questions about school. She explained that no matter what their program, every academy student spent most of their time doing compulsory subjects with others in their year. There was only one junior English class for example, which Starr and Joel would be in together.

'At least there'll be one class where I'll know someone,' he said, feeling relieved.

'My best friend, Tashi, will be in our English class as well. We've known each other since grade school. This is her third year here. She started in freshman year while I was stuck at Acadiaville High. She's really great, you'll love her. Her major is film. But her mom wants her to be a chef. Their family owns the café on the town square, Little Tibet. Her mom is Tibetan. My gran's quilting store is two doors up from the café, so Tashi and I spent every summer holiday since we were six hanging out in the square together.'

'I saw the quilting store when I got off the bus. Do you normally live with your gran?'

'Yeah.'

'Why are you boarding when you live so close?'

'My gran doesn't drive, never has, and there's no bus.'

'Don't I know it! I only made it halfway with my luggage before completely puffing out. How long is that walk? It said fifteen minutes online.'

'Oh, no, it's more like forty. In the summer that's thirty-five minutes too long.'

Joel nodded. It was far too humid to walk so far in the full summer heat. 'How long have you lived with your grandmother?' he asked.

'Since I was six. My dad died in the war in Afghanistan, so my mom and I moved in with gran. Then my mom left a couple of years ago. She couldn't accept that I'm a girl. She lives in Atlanta now.'

'I'm so sorry.'

'Thanks. They're old wounds. Not that they don't still hurt sometimes.' She played with her shoe-laces, hiding the sadness that shadowed her otherwise beautiful face. Joel knew that feeling – sadness mixed with embarrassment and shame. It was the shame that was hardest to deal with, because it made no sense. Why should they feel shame because of what other people had done to them? Joel's therapist had said it was misplaced blame. Rather than blame the people who had harmed them, kids often blamed themselves. It was easier to blame yourself than someone who was supposed to care for you, supposed to protect you. Like Patrick. Like Starr's mum.

Joel could feel his eyes starting to well up at the injustice of it so he distracted himself and Starr by raising the one topic certain to snag the attention of every gay kid and teen straight girl on the planet. Boys.

'So, you know I like boys. Do *you* like boys?'

'Oh, do I!' Starr exclaimed. 'I do so much. I'm a total fangirl for boys. Not all boys; some of them are sweaty and stupid and rude and horrible.'

'Yes, they can be all of that.'

'But then there are boys who are gentle, and sensitive, and kind—'

'Ugh,' Joel groaned. 'You sound like you're describing someone's grandma. Not hot.'

'Kind can be hot. I also like boys who are confident and brave and—'

'Super swol!' Joel pantomimed a swollen muscle boy by pushing out his chest and flexing his (almost non-existent) biceps.

'Yes, totally love a super swol boy!'

'You may be joking but I'm not. I like a man with muscles.' Joel waggled his eyebrows up and down to emphasize his enthusiasm for muscles.

'But muscles aren't everything, are they? A boy should be smart and kind too.'

'Sure, sure,' Joel said, 'smart and kind and all that stuff are great, but mostly really swol.' Joel did the best impression of a drooling, horny teen he could muster.

Starr laughed out loud.

'You look like such a creeper right now,' she said.

'Do I?' Joel licked his lips. 'Do I look like a creeper?'

'Yes, stop it!'

Aunt Penn chose that moment to arrive at Joel's door.

'Put that tongue away, Joel, and come help set the table for lunch. You too, Starr, if you don't mind.'

Joel and Starr both hopped up.

'Now, Starr,' Penn said when they reached the door, 'your grandmother entrusted me with your care, but you may regret that when you taste my cooking. There's a reason I am a principal and not a chef.'

'There really is,' Joel said, nodding fervently, 'and it is Aunt Penn's bean tacos. Making children eat that is a crime against humanity.'

'Joel!' Penn gasped. 'That's the one dish I thought I was okay at.'

Joel shook his head even more fervently than before. Starr chimed in:

'I'm sure whatever you make will be fine,' she said. 'What are we having?'

Penn's face was grim. She took ages to answer.

'Bean tacos.'

All three were silent. It was Joel who started laughing first, quickly followed by Penn and Starr. It took them a good ten minutes to settle down enough to go out to the kitchen and order pizza instead.

DISAPPEARANCE DREAM

The streetlights buzzed, their glow weak and yellow, struggling against the thick Louisiana night. The air was slow and heavy, swollen with the scent of hot pavement and honey-suckle. The only sound was the hum of cicadas, and the slow rustle of a breeze moving through the live-oaks that lined the small town square. Joel looked around. How did he come to be here?

A woman entered the square from the street opposite him. In her mid-twenties with long blonde hair woven into a braid and wearing a pretty yellow sundress, she glanced about as she walked, unnerved by walking through town alone so late at night. A strange sound caught her attention. The sound of shuffling feet on dry pavement. Alarm spread through Joel's body like an electric shock. He tried to shout a warning to the woman but no matter how loud he shouted, no sound came out. It was as if his voice was being absorbed by the darkness. A group of figures dashed out of the shadows of a nearby alley, bringing with them a fetid stench. They moved incredibly fast with an unnatural jerky gait. The woman turned to run, but they were already there, they already had her. Their bony fingers curled around her wrists, their dead arms folding around her waist. She screamed, tried to pull away, but their grip only tightened. They dragged her away, steady and deliberate, drawing her into the darkness of the alley where the light of the streetlamps didn't reach.

And then Joel woke, his skin damp with sweat, the echo of shuffling feet and screams still in his ears. Barefoot and only in his sleep shorts, he was standing in the middle of the wooden bridge that crossed the river separating the grounds of the academy from the rest of the swamp. A sign on the bridge read "Little Bayou River". The moon shone high overhead. He groaned. He'd obviously been sleepwalking. He'd started sleepwalking after the awful thing, after what Patrick, the boy he once really liked, had done to him last year.

'Dammit,' he said to himself, 'freaking zombies! Again! Why is my brain so broken?'

He turned around to head home, and stopped dead in his tracks. A boy was standing on the other side of the bridge, just by the entrance gate to the school. Dressed in an Acadia Academy uniform, the boy looked like a freshman. What was a freshman doing out by the bridge in the middle of the night? Joel walked a little closer, then stopped again. Something wasn't right. The uniform was a little different, and looked old fashioned somehow. Not only that, Joel could see through the boy all the way to Acadia House. Joel blinked. Was he seeing things? Was he still sleeping? Still dreaming? He pinched himself. *Ouch!* He'd pinched a little too hard. And the boy was still there, looking lost and lonely, watching the dark water of the river drift by. And he was completely see-through. Like a ghost. Joel's poor heart started hammering again. This can't be real, he thought, either I'm still dreaming, or I've lost my mind! The clouds overhead passed over the moon, casting the boy in shadow so that Joel could barely see him. Joel stared, and then the boy looked up and straight into his eyes. A feeling of sorrow passed over

Joel, and then the boy faded into the night, dissolving like a lump of sugar dropped into warm water. The exact same experience he'd had with the black man in the swamp.

Joel shook himself, making sure he was awake and not about to see anything else that defied the laws of nature. Then he crossed the bridge back onto academy grounds, and, with a huff and a groan, began the long, barefoot walk back to Oakshade Cottage.

Not. Fun. At. All.

HAMSTERS AND SQUIRRELS AND CURSES

Joel stared at his cereal. A bowl of Honey Nut Cheerios. He'd never had them before and didn't like the look of them. In Australia he would have just had toast for breakfast. Toast was familiar. Toast was safe. Starr was happily eating her Cheerios across the breakfast table from him. At least he knew they weren't lethal. He and Starr were wearing their school uniforms, complete with red junior ties, and were as ready as they could be for their first day of classes at their new school. But first he had to deal with this Cheerios situation.

'Just try them,' Starr said, 'they're good.'

He dipped his spoon in and raised it to his mouth, then plunged it in with his eyes closed. He chewed. Huh. Not bad at all.

'They *are* good! Honey-ish and nutty,' he said, surprised.

'Yes, that is in their name – Honey Nut Cheerios.' Starr shook her head at him and returned to her own bowl of Cheerios.

Penn came into the kitchen, all dressed in her principal garb, an elegant navy blue skirt suit. She had a newspaper in one hand and something small and brightly colored in the other. She dropped a small, palm-sized cloth bag on the table between them. It was bright red with an electric blue drawstring.

'I found this hanging on the porch railing,' she said. 'Any idea what it is?'

'It's a gris-gris bag,' Starr said immediately. 'A voodoo protection amulet.'

'Voodoo? How cool.' Joel picked up the bag and smelled it. It smelt of dry herbs.

'Why on earth would you smell it, Joel?' Penn asked. 'You don't know what's in it or who left it here.'

'It's perfectly safe,' Starr said. 'It's to ward off evil.' She turned to Joel. 'You're deep in the land of voodoo, hoodoo, curses and hexes now, Joel.'

'Cool,' Joel said, sniffing it again as though there were some evil up his nose he was in a hurry to get rid of.

'Joel,' Penn hissed. 'As a general rule please do not go around sniffing things you cannot identify.' She took the bag from his hand. 'So, what was it doing hanging on our porch railing?'

'T.J. probably put it there,' Starr said.

'T.J.?' Penn asked.

'T.J. Thibodaux. He delivered the pizza last night.'

'The pizza boy left this here?' Penn looked confused. 'Why?'

'Just being nice, I suppose. It's the sort of thing he does. His mother is a fortune teller. She reads tarot cards in town,' Starr explained. 'They're into all that stuff, voodoo, gris-gris and tarot cards and such. My gran thinks they're a bit "woo-woo" but I think they're okay. T.J. is home-schooled, so I don't know him very well, but he's always been kind to me.'

'Oh, that home-schooled boy. I thought his name was Thierry?'

'It is. Thierry Jean Thibodaux. T.J. for short,' Starr explained.

'I gave him permission to use our school library because it's much closer to his home than Acadiaville High. They live on the bayou quite close to here, don't they?'

Starr nodded.

'He was very polite when I met him,' Penn continued, 'and he did seem nice.'

'Polite, nice and kind, just your type, Starr,' Joel said, smirking.

'Oh, no, he's not my type at all. We've known each other since we were two. We're like cousins. He is super cute though, and bisexual.' Starr raised her eyebrows at Joel to emphasis this last point. Joel perked up. A super cute queer boy lived on the bayou nearby. Joel looked out the kitchen window as if in the hope of catching sight of him.

'He's not still here just hanging out in the yard, silly,' Starr said with a grin. 'But I think you would like him. Picture a young Elvis mixed with Shawn Mendes only hotter and with a thick Cajun accent.'

'Drool,' Joel said eagerly. 'Like, total drool.' Starr laughed in appreciation. It was fun for Joel to pretend that he was confident with boys. In reality he was terrified of them. If T.J. were actually here Joel would probably run to his room and hide, like a hamster. He was no lion. He wasn't even a spunky alley cat. Besides, his interest was in an altogether different boy, this one Creole.

Penn shook her head and muttered something about teenagers being the death of her. She sat down and started reading the newspaper, spreading it out on the table in front of her. The headline immediately caught Joel's attention: *SERIAL KILLER SUSPECTED*. The first few lines of the front page article were just as shocking:

> *Acadiaville Parish sheriff said the suspected kidnapping of Liz-Anne Landry could be the work of a serial killer. Liz-Anne's disappearance is the third of its kind in the last month.*

When Joel saw the picture of Liz-Anne in the paper he nearly fell of his chair. She looked exactly like the woman in his dream, the woman who'd been dragged away by … by what? By zombies? Just thinking that made him feel insane. It couldn't be the same woman. Dreams do not come true. Was he properly losing his mind now? What was happening to him?

Penn let out a frightened little sigh. 'This is getting scary now.'

Joel agreed, but for different reasons.

'Maybe we should get a few more gris-gris bags from T.J.,' he suggested, feeling more than a little scared.

'Maybe,' Penn said quietly, still reading the article. 'At the very least you two have to stick together, don't wander off school grounds, and be home when you're supposed to be home – straight after school. And keep all the doors locked.'

'I have no desire to be serial killed, so you'll get no arguments from me,' Joel said, pointedly burying any thoughts or worry he had about the weird dreams he was having.

'Me neither,' Starr added, shooting a worried look at the newspaper. 'I'll hang the gris-gris bag on the door handle of the front door. Gran says that's where they go.'

*** ***

Joel's first class was Creative Writing Studio, which he had every day for an hour. Starr dropped him off at the right building on her way to her own first class (Theater Studio) but he walked into the classroom alone. His stomach danced with both nerves and excitement. He took a seat at the back and straight away noticed that everyone in this class knew each other. They'd obviously all started in freshman year together and had already formed tight friendship groups. Some of them were juniors and seniors which meant they'd known each other for three or four years. He got a few sideways glances but no-one came up to him or said anything. The teacher entered and settled everyone down. She was a short, slightly chubby woman in jeans and an oversized top with an ice-cream cone pattern. She wore glasses with bright purple frames, which Joel appreciated. She had a stack of books under her arms, which she plonked on the desk at the front of the class. She tidied her wispy blonde hair, which she wore short, and wrote her name on the board in pink chalk: Miss Dill. Ah, Joel thought, the guardian of the female boarders' virtue.

'Most of you know who I am,' she said in a clear voice, 'but we have a new person today. Joel River, stand up please.'

Joel stood up, his knees instantly going a bit wobbly.

'Tell us a bit about yourself: where you're from, favorite hobbies or passions, preferred pronouns if you have any, any of those things would be a good start.'

'Err, right, well, I'm Joel, I'm from Australia, I don't really have any hobbies or passions—'

'No passions? What is this then?' Miss Dill pulled some sheets of paper out from among the stack of books on her desk.'

'I don't know what that is.'

'It's the portfolio of stories you submitted to join the writing program, Joel.'

'Oh, right.' Joel prepared himself to be told he was a terrible writer and was only in the program because of nepotism, because his aunt had got him in.

'I have been teaching at this academy for twenty years,' she said, 'and these stories are among the best I've ever read.'

Joel blinked. He couldn't believe his ears.

'In fact, they are so good I thought a junior could never have written them, though Principal Stacy assured me you had. I did a thorough investigation to determine if they were really yours, searched every dark space on the internet frequented by cheats to see if you'd bought or copied them. I was surprised, and really delighted, to decide in the end that you had written them yourself. They really are wonderful.'

Joel didn't know how to feel. In a few sentences she had accused and acquitted him of cheating, then said his writing was wonderful. His ears were now literally burning and his mouth was terribly dry.

'Welcome to the program and take a seat, Joel River, you have well and truly earned it.'

He sat, more heavily than he should have, which made his ears burn even more. He was aware of many students' eyes on him. One girl in particular, sitting right up front near Miss Dill's desk, had turned bodily around and was staring right at him. She was more than pretty, she was gorgeous, with long blonde hair and steely grey eyes. Her tie was gold, so she was a senior, a year above him. She was looking at Joel like he'd cussed her out, hard; like he was the worst thing to have happened to her in her whole blonde life.

'Now, as with last year,' Miss Dill said, 'this year we will be starting with poetry and lyrics, then after Christmas turning to the short story before finishing the school year by focusing on writing for the stage. At the Christmas showcase, the student with the best poetry or lyrics will be awarded the *Alice Dunbar Nelson Poetry Prize* and have their work performed by the music and theater students. This is a great honor, which, as you all know, Lana Beaux has won three years in a row now.' She smiled proudly at the girl in the front row. Death stare girl. 'Let's see if you can make it a full sweep, Lana. You've got some real competition now.' Miss Dill looked back at Joel with a similar smile. He shrank down in his chair, mortified. Reason for death stares from blonde bombshell ascertained. Joel had unwittingly moved into her territory and stolen her thunder, or so Lana Beaux clearly thought.

*** ***

The rest of the creative writing studio was pretty good. Joel thought a class about poetry would be dull, but Miss Dill had a way of making it fun. When she was talking about love poems she played a rap song that had all their heads bopping. When she talked about haiku, short three line poems, she wrote some examples on the board in multi-colored chalk. Though short poems they really painted a picture. Some of them were even funny. The fact that Lana Beaux raised her hand for every question Miss Dill asked, and answered every one correctly, was intimidating, sure, but not enough to spoil it for Joel. For the first time in his life he felt like he was in the right place; that this school and the creative writing program were where he was meant to be.

When the bell rang Miss Dill asked to see Joel before he went to his next class. If she hadn't already made such a fuss of his writing he might have been nervous. He went up to the desk and tried to thank her for the kind things she'd said, but his mouth betrayed him. Again.

'Thanks for, you know, liking my, um, stuff.'

'I see your gift for language does not extend to the spoken word. It's often that way. Some of the most gifted writers can't order a meal without messing it up.'

'I can order meals,' Joel mumbled, 'quite well.'

'Indeed,' Miss Dill said. 'I'm sure you order your Happy Meals with profound eloquence.'

Joel wanted to bite back at that. He didn't even like Happy Meals. He wasn't a child, but Miss Dill went on speaking.

'I wear many hats at this academy,' she said. 'I am Chair of the creative writing program, I teach English to sophomores, juniors and seniors, not the freshmen thank goodness, and I am also, believe it or not, the extracurricular sports coordinator.'

'Really?'

'Yes, I am as surprised as you. We are perpetually short staffed here at the academy and we must all fill multiple roles. Now, I'm not sure if your aunt filled you in, but all students do physical education, or gym, once a week—don't worry I do not teach that, I don't think I even know where our gym is—and all students must sign up for an extracurricular sport. The options we have here are swimming, track and field, archery, yoga, tai chi, kendo, and tennis.

That had to be the most boujee list of sports Joel had ever heard, some of them he didn't even recognize, but he thought tai chi wouldn't be so bad.

'Do I have to choose one now?'

'Choose? No, I'm afraid there is just the one spot left so you don't have a choice.'

'Please don't say I'm doing archery! I'll shoot myself straight in the head!'

'That would be a rather incredible feat, and also rather gruesome, so please don't do that. But no, you will be joining the boy's swim team.'

'What!' He didn't know how to tell her that he couldn't be on the swim team because that would involve taking his clothes off in front of human people with eyes and wearing a swimsuit. He could never do either of those things. 'But, I can't …'

'Oh, you can't swim?'

Joel didn't correct her. At least he didn't have to admit to his body shame issues.

'Never mind,' she said, 'the academy's swim team is our only real athletic strength and every place on the boy's squad is spoken for. You were only going to be a reserve anyway. Our sports-challenged students often join teams in a support role. As you can't swim that sounds like the ticket for you.'

'Support role?'

'Yes, like ball boy or girl in tennis, or water boy or girl in track and field.'

'So, what, I'm going to be—'

'The pool boy, yes.'

Oh. Sweet. Baby. Jesus. No.

'Do I have to?'

'Yes. No choice I'm afraid. It's all that's available to you. Report to the pool after classes today. And I hope you can sew?'

Wait. What?

'Do I have to make swimsuits for the team too?'

'No, this is about your minor. As with athletics all the places in the minors are full except one spot in Costume Design.'

'Right.'

Joel thought Costume Design could easily be as dangerous for him as archery, all those scissors, needles and pins, but what choice did he have? Besides, it might be fun, Starr was in costume design. He headed for his next class feeling despondent and a bit anxious. What does a pool boy even do?

His second class was math, which he had with other juniors, but not Starr, because she was doing advanced math, geometry or calculus or something. He was doing what he called "veggie math", which was math when you don't know how to do math. At Acadia Academy it was called Integrated Math. After math was American History, where he would see Starr again, and after that was lunch. He and Starr had planned to spend lunch together debriefing about their first day so far.

He was hurrying across the quad on his way to American History when a squirrel raced out of nowhere straight at him. It ran up his leg before bouncing off his thigh and tearing away in the opposite direction. Joel dropped his books, spun on the spot to make sure there were no more squirrels about to assault him, and let out an actual squeal. Not a roar like a lion or a yowl like a wily alley cat, but a high-pitched squeal like a petrified hamster. As he was spinning and squealing he collided with a hard fleshy object that turned out to be Royal Dumaine.

Why? Just why? What was it with this place? First alligators, then a storm, now a rampaging squirrel. Why did the wildlife and weather of Louisiana have it in for him? Why was nature bent on humiliating him in front of Royal Dumaine? Was it some kind of voodoo curse? And if so, who would want to curse him? He was a nobody, just a very awkward, very fainty boy.

Royal looked down at Joel with wide eyes (he really was rather tall) and his face flashed through emotions like a multi-colored neon sign: irritation, surprise, confusion and then something else that looked like embarrassment. What had Royal to be embarrassed about? He wasn't the one flailing about and squealing in the middle of the quad like a proper lunatic.

'Sorry,' Joel said in a hamsterish voice. He coughed to deepen his tone a bit. 'Sorry, squirrel, up my leg. Very fast!'

Royal blinked, staring down at him, silent. Joel felt his face flush with heat. He couldn't imagine a worse situation. He thought the limo ride had been bad, but this? Joel didn't have to imagine a worse scenario because at that moment Lana Beaux walked up behind Royal and slinked her arm into his and leaned into him like she owned him. Like he was hers.

'Who's your new friend?' she said to Royal in a sweet voice while directing a poisonous smile at Joel.

Joel fumed, she knew exactly who he was, but he communicated his irritation only through further flushing. He was probably as red as a beetroot by now.

'We're not friends,' Royal blurted out, his face now showing no emotion at all. 'He's just some junior.'

Joel felt like he'd been kicked in the stomach. Lana's poisonous smile deepened in toxicity. She pulled Royal a little closer to her.

'Off you go then, little junior, you wouldn't want to miss a class on your first day,' she said with mock concern.

She steered Royal away as Joel picked up his books as quickly as he could. He then marched across the quad feeling miserable, hurt and angry and arrived at American History a bit breathless. He found Starr in the back row, sitting with an Asian girl with bubble-gum pink hair and cool Beatnik style eyeglasses. Starr's best friend, Tashi Bellman. Starr introduced them and then said,

'Okay, Joel, Tashi, share fun facts about yourselves with each other, like in speed dating, only this is speed friending.'

Joel shared that he was Australian, in the creative writing program, was a secret bird watcher and recently appointed pool boy. Tashi laughed at the pool boy thing and shared that she was in the film program because she wanted to be a producer and in culinary arts because that made her café-owning mum happy. She said she was not only on the archery team, but the captain of it, which she loved, despite her mom being the instructor, because it was something she really enjoyed and was really good at. She also said she loved Joel's rainbow Chuck Taylors.

'Why thank you,' Joel said. 'I love your hair, and your glasses, and generally your whole look.'

'He's a keeper,' Tashi said to Starr.

'I know, right.' Starr smiled at them, happy that her newest friend and oldest one were getting along. 'Don't worry about the pool boy thing, Joel. You can change sport next year. I'm captain of the Kendo team, maybe you could join?'

'What's kendo?' Joel asked.

'It's a Japanese martial art using swords. We use bamboo swords, but this is Louisiana and we're all armed up to the hilt down here, so I've got a real sword too.'

'Seriously, you're like, a swordsperson?' Joel said, deeply impressed.

Starr nodded, smiling humbly.

'She's incredibly good at it,' Tashi said proudly. 'She's like Blade, you know the vampire-slayer, but pretty.'

'Swords are not my thing,' Joel said. 'Not if I want to keep my fingers, toes, hands, feet, and nose intact. Same goes for archery. Maybe I could join the Tai Chi team? Surely I couldn't hurt myself too much doing that?

Or maybe I could start my own team – a competitive evening strolling while eating Oreos team, or something.'

'I'd join that team,' Starr and Tashi said as one.

LIPSTICK, PLAGUES AND THE COLOR PURPLE

The American History teacher came in to the classroom followed by a few straggler students. He was a tall, solidly built African-American man with a perfectly shaped goatee. One of the straggler students was a handsome Latino kid with hair and eyes as black as each other. If Joel had to guess he would say this kid was in the theater program, an actor, because he was movie star material. When Tashi spotted this guy she tensed up, quickly dropping her eyes to her books. A weird reaction. Starr passed a glance and a smirk at Joel, letting him know that Tashi had a thing for this guy. Joel couldn't blame her. He was a solid eight. But he wasn't Joel's type; a bit too polished. Joel liked boys who were more naturally hot, like Royal Du—' No. He was not going to think anything positive about that particular boy. Not after he'd just snubbed him in front of Lana, who Royal seemed to be dating. There was no point Joel even thinking about a straight guy. Especially not a straight guy dating the very same girl who in the space of half a morning had become Joel's nemesis.

The polished actor guy strolled confidently to the back of the room and, on spotting Joel and Starr, stopped in front of their desks.

'Hi new kids,' he said to Starr and Joel. 'I'm Carter Herrera, welcome to Acadia Academy.'

Joel and Starr smiled and said hi in unison.

'Hey, is that an Australian accent?' Carter asked Joel.

'Um, yeah.'

'Holy shit, are you the fainting kid?' Carter looked around at some nearby students, who all looked at Joel as if they knew he had fainted on the porch of Acadia House. 'Hey, can you faint now so we can get out of history?' Everyone laughed.

Joel's throat tightened instantly and his stomach lurched. How could they know about that already? Who told them? Joel looked to Starr, his eyes asking that very question.

'It wasn't me,' she said. Joel already knew it hadn't been, had never thought it was. That only left Royal. So much for his so-called soft side. So much for his protective act. As soon as he'd had a chance, Royal had told everyone about the fainting kid. As if it was some hilarious joke. Then in front of Lana he'd acted like he and Joel had never met. Just some junior. Joel felt sick. He'd left Australia to get away from this kind of thing and it was happening here as well, happening all over again.

The teacher, Mr. Johnson, told the class to quieten down and started the lesson. Joel barely paid attention. His head was reeling. He knew Mr. Johnson was giving an overview of the class, that they would cover everything from the Civil War to the 1950s, but his mind was fixated on how Royal had betrayed him. Could someone betray you when you weren't even friends? Joel had felt something for Royal, had literally felt safe in his arms. For Royal to turn around and tell the whole school about what had happened felt like a betrayal. He still felt sick from it when the bell rang and he, Starr and Tashi headed to lunch together.

They got a bunch of sandwiches and fruit from the cafeteria and went to eat in the quad. They claimed a cool spot beneath a shady tree. Tashi laid out a blanket she'd brought from home and arranged their food on it like a picnic. Joel was still spinning from the realization that everyone knew he'd fainted on his first day at the academy, but he was glad to be out in the open air and away from the crowded cafeteria.

'The fake cheese on this vegan sandwich tastes like my old raincoat,' Tashi said with a grimace.

'How would you know?' Starr jibed. 'Did you eat your old raincoat?'

'No, obviously. The taste of the cheese just reminds me of how my old raincoat smelt.'

'Yeah, I know what you mean. Some candy tastes exactly like my gran's perfume.'

'I know, right.' Tashi glanced sideways at Joel.

He knew this food banter was their attempt at distracting him from his misery. He appreciated them for it but couldn't get out of his bad mood. He thought eating might help calm him down but chewing on his peanut butter and jelly sandwich felt like eating two pieces of cardboard stuck together with a lot of construction glue. Starr noticed him struggling and passed him a juice.

'Thanks,' he said in a dry voice. His throat felt glued closed. He put the rest of the sandwich down.

'I'm sorry about Carter.' Tashi said. 'What he did was very insensitive. He can be that way sometimes, but he's a good person deep down.'

'Very deep down,' Starr said.

'Thanks,' Joel said, 'but you don't have to apologize. You didn't do anything wrong.'

'I know, but I feel responsible because …'

'Because you like Carter?' Joel's voice was returning to normal thanks to the juice.

'Yeah. I've been suffering with an all-consuming crush on Carter Herrera since first day of freshman year.' Tashi shrugged apologetically.

Starr rolled her eyes.

'You make liking him sound like a disease that you have no control over,' she said. 'You can just stop liking him you know.'

'It *is* like a disease. A miserable plague. I've tried to stop liking him, I truly have. I'm just doomed to crush on Carter Herrera to the end of my days, no matter how much of a vain, insensitive jock he is. It'd be different if he had no redeeming qualities, but he is a brilliant actor.'

So Carter was an actor after all. Called it, Joel thought. He kind of knew how Tashi felt. He had kept liking Patrick, the boy from his old school, even though there'd been tons of red flags. It wasn't until after Patrick had really hurt him that Joel was able to finally let those feelings go.

'They say love is blind,' he said, giving Tashi an understanding smile.

'If I were blind I wouldn't be in this predicament,' Tashi said with a sigh. 'I mean, you *saw* him, Joel, you *saw* what I'm up against.'

'He is pretty hot,' Starr said, the way someone might say "I'm sorry you're sick with a debilitating disease". She patted Tashi on the hand soothingly.

'I know, right.' Tashi picked up another slice of her vegan sandwich and bit into it half-heartedly. 'He's one of the hottest boys to be born on this or any other world.'

'Yeah, one of,' Joel agreed, thinking of Royal Dumaine, who he should definitely not be thinking about. Because, straight. Because, Lana. Because, have some dignity, Joel.

They spent the rest of the lunch hour talking. Tashi gently asked Joel about the fainting thing and he explained NMH. She was cool about it – sympathetic but not over-the-top. Some people treated him like he was always on the verge of a near death experience, like some fragile, broken kid. They never relaxed around him. Others, the Carter Herrera's of the world, treated him like a freak or a joke. When those people looked at Joel all they saw was the fainting thing. Tashi and Starr weren't like that. When they looked at him they saw *him*, not just some kid with a fainting condition.

'Okay, you two,' Tashi began, flipping open a notepad and balancing it on her knees like she was about to conduct an official survey, 'it's time for the *Ultimate Get-To-Know-You Faves Quiz*. Here are the rules: No lying. No overthinking. Just blurt it out.' She clicked her pen dramatically.

'Pressure,' Joel joked, leaning back against the tree.

'First question,' Tashi said, 'favorite music genre?'

'Easy,' Joel said. "Eighties. Synths, big hair, way too much eyeliner. Heaven.'

'I like lots of things,' Starr said without hesitation, twirling a lock of her braids around her finger. 'Missy Elliott, Lizzo, Billie Eilish, Lil Nas X.'

Tashi then answered for herself. 'Mine is punk and nineties grunge. Give me angry guitars and emotional breakdowns set to a mad drum solo.' She scribbled notes and plowed on. 'Favorite band from your favorite genre?'

'Soft Cell,' Joel said immediately. "Or maybe The Cure, or Culture Club, or The Human League. Depends on my mood.'

Starr laughed. 'I'm gonna say Missy Elliott.'

'Mine is Dead Kennedys,' Tashi said with a grin. 'They are the punk blueprint. Oh, and MC5 and Bad Brains!' She jotted everyone's answers down. 'Favorite movie?'

Joel scratched his head. '*The Care Bears Movie*–don't laugh!–it's got a really well-developed plot!'

The girls laughed despite being warned not to and despite Joel's faux grumpy glares.

'*Love and Basketball*, is mine' Starr said with a dreamy sigh. 'Romance goals.'

'*10 Things I Hate About You*,' Tashi chimed. 'Kat Stratford was my childhood hero.' Tashi barely let them breathe before launching into the next question: 'Cuisine?'

'Southern,' Starr said. 'Give me cornbread, gumbo, and beignets. Please and thank you.'

'Italian,' Joel said. 'Veggie lasagna is my whole personality in food form. Cheesy, lumpy, messy.'

Tashi laughed. 'Mine is Thai. Spice it till I cry.' She entered their answers into her notebook. 'Favorite individual food item?'

'Chocolate pudding,' Joel said, like it was obvious.

'Mac and cheese,' Starr said with a small grin.

'Deep fried tofu, no, wait, sushi!' Tashi nearly shouted, punching the air like she'd scored a goal. 'Now, favorite color?'

'Blue,' Joel said, the image of Royal Dumaine's eyes flashing in his mind. 'Or maybe black.'

'Purple,' Starr said, stretching her legs out.

'Mine is pink, obviously,' Tashi said, then added, 'like neon, not natural. What about your favorite animal?'

'Sloths,' Joel said. 'They're like my spirit animal.'

'Panthers,' Starr said without missing a beat. 'Strong. Elegant. Quiet until they're not.'

Tashi pretended to think hard. 'Axolotl. Weird yet interesting. Much like me.' Tashi mimicked an axolotl's weird movements and under-water breathing.

Joel laughed so hard he banged his head on the tree trunk. 'Ouch!'

'How about artist?' Tashi asked. 'Anyone you really love? For me, it's Mark Rothco.'

Joel didn't know who Mark Rothco was, so made a mental note to Google him later. 'Mine is a bit cliché for a gay boy – Andy Warhol.'

'Oh, I love Andy,' Starr said, 'but my favorite is Basquiat.'

'Cool,' Joel said. 'Very cool.'

'Bonus question,' Tashi said, wiggling her eyebrows. 'Favorite thing about boys?'

Joel went red but answered anyway. 'Their eyes. I don't know why, just …' He gestured vaguely, embarrassed.

'Their smiles,' Starr said softly. 'Especially when they're being sweet without knowing it.'

Tashi grinned. 'I'm a mega-fangirl for their whole stupid, chaotic energy. Like they can't help but make everything a little bit mad and unpredictable. It's kinda adorable.' Tashi dropped her voice to a whisper. 'I'm also a big fan of their hot, hot bods!'

They all dissolved into giggles. Joel felt lit up on the inside with a rare, easy kind of happiness that he hadn't felt for years. He really liked these two awesome girls. Maybe this year he really could have a new, easier life?

*** ***

When the bell rang they all headed off to different classes. Joel got lost on his way to Earth Science, but other than that his next two classes were uneventful, except for the occasional kid whispering about him or giving him odd looks. He met up with Starr and Tashi again for their last class of the day – junior English with Miss Dill. Despite the presence of Carter Herrera, whom they all pointedly ignored, it was the best English class Joel had ever been in. Miss Dill was a great teacher, often using personal stories to make the topic relatable.

'When I was a junior, all those centuries ago,' Miss Dill said with a smirk, 'the assigned novel for English was the worst book I'd ever read. I hated it. A truly monstrous book full of backward ideas, and also terribly written. Every line on every page was like a razorblade to my eyeballs. In other words, it made my eyes bleed, figuratively speaking.' She shivered. 'An awful, awful book. I won't name it, for fear of summoning its spirit here to torment me further. Now, much time has passed since I was sixteen. Thankfully, the Louisiana Board of Education has evolved more or less apace with the many social movements that have enriched our lives – civil rights, women's rights, LGBTIQ+ rights. Of course, we still have a way to go but at least we can be grateful that the assigned novel for junior English is a work of beauty and insight penned by one of our nation's greatest writers. The novel you will be reading and discussing for this class has been banned by school boards and attacked by censors so often that it's in the top twenty most banned books in American high schools.'

Joel sat up in his seat, along with the rest of the class. They'd all come to attention as one at the exciting prospect of reading a banned book.

'I see that caught your interest.' Miss Dill said smiling. She tapped the lip of a large cardboard book box on her desk. 'The book in this box will be central to our focus in class this year, which is the way that literature can play a part in transforming society for the better. Let's get to it then.' She stood and opened the box. 'I'm going to need someone to hand these out.' She looked around the class. 'Carter, if you would help me please?'

Rather than just hand out the books, Carter made an Oprah style production of it.

'You get a book, and you get a book, even *you* get a book.' The class laughed along with him.

Joel, Starr and Tashi rolled their eyes in unison. Joel wondered if Carter would've got so many laughs if he wasn't one of the hottest boys alive. One of. No, absolutely no thinking about you know who. The Voldemort of hot boys who shall remain nameless.

When Carter reached Joel he said,

'And you get a book, fainting kid.'

Tashi stood up so fast Joel didn't realize she'd done so until she was face-to-face with Carter, or rather face-to-chest because Tashi was quite a bit shorter than Carter.

'That's not funny,' she hissed, snatching the last two books from Carter's hands (hers and Starr's). 'It's not clever or amusing to tease someone about a serious medical condition, you … you … you absolute plague!'

Carter blinked, looking down at Tashi in shock. Miss Dill raised her voice over the class's Oohs and giggles.

'Carter Herrera and Tashi Bellman, take your seats please, and Carter, see me after class.'

Tashi dropped into her seat, her face flushed. Joel could have hugged her. On his way back to his seat, Carter asked some kids sitting nearby:

'Did she just call me a plague? That's not good, right?'

It was only then that Joel noticed the novel on his desk. *The Color Purple* by Alice Walker. He felt the smile blooming on his face. He had a feeling he was going to do pretty well in his junior English class. He turned to Starr and Tashi.

'I *love* this book,' he said. 'I read it last year, like twice, and I've seen the movie at least a dozen times.'

'Me too,' said Tashi. 'I love Alice Walker.'

'I got you both beat,' Starr said smugly, 'I've read it at least a dozen times and seen the movie twice as often as that.'

'We are so getting an A in this class.' Tashi high-fived them both.

'Tashi Bellman,' Miss Dill said from the front of the class, 'I appreciate your exuberance for English literature but please dial it down just a little.'

'Sorry, Miss Dill.'

Tashi smirked behind the cover of *The Color Purple*, silently mouthing 'We gonna get As, we gonna get As.'

*** ***

When the bell rang signaling the end of class and the end of the school day, Joel got a strong feeling of relief and satisfaction. Despite the thing with Carter, and the thing with Lana in creative writing, and colliding bodily with Royal after the squirrel sneak attack, his first day at the academy hadn't been that bad. He loved creative writing, really liked Miss Dill and had made two new friends in as many days – Starr first and now Tashi. Things were looking up. Maybe he really was going to be able to put his past behind him? Miss Dill chose that moment to pop that small bubble of hope by reminding him he had to report to the pool for his first stint as pool boy for the swim team.

'You've got pool boy duty now, on day one?' Tashi asked.

'Yeah, unless you strangle me with my tie.' He offered the end of his tie to them. 'Please, strangle me with my tie right now.'

'No need for that, Joel,' Starr said, 'we are coming with you.'

'You are?' Joel said simultaneous with Tashi's 'We are?'

'We are. Carter Herrera's on the Swim team.' Starr looked at them as though her meaning was clear. It wasn't. Joel and Tashi looked at each other, confused.

Starr explained, taking Tashi's hand.

'You've been complaining to me for a full twelve months that Carter doesn't know you exist. I think we can be sure he does now. You've made your existence well and truly known to him. And increased his vocabulary. I bet he's googling the definition of plague right now.'

Joel and Tashi glanced at each other again, even more confused. Starr continued explaining.

'You need to strike while the iron's hot, seize the day, close the deal – please add in any other metaphors that work for you. When he sees you again he will take notice, so we're going to spruce you up a bit and go with Joel to the pool. We can keep Joel company, and display your feminine charms for Carter Herrera at the same time.'

'Spruce me up? Display my charms?' Tashi said indignantly. 'I'm not a heifer at a cattle auction! I'm not an object of the male gaze, I'm a—'

Joel interjected: 'A human girl with feelings.'

'Yes, that! I'm a human girl with feelings. I'm not going to prance about in front of some stupid boy—'

'His eyes are the deep dark brown of a Hershey's Kiss,' Starr whispered as she pulled a small make-up case out of her blazer pocket. 'And I'll let you borrow my Pink

Blaze lipstick.' She took a small, silver lipstick cylinder out of the case and passed it before Tashi's eyes like a hypnotist. 'With the Pink Blaze and your hair, your whole look will be *life*.'

Joel nodded. That lipstick and that hair would be life indeed. Carter Herrera wouldn't know what hit him. Tashi stared at the lipstick like it was a magic bullet.

'Vegan and cruelty free?' she asked, the reflection of the lipstick looming large in her glasses.

'Yes,' Starr answered, still waving the lipstick from side to side right in front of Tashi's face. Tashi closed her eyes and nodded, giving in to the twin temptation of Carter's deep brown eyes and the luscious pink, cruelty-free lipstick.

'We're going to display your charms right up in his face!' Joel said.

*** ***

They were back under the tree in the quad. Joel realized they were a "they" now and they already had a special place. He straightened Tashi's tie and picked lint off her blazer while she ran her fingers through her pink hair.

'I feel like I'm betraying my feminist sisters,' Tashi whined as Starr finished applying the lipstick. Starr shushed her to keep her lips still. When they were done Starr and Joel stepped back to check their handiwork. They nodded in approval. Tashi looked seriously cool and seriously pretty, her pink hair and lips popping.

'Carter is a dead man walking,' Starr said. Joel nodded in agreement, though the mention of walking dead woke that lurking anxiety about his weird dreams that seemed to be coming true.

'A total zombie hottie,' he said, facing his fear. 'Okay, that came out wrong. Zombies are not hot.'

'They are not,' Starr agreed.

'I meant, you look great, Tashi, and Carter Herrera would have to be a corpse not to notice you. A hot corpse but still a corpse.'

'Okay, totally dark turn there, Joel,' Tashi said smirking, 'but thanks.'

LOCKER ROOMS, SPEEDOS AND NUMB NOSES

They headed to the pool, both Joel and Tashi visibly more tense with every step. Joel's stomach was both tight and squirming at the same time. The athletics building, which housed indoor tennis courts, the gym and the pool, was the newest building on campus, by a good fifty years. It was barely two years old and faced the playing fields rather than the quad. Joel stopped when he saw the name emblazoned on the concrete façade: Dumaine Athletics Building. He looked at Starr and Tashi. Seriously? They nodded.

'Royal's father is an alumni of the academy,' Starr said. 'He donated the funds for this.' She gestured to the large edifice before them. 'He was a track star and captain of the swim team when he was here.'

Joel thought that sounded about right. Though in his forties Mr. Dumaine still had the body of an athlete. Like his son. No, Joel would not be thinking about Royal's athletic body. Absolutely not. Starr led them into the building, steering them to the left following a sign that read "Aquatic Center". The pool was Olympic size and shimmered beneath a row of sun-lights. Perhaps because it was brand new it didn't give Joel the sad and kind of creepy feeling that most indoor pools did. It didn't smell damp or of too much chlorine either. It was a light-filled, almost beautiful space. For a pool. Joel didn't like pools. They made him anxious because of the whole minimal clothing thing. He was a maximum clothing kind of kid. At least, he had been since his whole life broke apart last year. He used to really love swimming but because of NMH his doctor had given him strict orders that he should never swim alone. If he fainted in the water he'd drown. A dark part of Joel felt drowning was preferable to the humiliation of people seeing his body. After the awful thing with Patrick and the other boys from his old school he hadn't felt comfortable taking his shirt off in front of anyone, not even his parents or doctor; so swimming was one more thing he loved that he'd lost.

'Joel River.' It was the booming voice of Joel's American History teacher, Mr. Johnson, who apparently was also coach of the swim team.

'Yes.' Joel had to crane his neck upwards as the massive teacher came up to him.

'Miss Dill tells me you can't swim. Never had a kid on the swim team who can't swim, but here we are. Athletics is compulsory at Acadia Academy and this is the last team with an open spot, so we're both going to have to make the most of it. Did Miss Dill tell you what you'd be doing on the team?'

'Pool boy,' Joel said embarrassed.

'More or less. You and I will both be support members of the team,' Mr. Johnson said kindly. 'You'll be keeping the locker room tidy, making sure towels are in the laundry hamper and the floors are mopped.'

Right, Joel thought, so basically a maid. His face reddened.

'You'll also be keeping track of equipment and helping me keep time as the boy's train.' Mr. Johnson looked over Joel's shoulder at Starr and Tashi. 'There's only one spot on the team so why are you two here? Are you the cheer squad?'

'Because we're girls we have to be here to cheer on boys?' Tashi bristled. 'We are not here to cheer. I'm realizing I'm rhyming now which is undermining my point.'

'And it's a point I take on board,' Miss Bellman. 'I apologize and applaud your spunk. So why are you here then?'

'As emotional support for Joel,' Starr said.

'Emotional support?' Mr. Johnson's eyebrows arched. 'In other words you are here to lift Mr. River's spirits, to cheer him on as it were.'

'Um, yeah,' Tashi said somewhat weakly.

'Do you need your spirits cheered, Joel? Are you feeling low?' he asked.

Mr. Johnson's tone told Joel that he was expected to say no, that he shouldn't need emotional support for a short stint as pool boy.

'No,' he said. He kind of did though.

'There you have it, ladies,' Mr. Johnson said. Your services are not required. Now off you go. As for you, Joel, the locker room is that way.' He pointed in the general direction of the locker room as he strode away.

Starr and Tashi waived sadly at Joel and turned to leave. A loud laugh from behind them made them all turn back. Coming out of the boy's locker room was Carter Herrera and a bunch of other boys, all wearing the bright red speedos that were the swim team uniform. And nothing else. Joel's, Starr's and Tashi's mouths all dropped open. Synchronous drool response.

'Okay, so everyone on the boy's swim team is incredibly hot,' Joel said.

'Yes,' Starr agreed. 'They truly are.'

The Acadia Academy boy's swim team had been hit hard with the hot gene, like really hard. Every boy on the team was an easy seven, with Carter rising from an eight to a nine because of his appeal increasing in direct proportion to the decrease in clothing.

'My nose feels numb,' Tashi said in a whisper. 'Does anyone else's nose feel numb? Is that something that happens when you see the guy you've pined over for a year wearing the skimpiest swimsuit imaginable?'

'No, I don't think that's a thing that normally happens,' Joel said, smiling at Tashi.

'It is for me.' Tashi's eyes were glued on Carter.

Joel and Starr shared a sideways glance and amused smiles with each other. When they looked back at Tashi her face was screwed up, as if in thought.

'What are you doing?' Starr asked.

'Trying to imagine a skimpier swimsuit.'

They all laughed. Their laugh caught the attention of Carter. His eyes were drawn straight to Tashi's pink hair and lips. He took her in appreciatively. Their job was done. Carter not only knew Tashi existed but liked what he saw. He acknowledged her with a nod of his head and said:

'Hey, plague girl.'

'Plague girl?' Tashi cringed. 'Did he just call me *plague girl?*'

Before Joel or Starr could answer Mr. Johnson spotted them. He impatiently waived the girls towards the exit, then with a jabbing finger directed Joel to the boy's locker room. His expression made it clear that Joel better get a move on and start his pool boy duties immediately.

The girls left, with Tashi muttering "plague girl" under her breath. Joel went through the door to the locker room as Mr. Johnson began addressing the team, telling them they were going to be doing laps to establish their base times.

'Coach, why's fainting kid here?' It was Carter's voice. Joel flinched and involuntarily shut his eyes, blocking out whatever Carter and the coach said next. He didn't want to hear it. As a result he walked into the locker room blind and collided with a wall of bare skin. He opened his eyes. Oh no, no, no, no. Royal Dumaine. Practically naked. Just wearing those skimpy red Speedos. He towered over Joel, so close, looking down with that same expression of surprise and confusion that was his default face when Joel was around.

If Carter Herrera was a nine, Royal Dumaine was a ten by ten million. It should be a crime for a boy to be so stupendously and mathematically incalculably handsome. He reminded Joel of James Dean only hotter and fitter and much more muscled, so kind of not like James Dean at all. And those Speedos. There should be a law against those. The Royal Dumaine statute: Guys as hot as Royal Dumaine shall henceforth and forthwith be banned from wearing skimpy swimsuits, especially red Speedos. Joel averted his eyes by staring at the grey locker room ceiling.

'Sorry,' Joel mumbled, 'eyes were closed, didn't see you.' He glanced back at Royal, took in that wall of smooth, olive skin, and quickly looked away again. 'Sorry for looking,' he stuttered. 'Should be a crime,' he gestured in the direction of Royal's body, 'skimpy!'

Oh. God. No. Stupid mouth!

Out of the corner of his eyes Joel saw the expression on Royal's face change from surprise and confusion to something else. His blue eyes blinked in rapid fire and he flushed. He opened his mouth to say something to Joel but then closed it again. He silently stepped around Joel and walked out of the locker room. Joel staggered to a bench and collapsed face down on it, not because he was having an NMH episode but because he had never been so mortified in his entire life. His arms and legs went limp and hung to the floor either side of the bench. He lay there, belly pressed to the cold wood, like an exhausted sloth slung over a tree branch.

'Royal Dumaine,' he said with lips pressed against the bench and voice muffled, 'is going to be the total end of me.'

It took Joel ages to haul himself up off the bench and do a check of the locker room, making sure all the soap dispensers were full and doing a general tidy up. He went out to get further instructions from Coach Johnson and was given a pocket watch to time the junior and senior boy's laps while coach timed the freshmen and sophomores. The time-keeping went reasonably well. The boys were for the most part pleased with their times and clapped Joel gratefully on the shoulders as if he'd somehow contributed to them. The last kid off the block was Royal. Joel kept his traitor eyes on the stop watch, making sure not to look even once while Royal was in the water doing his laps. He didn't even look up when Royal walked over to him, wet and dripping, to get his lap time. Joel gave it to him and coach wrote it down.

'That's a real good time, son,' coach remarked. 'Something must've been pushing you to perform today.'

Joel felt eyes on him and glanced up to find Royal looking right at him, but he looked away so fast the boy could've given himself whiplash.

What. Was. That?

'New school,' Royal said, 'that's all,' and stalked off.

Joel fumed, irritated and confused by Royal's weird behavior. Maybe he thought Joel was some kind of pervert because of the whole shouting "skimpy" in the locker room thing? The rest of the training session was uneventful, except for Carter calling him "fainting kid" again, which was annoying but not as annoying as catching Royal and Carter in a huddle minutes later, clearly talking about Joel. Carter's eyes darted over at Joel not once but three times while Royal whispered something to him. After that Carter could barely look at Joel, which was worrying. What had Royal said that was so bad that Carter couldn't even look at him let alone make any more fainting kid jokes? So, yeah, that sucked.

It seemed Royal had graduated from stranger to clear enemy in a little over twenty-four hours. That had to be a Joel record. His list of enemies was already longer than the number of days he'd been in America – Lana, Carter and Royal. If he didn't have Starr, Tashi and Aunt Penn he might've walked out of the Dumaine Athletics Building, packed his bags and caught the first available flight back to Australia. But he did have Aunt Penn and his new friends, so he gritted his teeth and tried to pretend that Royal didn't exist.

When training was finally over Joel stayed out by the pool, taking his time winding in the lane dividers so that the team would be showered and changed back into their uniforms before he went into the locker room again. He didn't want to be mistaken for a locker room perv, just hanging around while the team got naked and showered. He took so long with the lane ropes that by the time he finished most of the team had already gone. He felt sure that whoever was left behind would be well-and-truly dressed by then. He steeled himself and headed into the locker room to tidy up. Picking up dirty towels after sweaty teenagers. Yay. He wished Starr and Tashi really had strangled him with his own tie.

When he entered the locker room he was surprised to find it already tidy. No towels lying around, no pools of water all over the floor. Either these were some of the neatest teenage boys on the planet or someone had already cleaned up. The sound of a bucket and mop being put away let him know that someone else was in the locker room. It wasn't the coach. Mr. Johnson was doing a last-minute check of the building before locking it up for the night.

'Hello?' Joel headed toward the room where the laundry hamper and cleaning stuff were kept. Royal came around the corner, tall and handsome as always but thankfully fully dressed. He stopped still when he spotted Joel. Neither of them said anything. Coach Johnson entered behind Joel, whistling when he saw how tidy the locker room was.

'Joel, you've done a bang up job here,' he said. 'You could never tell a bunch of teenage boys had just showered and changed in here.'

Joel and Royal looked at each other. Royal said:

'See you next time, coach,' grabbed his gym bag and left.

Joel watched him go feeling seriously confused. Thunder rumbled overhead. Joel jumped and made some more hamster-like sounds.

'Storm coming,' coach said. 'Already pretty dark out there. You'd better get going too.'

Joel didn't need further encouragement. On his way out his mind was full of questions. Had Royal tidied the locker room so that Joel didn't have to do it? Why would he do that for someone he clearly hated? It was a very weird thing for a sixteen year old boy to do. What was that look on his face he always seemed to get around Joel? Embarrassment or a flush of irritation or what?

When Joel exited the building a flash of lightning made him flinch. The boom of thunder that followed it was deafening. The sky was a mass of roiling purple-black clouds, moving in fast from the south. Joel headed back toward the main building to get his bag and books from his locker. Across the playing fields lights were on in the windows of Oakshade Cottage, so Penn and Starr were home. Given how quickly the storm was rolling in he probably should have gone straight there but he needed his books for homework. He only got as far as the library before the sky opened up and rain poured down. Drenched, he took refuge on the library porch to wait it out. He pulled off his blazer to shake some of the water out. The front of his shirt was wet where it hadn't been covered by the blazer, but the rest was thankfully dry. His hair was dripping on his shoulders though.

The rain intensified as he stood there. Lightning flashed overhead like fireworks and the thunder boomed as if from very close by. Storms in Louisiana seemed to happen right on top of you. Joel shivered as the temperature dropped fast. A few minutes later Royal came out of the library and, once again, stopped in his tracks at the sight of Joel standing there, dripping wet and shivering, like a defeated, half-drowned sloth. Another awkward silence descended, as heavy as the rain falling all around them. Joel fixed his eyes out on the quad, as though watching the puddles of storm water grow. He silently cursed the weather, Louisiana and nature in general. It had been a storm like this one that prompted Royal to carry Joel up to his dorm room, to get him out of the weather but inflicting the greater suffering of humiliation. Now a storm had him bailed up on a porch with the one person he least wanted to be near.

This place was out to get him. The Louisiana heat had forced him to rest on that shady bend of road, where the alligator promptly scared him half to death, all leading to him getting into the Dumaine's limo and coming face-to-face with Royal. A swamp bird had lulled him into a false sense of security and then made him feel that maybe there was something there with Royal. A possibly rabid ninja squirrel had used Joel's thigh as a springboard, causing him to collide face-first into Royal's muscled chest, right in front of Lana Beaux, his newly minted nemesis and Royal's girlfriend. Yes, this must all be the unfolding of some voodoo curse. That was why the pizza boy, T.J., had left the gris-gris bag. He had sensed there was a curse on someone in Aunt Penn's house.

Joel felt Royal's eyes on him but didn't look over. Why was Royal staring at him? Joel fixed his gaze on the growing puddles until Royal looked away, and then kept staring in every direction but Royal's. Ten minutes that felt like a billion later the rain eased. To get to the steps Joel had to pass Royal, who was looking at him again but who quickly averted his eyes when Joel moved. Joel put his blazer back on as he dashed across the quad, aware of Royal descending the library stairs behind him and jogging towards the boys dorm in Nottoway House.

*** ***

Fifteen minutes later Joel dropped his school bag on the porch at home and took off his shoes, socks and blazer before going inside. He found Penn and Starr in the kitchen, irritatingly dry. They were dishing out Chinese food Penn had clearly just picked up from town.

'You're wet,' Penn said in a deadpan voice on spotting him in the doorway. Joel wiped his dripping hair out of his eyes.

'Yes, I've just walked home in a hurricane. I was lucky to make it back alive.'

'I'm glad we don't have company for dinner tonight,' Starr said, 'no decent company would approve of that.' She gestured at Joel's wct shirt.

'What? Southerners don't approve of boys being a bit wet because they nearly died in a hurricane?' Joel dramatically blew wet hair away from his eyes.

'No, Southerners are fine with that. I'm talking about *those*.' She gestured at Joel's shirt gain. Aunt Penn followed her gesture then looked alarmed, and a bit amused.

'What are you talking about?' Joel asked.

'Err,' Penn began, 'your shirt's very wet Joel and, err, well …'

He looked down at his shirt.

'It's wet, so what —' Oh. My. God. 'It's see through!' Joel's voice sounded as horrified as his face must've looked. By "those" Starr had clearly meant his nipples, which were alarmingly visible and prominent through his wet shirt.

'It's like an owl with very pointy eyes is staring at us through your shirt,' Starr said.

'Starr!' Joel slapped his hands over his nipples and half-turned away to preserve what was left of his modesty. Then he realized why Royal had been staring at him while they were stuck on the library porch together. Joel had been doing an inadvertent wet t-shirt show.

'Oh my god.'

'What?' Starr and Penn asked as one.

'Royal!'

'Sorry, I'm not following,' Penn said.

'I took cover from the rain on the library porch and Royal was there too. He kept staring at me. Now I know why. I was pointing these *things* at him. He must think I'm a total pervert!'

'Why would he think that?' Penn asked.

Joel didn't have the words or the desire to tell her about how twice in one day he'd bodily collided with

Royal. The second time when Royal was only wearing Speedos and Joel had shouted the word "skimpy" at him.

'I know that's what he thought,' Joel said miserably.

'Joel,' Starr said in a mischievous voice, 'he was probably just checking out your rack.'

'Ugh, don't say *rack*!' Joel practically dry-retched.

'Yes, definitely don't say rack,' Penn said smirking. 'Whether you're speaking about boys or girls, always say chest or bosom.'

'Sorry,' Starr said mock seriously, 'Royal was just checking out Joel's bosom.'

'That's better,' Penn said.

Joel nearly dry-retched again.

'Buff straight boys don't check out awkward gay boy's nipples,' Joel said crankily.

'They can, though,' Starr said. 'It's a non-binary, pansexual world. Straight guys are free to appreciate gay boy nipples. It's their human right.'

'Stop saying nipples!' Joel shouted.

'Yes, let's,' Penn said. 'I barely understood half of what Starr just said, but what we're both trying to say, Joel, is no-one thinks you're a pervert.'

'And you should let your nipples be out and proud!' Starr blinked at Joel's nipples rather deliberately. 'Though they're already quite out.'

Penn suppressed a laugh and quickly rearranged her face to show the sympathy Joel clearly expected. Then she broke down and guffawed. Guffawed!

'That's it!' Joel stormed out of the kitchen and headed for his room. He shouted after himself: 'I don't want to hear a peep out of either of you until you can show some maturity!'

Their laughter followed him down the hall.

WOLF DREAM

Yellow eyes stared at him through the mist. Other than the mist, he was shrouded in a kind of heavy silence. The frogs and bugs and birds had all gone silent. It was twilight, the sun was very low on the horizon, but the mist made it almost as dark as night. He startled at a low, rumbling growl. It sent shivers up his spine. Was that a wolf? Were there wolves in Louisiana? It growled again, this time louder. He couldn't see it clearly, it was on the other side of a murky pond, all fallen logs and moss and half-sunk swamp cedar trees. Whatever it was, it paced to and fro, its eyes never off him. Those eyes! Those he could see despite the heavy mist. They were lit with an unnatural light. They glowed like flames! A howl rent the air. Joel nearly jumped out of his skin.

He woke standing beneath a grizzled live-oak tree on the edge of the bayou at the back of Oakshade Cottage. The first thing he noticed was that his feet were cold and damp. He was standing barefoot in mud. The next thing he noticed was that he was in his underwear and absolutely nothing else.

'Oh, crap,' he said, 'sleepwalking, again.' He must've fallen asleep after he'd stripped off his wet clothes, dried off, and slumped onto his bed in irritated humiliation at the afternoon he'd had. He wasn't normally the type for afternoon naps, maybe it was a jet lag thing. He turned around and saw Oakshade cottage up the slope a little. The lights were all on. It looked safe and warm. He headed towards it, doing that walk you do when you go outside after watching a horror movie – when you're really scared but are acting like you're not because you know you shouldn't be, because horror movies aren't real. He glanced over his shoulder, more to confirm that he had dreamed those eyes and that growl than to check if anything was actually there.

Something *was* there. He stopped dead still. Dashing through the trees on the far side of the bayou were many shadows. Shadows in the shape of wolves. He ran back to the house, mounted the back stairs in a single leap, got the door open with a little too much fumbling and shut it and locked it behind him. He leant against the door, panting, his chest pounding, his ears ringing. Was he going to faint? He started his breathing exercises to calm down. As he was breathing he remembered a dream he'd had back home. He'd dreamt he was in a fancy restaurant eating pizza with Brad Pitt. He'd recently re-watched *Troy*, and for reasons that don't need to be explained to any teenage girl or gay boy, he'd been crushing hard on Brad. Then he woke to find that he'd been sleepwalking again and wasn't in a restaurant with Brad Pitt at all, but at his own kitchen table, in his rainbow unicorn pajamas. The disappointment of waking up with no Brad Pitt and no pizza had taken weeks to shake. Even so, the taste of the pizza had lingered in his mouth for ages after he woke up. His therapist said that sometimes happened with sleepwalking dreams, some parts of them could seem real even after waking. That must be what had happened just now. The shadow-shapes of the wolves was just a hangover from the sleepwalking dream. That had to be it. His heart was calming and the ringing in his ears had stopped. He crept back into his bedroom. Even though he had only dreamed those firelight eyes and despite the heat, he shut his bedroom window and locked it.

He crept to his bed where he kept his most valued, most secret possession hidden under his pillows. He slipped his hand beneath the pillows and sighed when the familiar softness met his fingers, and the tight knot in his chest eased. He carefully tucked it back under his pillows, hidden from view. It was silly, maybe, but just knowing it was nearby helped him feel a little less like the world was about to split open under his feet. And then he crawled into bed and tried not to think about those firelight eyes.

THE FALL

HALLOWEEN BIRTHDAY

It had been nearly three months since *The Wet Shirt Incident*, otherwise known as the day Joel's life was ruined. Also the day Joel's brain had been fried by the sight of Royal Dumaine in a tiny, traitorous red speedo. Yet, somehow, he had survived. Barely. Once a week, without fail, he'd been roped into pool boy duties at swim team practice, ferrying towels, checking chlorine levels, and enduring the exquisite torture of Royal gliding through the water like some perfect, impossible dream. At least creative writing studio had been a saving grace. Joel had been quietly crushing it, earning the kind of praise from Ms. Dill that almost made up for the slow death of his dignity on the pool deck.

Week after week, Joel found himself tagging along to Starr's kendo practice and Tashi's archery training, growing more and more impressed—and a little envious—of their ninja-level reflexes while he remained about as graceful as a sleepy sloth on roller skates. Watching them slice through the air and hit bullseyes with ease made him feel like he was still figuring out how his own limbs were supposed to work.

Other than martial arts practice and pool boy duty, Joel, Starr and Tashi had spent the last months focused on schoolwork and avoiding certain boys (Carter and

Royal). Joel had vowed to avoid Royal at all costs since the aforementioned incident. He didn't think he could ever look him in the face again. Besides, no matter how attractive Joel found him, Royal was straight and dating Lana; and had also made it clear he thought Joel was a loser. "Just some junior". That phrase had echoed in Joel's head for weeks. Each time he remembered it, he felt stung all over again, so he made up his mind never to think about or speak to Royal ever again.

Now, with the humid air finally cooling and jack-o'-lanterns leering from every porch, it was Halloween night, which also happened to be Starr's seventeenth birthday. Joel had organized a low-key celebration – a movie night for Starr, Tashi and himself, complete with blood-colored popcorn. He'd planned the perfect 1980s fright-show festival. The main feature, *The Hunger*, was a true classic of the vampire genre starring David Bowie, who also happened to be one of Joel's musical heroes. After *The Hunger*, they'd watch *A Nightmare on Elm Street*, and then *Beetlejuice* to close out the evening. It was going to be a long, spooky, and super fun night.

Joel stood in the living room of Oakshade Cottage, surveying his Halloween decoration masterpiece with his hands on his hips like a very proud, very gay, very exhausted BFF. He'd strung fake cobwebs across the curtain rods, tacked paper bats and ghosts to the walls, and even arranged a shrine of jack-o'-lantern candles on the coffee table so it looked like a low-budget séance was about to go down. On the couch, he'd spread a big velvet throw blanket he'd found in Aunt Penn's linen cupboard—dark purple, appropriately witchy—and stacked it with a mountain of pillows for maximum cozy vibes. The TV was cued up, waiting for their 1980s horror movie extravaganza. The popcorn—a menacing shade of blood-red—sat proudly in a giant plastic cauldron he'd found in Aunt Penn's big box of decorations. Joel smiled from ear to ear, surveying his work.

Best. BFF. Ever.

The front door burst open and Tashi stumbled in backwards, her arms full of Tupperware containers. She was wearing a black hoodie with pink devil horns stitched onto the hood and combat boots that looked like they could survive an actual apocalypse.

'Halloween slash birthday party cuisine delivery!' she announced. 'Help! I can't feel my hands!'

Joel dashed over, taking the topmost container just as it started to slide. He set it on the coffee table and peered inside.

'Oh my god, Tashi, what is all this?'

'Ghost cake,' Tashi said, pulling down her hood and pointing to the delicious-looking marvel in the container Joel had rescued. 'And vampire cookies. And caramel apple bites. And graveyard cupcakes. And something I'm calling swamp punch but which may actually be a health violation.'

'You are the absolute best,' Joel said.

They quickly unpacked the spoils. Tashi had seriously gone all out: vampire-bat-shaped cookies, cupcakes like graveyards with candy tombstones, a Black Bavarian cake with edible cobwebs and candy ghosts, a punch that was 1% Blackberry, 1% lime, and 98% sugar, and a "salad" made with green gummy leaves and candy eyeballs and teeth.

'You are a Halloween goddess,' Joel said, popping a candy eyeball into his mouth.

'Why, thank you, Joel, I do my best.'

They'd barely finished setting up the food when they heard Aunt Penn's car pull into the drive. Penn had taken Starr to her grandmother's place for a birthday visit.

'Birthday girl incoming!' Joel announced, as he bounded over and flung open the door like he was hosting the Oscars.

Starr stood on the porch, all dramatic eyeliner and smoky eyes. A vintage diamante tiara was perched in her braided hair. A gift from her grandmother. Otherwise, she was wearing a black velvet dress, sparkly black tights, and combat boots that matched Tashi's.

'You both wore boots?' Joel said. 'Was there a memo?'

'Combat boots are year-round appropriate,' Starr said, breezing past him into the living room.

'They really are,' Tashi agreed, handing Starr a cupcake immediately.

'Happy Birthday!' she said, echoed quickly by Joel.

'Presents first!' Joel declared, 'horror later.' He gestured to the TV where the opening credits of *The Hunger* were on pause.

Starr's eyes sparkled as she sat down on the velvet-draped couch. 'You guys didn't have to get me anything.'

'Hush,' Tashi said, thrusting a gift wrapped in silver paper into her hands. 'Open mine first.'

Starr ripped off the paper and gasped. It was a vintage hardcover copy of *The Complete Plays of Oscar Wilde*. Starr held it like it was made of gold.

'Tashi!' she cried. 'You know I love Oscar! I've been wanting a complete plays forever!'

'My Dad took me all over New Orleans looking for it,' Tashi said smugly. 'I found it at a second-hand bookstore on the edge of the French Quarter.'

'You are an angel in pink hair,' Starr said, hugging her.

'My turn!' Joel said, bouncing in place. He thrust his present forward. Wrapped in pink paper, with a huge pink bow stuck on the top, it was an explosion of camp in contrast to Tashi's elegant wrapping. Starr unwrapped it and let out a delighted squeal. It was a vintage black Barbie doll, still in its original box, looking just as new as it'd been in 1980.

'Joel,' Starr breathed, running her hands over the box. 'How did you find this? They're so rare. '

He shrugged, trying and failing to act casual. 'That's top secret. It's from me and Aunt Penn. It cost *way* more than I had in my piggy bank. Do you like her?'

'Like her? I *love* her!'

Starr launched herself at him, knocking him back into the pile of pillows.

'I love you, Joel River!' she declared.

'Love you too, birthday queen,' he said, laughing.

Tashi threw herself into the dog pile, and soon they were all tangled up in a heap of limbs and laughter and too many cushions. When they finally untangled themselves and got semi-upright again, Joel flung himself at the remote.

'Okay,' he said, grinning. 'Enough feelings. It's time for a 1980s fright-show extravaganza.'

He hit play, and *The Hunger* flickered to life on the TV, all moody lighting and velvet darkness. David Bowie appeared on screen, impossibly cool in his round sunglasses and eternal cheekbones. Tashi shrieked immediately, stuffing a handful of blood-red popcorn into her mouth.

'David Bowie is literally a bisexual fever dream,' she said through popcorn crumbs.

'Preach,' Starr said, nodding solemnly.

Their 1980s movie fright-show was everything Joel had hoped it would be. They screamed at the scary parts, cheered when things got hot, and argued (loudly) over whether the vampire Miriam from *The Hunger* was a villain or an icon. By the time the *Beetlejuice* credits were rolling, they were all glassy-eyed and yawning. Joel stretched, and blinked at the clock. Nearly midnight.

'Pumpkin time, Cinderellas,' Tashi said, groaning as she sat up.

'Noooo,' Starr protested. 'Stay. We'll braid each other's hair. Watch *The Hunger* again. Eat some more popcorn.'

'I wish I could,' Tashi said, pulling on her hoodie. 'But my mom will turn into a yeti if I'm not home by twelve-thirty. It took months of begging to get her to agree to such a late night in the first place.' She texted her mom, who came to pick her up surprisingly quickly for midnight on Halloween. Joel and Starr walked her to the door, each with an arm slung companionably around her shoulder.

'You were the best party guest ever,' Joel said.

'You were the best party planner ever,' Tashi said, booping his nose.

'And I was the best birthday girl ever,' Starr said, laughing.

'No contest,' Joel said.

'Definitely,' Tashi agreed.

'It was the best birthday ever,' Starr said, beaming at them both.

Tashi's mom flashed the headlights and waved at Joel and Starr.

'Happy Birthday again, Starr!' Tashi called over her shoulder as she jogged down the steps.

'Thanks, Tash!' Starr called back, waving dramatically.

Joel and Starr watched until the car disappeared among the grove of live-oaks bordering the school, then closed the door and turned to the mess in the living room.

'Oh dear,' Starr said.

'Just ignore the mess and go to bed,' Joel ordered. 'Birthday girls don't clean up after their own parties.' Joel said it forcefully enough that Starr acquiesced and traipsed off to bed, yawning. Joel set to cleaning up. He was happy to do it, exhausting though it was, because the mess was the evidence that he had thrown Starr a great little birthday party, and that he'd made his friend happy. He felt warm and light all over and a sudden gladness that he'd made such good friends. It wouldn't have happened if he hadn't left home to attend Acadiaville Academy. He would never have left if the awful thing with Patrick hadn't happened. Maybe what everyone said was right – everything works out in the end.

***   ***

Once the living room was clean as a whistle, Joel lugged a garbage bag as big as Santa's sack outside to the trash bin. The screen door groaned on its hinges as Joel nudged it open with his hip, the heavy garbage bag swinging against his leg. The night air was thick and close, full of the sour-sweet smell of fallen magnolias and the distant, muddy scent of the bayou. The old live-oak trees loomed along the fence line, their gnarled arms dripping with moss that swayed ever so slightly in the stale breeze. Crickets pulsed in the grass, their song a low, relentless hum.

Joel yawned, blinking against the darkness, and shuffled toward the trash bins set beneath the lattice lean-to at the side of the house. His bare feet whispered over the damp grass, the bag rustling like dry leaves. Just as he lifted the lid with one hand and dropped the bag in with the other, he caught a flicker of movement out of the corner of his eye.

Someone was standing at the edge of the yard. Joel froze, his heart knocking once, hard, against his ribs. Beneath the massive live-oak that marked the far boundary of the property stood a figure, dark and still, holding a blue glass lamp that flickered dimly in the heavy shadows. The candle inside the lamp guttered, sending warped shadows crawling over the grass.

'Hello?' Joel called out, his voice breaking the hush of the night.

The figure didn't move. Didn't answer.

Joel squinted. The live-oak's limbs kept the silhouette in deep shadow, but he could just make out the person's outline. It was a woman, an elderly, black woman with long dreadlocks.

Joel took a cautious step forward. 'Who are you? You need something?'

Still no answer. Just the slow, rhythmic flicker of the candle in that blue glass. The crickets quieted all at once, as if fear had muffled them. Joel became suddenly aware of the silence, heavy and expectant. Then, out of nowhere, birds began to sing. First one or two, then quickly joined by more. Wild, bright trills from the trees above. One by one, birds descended from the dark sky. Sparrows, thrushes, and tiny warblers fluttered down onto the fence near where the old woman stood, their small bodies lined up along the fence. Others alighted on the sagging branches of the live-oak above her, sending thin showers of lichen drifting down.

Joel stumbled back a step. A raven swooped in from nowhere and landed with a heavy thunk on the rim of an old tin trashcan, its beady eyes fixed on Joel. The birdsong swelled, a chaotic, crazy roar that seemed to pour into Joel's ears, pressing against his skull, trying to force its way into his brain. He clapped his hands over his ears. The air itself seemed to vibrate with the shrill noise. Then … Snap.

Something broke in Joel's mind, a hairline crack that split wide open. All sound vanished in an instant. The silence that replaced it was absolute. It wasn't mere quiet. It was dense, total, a wall of stillness so complete it seemed to hum against his skin and sing in his ears. Joel staggered, disoriented, the world around him drained of all noise, as if he had fallen into a deep, silent well.

The blue glass lamp began to glow brighter, the candle flame blazing. The silhouette of the woman shimmered, her edges blurring. The birds, motionless as figurines, turned their heads toward Joel in unison, black bead-eyes shining. Joel tried to move, to speak, but his body refused him. The raven let out a cry. Joel heard it as a vibration in his bones. It lifted its wings, feathers unfolding like slow explosions, and rose into the air. As it flew, the others followed, birds streaming upward into a whirling column of wings and bodies that spiraled above the live-oak, forming a swirling circle like the eye of a feathered tornado.

The woman's form lifted too, her feet leaving the ground. Her lamp swung back and forth, casting rings of blue light that pulsed outward, washing over the fence, the yard, the house itself. With each pulse, the world seemed to peel back, like a thin film being stripped away, revealing flashes of something deeper beneath: a swamp teeming with flickering ghost lights; ancient trees twisted into impossible shapes; a timber church, leaning and half sunk, and shadows, bodies, twisted and unnatural, moving toward him.

Joel's breath caught in his throat as the woman's face emerged from the shadows. Her eyes were luminous blue, not reflecting light but radiating it. Her lips moved soundlessly, mouthing words Joel could not hear but somehow understood in his gut.

They are coming.

The blue light flared one last time, a blinding flash, and then Joel saw nothing but white. He collapsed to his knees, the grass cool and real beneath his palms. The normal sounds of night came back slowly: the creak of the porch swing, the rustle of the breeze, the low hum of insects.

The dreadlocked woman was gone. The birds were gone. Even the raven had vanished, leaving only a single black feather spinning lazily to the ground. Joel sat back on his heels, heart hammering, staring at the spot where she had stood. A faint whiff of candle smoke hung in the air. He reached out and picked up the fallen feather, turning it over in his fingers. It was still warm.

From deep in the bayou, something called out – a sound so ancient and mournful it made the hairs on Joel's arms stand straight up. Some deep, hidden part of his mind or heart recognized the sound. It was the voice of nature itself. He stumbled to his feet, eyes scanning the darkness. Far off in the distance, on the other side of the bayou, a blue light flickered once more, tiny as a firefly, and then was gone.

Joel didn't realize he was running until he was halfway up the porch steps, the screen door banging open against the wall as he hurtled inside. He quickly shut the screen and the door behind him. His heart rattled like a trapped bird against his ribs. He slid down against the door, the raven feather still clutched tight in his trembling hand. "They are coming" the voice in his mind had said. He didn't know who or what was coming. But he knew it had already begun. A heavy fear hit him. Had any of that been real? What if it was a hallucination? Was the thing that was coming his own insanity? What if the dreams and whatever he'd just experienced outside meant he was going crazy? Tears welled up in his eyes. He took himself to bed and cried himself to sleep, hugging his most valued, most secret possession tightly to his chest.

UNICORNS AND THE GARDEN OF GOOD AND EVIL

Starr's grandmother, Mrs. Ursuline Davis, was the coolest grandmother Joel had ever met. It was mid-November before she managed to come over for dinner, because her church schedule often clashed with Aunt Penn's work schedule. Mrs. Davis went to night mass at Saint Augustine's Catholic Church at least three times a week. Then she went again on Sunday mornings. Joel hadn't been in a rush to meet her, assuming such a religious woman would not like him at all. He was very pleasantly surprised to be wrong.

Because Mrs. Davis didn't drive, Penn had picked her up from her apartment behind the quilting shop and driven her over to Oakshade Cottage. The first Joel knew of her arrival was the laughter coming in from the yard through the open windows. Mrs. Davis had one of those laughs that gave you a warm feeling in the chest. She and Penn had got out of the car laughing, come up the stairs laughing and walked through the house laughing the whole way. By the time they entered the kitchen Joel was beaming from ear to ear. The joy was that contagious.

Like Starr, Mrs. Davis was an African-American woman with perfectly formed plaits that hung down to her waist. She was young for a grandmother, with only a few grey hairs flecked through the rich brown. She was wearing what looked like a Chanel skirt suit in sky blue. Starr noticed Joel admiring it and whispered:

'I made that myself. Turned out okay.'

'Turned out amazing,' Joel replied.

Dinner was a success with Mrs. Davis congratulating Penn on the flavor of the food. Mrs. Davis wasn't aware that earlier that day Joel had found Penn and Starr in the kitchen emptying Tupperware containers of delicious-smelling food into proper dishes. Starr had arranged for Tashi to make the food so that Mrs. Davis didn't discover that Penn couldn't cook. Putting the food in Penn's dishes as though she'd cooked it herself had been part of the subterfuge.

'This tastes as good as any gumbo I've ever had. Gumbo without meat is hard to pull off but you've made this delicious.'

Penn quickly changed the subject. Joel and Starr smirked at each other. Joel made a mental note to tell Tashi, yet again, that she was an amazing cook. Mrs. Davis brought home-made banana pudding for dessert. Joel had never had it before. After one spoonful he hugged the bowl to his chest and whispered lovingly:

'Where have you been all my life', which got a laugh from everyone at the table.

The rest of the night went really well. Mrs. Davis took to Joel straight away, spending half the time talking to Joel about his writing.

'Being a writer isn't going to be an easy life,' she'd said. 'The world makes everything harder for artists, but you stick with it, Joel. Never let yourself be discouraged. I'm always telling Starr, our most precious dreams don't just come true by themselves. We have to make them come true with our own hard work and perseverance.'

That was some of the best advice Joel had ever been given. It wasn't the only precious advice Mrs. Davis gave that night. After dessert, with the empty bowls pushed to the side and the table cleared of everything but mugs of coffee, Mrs. Davis turned her thoughtful gaze on Joel.

'So, Joel,' she said, wrapping her fingers around her mug, 'how are you finding life in the South? I imagine it's a little different to what you're used to.'

Joel sat up a little straighter. 'It's been … an adjustment,' he admitted. 'The weather's different to home, the bugs are braver, and people here believe in all kinds of things I thought only existed in movies and books.' He hesitated, then added with a crooked smile, 'Southerners are superstitious. *Super* superstitious.'

Mrs. Davis gave a slow, knowing nod. 'That we are. My family, the Davis line, we have tales going back generations about them superstitions.' She glanced sideways at Starr with a sly look. 'You know the one I mean, baby?'

Starr rolled her eyes. 'The ghost protector?'

'That's the one.' Mrs. Davis turned back to Joel. 'Our family lore says we have a protector, following the Davis clan down the generations. Some say it's a ghost, some say a voodoo priest, and some swear it's a demon. Whatever it is, the story goes that this … being … has shadowed the Davis family for over two hundred years. It protects us, in its own strange way. But there are rumors it's done … terrible things too.' She took a sip of her coffee. 'My own grandma, Francine Davis, swore she saw it once, when she was just five years old. She didn't describe no ghost, no monster. Said it was a *white man*, dressed fine as you please – brocade vest, gold watch chain, and a top hat. She saw him standing at the edge of the woods, watching her like he was making sure she was safe, or maybe sizing up his next meal.'

Joel's mouth had gone dry. He tried to laugh it off, but his voice caught. 'That sounds like something out of a very scary movie.'

Mrs. Davis smiled kindly. 'That's exactly what I think. Scary movies aren't real, are they? The South has a way of getting inside your head, Joel. The heat, the shadows, the quiet bayou, all these stories passed around like sweet tea, it can mess with your mind. My advice? Don't get too carried away with what you *think* you see or hear around here. The mind plays tricks. And in this part of the world, the mind is encouraged to play even more and bigger tricks.'

Joel let out a breath he hadn't realized he'd been holding. He felt like someone had just opened a window in a stuffy room. Maybe he wasn't losing his mind? Maybe it was just the atmosphere of this place that was causing his dreams and making him think they were coming true. Things did seem stranger than they actually were around here. He nodded and said, 'That's super wise. Thank you, Mrs. Davis.'

'You're welcome, sugar,' she said, sipping her coffee. 'Now, Starr, lead me to the bathroom. I need to freshen up before Penn drives me home.'

Mrs. Davis left saying she could rest easy that her baby child Starr was in good hands. She gave Joel a bear hug that made him breathless but happy, then Penn drove her home, leaving Starr and Joel alone in the house.

'I guess this means I've been assessed as no threat to your virtue?'

'It does,' Starr said, smiling. 'You make a good first impression. Gran told me she loved you when you were helping Penn serve up the gumbo.'

'That quick! Wow, I'm so good at charming grandmas.'

'Yeah, she said the rule still stands though, I'm not to be alone with any boys she doesn't know, but she said you don't count as a boy.'

'What! But I *am* a boy! A proper human boy!'

'I don't know what to tell you. Gran just doesn't see you as a threat to my virtue. It's a compliment. Gran thinks teenage boys are the worst. But she likes gay people. Her best friend for her whole life, since she was five years old, is a gay guy, Bertrand Dushamel. He owns the antique store in town, and he's very sweet, gentle and harmless. Gran said you remind her of him.'

'I should be offended, but I feel weirdly flattered.'

'Come on, let's get the dishes done as a surprise for when Penn gets back.'

'Ugh, what kind of teenager are you? We should be going wild when we're home alone, not planning thoughtful surprises.'

Starr looked at him as though seeing him for the first time.

'Huh, you are a real boy after all.'

'I really am.' Joel smirked before dashing into the sitting room to put on some music. Classic Billie Eilish – "Bad Guy". He turned the volume right up and danced back into the kitchen where Starr was dancing too. Then he helped her to wash and put away the dishes, like a real rebel.

Outside, the wind rattled the windows gently. Since Halloween, Joel had avoided going outside after dark, and had tried not to dwell on the fact that either he was having dreams and hallucinations that meant he was going crazy, or something freaky and paranormal was going on in Acadiaville. Either way, he didn't want to think about it. He chose instead to think about how good things were for him here. Oakshade Cottage was warm and safe and full of a kind of magic that no darkness could ever touch. The magic that was friendship and *Home*.

*** ***

The rest of the week at school, Joel, Starr and Tashi focused on homework and continued avoiding Carter and Royal, as they had done for weeks now. It had become second nature to them to stay away from the places where Royal and Carter hung out. It was easy enough to avoid Royal – he was a senior and not in any of their compulsory classes. Avoiding Carter wasn't as easy. As a junior he was in both their English and American History classes. Even so, they did their utmost to pretend he didn't exist. This wasn't so hard for Joel because Carter had neither looked at nor said a word to Joel since the first swim training session. What had Royal said to the irritatingly smooth and handsome theater major to make him avoid Joel so completely?

Tashi had extra motivation to ignore Carter. She didn't want the nickname "plague girl" to stick. Joel didn't blame her, it was as bad as "fainting kid". Unfortunately, it was quite hard for Tashi to ignore Carter because he kept trying to get her attention by waving and smiling and pantomime pouting when she didn't acknowledge him. She made an admirable attempt to pretend she didn't notice all this but the flush to her cheeks proved she had indeed noticed.

They all had their minor studios as their last class for the week, which meant that Joel and Starr said goodbye to Tashi in the quad as she headed to Culinary Arts and they went together to Costume Design. Barely a minute later Joel and Starr got a group text from Tashi: *I miss you already! Come to my place tomorrow to hang?* They texted back a *YES* straight away. Look at me, Joel thought, a proper human boy with weekend plans with friends. No. Weekend plans with a set of BFFs!

The Costume Design studio was held in one of the basement rooms of the theater building. Weeks before, as Starr had led him there for their first costume design class, she'd told him that the students called it 'the frock dungeon'. Joel had smirked at that, picturing a space that was part dungeon, part drag queen bar. Not that he'd ever been in a drag bar. He'd only ever seen such magical places in movies or on TV.

The theater building was opposite the library and was another old, red brick structure that looked more like a mansion than a school building. On their way now Joel remembered with a shiver of shame what had happened before that first class. The memory triggered another visceral flashback, this one the longest he'd ever had.

*** ***

Starr stopped Joel on the porch before they went inside the theater building for their first costume design studio.

'Are you ready?' she asked, just as she had that first time.

'Yeah, sure. Wait, why do you look so worried?'

'Because this is your first Costume Design class.'

'Yours too,' Joel had said, not sure what the big deal was.

'Yes, but—'

'But what? Are you worried I'm going to be terrible at costume design and embarrass you? Well, I am, I'm going to be awful at it, just horrendous. Whether or not you're embarrassed is up to you. You can pretend you don't know me if you like.'

'I'm not going to pretend I don't know you!'

Joel let out a small sigh of relief. 'Okay, we're in this together then,' he said. When he went to step through the door he found himself held in place by Starr's hand on his arm. It felt just as real as it had when it'd happened.

'Joel, do you remember when we were chatting in your room that first night—'

'When we both expressed our mutual appreciation of super swol guys?'

'Yes, then. Do you remember that you asked me what Royal's major program was?'

'Yeah, you said it was music.' Joel started worrying about the direction the conversation was going. Anything to do with Royal inevitably led to embarrassment and mad squirrels and freak storms and humiliatingly visible nipples.

'No, I said his passion was Blues music and that his *minor* was music, but that he had a different major program because there were no other spaces left.'

Joel thought back to the conversation in his bedroom and realized she was right. He had misremembered it. 'Oh, right, yeah,' he'd said. Starr took his hand and squeezed.

'And do you remember I said that the only major that had room for Royal to join was—'

'Oh, god. Oh no.' Joel stared into Starr's eyes in horror. With everything that had been going on in that first week of school he had forgotten it. 'He's a Costume Design major,' he said in a choked voice. He remembered that moment so clearly now, weeks later, that gut-wrenching feeling. And now it seemed like he was standing there all over again, reliving it – standing there on the theater building porch, his face constricted in alarm, his mouth agape like a fish suffocating out of water.

'He's a Costume Design major,' Starr echoed, giving his hand another reassuring squeeze.

Joel lifted the end of his red tie and offered it to her. 'Please, strangle me now,' he said.

Starr batted the tie away. 'Just take a deep breath and calm yourself. We don't have to talk to him. We don't even have to acknowledge his existence.'

Joel nodded half-heartedly, dazed.

'And don't ask me to strangle you. Suicide jokes are not funny.'

Joel blinked. Starr was right about that. He muttered a weak 'Okay'. Then he offered her his tie again. 'Will you at least tie me to a tree somewhere far away from here, so that I don't humiliate myself again? Somewhere deep in the swamp. Not forever, just until the end of the school year.'

'Don't be so dramatic. It'll be fine. It's one class a week. Now come on.' She tugged on his hand but Joel stayed rooted in place.

'Please tie me up somewhere far away from here. It's for my own good. Please! Bind and gag me now!'

'Stop begging me to bind and gag you!'

A cough behind them had made them both jump.

'Excuse me, can I get by?' Royal Dumaine. Of course it was. By the flushed look on his face and the alarmed glance he shot Joel, he'd heard Starr tell off Joel for begging to be tied up.

'No,' Joel said loudly, waving his tie about, 'I wasn't begging to be tied up! Well, I was, but not for real! I wanted her to strangle me—'

Starr clamped a hand over Joel's mouth before he dug himself any deeper. Royal looked down at him, his eyebrows furrowed with disbelief but his lips quirking into an almost smile.

'Okay, whatever,' he muttered, before he shook his head and walked inside. Joel and Starr looked into each other's dumbfounded eyes. Starr's hand was still clamped to his lips so Joel had mumbled through her fingers a pathetic: 'Thank you for saving me from myself.'

'Yeah, should've tied you up,' she said, smirking. She removed her hand from his mouth and dragged him inside the building and down the stairs to the Costume Design studio before he regained his wits enough to resist.

*** ***

Whoa. That was a doozy. That was all months ago. He checked his surroundings to see how much time had passed while he was flashbacking, but everything looked exactly as it did before. It must've been just a few seconds. Starr was looking at him with concern.

'Are you okay, Joel? She asked.'

'Sorry, I was … somewhere else.' He shuddered, shook his head and tried to act normal.

'Did you have another flashback about Royal?'

'Um, yeah. It was of that time he overheard me asking you to tie me up.' He wiggled his tie to help her remember.

'Oh,' she said, 'that was a very awkward moment.'

Joel nodded. He wished he could forget it. But now they were on their way back to the scene of the crime, as they'd done week after week since it'd happened, but now all that humiliation felt completely fresh again.

The presence of Royal in their Costume Design class was made worse by the fact that the design program didn't have anywhere near as many students as the creative writing program. It meant Joel couldn't avoid Royal by blending into a crowd. There were only twelve students in total. Joel had worked out straight away that costume design at Acadia Academy might as well have been the LGBTIQ+ club. Every kid in the room was somewhere on the rainbow spectrum; except for Royal, who stood out like a sore thumb. Joel wasn't the only one to notice that. When they arrived for class that day, a boyish girl dressed in a boy's senior year uniform (gold tie) walked up to Royal and looked him over as though he were a museum exhibit.

'I heard the whispers but I didn't believe they were true,' she said.

'What rumors?' Royal asked, looking around nervously.

'That a unicorn had come to Hogwarts.'

'What?' Royal looked around at the other kids in the class, wondering if anyone understood what this girl was talking about. They were all smirking.

'You are a unicorn,' the girl said. 'I just heard from Lana Beaux that you're straight. All this time I'd assumed you were just straight-acting. But you're an actual straight boy doing costume design. In other words, an imaginary creature.'

'Funny,' Royal mumbled before taking a chair in the corner and shrinking down into the seat to make himself less conspicuous. It didn't work. Everyone was looking at him, except Joel who was pointedly looking at his shoes as though he had never seen them before.

'Okay, class, settle down' said a thin, breathy voice. The costume design teacher, Miss Lawson, had entered the room behind them. She was as delicate and thin as her voice. Her pale skin made Joel think of butterfly wings, almost translucent when the light was shining from behind. As always, she drifted to the front of the class and sat behind the desk, perched on the very edge of her seat like it might try to eat her. In that same breathy voice she outlined their focus for the next few weeks –

to form teams and design the costumes for the end of semester showcase at Christmas time. These were the costumes the music and theater students would wear during their performances. The theme for this year's Christmas showcase was Nineties Hollywood Retro Glamour.

Joel glanced at Starr with a raised eyebrow and whispered. 'The Nineties are retro?'

Starr smirked. 'Anything that happened before *we* were born, babe, *is* retro.'

'You will work in teams of three,' Miss Lawson continued. 'Each team will pitch their costume ideas and the class will vote on which design idea is selected. Then the whole class will make the costumes for the showcase.'

Joel put his hand up and said: 'You mean, we're going to be making *actual* costumes that *actual* people will wear on an *actual* stage?' Up until that point their costume class had not been practical. They'd mostly been learning about the history of fashion and costumes.

'That is *actually* correct,' Miss Lawson said with a meek smile.

Joel looked to Starr and whispered, 'I can't fix a hole in a sock let alone make a costume good enough for someone to wear.'

'You'll be fine,' Starr whispered back.

'Form teams and start brainstorming,' Miss Lawson said to the class, 'and make sure you let your team mates know what your strengths and passions are, if you haven't already shared that with them over the last months. November is nearly gone and we don't have a lot of time to prepare fr this showcase, which is entirely my fault. I spent far too much time teaching you about the under-appreciated art of crochet fashion! Now get to work!'

Joel turned to Starr in a panic. 'My strengths are zero and my passions are not being humiliated, so maybe I should drop this class and take up Culinary Arts instead?'

'Do you cook better than you sew?' Starr asked.

'No, worse.'

'You'll have to stay here then. Besides, it's too late to drop the class, we're nearly through the semester. And there are no places in any other class. That's why you were put in this program in the first place, remember?'

Joel acknowledged she was right with a weak nod.

'Same for me,' an all too familiar voice said. Joel looked up. Royal Dumaine was standing immediately behind him. Joel lurched sideways in surprise and nearly fell out of his chair.

Starr gave him an exasperated look before smiling up at Royal. 'Same for you, how?' she asked.

'I'm in this class because all the other classes were full. I didn't have a choice. I'm also terrible at everything to do with fashion. Drawing, sewing, you name it, I'm bad at it.'

'Pretty good at eavesdropping though,' Joel muttered. Clearly Royal had heard him confess his own weakness with a needle to Starr.

Starr shot Joel another exasperated look.

Royal pretended not to hear Joel's mutterings and spoke over his head to Starr. 'All the other teams are full.'

Joel looked around. Everyone else in class had already formed teams of three.

At that point Miss Lawson came over. 'You three make the last team. Take a seat, Royal.'

No. No. No. No.

Royal's sapphire blue eyes met Joel's grey ones. Joel looked away first. Then Royal did as he was told, taking the seat right next to Joel. Joel scooted his chair away, which made a deafening scraping sound on the floor. The sound was like a million needles stabbing Joel all along his spine. Joel shuddered and turned his back on the all-too-handsome senior boy now sitting next to him.

Royal couldn't help but notice all this and took immediate offence. He crossed his arms over his chest and stared at the ceiling. Joel crossed his arms over his own chest and stared at the floor. Starr looked from Joel to Royal and back again, unsure what to do. Miss Lawson looked confused.

'Start brainstorming, please,' she said, before drifting away to make sure the other teams had started discussing ideas.

Joel's stomach tightened. So much for not thinking about or speaking to Royal Dumaine ever again. Now they were on the same stupid costume design team and had to brainstorm stupid ideas, which meant Joel having to use his stupid mouth to speak actual intelligible words to stupidly hot Royal Dumaine. Dammit.

Starr looked from Joel to Royal some more, then leant forward in her chair and slapped her hand on the table, making Joel and Royal jump. 'No,' she said, looking from one to the other, 'I will not miss out on the opportunity to have my designs made for the showcase because of two silly boys. I'm in this costume design studio because I want to be, not because there weren't any other spots left. Costume Design is integral to my future career in the theater. You two are not going to ruin this for me.' She glared at them. 'You will behave like normal people, talk to each other like normal people, and get along. Have I made myself clear?'

Joel nodded. Royal straightened up in his chair and shrugged half-heartedly.

'That will not do,' Starr said coldly to Royal. 'Have I made myself clear?'

'Yes, Starr Davis, student ambassador, you have made yourself clear. The problem is, your designs are not going to be selected for the showcase with me on your team. I don't know what I'm doing. I can't draw, stitch or sew and, from the sound of it, neither can Joel.'

Joel wanted to hate Royal and disagree with everything he was saying with that super sexy Creole accented voice of his, but he was kind of right. Joel use scissors without nearly losing a thumb. Royal being right irritated Joel. It irritated him a lot. There should be a law against hot people ever being right. Hot people should always be wrong about everything. He put his irritation to one side. This was about Starr and her dream of having her costumes on stage.

'He's got a point,' he said. 'I can draw a bit but I can't do any of the other stuff either. You should talk to Miss Lawson and get her to put you on another team.

Starr thought a moment. 'No. We are keeping this team as is. You don't have to know how to make clothes. The first step is design. That's just having an idea. It's the designs that'll get us selected to do the showcase. Once our designs are chosen the whole class will be pitching in to make the costumes.'

'What will my contribution be?' Royal asked. 'I can't coast along doing nothing and expect to share the grade.'

'First off, you'll help brainstorm the designs.'

Royal looked worried. 'I don't know anything about costumes or fashion.'

'You have two gay dads,' Joel said 'and you don't know anything about fashion?' He surprised himself by managing to say a complete sentence to Royal without stuttering, waving his arms about or shouting. Or being attacked by a squirrel.

'Only *one* of my dads is gay,' Royal said to Joel with a frown. 'The other one, the one you met, is bisexual. Bisexual people exist you know, and bi people can be in same-sex marriages too.'

Oh, right, sorry.' Joel flushed a little but nodded in agreement. Another true thing said by a hot person. Dammit.

'Point taken though,' Royal continued. 'I do know the difference between a Gucci suit and a Prada one.'

'That's a beginning,' Starr said with a smile. She pulled out her sketchbook and wrote "Nineties Hollywood Retro Glamour" across the top of a new page. 'So, what do you think of when you hear Nineties Hollywood Retro Glamour?'

Joel shrugged.

Royal took a minute to think then said, 'When I think of the Nineties, I don't think of glamour at all. I think of Grunge music, like Soundgarden, Nirvana, bands like that.'

'And the Smashing Pumpkins,' Joel added.

'Exactly,' Royal said, smiling at Joel for the first time ever. It had a curious effect on Joel. He felt kind of giddy and giggled like a girl. He cut the giggle off as quick as he could, which turned it into a kind of snort. Royal barked with laughter at that.

'Well, look at you two,' Starr said, 'behaving just like proper adult people.'

'Ugh,' Joel said with a scowl, 'don't use that word to describe me ever again.'

'What word?' asked Royal. 'Adult?'

'No, "behaving".' Joel shuddered. 'Dogs behave. Trained parrots behave. Hamsters behave. I am a proper human boy, not a pet. I do not behave.'

'Never a truer word has been spoken,' Starr said. 'But, we still need to think what Nineties Hollywood Retro Glamour means for us.'

'What movies even came out in the Nineties?' Joel asked. 'We weren't even born then.'

'The only movie from the Nineties I can think of is *Midnight in the Garden of Good and Evil*,' Royal said.

'The one set in Savannah?' Starr asked.

'Yeah. I only know that one because my dad, the gay one, made me watch it with him about a dozen times. He's from Savannah. And *very gay*.'

'I think I've seen that film. Is that the one with the Voodoo priestess?' Joel asked.

Royal nodded. 'There's a bisexual hustler too.'

Joel noted that was the third or fourth time Royal had said the word "bisexual". Was Royal trying to tell them something? Joel hoped he wouldn't say it again, because every time he said "bisexual" with that accent of his it made Joel tingle all over. New Law: Hot guys with Creole accents should never say the words "bisexual hustler".

'There's a trans character too,' Starr said. 'The Lady Chablis, she's very glamorous.'

'So that's one Nineties film we've all seen,' Royal said.

Starr thought a moment. 'We could do a reimagining of some of the costumes from that film. There's the drag bar scene with some cool costumes and a party scene with people all glammed up, and we could bring in some of the voodoo elements!' Starr's eyes shone. She was clearly excited.

'That sounds cool,' Joel said.

'Yeah, it docs,' Royal added.

'That's our first group decision made,' Starr noted. 'And it wasn't hard at all, was it?'

Joel shook his head.

'No, it wasn't hard at all,' Royal said before adding: 'My dad, the gay one, he's moved back to Savannah, you know, after the break up. I could ask him for some insider stories to give us ideas.'

'That'd be great, Royal,' Starr said. 'Thanks.'

'No problem.'

'I think our next step,' Starr said, her eyes twinkling with mischief, 'is to watch the movie together.'

Wait. What?

Starr continued: 'Joel and I could come to your dorm room …'

What was Starr doing? It was bad enough having to sit in a classroom with Royal week after week. Joel didn't want to watch a movie with him. He certainly wouldn't be going to the Nottoway House dorm room, the scene of his humiliation.

'I share a room with Carter.' Royal shot a look at Joel. 'I'll come to your place if that's okay?'

So, Joel thought, Royal doesn't want his roommate to know he's hanging out with a loser junior.

'We're free tonight,' Starr said. 'Aren't we, Joel?'

Joel didn't move or speak. He doubted he was even breathing.

'I can't tonight. I've got an, err, a thing. I can do Saturday though.'

Joel guessed the "err, thing" was a date with Lana Beaux.

'We've got stuff tomorrow,' Starr said, 'but we can do Sunday night.'

Starr and Royal agreed on the time. Joel sat still as a stone. Royal Dumaine was coming to his place to watch a movie. If only he really had been tied to a tree in the swamp all those months ago. If he had, this wouldn't be happening. He'd managed to avoid Royal for weeks. He had sworn to himself he wouldn't think about let alone talk to him. Now, after mere minutes in a class team with him, Starr had succumbed to his broody charm and invited him over. To his own place, where he lived, slept, showered, ate Honey Nut Cheerios and kept his underwear in a draw, right where anyone could see them. Joel's head swam. But thankfully he didn't faint. He just sat there, looking pale and empty-headed.

*** ***

Starr had a team meeting for kendo after school that day, so Joel started the walk home alone. His brain had cleared since the shock of having to speak to Royal, and the terror of the impending movie night had eased off to just a nagging anxiety, so he was able to appreciate the late afternoon light and the blueness of the clear sky. It was a perfect late autumn afternoon. As he took the shortcut home between Rosedawn House and the library, he noticed a woman standing on the porch of the girl's dorm. Sunlight streamed through the boughs of the live-oak shading the porch, dappling her in flickering patches of gold and dusky orange. She looked out of place, like someone caught between time periods. Her clothes were formal but old-fashioned: a long wool skirt, a high-collared blouse, and a brooch at her throat that glinted in the sinking sunlight. Her hair was in a tight bun and she wore horn-rimmed glasses of a pale olive green. She didn't look like one of the staff, though she had a book in her hands and chalk on her fingers, clear signs of a teacher. She didn't look like anyone he'd seen around campus before. Her expression, though kind, had a hint of sadness to it, of loneliness. And she seemed too … still. Far too still.

Joel stopped. Something wasn't right. The woman's glasses didn't reflect the sun. Her skirt fluttered faintly in a wind he couldn't feel. Then there was the impossible fact that he could see the shape of the porch swing *through* her blouse. She was hollow, see-through, like a ghost. Joel's breath caught in his throat.

Not. This. Again.

Joel's mind scrambled for sense. Was he hallucinating? Was this another dream? Was he having a stroke? But he could feel the gentle heat of the autumn day on his skin, and the crisp air on his cheeks. He was very much awake. Was he actually looking at a ghost?

Joel swallowed and put his head down. He had no intention of engaging with this …this … what was she? A phantom? An apparition? A ghost? Whatever she was, it didn't matter. He averted his eyes and sped down the path until the porch of Rosedawn house was well out of site. He crossed the playing fields to Oakshade Cottage in record time, mounting the porch and dashing inside. He shut the door firmly behind him and went straight to his bedroom and took out his most valued, most secret possession. If ever he'd needed some comfort, it was now.

CARE BEARS, TAROT CARDS AND THE AWFUL THING

The next morning Joel woke feeling surprisingly light and optimistic. Starr had spent most of the night before convincing him that everything was going to be okay. He still only had to see Royal in one class a week and work with him on one assignment. He could deal with that. He'd dealt with a lot worse. He put Royal out of his mind and got ready for his Saturday visit to Acadiaville. He and Starr were going over to Tashi's to hang out. He still wasn't used to just hanging out with friends. For so long his life had been taken over by the trauma he'd experienced at his old school. Now he had moved on. New school, new country, new friends, new life.

It was forecast to be an unusually warm November day, so he dressed in jeans, a vintage pair of 501s he got from a thrift store, and a white t-shirt featuring his favorite cartoon characters – the Care Bears. He pulled on his rainbow Converse sneakers and headed to the kitchen for some Honey Nut cereal. Starr was already there, finishing up some toast. Joel stared at her and she stared back at Joel. They were dressed almost identically, except Starr's t-shirt was blue and featured Smurfette. Instead of sneakers she was wearing cherry red Doc Martin boots.

Joel spoke first. 'Umm, should we change?'

'Nah, we'll just pretend these are our gang threads.'

'Right, the cartoon thugz. Thugz with a Z.'

Starr blinked. 'Gosh, you really are very, very white, aren't you?'

'Yeah, I'm so white you should call me Creamy Z.'

'Never say that in public.'

They were both giggling when Penn came into the room.

'Ready to go? I'll drop you off at Tashi's on my way to do some errands in town.'

'Just gotta finish my Honey Nuts,' Joel said. He shoveled the cereal into his mouth, swallowing without bothering to chew or breathe. Starr and Penn watched with looks of growing horror.

'I'm going to wait in the car,' Penn said, 'before this makes me puke.'

Starr followed her out, calling shotgun.

Joel finished his cereal then jogged out to the car and settled himself in the backseat. Once they were off, he kept mental note of the route they were taking from the school to Tashi's place, just in case he had to get there by foot one day. He committed every turn to memory. The only part he didn't need to memorize was the stretch of road where he'd met Royal, in the middle of the alligator infested swamp. That part of the road was seared into his brain, like a scarred brand. As they drove through the shady bend where he'd seen an alligator, and maybe a ghost, and nearly fainted he rolled his window up, leaving just a thin gap for the breeze to get in.

'Anything wrong?' Penn asked, watching him in the rearview mirror.

'No, nothing wrong,' he said out loud before mumbling to himself, 'unless you call a congregation of homicidal alligators who are all hungry for sixteen-year-old boy flesh wrong, which I certainly do.'

Penn and Starr glanced at each other but chose to pretend they hadn't heard anything and kept quiet.

Tashi lived in an apartment above *Little Tibet,* the café that her mum ran on the town square. The door to the apartment was on the street next to the entrance to the café. Starr knocked on the door while Joel peered curiously through the café window. It looked fancy and exotic. Joel pressed his nose to the glass trying to get a better look but Starr pulled him away. Just then Tashi opened the door. She was wearing cherry Doc Martens, a denim mini-skirt and a yellow He-Man t-shirt. From the car, Penn called out:

'Was this planned?' She gestured to the three of them and their cartoon t-shirt looks. The three of them shook their heads, no.

'It's just auspicious coincidence,' Tashi called out as she hugged Starr, then Joel. Penn smiled, waved and drove off. Tashi led them up the stairs and across a hallway into a family room at the front of the apartment with large bay windows that looked over the square. It was furnished in what Joel guessed must have been a Tibetan style. Tashi had already laid out an array of vegan snacks on a sideboard beneath the windows.

'Did you make all this for us,' Starr asked, her eyes raking the buffet.

'Yep,' Tashi said. 'Getting in practice for Culinary Arts class. I need an A in that class to keep my mom off my back.'

Joel positioned himself next to the California Rolls, one of his favorite foods. 'It all looks delicious.' He had half a California roll stuffed in his mouth when Tashi's mother, Mrs. Bellman, came in a moment later.

'Hi Mum,' Tashi said, 'Starr and Joel are here.'

'I see that, yes.' Mrs. Bellman was a dignified looking Tibetan woman with long black hair and warm brown eyes.

'You remember Joel,' Tashi said, gesturing at Joel.

Mrs. Bellman watched Joel with a slight look of disgust as he tried to scoff down the sushi before having to say hello. He couldn't quite get it down quick enough so he mumbled through a mash of seaweed, avocado and rice.

'Hi! Fanks for letting me come ovfer fer a play dwate with Tashi!' Starr and Tashi looked at him like he'd lost his mind. Starr mouthed "play date" and shook her head in disbelief.

'Anyway, fanks,' Joel said, still wrestling with the California Roll. Miss Bellman stretched out her hand to pat him on the back as he struggled to swallow. Right then his sneaker snagged on the rug and he tripped, causing him to half cough, half spit. A damp wad of green something-or-other landed on Mrs. Bellman's extended hand. They all stared at it. No-one moved. Right at that moment a man walked in, a professorial-looking fellow with thick glasses like Tashi's who reminded Joel of his Jewish math teacher back in Australia. Clearly this was Tashi's dad, who Joel hadn't met yet. He spotted the green wad on his wife's outstretched hand and took a step back.

'Oh, ick, what on earth is that?' he asked.

Joel swallowed and said, 'Would anyone believe a bizarre Australian greeting ritual?' Everyone stared at him, silent. 'No?'

Mrs. Bellman composed herself. 'If it's okay with you all, I'll go wash my hands now.'

'Oh yes, please do,' Joel said.

'Yes, darling, please do,' Mr. Bellman said, looking a little nauseated. He turned to Joel. 'Nice to meet you, son,' he added, waving at Joel awkwardly before following Mrs. Bellman out, pointedly not looking at her still outstretched hand and the green dollop of goo.

'Can't take you anywhere,' Starr said once they were alone, smirking.

'Yes, best not to,' Joel muttered, his face red.

'Don't fret about it,' Tashi said, 'my parents are cool with my friends. Evil task masters with me, but very cool with my friends. By tomorrow they won't remember that happened.'

Joel shot her an arched eyebrow.

'Okay, so maybe they'll still remember tomorrow but in twenty or thirty years it will definitely be forgotten.'

'God, why can I not make a good impression, like, ever?' Joel felt mortified. His time in Acadiaville was one humiliating episode after another. How was he supposed to start a new life when all he did was make a fool of himself?

'This'll cheer you up,' Tashi said, 'I've booked you in for a tarot card reading this morning!'

Joel blinked. 'You what now?'

'I booked you in for a tarot reading with Miss Thibodeaux.'

'Miss Tee-bow-doh? Is she your local voodoo queen?'

'Hoodoo,' Starr said.

'Who does what now?' Joel looked form Starr to Tashi and back again. Were they speaking a foreign language?

'Hoodoo,' Tashi repeated. 'She's a Hoodoo psychic.'

Joel felt both perplexed and a little bit spooked. His worried face prompted Starr to explain.

'Hoodoo is the white version of Voodoo,' she said. 'A lot of back country Cajuns practice Hoodoo on the side.'

'On the side of what?' Joel smirked.

'Oh, for goodness sake,' Tashi chided, 'you're just being silly now.'

'Well, it is a play date,' Joel said.

'Don't say *play date*,' the girls sang as one.

'Okay, okay, I get it. I won't say it again.' He felt it best he change the topic. 'So, Hoodoo is white folks Voodoo?'

'Yes,' Starr answered. 'A lot of the swamp people practice it alongside Christianity.'

'Swamp people?' Joel thought he'd seen a horror movie called *Swamp People*.'

'Folks who live in the bayou,' Tashi said, 'off the grid mostly.'

'So I'm getting a Hoodoo reading from a swamp person?' Joel asked.

'Just a tarot reading,' Tashi said, 'by Miss Thibodeaux.'

'Not miss Tee-boo-doo?' Joel smirked broadly, reaching for another California Roll.

'He's just incorrigible,' Tashi said to Starr.

'He wouldn't get away with it if he wasn't so cute.' Starr said frowning.

'You think I'm cute?' Joel blushed.

'You know you are,' the girls said in unison.

'I really don't. Really. I don't feel cute at all.'

'Well you are,' Starr said kindly. 'But don't get a big head over it.'

Joel didn't know what to say. Tashi stepped close to him and squeezed his arm.

'Come on,' she said, 'eat up and then we'll head across the square to get your tarot reading.'

Joel made a bee line for the California Rolls again. The girls stepped out of his way – fearful of flying wads of green goo.

*** ***

After Joel had finished stuffing his face, Tashi took him to see a new poster in her bedroom. Her room was exactly what Joel had expected it to be – a mishmash of movie and band posters and Buddhist stuff. Joel noticed that her room was very neat, which made him think he'd better tidy his room before Royal came over. Not that he cared what Royal thought of him, of course. A large poster of the Swedish Chef from *The Muppets* loomed over a small vintage desk in the corner of Tashi's room. The new acquisition.

'My nod to the culinary arts,' Tashi explained, 'to keep my mother off my back.'

Joel smirked and did a very poor impersonation of the Swedish Chef saying 'I love meatballs.'

Starr asked 'Why do you sound Indian?'

'Because I'm very bad at impressions,' he said.

'Very bad,' Tashi confirmed.

'So your mother really wants you to be a chef, huh?' Joel asked.

'She wants me to be the Momo queen of Louisiana, if not the whole South.'

'Momo?' Joel had no idea what a momo might be.

'Tibetan dumplings,' Tashi explained.

'They're delicious,' Starr added enthusiastically.

Tashi smiled proudly. 'They're my mum's specialty,' she said. 'They're the stars of the café's menu.'

'I'll have to get Penn to order some for our next take-out night.'

'Yes please,' Starr said, practically drooling. 'I love me some momos.'

They spent the next hour or so listening to Tashi's favorite music – a mix of old school be-pop, Nineties grunge and, weirdly, K-pop.

'K-pop is my shameful pleasure,' Tashi said as she put on a very high energy track and bopped up and down to a tune Joel kind of recognized but couldn't distinguish from any other Korean pop song.

Starr and Joel looked at each other, feeling awkward. K-Pop was definitely not their thing. Tashi continued to bop. Joel and Starr tried some of Tashi's perfume, which was very sweet-smelling, a sandalwood and vanilla mix. Joel thought all three of them smelt like custard now. Not a bad thing. Custard is delicious! After a while, Tashi's bop finally ran out, so they set to tidying up the dishes from the excellent vegan buffet (of which Joel calculated he'd eaten about 98% all by himself). As he'd eaten the most, he decided he'd carry the most platters to the kitchen. On his way there, with a pile of carefully piled platters in his arms, a glimmer of gold and bronze caught his attention. It was coming from a room opposite the living room he hadn't noticed before. He stopped by the doorway and peered in. A large Buddha statue sat on a beautiful wooden cabinet beneath a tall window. A little electric lamp in the shape of a lotus flower cast a soft light that made the Buddha's skin seem to shimmer. Three brocade meditation cushions sat on the polished floor boards at an equal distance from each other. One each for Tashi, her mum and her dad. The room felt deeply calm and quiet, and smelled of sandalwood and rose. Joel wanted to go in but felt that doing so would be an intrusion. He quietly continued to the kitchen.

After they'd stacked the dishwasher they headed downstairs on the way to Joel's tarot reading. Joel felt quite nervous at the prospect but didn't say anything, not wanting to disappoint his friends who were very keen that Joel should be told his future by some swamp Voodoo queen.

'So where's this psychic reading happening,' Joel asked when they hit the street. 'Is there a Hoodoo temple or something?' He scanned the square, half expecting to see a big neon sign blinking "Hoodoo Temple" in red letters.

'No, Miss Thibodeaux does readings out the back of the car wash,' Tashi explained.

'Out the back of a car wash? This is not sounding like a legitimate enterprise!' Joel felt even more nervous now.

'She's got the space set up real nice,' Starr said. 'She's got a futon sofa in the waiting room and everything.'

'Oh, well, if she has a futon sofa it must be legit.' Joel noticed his voiced sounded a little high pitched.

They crossed the square and turned down Main Street heading away from the center of town. About three blocks from the square they came to the car wash. It did have a neon sign but it spelt "Automated Car Wash" rather than "Hoodoo Temple", only with the W missing. Joel looked at his friends, eyebrow cocked. Were they serious? Were they taking him to get his future told at this broken down place? Before he could voice the scathing remarks that had formed in his mind he stopped in his tracks. Coming toward them was a guy a little older than them, probably seventeen, shirtless and drenched from head to toe. He was barefoot too, just wearing a pair of black jeans. Joel scanned the guy from his black hair, full lips and muscled chest to the perfectly tight jeans. Every inch of him was soaked and dripping. Joel swallowed hard.

'Hey, Tash,' the guy said with the thickest Cajun accent Joel had ever heard.

'Hey, T.J.,' Tashi said, echoed by Starr.

'Hey, Starr,' he said, smiling. He stopped in front of them and tussled his wet hair so that droplets hit all of them. The girls groaned and flinched but Joel didn't feel like flinching. He felt something altogether different.

'It's *late November*,' Starr said, 'aren't you freezing to death?'

'Nah,' the wet guy said, 'I run pretty hot.' He looked at Joel and winked. 'Who's this kid,' he asked, looking Joel over.

'This is Joel,' Tashi answered. 'Joel, this weather-inappropriate lunatic is T.J.'

'Hi Kid,' T.J. said with a smile so big and unguarded that Joel beamed back without even meaning to.

'Hi,' Joel squeaked, acutely aware that one of the droplets from T.J.'s hair had made its way to his top lip. It sat there, cool and heavy, like a jewel pressed to his skin. He figured he should wipe it away, but he just left it there, too anxious to wipe it away in case T.J. took offence.

'You here for Ma?' T.J. asked the girls.

'Yeah, we're bringing Joel for a reading,' Tashi explained.

'Cool,' T.J. said.

Joel smiled meekly, making sure his gaze stayed on T.J.'s face, and didn't drop down to his chest or glistening abs. T.J.'s eyes were bright and the color of caramel toffee.

'Ma will treat you right,' he said to Joel, before reaching out and gently tugging on Joel's t-shirt. 'Little bears,' he said. 'Cute.'

'Thanks,' Joel squeaked. 'Care Bears are, like, real super cute.' *Real super cute?* OMG. Shut your stupid mouth.

'Sure they are,' T.J. said, smirking. 'Just like that accent of yours.' He winked at Joel and headed back into the car wash where he resumed hosing down a bright red dirt bike. Joel's mouth dropped open and his face flushed as red as the bike.

Starr and Tashi took one of his hands each and led him around the back of the building.

'Was he,' Joel stuttered, 'did he, did he—'

'Flirt with you and call you cute?' Starr said, smiling.

'He sure did,' Tashi added.

'And that boy gives Royal Dumaine a run for his money in the looks department.' Starr declared, squeezing his hand for emphasis.

'If you like that hot, young, redneck Elvis thing that T.J.'s got going on,' Tashi said.

'Oh me do, me do like,' Joel spluttered.

The girls laughed in unison and dragged him through a bright blue door with a sign above it that read: "Fortunes Told Here. No Credit." The waiting room of Miss Thibodeaux's fortune-telling parlor made Joel blink. The walls were painted an eye-watering orange. There was indeed a futon sofa, covered with cushions of every color in the rainbow. There was also a sideboard showcasing a collection of crystals and scented candles. The one window was hung with almost see-through purple curtains. A colored glass wind chime tinkled with the light breeze and reflected rainbows around the room. A beaded curtain separated the parlor from another room. Joel was still adjusting to the riot of color and smells when a woman parted the beaded curtain and greeted them.

'Morning all.' She had the same thick Cajun accent as T.J. and was not what Joel expected. She was a completely ordinary-looking woman, good-looking in her way, with warm amber eyes, black hair hanging softly at her shoulders, and dressed in a simple black top and jeans. She didn't look like a witch at all. Joel felt a little disappointed. She smiled at him kindly.

'You must be my next appointment, Joel River.'

Joel nodded. 'I guess so.'

'Don't be nervous, puddin', a tarot card reading is perfectly harmless. Come in to my reading room.' She gestured through the beaded curtain. Joel and the girls followed her through into a smaller room with another purple-curtained window. This room had a small table with two wooden chairs and a blue velvet loveseat in the corner. Starr and Tashi squeezed into the loveseat together. Miss Thibodeaux sat on one side of the table and invited Joel to take the other chair. He sat down, aware that his heart was beating a little fast and his mouth was dry.

'I'm Rose-Marie Thibodeaux, I'll be tellin' your fortune today. I'm guessin' you've never had your tarot read before?'

'No, never,' Joel said.

'Okay, puddin', the first thing we'll do is get you to shuffle and cut the cards.' She gestured to a set of tarot cards on the table between them. Joel picked them up and shuffled them.

'Now cut them three times, divide them into three piles and pop them here.' She tapped the table between them. Joel split the pack into three piles. Miss Thibodeaux, Rose-Marie, picked them up and held them for a moment, her eyes closed.

Joel looked to the girls, mouthing 'What's she doing?' The girls shrugged in unison.

'Okay, pudding, Joel,' she said, making Joel jump with fright, 'I'm gonna lay out your cards in three sets of three. Three cards for the past, three for the present and three for the future.' She dealt the cards in three rows, with only the backs showing. 'First we read the past.' She turned over the first card, looked at it a moment then turned over the next one. She sighed, looking at Joel sadly and then turned over the third card. 'Oh, Joel, you poor, sweet boy.' She slid her hand across the table to rest on his. She squeezed it and held on. Her eyes were soft with forming tears.

Joel swallowed hard. Did she know? Did the cards show what had happened to him last year? He looked to the girls. They looked worried, their eyes fixed on the cards on the table. Joel looked down at them. The first card was an upside down three of swords, the second was a man hanging upside down, and the last card was an eight of swords, also upside down. 'What do these cards mean?' Joel asked.

'They point to what happened to you recently,' she said. She tapped her finger on the first card, with three swords stabbing a red heart. Joel's ears started ringing. His heart kicked into a rapid beat. Miss Thibodeaux squeezed his hand tighter, as if to anchor him, hold him in place. 'You are safe here, puddin', nobody here is gonna hurt you.' She gathered the cards up and put them back in the deck, as if to shield Joel from the truth they showed. 'These cards tell of a betrayal, of a terrible violation, and of the shame you feel over it. But puddin', you have to know that you shouldn't feel shame about what happened. It wasn't your fault. The only ones at fault were the three who did that to you, the three who hurt you.'

Joel's head spun. How did she know there'd been three of them, three guys in the room when it'd happened? He remembered the card with three swords piercing a red heart. He put his hands in his lap, holding them tight, holding himself tight. His stomach churned. He felt sick. He looked over at Starr and Tashi. Starr was wiping tears away from her eyes. Tashi was covering her mouth with her hand. Her hand was trembling.

'These sorts of traumas fester unless we speak about them, Joel,' Rose-Marie said gently. 'But only you can decide when to talk, who to talk to and how much to tell. It has to be up to you and you alone. Let me just say this – these girls here, these girls are rock solid. I've known both of them since they were itty-bitty babies in diapers. They're good kids. You can trust them. You could tell them, if you wanted to.'

Joel started to talk. He didn't know what had come over him. He just felt he had to get the secret out of him immediately, so that it couldn't poison him anymore. Rose-Marie looked even more surprised than he felt. Clearly she hadn't expected him to tell them right now.

'Last year, at my old school, this awful thing happened. There was this kid, Patrick. He was two years older than me. I thought he was nice. He'd smile and say hi to me all the time. I kind of fell in love with him. It was the first time I'd ever felt like that for anyone. Then at the end of term there was a big party. Patrick said he was going, everyone was going, and Patrick said that I should go too. So I talked my parents into letting me go and I went. Not long after I got there someone handed me a drink, some kind of punch. I'd never had any alcohol before, I was only fourteen, but Patrick was right there and I didn't want to look like a loser in front of him so I drank it.' Joel's voice was shaking now. He paused to take a deep breath. 'Almost straight away I felt sick, kind of woozy and confused. I stumbled off to a bedroom to lie down. The next thing I remember was waking up back at home, in my own bed, without my clothes, just in my underwear.' Joel's voice broke on the last few words.

Starr and Tashi gasped. Rose-Marie got up and got him a glass of water. Joel felt a tear roll onto his cheek. He wiped it away.

'I don't remember what happened, but I *know* what happened because, because of the pictures.

'Pictures?' Starr whispered, looking horrified.

'These three guys, one of them Patrick, the guy I liked, found me passed out in the bedroom and thought it'd be fun to take some pics. I think my drink was spiked, that I'd been drugged. They stripped me down to my underwear and took a bunch of selfies with me, putting me in all these gross positions with them, like it was a foursome … like an orgy. They sent the pics to everyone at the party and posted them online.' Joel's voice cracked so that he couldn't speak anymore. Starr and Tashi rushed over and hugged him, hugging him so tight he couldn't move at all. He felt wonderful being held like that. After a long while, he squeaked that he needed some water so the girls let him go. Miss Thibodeaux rubbed his shoulder as he drank the water. He took a deep breath and finished the story.

'Someone at the party called the cops. The cops came and took me home. The three boys were all charged, but it was too late. Everyone had seen the pics. After that my nickname at school was "Foursome". People graffitied it on my locker, and a lot of worse things too. I got bullied so bad after that. It just never eased off. All of that really hurt, especially because I was fourteen and, like, you know, a total virgin. I'd never even kissed a boy. Still haven't. The worst thing was that Patrick never said another word to me, not "sorry", not "how are you?", nothing. He acted like it was my fault he was in trouble with the cops, that it was my fault he got suspended from school.'

'Suspended!' Starr said with outrage. 'That creep should have been expelled and sent to jail.'

'Yeah,' Tashi echoed, 'please tell me he went to jail?'

'No, just got suspended and some community service.' This fact still hurt Joel. It made him feel that no-one, not the cops, not the judge who handed down the sentence, and not the headmaster of his old school, really understood how much he'd been hurt by what had happened, how emotionally devastating it had been to him. Because of those pics, he had been mercilessly bullied, day in and day out for months until he left for America. Starr enfolded him in her arms again.

'I am so, so sorry, Joel, for what I did your first night here, making you stay in the room with Royal. That was the absolutely worst thing I could've done to you.'

'It's okay,' Joel said, truly meaning it. 'You didn't know. How could you have known?'

'Still, it makes me feel sick to think what you must have been going through. I am so sorry.'

'Apology well and truly accepted,' Joel said, squeezing Starr hard.

'Puddin', Joel,' Rose-Marie said gently, 'we don't need to finish your reading now. You've had a big emotional moment. How about I take you kids to the ice-cream parlor, my treat?'

'You don't have to do that,' Joel said. 'I'm okay, besides, I want to see what my future holds. But, if it's bad, please don't tell me, just make up some lie about how I'm going to meet someone tall, dark and handsome and fall in love and get married and adopt a dozen Golden Retriever puppies and live happily ever after.'

'Okay, I can do that,' Rose-Marie said, smiling. Everyone went back to their places. Starr and Tashi to the velvet loveseat, Rose-Marie to the chair opposite Joel. Joel smiled bravely even though he didn't feel very brave.

CAJUN PRINCES AND PEEPING TOMS

Miss Thibodeaux turned over the first card for the present. It was a three of cups. The next two were a Princess of Cups and a Princess of Wands. Joel looked at the cards nervously.

"So, is it Golden Retrievers?' he asked.

'You may have Golden Retrievers in your future, Joel, puddin', but these cards are for your present. These cards are all about friendship.' She looked over at Starr and Tashi. 'These cards show you have met some true, lifelong friends, and these friends will help you move beyond the past and prepare for the future.'

'I think she's talking about us,' Tashi said, waving from the corner.

'Yeah, I got that,' Joel said, smirking.

'Now, let's see what the future is like for you,' Rose-Marie said, slowly turning over the last three cards with quite a bit of dramatic flourish. Joel took a sip of water. The first card was the Prince of Cups. The second one was the Prince of Pentacles. The third card was a surprise – The Lovers. Joel nearly choked on the sip of water he'd just taken.

'Well, puddin', this is interesting.'

'Retrievers?' Joel asked, half-joking, half-worried.

'No, no retrievers, but there is a happily ever after, and there really is someone tall, dark and handsome,' she tapped her finger on the Prince of Pentacles. '*And* someone tall and not so dark.' She tapped her finger on the Prince of Cups.

'What, two dudes?' Tashi said from the corner.

'Two princes,' Rose-Marie said, quietly thinking. She glanced out the window toward the car wash. 'These cards,' she tapped the two princes, 'generally indicate people with male energy, if not actual males. The Prince of Cups is someone who is intelligent and creative, a dreamer, but also easily swayed by the opinions of others. The Prince of Pentacles is someone who is serious and hard-working, very down-to-earth, but also too stubborn for his own good. The prince cards usually represent someone young, someone in their teens or early adulthood. I think we can assume that these are actual males.'

'So, what, I'm going to fall in love with two guys?'

'You might, but what the cards are saying is that these two princes will fall in love with you. Both of them will love you, and love you deeply.'

'A love triangle,' said Starr. 'My absolute favorite kind of geometry.'

Joel felt uncomfortable. Two guys? When your school nickname was "Foursome" the very idea of more than one guy in your life was unsettling. Joel was about to ask a follow up question along the lines of "How can I make sure this never, ever happens?" when Tashi piped up from the corner.

'Do you know who these guys are?'

'There are indications,' Rose-Marie began. 'Normally, the prince cards are seen as symbolic, but in this case I think these are actual princes.'

Joel blinked. 'What the unholy what now? Actual princes, but we're in Louisiana!'

'Not a lot of people know this,' Rose-Marie said, 'but there are two families in Louisiana descended from French royalty.'

'Seriously?' Joel was becoming very skeptical now.

'Yes. After the French Revolution the heir to the French throne fled to America to avoid the guillotine.'

'Oh, I've heard this story,' Starr said. Rose-Marie smiled at her and continued.

'His name was Louis Philippe and he was the cousin of King Louis the Sixteenth, the one who got his head cut off. Louis Philippe came to America in 1796 and travelled the length of the East Coast, finally coming to New Orleans in February of 1798. He only spent five weeks in New Orleans, but that was long enough for him to have an affair with a Creole girl named Semanthe. They called Semanthe the prize of New Orleans because she was so beautiful. She was also rumored to be a powerful voodoo priestess. After Louis Philippe left America to return to Europe, Semanthe gave birth to twin girls, the daughters of a would-be French king. The girls grew up in secret in the French Quarter of New Orleans, learning the art of voodoo from their mother. When they came of age, one made a good marriage to a rich Creole businessman from the Garden District. They started a family that became one of the most prominent in Louisiana. The other daughter married for love, choosing as a husband a Cajun boy, dirt poor but incredibly handsome. They settled in bayou country and also started a family that survives to this day. The two families couldn't be more different. One family is Creole, from the city and wealthy, the other is Cajun, from the backwoods and poor. The Creole family turned their back on voodoo, but the Cajun line kept it up. The sons of both families would technically be princes, technically, though they are so many generations removed from the throne that it hardly matters.' She glanced out the window towards the car wash again.

'So, two actual freaking princes are going to fall in love with me? With, like, *me*?' Joel couldn't believe that one prince, let alone two, would ever find him anything more than a weird, awkward, fainty loser.

'Weirder things have happened, Joel,' Tashi said.

'Especially in Louisiana,' Rose-Marie added. 'Besides, you are very sweet, puddin', why wouldn't somebody fall in love with you?'

'One somebody, maybe. A hunch-backed somebody with very bad eyesight, for sure. But two somebodies? No, not possible.'

'You don't give yourself enough credit, Joel,' Starr said. 'Your eating habits aside, you're a real catch.'

'The cards definitely say you are worthy of love,' Rose-Marie added. 'They also indicate that the boy who captures your heart will feel very fortunate, and the other one, well, he will be heartbroken.'

Joel's stomach turned. 'How is it possible that I feel guilty already, without having done anything wrong, or having even met these so-called princes?'

'Because you have a good heart,' Starr said. 'You care about people's feelings. That's why whichever prince you choose will be the luckiest guy alive.'

Joel beamed. That was one of the nicest things anyone had ever said to him.

'I can draw another card if you'd like to know more,' Rose-Marie said.

'Yes, please,' Joel, Starr and Tashi all said at once.

She drew another card and placed it beneath the cards for the future. This card was The High Priestess. Joel looked down at the card and then up at Rose-Marie.

'Is that you?' he asked.

'No, I think in this case this card represents the forces of nature and fate. It means that you are fated to be with one of these princes, and the forces of nature will keep pushing you together until you accept that you are meant to be together.'

'The forces of nature? I don't understand.' Joel said.

'You will understand soon. In the not too distant future some natural occurrence will bring you and your fated prince together, making it clear to you that he loves you and that you love him.'

'That's all very dramatic and cool,' Tashi said. 'The only interesting thing in the tarot reading you did for me was that I'd get an A in English. Why is my life so dull?'

'It's not dull,' Starr said, 'just different.'

Rose-Marie ended the reading with some general advice about how to "integrate" the messages of the reading and how to "listen to nature" more. Joel was barely listening. Two princes! Not one but two! How could that ever happen? Just as they finished up, Rose-Marie's phone rang and she excused herself to answer it before they could pay her for the reading. The three of them waited for her to come back, gazing at crystals and smelling the scented candles. When Rose-Marie came back she looked a bit irritated.

'Have you kids seen my boy, T.J., today? I need him to run an urgent errand.'

'He was just outside washing his dirt bike,' Starr said.

Rose-Marie went to the door and hollered. 'T.J.! T.J.! You there?'

T.J.'s deep, Cajun-accented voice came back. 'Yeah, I'm here, what you want Ma?'

'I want you to run somethin' over to the Beaux place.'

'We have to pay?' Tashi said before anyone could yell any more. She handed over the money rolled up like a little cigar.

'Oh thanks, sugar, thanks so much.' Rose-Marie slipped the cigar of money into her jeans pocket.

A moment later T.J. appeared at the door. He was still shirtless but not quite as wet as he was before. The Louisiana sun had dried him off a bit. He still looked damn hot. Joel averted his eyes, pretending that the glass wind chime was the most interesting thing he'd ever seen in his life. His usual tactic when hot boys were around. Stare at something else like a hypnotized sloth.

'That entitled you-know-what Mrs. Beaux called and wants a stack of things taken over right now, juju bags and ah, herbs, and the like. Can you haul it over there for me, T.J.?'

'I would but I got no way of carryin' stuff on my bike. I left my backpack at home. Can't I take it over tomorrow?'

'Mrs. Beaux's mad on having this stuff delivered today. You know what she gets like, that whole Beaux family is angry as snakes.' Rose-Marie thought a minute, then her eyes fell on Joel and an idea lit up her face. She looked positively mischievous. 'Joel, puddin', would you mind going with T.J. and holding onto the juju-bags and things? He can't hold onto all I got to send and steer his dirt bike at the same time.'

What the hell was happening? What was she asking? Where did she want him to go? Starr and Tashi stepped forward protectively.

'Joel doesn't know T.J. at all, Miss Thibodeaux,' Starr said. 'He wouldn't be comfortable doing that.'

'I might look like a redneck savage,' T.J. said, 'but I ain't dangerous, promise.' He smiled that wide, unguarded smile right at Joel and Joel couldn't help but smile back, his anxiety dissipating somewhat.

'Joel,' Miss Thibodeaux said, 'it's totally up to you if you go along with T.J. or not, no pressure. And T.J., you listen to me – if Joel does agree to go along, you will be more careful on that bike than you ever been in your life. You hear me? You are not to mess about at all. You do the speed limit and you be careful as you can be. You act like you got a fragile old grandma on the back of the bike with ya, you hear?'

Grandma? Fragile? Joel's temper flared.

'I am not a fragile old grandma. I'm a teenage boy with a perfectly normal level of fragility and I can ride on the back of a dirt bike if I want.'

'It's settled then,' T.J. said quickly, seizing on Joel's outburst, 'he's coming along.'

Wait. What?

'Are you sure you want to go along, Joel,' Rose-Marie asked, with Starr and Tashi behind her looking anxious and concerned.

'Well, um—'

'Sure he do,' T.J. said. 'It's just a five minute ride each way. It'll be fun.' And there was that smile again, wide-open, so completely disarming that it made Joel feel unusually safe. Joel never felt safe with boys. Never. Like, not ever. It was a shock to him to feel that way. A nice shock but a shock just the same. It was a further shock when he heard himself say that he would help T.J. with the errand.

'Okay, yes, I'll go.'

Starr and Tashi both mouthed "Are you sure" and he nodded, yes. It wasn't a vigorous nod, because though he did, for some unknown reason, feel safe with T.J., he wasn't completely sure he wanted to go for a ride on a dirt bike with him.

'We'll meet you back home afterwards,' Starr said. Joel nodded, his throat suddenly dry. If it truly was only five minutes each way, how bad could it be?

*** ***

It was bad. It was really, really bad. Not scary, dizzy, passing out bad. No, not that kind of bad. It was bodies pressed too close together on the back of a dirt bike bad. A whole different kind of bad that Joel had never experienced before. Joel was seated behind T.J., with his arms wrapped tightly around the other boy's waist. He hadn't been holding on so tight when he'd first got on the back of the bike, but T.J. had smirked and said 'safety first' and taken hold of Joel's hands and drawn them closer together, until his chest was pressed hard against T.J.s muscled back.

As they zoomed along the country road he could feel each and every one of T.J's six-pack abs. It was closer than he'd ever been to another boy. And yet he wasn't freaking out. Well, yes, he was kind of freaking out, but it wasn't a panic-stricken, anxious freak out. It was a different kind of freak out. An almost nice freak out. Like going on a Roller-Coaster ride – scary and thrilling and exhilarating all at once. As they slowed down on the approach to a long plantation driveway lined with magnolia trees, T.J. reached back and tapped Joel's thigh. It could have been just a friendly gesture, but it felt like more than that. 'You okay back there, kid?' T.J. asked, the thrum of the motor half drowning him out.

'Yeah,' Joel yelled back, 'yeah, I'm okay.' He wasn't lying. He felt okay, despite the fact that ninety percent of his body was in contact with T.J.'s body. Despite the fact that he could feel every muscle in T.J's stomach flex as he leaned into the turn onto the driveway. But why was he okay? Ever since Patrick had betrayed him and posted those awful pics online he hadn't felt safe with any boy, not one. Yet he did feel safe with T.J. On the surface, T.J. seemed like exactly the kind of boy Joel shouldn't trust – a very good-looking, horny teenager. Despite that, Joel did seem to trust him. He couldn't think of a single reason why he should feel so differently about T.J. compared to boys like Patrick or Royal. Maybe this was how it was supposed to feel when you met a boy you liked for real? Maybe the way he'd felt about Patrick, and even how he felt about Royal—like his stomach was a swarm of butterflies and his heart was exploding over and over again like a New Year's fireworks show—were how you felt when it wasn't real, when a boy was wrong for you? He didn't feel any of that with T.J. He simply liked him.

The long driveway ended in front of a modern, two story plantation house. Well, it was more a mansion than a house. The house exuded an air of opulence, with towering columns lining its façade. A sweeping veranda wrapped around three sides, shaded by the stately columns and offering expansive views of manicured lawns and ancient oak trees, their branches draped in wisps of Spanish moss swaying in the slight breeze coming off a nearby bayou. This Mrs. Beaux must be proper rich.

Joel dismounted the dirt bike inelegantly, but without falling over, a small mercy. The driveway was filled with cars, most nondescript but one was the most glorious thing Joel had ever seen. Brand new, cherry red, shiny and sleek, the medallion on the hood said it was a Mustang. Joel didn't know anything about cars, and was generally not interested in them, apart from enjoying the fact that they took him from point A to point B and back again without him having to use his legs. He liked that about them very much. Joel went over to the cherry red beauty and resisted the urge to stroke it.

'Ford Mustang Mach-E GT,' T.J. said, coming up behind him. 'Hot, ain't it? And it's electric too. Gotta love somethin' that handsome that's good for the environment too, like a hot guy who pays your bills.' T.J smirked in that flirty way of his.

'It's very pretty,' Joel said.

'Belongs to one of them rich kids in your school, that Royal Du—'

'Dumaine.'

You've. Got. To. Be. Kidding.

'Yeah, that kid,' T.J. said. 'Got it for his seventeenth birthday.' He rolled his eyes as if such a thing was completely over the top. 'So, I got to take the delivery round the back. You comin' or you want to wait here?'

Joel had to think about that. He didn't want to see Royal but also didn't want to be caught lurking around the parked cars like a criminal. 'I'll come,' he said. He juggled the bag of goods Rose-Marie had given him and followed T.J. around to the back of the mansion. On the way he peaked into the bag, wondering what the wealthy inhabitant of this mansion could want so desperately from T.J.'s mum that it had to be delivered immediately. It was a jumble of small packages. Joel had no idea what any of it was, but wouldn't be surprised if it was snake's innards and other weird stuff like that. One small parcel wrapped in foil looked suspiciously like marijuana. Had he been duped into being a drug mule for a Hoodoo card reader slash drug dealer? He carried the bag gingerly, as though it might bite him or get him high if he held it too close.

Behind the mansion was one of the biggest backyard pools Joel had ever seen. Some kids Joel's age were in the pool and he thought he recognized a few of them from Acadia Academy. More kids were in a pool house as big as Penn's cottage listening to music and dancing around. The strains of a Taylor Swift song he recognized but couldn't name drifted out to him.

'You right to wait here while I take the delivery in to Mrs. Beaux?' T.J. asked. Joel nodded and looked around for a place to wait without looking like an interloper. He found a large pot plant beneath an open window that he could stand behind so that he was out of view of the people in the pool and pool house. He leant against the back wall of the mansion and tried to identify the people in the pool. He was pretty sure they were mostly seniors, with just a couple of juniors. Then from inside the pool house he thought he heard the booming voice of Carter Herrera, a junior and Royal's roommate. The voice acted on Joel like a shot of adrenaline – his heart kicked into a rapid beat and his mouth went dry.

The last thing he wanted was to run into Royal Dumaine while acting as a drug mule for a Hoodoo fortune-teller. He decided to sneak back to the dirt bike and wait for T.J. there. Before he'd gone more than two steps thunder boomed in the perfectly blue sky. Joel involuntarily ducked low. Kids in the pool shrieked. As Joel straightened up he heard footsteps in the house, rushing toward the open window, no doubt the footsteps of someone intent to investigate the source of the boom. The next minute two heads popped out of the window, spotted Joel half hunched beneath them, and started screaming. One of the screaming heads was Lana Beaux. Beaux! Of course, this huge mansion was her house. The other screaming head belonged to a senior girl Joel didn't know the name of.

At the sound of screaming, all the kids came running from the pool house, a shirtless Carter Herrera in the lead. The girls in the window stopped screaming and raced outside to join the mob surrounding Joel. Lana was wearing the skimpiest, pink bikini he had ever seen in his life. Her face was plastered with a sneer that looked even more murderous than usual, a sneer mirrored by the pack of bikini-clad girls around her.

'Fainting kid!' Carter said, 'Why are you hiding behind that bush?'

'His name is Joel,' a horrifyingly familiar voice said from behind Carter. Royal Dumaine stepped from behind the crush of other kids, shirtless as well, wearing red board shorts that were annoyingly well-fitted. He had that perplexed and alarmed look on his face that he always had when Joel was around. 'His name is Joel, I've told you.'

'Right, sorry,' Carter said to Royal before turning back to Joel. 'Joel, what are you doing behind that bush, man?'

'Isn't it obvious,' Lana said, 'he's a peeping tom!' She covered her breasts with her arms. Many of the other girls followed suit.

Joel's heart thumped, his throat tightened, his palms sweated and his mind raced with a million things he could say to defend himself but all that came out was:

'Not peeping! Just, sort of, leaning … waiting! Thunder! Marijuana delivery!'

Everyone's mouth dropped open.

'I wasn't peeping,' Joel pressed on. 'I'm not even interested in your boobs! Not *your* boobs specifically, I mean boobs in general. I have no interest in boobs at all. Not that your boobs aren't all fine. Not just fine, I mean *yours* are exceptional,' he said to a senior girl he recognized as one of the acting majors. 'Congratulations!'

The acting major smiled proudly, hitching her bikini to better display her assets.

'But generally speaking,' Joel continued, I am not at all interested in any boobs whatsoever. I have zero sexual interest in the female chest region.'

'Clearly brain damaged,' someone in the back muttered, 'poor kid.'

A murmur of understanding broke out. Once they'd all decided that Joel was brain damaged rather than a pervert, everyone wandered back to the pool. Joel was left alone with Lana and Royal. Lana leaned in close to Royal and linked her arm in his. Another statement of ownership.

'Why are you here?' she hissed.

'He's here with me.' T.J. had returned. 'I was dropping something off to your mom and Joel came along for the ride. Is there a problem?' He flashed that broad smile as though nothing could ever be wrong wherever he happened to be. Lana went to say something, presumably something very hateful, but Royal cut her off.

'No, there's no problem.'

'Great. Come on kid, let's get out of here.' He slung his arm around Joel's shoulder and began steering him away. Joel tensed but was very glad to be steered out of there.

'I didn't know you two knew each other,' Royal said, his eyes on T.J.'s arm over Joel's shoulder and his tone cold.

'We're only just now getting acquainted,' T.J. said. 'But we're gonna be *fast* friends, aren't we, Joel?'

Joel nodded because he didn't know what else to do. What was happening? Why were Royal and T.J. behaving like this? It was like they were at a buffet and were fighting over the last good sandwich. Did Royal and T.J. both like Lana? Was Lana the sandwich? Joel had suspected Royal had a date with Lana today when they were planning their design studio project get together, and here he was, arm in arm with her. As for T.J., he had flirted with Joel, but he seemed the type to flirt with everyone. Flirting was probably T.J.'s primary means of communication. Also, when Starr first told Joel about T.J., she had mentioned that he was bisexual. Yes, that was the only reasonable explanation for what was happening – they both liked Lana. Of course they did. Of course the two hottest guys in Acadiaville both liked the same (incredibly mean) girl. Joel wouldn't have expected anything else. The universe sucked like that. And of course Joel would be forced to watch those two hot guys square up against each other like two Spider Monkeys about to fight over a banana. Brilliant.

'Ugh,' Joel said louder than he'd meant to, 'I don't care who gets the damn banana.' He stalked off. Those two hot idiots could have Lana for all he cared. When he got to the front of the house and saw the long driveway he wondered how long it would take him to walk home. It'd been about a ten minute ride on the dirt bike, he figured that'd translate to a long walk that would get him home well after dinner had gone cold. Great. Just great. He suppressed a very strong urge to kick the red Mustang and stomped down the drive.

A rumble of thunder echoed his mood. And then he remembered what Rose-Marie had said about the forces of nature pushing him to be with some Louisiana prince. It had been a crack of thunder that had led Royal, and half of the academy, to see Joel hiding behind that potted bush. He scoffed out loud at the sky.

No. Damn. Way. Is. Royal. Dumain. A. Freaking. Prince.

And there was no way he would let stupid storms or stupid squirrels or stupid alligators push him in Royal's direction. Or in any boy's direction. Mother Nature can suck it.

Half way down the drive T.J. pulled up alongside him.

'Hop on, you can't walk home.'

'Sure I can,' Joel said.

'It's more than ten miles to your place.'

Joel stopped in his tracks. With a huff he hopped onto the bike behind T.J. Ten miles was ten miles.

'Want to clue me in to what happened back there?' T.J. asked. 'And why were you muttering about bananas?'

'Because I'm a lunatic, clearly,' Joel said, thinking he had to be a lunatic to believe either T.J. or Royal could possibly like someone like him. Even if Royal were into guys he'd never be into a guy like Joel. 'Just take me home, please,' Joel said, sounding as hopeless and defeated as he felt.

PORCH-LIGHT KISSES AND A BROKEN BOY

T.J. didn't insist Joel hold on as tightly on the way back as he had on the way there, probably sensing that Joel was upset about something but not likely knowing what. When they got to Penn's place it was already twilight and the porch light was on. Joel jumped off the bike and gave T.J. a cursory wave goodbye as he headed straight for the house. He was already on the porch about to open the front door when T.J. caught up with him and took hold of his elbow.

'Hey, kid, what's wrong? Did I do something?'

'Stop calling me *kid*! I am almost the same age as you.'

'Okay, okay, sorry, *Joel*. Want to tell me what I did to upset you?'

'Nothing. You did nothing. It's not you I'm upset with. I'm upset with myself.'

'Well, that makes two of us upset with you,' T.J. said.

That took Joel by surprise. 'What?'

'I've been layin' on the charm as thick as snow on the North Pole and you ain't barely noticed.' He leant in and tugged on Joel's t-shirt again.

What. Was. Happening.

'What?' Joel repeated.

'I think you're cute, Joel, weird for sure, but awful cute, and I'd like to get to know you better. A whole lot better.'

'What?'

'What do you mean *what*?'

Joel shook his head, confused. 'I, I don't understand. What about Lana?'

'Lana? Do you got a thing for Lana?' A flash of disappointment crossed T.J.'s face.

'No! *You* do!'

'I do what?'

'You like Lana.'

Now it was time for T.J. to shake his head all confused. '*What*?'

'You like Lana. Don't you?' Joel was feeling deeply confused now.

'Me, like Lana Beaux? Lord no, never. That girl is meaner than a viper fed on a diet of nothin' but pure caffeine and refined sugar.'

'You *don't* like Lana?'

'I do not.'

'But you *are* bisexual?'

'That I am. Are you saying that all bisexuals in Acadiaville have to like Lana?'

'No, of course not.'

'I'm glad, 'cause that girl ain't my type at all.'

'What is your type?'

'Boys like you, and girls who ain't Lana Beaux.'

'So, all other girls then.'

'Pretty much.' He smirked and stepped closer to Joel. 'But there's only one person I like right now, boy or girl, and that's you. You're real cute to me, Joel River, and it ain't just your little bears t-shirt.'

'Care Bears.'

'Yeah, them. So, could I come collect you sometime and take you for another ride?'

Joel blinked. Was T.J. actually asking him out on a real live date? He didn't know what to say. T.J. was good looking, ridiculously hot, and currently the only human on earth showing any romantic interest in him. He would be stupid not to say yes. Even so, Joel didn't know if he had those kind of feelings for T.J. He liked him, but didn't know if he 'like' liked him. But wasn't that what dating was for? To work out if you truly liked someone?

T.J. waited for an answer, his toffee-colored eyes watching Joel closely. Even though Joel didn't know for sure how he felt about T.J., he knew he found him supremely hot, and knew that he felt safe with him. He hadn't felt safe with a boy since the awful thing with Patrick at his old school. That must mean *something*, right? T.J. was also fun to be around, and really charming. What could it hurt to go on a date?

'Okay, sure, that'd be cool.'

T.J. beamed. 'Super. Maybe I could take you out for a moonlit boat ride on the bayou?'

'Sure, that'd be cool.' Joel smiled nervously.

T.J. leaned in and gave Joel a slow kiss on the cheek. The porch-light flickered, as if something momentous was happening. Joel flushed from head to toe. T.J. stepped back, his grin wide and infectious. 'I'll text you to work out when we can hang.' He loped down the steps and hopped on his bike. It seemed to purr when he started it up, echoing the smug look on T.J.'s face.

As T.J. rode off, Joel touched his cheek, still feeling the warmth of the kiss. He had agreed to a date with T.J., a possibility that seemed as surreal as it was daunting. He turned and went inside, his mind a whirlwind of thoughts and emotions.

As soon as Joel was through the door, Starr and Tashi were on him, like a pair of pretty, custard-sweet-smelling owls swooping down on a startled mouse, each taking one of his hands and asking in unison:

'Are you okay?'

'I'm fine.' Joel let them scan his face to reassure themselves he was telling the truth. 'I am fine, honestly.'

'Why did you go on the errand with T.J.?' Starr asked, squeezing his hand. 'We were terrified you'd—'

'Have a fit and pass out like a freak?' Joel interrupted, feeling defensive. He didn't like being treated like an invalid.

'No,' Tashi chided, 'you know we don't think you're a freak. We were worried you'd be very legitimately overwhelmed by being alone with a strange guy.'

'Especially after just telling us about what happened to you,' Starr added.

Joel relaxed and squeezed each of their hands. 'Weirdly,' he said, 'I was fine with T.J. Normally, being on the back of a bike with a hormonal teenager of the male variety would be my biggest nightmare, but with T.J. it was okay.' He looked at them each in turn and shrugged, confused.

They steered him to the couch and sat him down, taking position either side of him so he was comfortingly surrounded.

'Spill,' Tashi said. 'Do you like T.J.?'

'I like him, but I don't know if I "like" like him'. Joel explained how he'd been feeling while he was with T.J. Safe and kind of calm, especially on the ride home and their moment together on the porch. He blushed when he told them that T.J. had kissed him, not that the girls noticed, they were too busy acting like he'd shown them a picture of a basketful of Golden Retriever puppies.

'He kissed you!' Starr said.

'On the cheek.' Tashi sighed.

They even made the awww sounds, just like you would at a basket of adorable puppies. He rolled his eyes at that and explained that he didn't know if feeling safe with T.J. meant that he "like" liked him, or the opposite. Both gave him curious looks. 'It's confusing,' Joel said, 'but I don't know if I'm not afraid of guys I actually like, or if I'm *only* afraid of guys I like.' The girls blinked at him in confusion, looking like pretty owls again. He slumped back into the couch and moaned. 'I'm a mess!'

Starr patted his hand and gave his fingers a squeeze.

Tashi said, 'Let's work this out scientifically.'

'How?' Joel asked, slumping down a little further.

'Let's go through the evidence. We know you liked the guy who hurt you.'

'Patrick.'

'Yes, that creep,' Tashi said. 'And are you afraid of him?'

'Very much, yes,' Joel said without thinking.

'And we know you fainted when you thought you had to share a room with Royal, right?'

'Yes, keeled right over.'

'I can vouch for that,' Starr said. 'He went down like a sack of potatoes.'

Joel moaned at the memory of it.

'So, do you find Royal attractive?' Tashi asked quietly, as though worried the question might make him faint all over gain.

'Of course I do,' Joel said. 'You've seen him, right? I mean, he's the textbook definition of hot.'

Tashi and Starr shot each other furtive glances.

'What?' Joel demanded. 'What were those looks for?'

'We must be reading different textbooks,' Tashi said with a smirk. 'Royal is not my definition of hot.'

'Mine neither,' Starr added.

'But he's so totally hot!' Joel was almost shouting.

'He's objectively good-looking,' Tashi said, 'but my tastes lean in another direction.'

'In the direction of Carter Herrera?' Joel asked.

'Yes, in that direction.' Tashi was properly blushing.

'The point is,' Starr interrupted, 'you are attracted to Royal and are terrified of him. You were attracted to Patrick and became terrified of him. You are not terrified of T.J. Are you attracted to him?'

'He's very cute,' Joel said, 'I'd be mad not to like him.'

'Well, that's the answer. You're not really attracted to T.J., so you're not afraid of him.' Starr said this with the tone of a lawyer summing up her case. 'Because of what happened with Patrick, you associate attraction with being betrayed and hurt. Thus, whenever you "like" like someone you feel terrified.'

'So ... ' Joel was still confused.

'You are only afraid of guys you "like" like,' Starr said.

Tashi nodded in agreement. Joel groaned.

'I'm broken. I'm a broken human boy.'

'You're not broken,' Starr chided. 'You went through a terrible thing and are still dealing with the after-effects.'

'That's right,' Tashi added. 'You're not broken, you're healing.'

'Healing,' Joel mumbled, not feeling very reassured. 'A healing human boy.'

'A healing human boy,' Starr and Tashi echoed.

Joel jerked forward in his seat. 'Oh no! You know what this means?'

'What?' Starr and Tashi asked in unison.

'I "like" like Royal Dumaine! And he's the absolute worst!'

'Keep telling yourself that,' Tashi said, smirking and jabbing him in the shoulder, 'and one day you might believe it.'

Joel moaned and slumped back into his seat. His stomach grumbled loudly at the same time. They all laughed.

'I'm starving,' Joel said unnecessarily.

'Penn's making vegan schnitzel, especially for Tashi,' Starr whispered. 'Hopefully it's better than her bean tacos.'

The girls dragged Joel up and slow-marched him into the kitchen, where Penn was humming to some jazz tune as she cooked.

'You're back,' she observed, her eyes on the stove and the vegan schnitzel. 'How was your day?'

Joel slumped into a chair, his mind still on T.J.'s smile and the unexpected turn of events – namely the impending date with a boy he liked but didn't "like" like.

'It was ... interesting,' he said.

Penn turned, a look of concern on her face.

'Everything okay?'

'Yeah, just a lot to process.' Joel wasn't ready to spill the details to his aunt, not yet.

Penn nodded, understanding. 'Well, dinner's almost ready. You can process and eat at the same time.'

Dinner passed in a blur for Joel. He was there but not quite there, his thoughts continuously drifting back to T.J. and Royal. That moment on the porch when T.J. had kissed his cheek. The fact that Royal was coming to their house to work on their costume design project.

About an hour after dinner, Tashi's parents came to pick her up. He said his goodbyes and excused himself and went to his room, lying on his bed and staring at the ceiling. His phone buzzed. A message from T.J.:

Looking forward to our date 😊

Joel's gut clenched. He typed a quick response—a speedboat emoji, a moon emoji and a smiley face—and then set the phone aside, his heart feeling heavy. As he lay there, his mind wandered to Royal. He couldn't deny the flutter in his stomach whenever Royal was near, the way his heart seemed to beat in a different rhythm in response to Royal's presence. But with T.J., it was different. It was easy, comfortable, and maybe that's what he needed right now. A *friend* not a *boy*friend. His stomach sank. How was he going to explain this to T.J. without hurting his feelings?

He took out his most valued, most secret possession and hugged it to his chest. He fell asleep thinking about the two boys, the complexities of his feelings, and the unknown territory he was about to navigate.

MOTORCYCLE DREAM

Joel was on the back of T.J.'s bike again, but this time they were riding under a nighttime sky filled with stars. An open road lay ahead of them, stretching far off into the distance. All around them was a creeping mist that shrouded the road. The mist moved as if it had a mind of its own, deliberately closing them in, blocking their vision.

A strange shriek rent the air. The mist thickened even more. He couldn't see more than a foot ahead of him, but still T.J. sped ahead, no concern for the danger. A shape lunged at them from the side of the road. A shape that smelt of death. T.J. swerved and lost control of the bike, striking another figure that loomed out of the mist directly in front of them. Suddenly Joel was soaring through the air, that strange shrieking all around him.

He hit the dirt hard. He sat up, shaking his head. T.J. lay on the road beside him, on his stomach, not moving. Joel rolled him over. It wasn't T.J. It was Carter Herrera. Carter's eyes were wide open, staring blankly upwards. He was dead. In the distance, the shape of a man emerged from the mist, slowly walking down the road towards them, a man dressed as if he were from another time, centuries ago, complete with a long, hooded cloak. The cloaked figure stretched out his hand

and made a grasping motion. Simultaneously a hand grabbed him. Carter's hand. Joel tried to pull away, but Carter held tight, his fingers cold and hard, his eyes gleaming like dull, wet coins. Zombie!

CRIMINALLY HOT PIZZA SAUCE AND PINK BIKINIS

Joel stood in the shower, letting the hot water flow over him. Aunt Penn and Starr had left him to get ready while they went in to town to pick up pizza for the movie night with Royal. He'd spent the day with Starr and Penn, hanging out, talking about books and movies, doing laundry for the upcoming school week. It hadn't taken long for the three of them to fall into a comfortable domestic routine. Like a proper little family. Joel smiled to himself. He realized he'd felt at home here for weeks now.

He got out of the shower and toweled himself off, thinking about what he'd wear for the movie night. He was nervous about it and wanted to feel comfortable without looking like a couch-sloth. He wrapped the towel around his waist and, because he was home alone, went out to the kitchen to grab a glass of water without getting dressed first. He decided on his outfit on the way – jeans and his vintage, red T-Rex t-shirt. When he got to the kitchen he stopped in his tracks. The kitchen was full of people. Well, not full exactly. Starr was by the overhead cabinets taking down plates. Aunt Penn was standing at the kitchen table, where she'd just placed a stack of pizza boxes. And beside Penn was Royal Dumaine, hot as ever in a snug white Jazz Fest t-shirt and blue jeans.

Oh. My. Good. God. Horror of horrors!

The three of them stared at Joel. Joel quickly covered his nipples and stared back, his mouth moving but no words coming out. If he had been able to make any sounds in that moment they would have been: Aaagh! No, no, no, no! Aaagh!

Penn spoke first. 'Ah, Joel, we're back from picking up the pizza, and, ah, Royal is here a little early.'

Royal had his hands in his jean pockets and was staring at the kitchen floor like his life depended on it. Joel couldn't bring himself to say anything. He slowly backed out of the room, then ran to his bedroom. He shut and locked the door behind him and dove face-first into the bed, horrified and dizzy and sick to his stomach. He muffle-shouted 'Humiliating!' into his pillow and pounded it with his fists for good measure. His hand automatically went beneath the pillows and found the familiar softness of his most valued, most secret possession, and he let out a quiet breath as the humiliated tightness in his chest loosened. Mere seconds later, Penn tapped on the door and asked if she could come in.

'No, please, just leave me alone to die of shame.'

'There's no need to die of shame,' she whispered through the keyhole. 'No-one in this house thinks any less of you because they saw you in a towel.'

Joel huffed into the pillow in indignant disbelief. He was pretty sure that Royal would think less of him. He probably thinks Joel was a total thirsty pervert – first colliding with him in the quad, then the pool locker room, then the wet shirt thing.

'Joel, are you really not coming out?' Penn sounded worried.

'No, I'm not, Aunt Penn, never, or at least not for the next fifty years!'

'Fifty years? Goodness. I'd better bring you some pizza then.'

Joel felt ashamed as Penn's footsteps receded down the hall. He was behaving like an absolute baby. What would Royal think of him locking himself in his room like a five-year old throwing a tantrum? He sat up, considering if he should just pull himself together and go out there and pretend that nothing had happened. Penn knocked on the door again.

'There's some pizza by the door, Joel. You can eat it in your room or come out and join us. It's just Starr and me. Royal left.'

Joel's heart sank. There was no way to fix this now. By morning Royal will have told Carter, and Carter will have spread it all over school. It would be "fainting boy" all over again, but this time they'd be calling him "tantrum boy", or something worse. Joel dragged himself up to get the pizza. Yes, his life was over, but the smell of the veggie pizza was drifting under the door and he was too weak to resist. He may be in the depths of humiliation, but a boy still has to eat.

Penn had left three big slices piled onto one of her sunflower plates. She was trying to cheer him up. He took it back to bed and started eating, his mind more on the nightmare he'd be facing at school the next day than on the chewing and swallowing. It was good though, and he tore into the second slice while wondering if Penn would consider home-schooling him. He'd half convinced himself the home-school thing was a possibility, and half-finished his second slice, when a hot sting of pain made him jump and curse.

'What the fu—'

A glob of hot pizza sauce had slopped onto his chest. It was criminally hot. It should be illegal for pizza sauce to be that hot. When he tried to wipe it away he dropped the whole slice of pizza in his lap. And on a white towel too! He lurched to his feet. The slice fell from his lap and hit the floorboards with a loud splat. He started wiping the mess up as best he could, mumbling to himself the whole time.

'Oh. My. God. Total absolute mess. Typical, clumsy … '

A light tap at the window and the whisper of his name made him freeze.

'Err, hey, Joel.' Royal Dumaine! Royal Dumaine was standing in the yard outside his window. 'Err, can we talk, please?'

Joel lunged sideways, to get out of sight of the window. He slipped on the slice on the floor on the way and thudded into his chest of drawers. He scrambled to stay upright and then lodged himself between the dresser and the wall, using the drawers as a modesty screen.

'Sorry!' Royal whispered, 'Sorry for startling you! I'm not looking. I'm looking away.'

Joel peered over the dresser. Royal had one hand raised, as one might when trying to calm a skittish pony, and had his face turned away from the window.

'I'm looking totally in the other direction, way off into the yard. I can't see you at all.'

Joel mustered his voice. 'Why are you here, Royal? Why are you tapping on my window?'

'I think we need to talk.'

'What about?'

'I don't want you to … well, I don't want you to be scared of me.'

'I'm not scared of you.' Joel worried that it was obvious he was lying. His voice was shaking.

'Okay, *uncomfortable* then. I don't want you to be uncomfortable around me. We go to the same school. I don't want you to feel, like, unsafe and stuff at school.'

Joel said nothing, just stayed out of sight.

'We got off to a bad start. That day we gave you a ride to school, I'd just had a massive fight with my dad, about him cheating on my other dad with my surrogate mom. I was really pissed. Like, *really* pissed. I've never been that angry. And then you got in the car and you were all, well, *you*. Very, very you. It threw me. You threw me. Then, when we got to school, my dad was being a dick and then you fainted and that threw me too. I felt so bad for you, so bad. All I wanted to do was help, but I think I made it worse. And then there was the squirrel thing and the locker room, they threw me too, and the thing on the library porch during the thunder storm, with the, the—'

'Wet nipples,' Joel interjected.

Royal half coughed, half choked.

'Err, yeah. It's just been a string of really, weird, err, encounters. But I meant what I said that first day. I would never do anything to hurt you.'

'Then why'd you tell Carter I fainted? Everyone's calling me "fainting boy" now.'

'I didn't tell him.'

'Then who did? It wasn't Starr, and she was the only other person there.'

'Carter was there. He arrived when I was carrying you up the stairs. He saw. But then that day at the pool, I told him not to call you fainting boy, and he hasn't since, has he?'

Joel had to admit that was true. So, that was why Royal and Carter had been talking about him at the pool. Joel started to feel he may have misjudged Royal. But he still had doubts.

'So, why do you always look at me with that weird face?'

'What weird face?'

'Like I bother you or something.'

'You don't bother me, Joel. You confuse me. That is a confused face. I thought maybe we could be friends, but then every time I ran into you, it's like you couldn't get away from me fast enough, you ran in the total opposite direction, or you acted like just my existing freaked you out. I got the feeling you 100% hated me.'

'I don't 100% hate you,' Joel said from behind the drawers, still staying out of sight.

'So just 99% then,' Royal joked.

'No, maybe 70%.' Joel pitched his voice so that it was clear he was teasing.

'70% isn't too bad!' Royal paused, shifted on his feet. Joel could almost hear him breathing. 'I don't want to freak you out, Joel. I want you to be, like, cool with me. Cool around me.'

'Cool around you?'

'Yeah, like two people who get along.'

'Two people who get along?'

'Yeah, like friends.'

'Friends.'

'Are you just repeating what I say now?'

'Yes, but not deliberately. I don't know what else to say.'

'Just tell me why I freak you out. Is it because I did the wrong thing when you fainted?'

Joel couldn't tell him the truth. He couldn't tell him that it was because of his hotness. His absolute and immense Creole, blue-eyed, red Speedo hotness. And because of what Patrick had done to him back home. He couldn't share either of those things, not yet anyway.

'I'm just embarrassed,' he said instead. 'Embarrassed about the fainting, and the squirrel, and the locker room and, well, everything really. I'm embarrassed about everything.'

'Don't be embarrassed. None of it's your fault. I mean, that squirrel was clearly insane, and you can't help your medical condition, and the locker room was—'.

'Mortifying.'

'I was going to say it was just a little bit awkward, that's all. Can't we move past it?'

Joel thought for a long moment before answering, 'Okay'.

Royal sighed with relief. 'Can I stay for the movie then?'

Joel hesitated only briefly. 'Sure.'

'Great. Here, take my phone.'

'Your phone? Why?'

'So I can tell your aunt I left it behind and had to come back for it. I can meet you at the front door in five minutes. I don't think your aunt would like that I came to your window, especially when you're, like, completely naked.'

'I am not completely naked! I'm semi-clothed!'

'Towels aren't clothes. So, yeah, you're fully naked. Will you take my phone or not?'

'Okay, but just leave it on the windowsill.'

'You're not still embarrassed are you, Joel?'

'No, just not decent. As you said, towels aren't clothes.' This was not exactly true. He was very much embarrassed. He currently had pizza sauce all over his bare chest, all over the towel, and not a small amount oozing between his toes.

'Look, Joel, don't freak out, but I already saw you drop the pizza in your lap, so you might as well come get my phone.'

Joel groaned. 'Okay, so now I am fully embarrassed again.'

'Who hasn't done embarrassing stuff like that?'

'Almost everyone, I'm sure of it.'

'Oh, come on, everybody's dropped pizza on themselves. It's what keeps the laundry detergent industry in business.'

Joel groaned again, this time pairing it with a deep sigh.

'Besides,' Royal continued, 'I don't care. It doesn't make me like you any less. Now come get my phone.'

Joel went through a few scenarios in his head. Could he get dressed while squeezed in the corner between the dresser and the wall, without Royal seeing anything? No, not likely. Besides, there was only underwear and t-shirts in the drawers. His jeans and chinos were in the wardrobe on the other side of the room. So, no, not at all possible. Could he hug the wall around to the window and take the phone while staying out of sight? No, not likely. Could he crawl along the floor commando style and get the phone without being seen? Definitely not. A minute or so of frustrated irritation passed before he just gave up. The arrangement of the furniture in his room had defeated him. He'd not considered having to navigate the space while avoiding being seen by a hot boy standing outside the window when he'd moved it all into place. He wouldn't make that rookie mistake again. He stepped out from behind the dresser drawers and, his heart pounding like a crazy techno beat, paced over to the window and held out his hand for the phone. All while pretending that he wasn't completely mortified.

'Whoa, Joel, you look like a victim in a horror movie.' Royal was grinning ear to ear, taking in the sauce all over Joel's chest, and in his lap. His annoyingly handsome face was positively lit up with amusement.

Joel fumed and silently gave off rage vibes.

'A totally cute horror movie victim,' Royal added quickly, toning down the glee on his face.

Wait. What?

Did Royal just call him cute? Royal looked as shocked by what he'd said as Joel felt.

'Are you … are you actually *flirting* with me, Royal Dumaine?'

'Will it get me below the 70% hate level?' he asked sheepishly.

'Yes, yes it will.' Joel swallowed hard. What was happening here?

'Okay, then, I am. And I can't believe I just said that.' Royal's face was a mixture of emotions – partly surprised, partly amused, and partly confused.

Joel's heart skipped into a much happier rhythm. Royal Dumaine was actually *flirting* with him.

'So, maybe I don't 70% hate you now,' Joel said. 'Maybe you're at just 30%.'

'Wow, 30% is progress.' Royal was smiling in a bashful way, which was all kinds of adorable, but he still looked confused. No, baffled. He looked positively baffled.

'What's wrong?' Joel asked.

'Err, well, I think … well the truth is I think I must be bisexual, or something, definitely something, and that's a bit of a shock to be honest.' He reached out his hand and gave his phone to Joel. 'I'll see you at the front door in five.' He walked away without saying another word.

Joel listened, rooted to the spot, his heart singing like a swamp bird, as Royal's grass-muffled footsteps moved steadily away.

*** ***

Joel tore to the bathroom to wash up. He dropped the soiled towel on the floor, then picked it up again and dropped it in the laundry hamper, so that Aunt Penn wouldn't strangle him later. The sight of himself in the mirror gave him a jolt. He really did look like a horror movie victim. There was pizza sauce everywhere!! His hands shook as he cleaned himself up. Royal had called him cute. His heart raced and pounded in his ears. Royal had basically come out to him as bi. His stomach roiled. What did all this mean?

He tore back to his bedroom, threw on some underwear, realized they were on back to front, so took them off and put them on again, the right way. He grabbed the first pair of jeans he could find and grabbed his vintage, red T-Rex t-shirt from the pile of clothes Penn had put away earlier. He grabbed Royal's phone, put on the t-shirt and his Vans slip-ons, and tore down the hall; all the while tugging on the t-shirt because it felt tighter than it usually did. Maybe it'd shrunk in the wash? When he got to the kitchen he found Starr and Aunt Penn quietly eating pizza.

'Joel,' Penn said, 'you're out of your room early. It's not quite been fifty years yet.'

'Err, yeah, sorry about that, over-reacted!'

Starr was smiling at him in a way he couldn't quite read. She was just about to say something when there was a knock at the door.

'I'll get it', Joel said, already on the way to the door, his heart still racing madly.

Royal was just about to knock again when Joel opened the door.

'I forgot my phone', he said, loud enough for everyone in the house to hear. They locked eyes. Joel smiled. Royal smiled. Oh my, he was gorgeous when he smiled. Then Royal's face got that confused or bothered or embarrassed look again.

'You've got that face again.' Joel pointed at Royal's face.

'No, I don't.' Royal quickly re-arranged his face to look normal.

'Yeah, you do. What's it about this time? I couldn't possibly have done anything confusing or baffling already. I literally just opened the door!'

Royal meekly pointed at Joel's chest. Joel looked down, thinking maybe pizza sauce had somehow got on his shirt. That's when he understood why the t-shirt was tighter than normal. It wasn't his vintage, red T-Rex t-shirt. It was a girl's t-shirt that had the words HOT STUFF emblazoned across the front in lurid rainbow letters and beneath that: "Come and Get It!" in silver glitter.

Oh. My. Wicked. Hellscape. Why?

'I didn't wear this on purpose!' Joel blurted. 'Honestly, this isn't my shirt!'

'It's my shirt, Joel,' Starr said coming up behind him. 'It must've got mixed up with your things when Penn sorted the laundry.'

'And before I get in trouble for that,' Penn called from inside, 'I'm going to my room to read. Make sure movie night is wrapped up by ten.'

'Ten!' Joel and Starr exclaimed together. What, were they children?

'Or nine if you choose.' Penn was messing with them.

'Ten's fine', Joel said. Starr nodded vigorously in agreement.

'Starr,' Joel whispered, 'could you please get the movie sorted? I have to change my shirt.'

188

'Err,' Royal said, coughing, 'don't change the shirt. It's, it's really cute.'

Joel's mouth dropped right open. He and Starr passed meaningful glances.

'Unless you really want to change,' Royal added. 'It's up to you, but we don't have a lot of time.'

Starr turned so that only Joel could see her face. She wiggled her eyebrows and mouthed: 'He *likes* you.'

They ate pizza and watched *Midnight in the Garden of Good and Evil* without anything else going wrong. Starr took notes for their costume project. Joel caught Royal sneaking peeks at him about five times. Each time they both blushed and went straight back to watching the movie. After the film finished, the three of them went over some ideas for costumes. Joel didn't think he or Royal contributed much, they were both too busy being ridiculously awkward, but Starr didn't seem to mind. At nine-thirty Joel offered to get them all some iced-tea, and Starr went to get her sketch book to start tracing out some designs. Joel was taking down glasses when Royal followed him into the kitchen. They smiled awkwardly at each other. Royal leant against the bench quite close to Joel, who felt as though the Hot Stuff t-shirt was tightening around his neck. He tugged at the collar and made a mess of pouring the first glass of tea.

'Here, let me,' Royal said, taking the bottle and filling the other two glasses without spilling a drop. His face was very close to Joel's. Joel could almost feel the warmth radiating from his body. A very large part of Joel wanted to run from the room, but with a massive effort he resisted the impulse. Royal put the ice-tea bottle down right by Joel and stepped a little closer.

'I, uh, want to try something,' he said.

'What?' Joel squeaked in a very hamsterish voice.

'Uh … kissing a boy. I mean, um … kissing you.'

Joel cough-choked, recovered, then whispered:

'Yes, please …. Err, I mean, sure.'

Royal smiled and leaned in. Now Joel could definitely feel the heat radiating from Royal's body, from his lips. It was like sitting in the sunshine on a cold, windless day. Joel was about to freak out and back away, before their lips could touch, but then a loud rap on the door interrupted them. Starr called from the hallway saying she'd get it. Royal took a step away, creating a space between them that felt like a million miles to Joel. Then another voice was in the house. Joel and Royal recognized it at the same time. Carter Herrera. Royal took another step away. Starr came into the kitchen, with Carter following behind her. Carter looked like a movie star, in black sneakers, black jeans and a black t-shirt.

'Hey, dude,' he said to Royal. 'Hey, ah, Joel.' He noticed the Hot Stuff t-shirt but didn't say anything. An awkward moment followed with them all standing in the kitchen not knowing what to say. Carter broke the silence.

'Sorry to interrupt your project meeting, guys,' he said. 'Royal, I came to get you because you didn't answer your phone.'

'Oh, I put it on mute for the movie.'

'Right, well, Lana's on her way to pick us up at Nottoway House.'

'Lana?' Royal had a different confused look on his face now. Was it confusion mixed with guilt?

Joel's stomach tightened. He had somehow completely forgotten about Lana's existence. How could he have done that? Lana was Royal's girlfriend. Joel wasn't the kind of person who kissed other people's boyfriends. What had he almost done? Was he so overwhelmed by Royal Dumaine's epic hotness that he had let all of his principles go out the window? Shame washed over him.

'Yeah, Lana,' Carter said. 'There's a late night pool party at her place. Come on, she might already be waiting.'

Joel's gaze had dropped to the floor the minute Lana's name was mentioned. It was still there. He couldn't bring himself to look up. He could feel Royal trying to catch his eye. He ignored him. He grabbed a glass of iced-tea and headed out of the kitchen.

'Bye, Royal, Bye, Carter,' he said as normally as he could. It didn't sound normal at all. It sounded like the voice of a broken-hearted boy, because that was what he was.

'Joel,' Royal said, but Joel kept going.

When he got to his bedroom he shut and locked the door, shut and locked the window, and closed the curtains, blocking every possible way Royal might use to speak to him. But he knew Royal wouldn't be coming. He'd be going with Carter to meet Lana. His girlfriend. He'd spend the night in the pool with her, him in his snug red board shorts and Lana in her extremely skimpy pink bikini. Joel felt sick. His ears were ringing. His mouth felt as dry as moth wings. He dropped onto the bed, and was suddenly filled to the brim with an irrational, seething hatred of pool parties and pink bikinis.

THE BOY WHO WAS TAKEN

Joel woke at midnight to the unmistakable sight of police lights flashing outside the house. Something bad had happened. He jumped up and opened his bedroom door, realizing only then that he was still wearing the Hot Stuff t-shirt. He figured it probably wasn't appropriate for him to go out wearing that, so he switched it for a plain blue one.

Starr's door was closed, so she must still be asleep. When he got to the living room, Penn was there with Sheriff Claiborne, who he recognized from the newspapers. Penn was sitting in the armchair, in her pajamas and a light silk bathrobe. She looked pale and small. Sherriff Claiborne was on the sofa looking grim. Joel lingered in the doorway, listening. The sheriff was explaining something to Penn, something about a search party.

'We've got a team of dogs following the scent, and three deputies heading up groups of volunteers to widen the search for the boy. Joel's heart dropped to his stomach. Who were they talking about?

Penn nodded and asked, 'How long has he been missing now?' Her voice was strained.

'Two hours, max.'

'And he was definitely *taken?*' Penn barely got the word "taken" out. Her hands were trembling. 'He didn't just wander off into the woods and get lost?'

'The witness was very clear. Someone came out of the woods, just ahead of the bridge onto school grounds at Little Bayou River, grabbed the boy and dragged him off. With what's been happening in Acadiaville lately, with the other disappearances, we have to take this seriously.'

Penn nodded that she understood, and clasped her hands together to stop them shaking. The sheriff flipped open his notebook.

'Can I just confirm the description of the boy? The witness was shaken up.'

Penn nodded. The sheriff read from his notes.

'Six foot tall, athletic build, dark hair, olive complexion, 17 years old, last seen wearing a white Jazz Fest t-shirt and blue jeans.'

That described Royal! The room spun around Joel. He had to steady himself against the door jam. He couldn't comprehend what had happened. Someone had grabbed Royal and dragged him into the woods? Why? Whatever the reason, it couldn't be good. The headlines about the disappearances flashed through Joel's mind and without meaning to he found himself saying the words 'serial killer'.

The sheriff and Penn heard him and looked over to where he was hovering in the doorway.

'Joel,' Penn said, 'go back to your room. This conversation is not for your ears.'

Joel didn't resist. He forced himself to turn and head down the hallway. He only made it a few steps before he had to stop and lean against the wall. His head was spinning. He was out of sight of Aunt Penn and the sheriff, so he just stayed there waiting for the dizziness to pass. The sheriff started talking again.

'Can I leave the witness in your care?' he said. 'I need to get back to the search.' Penn must've agreed because the Sheriff went outside. There was the sound of a car door opening and closing and then the sheriff came back in with someone.

Penn said to this new person, 'You're covered in leaves and mud, you need a hot shower.' Her voice was soft and kind and very gentle. 'Come on, I'll take you to the bathroom.' Joel shook away the dizziness as best he could and compelled himself to go to his room. He quietly closed the door behind him and sat on the edge of his bed. His mind was reeling. Was this real? Had Royal been taken? He prayed it was just one of his vivid dreams, but knew it wasn't.

In the hallway, Aunt Penn was showing someone to the bathroom. The witness. Who was it? Carter? Lana? A few minutes later, the shower came on. A knock on the door preceded Aunt Penn asking if she could come in.

'Yes,' Joel stuttered.

Penn was still pale and shaking. Joel got up and hugged her. She embraced him tightly and took a long time to let him go.

'What happened?' Joel asked.

'A student was taken,' Penn said. 'On his way back to school from a pool party off campus, where he should not have been.'

Joel's heart sank even further into his stomach than he thought was possible. He wanted to ask if it was really Royal who'd been taken, but he couldn't bring himself to do it. He couldn't bear to have it confirmed, to know for certain.

'We have a house guest for the night,' she said. 'I'll make up the sofa bed in the living room. I wanted you to be warned, in case you run into him in the hallway.'

Him. So maybe Carter was the witness?

'Who is it?'

Before Penn could tell him, someone tapped on the bedroom door. Joel couldn't believe his eyes. Standing in the doorway, in nothing but his red board shorts and recently showered, was Royal Dumaine. He was so handsome, so hot, so beautiful, more so than ever because just minutes before Joel believed he would never see him again. Joel's breath caught in his throat. It was a long moment before he took another breath.

'Sorry for interrupting,' Royal said, 'I didn't know where to go.' His eyes were a little red and his face looked haunted, ashen.

'I'll make up the sofa bed in the living room for you, Royal. Do you need to borrow some clothes from Joel, maybe a t-shirt and some sleep shorts?'

Of all the things Joel could have said—like "I'm glad you're safe, Royal" or "It's great you didn't get serial killed, Royal" or even "Sure, you can borrow some of my clothes"—he chose to say instead:

'There's no way he'll fit into my shorts, he's *huge*!'

Penn stared at Joel, gobsmacked. Royal flushed from head to toe. His face was doing that confused and embarrassed thing again.

Oh. My. Lord. Stupid, stupid mouth!

'It's fine,' Royal said, his voice rough, 'I don't need to borrow anything.'

'Okay then,' Penn said, still staring at Joel. 'I'll go get the sofa bed set up.' She left the bedroom, leaving Joel and Royal alone.

'Sorry,' Joel said, 'so sorry, just flustered.' He tried to act normal by asking what he thought was a normal question. 'What happened to your clothes?'

Royal took a moment to answer.

'Carter was wearing them,' he said.

Joel remembered what the sheriff had read out about the boy who'd been taken – 'Last seen wearing blue jeans and a Jazz Fest t-shirt.'

'It was Carter who was taken?'

Royal nodded, swallowed, sighed, and wiped his eyes even though they were dry. Joel wanted to hug him. Instead, he asked him why Carter was wearing his clothes.

'Carter's clothes went missing at the party. Someone playing a prank. He'd been in the pool all night and was cold in just his wet board shorts, so when we were heading home I loaned him my clothes.'

'You weren't cold?'

'I didn't get in the pool,' Royal explained. I spent the whole night … err … well, with Lana.'

Joel thought he understood what "with" Lana meant. His heart had now dropped to the tips of his toes. It would exit his body if one more even slightly bad thing happened, and then his heart would flap about on the floor like a gory fish out of water until it finally went still for good. Royal talked over the awkwardness.

'Some of Carter's friends from Acadiaville drove us back, they dropped us off just the other side of the bridge, so we could sneak back into the dorm without getting busted … I was a few yards ahead of Carter, in a hurry to get back. I'd had a bad night to be honest. I was on the bridge when I heard a weird sound, like scuffling feet, and then Carter shouted. He was being dragged into the woods. Carter's strong, you know, so the … the … whoever was dragging him away must've been, like, really strong, and fast. He was gone so fast. I ran after him, to help. I must've run a few miles into the woods searching for him, but I couldn't find him. It was really dark in the woods, there's no moon tonight. So I ran back to school and told Mr. Prince, the boy's dorm master, and he called the sheriff.

'They'll find him,' Joel said, hoping it was true more than believing it. 'They'll find him.'

'I hope so,' Royal said, his voice shaking. He took a step into the room and looked Joel over.

'Are you okay?' he asked.

'Me? You're the one who saw Carter get taken—'

'It's just that I ... I was worried all this would trigger your condition, especially with me staying the night.'

Joel blinked, surprised. Royal Dumaine was more concerned about Joel than himself, even after what he'd been through. He couldn't be any sweeter.

'Thanks, but I'm fine,' Joel said. 'How are you?'

'Freaked out. Really freaked out. I couldn't go back to the dorm. I share a room with Carter.'

'Ah,' Joel said, 'I totally understand.'

'You sure you'll be okay with me staying here?'

'Yes,' Joel said, once again hoping it was true more than believing it. 'I'll be fine.'

Penn came back into the room.

'Okay,' she said, 'your bed's ready, Royal. Come on, you need some sleep. You too, Joel. Back into bed.'

'Night, Joel,' Royal said before following Penn out.

'Night,' Joel replied.

Joel dropped down onto his bed again. He had dreamt of Carter's death. Had the dream come true? He'd had a strange dream before Liz-Anne Landry's disappearance as well. Did that mean all of the dreams he'd been having would come true? Were they visions of the future? He had to tell someone about them. But who? The sheriff? He'd probably think Joel was crazy or making it up for attention, especially if he told him about the zombie cheerleaders and the freaky priest with the red eyes. Aunt Penn? Somehow he didn't think Penn would believe him any more than the sheriff would. Maybe Starr or Tashi would know what to do? He decided he'd tell the girls in the morning. For now, he was so exhausted he had to go to bed. He peeled off his jeans and climbed under the covers in his t-shirt and underwear. He lay on his back, thinking about everything that had happened. He hoped Carter was alright, and hoped also that sleep would take him soon, and take away the fear and worry of this awful night.

*** ***

It turned out that hoping for sleep didn't make it come. Joel was still staring at the ceiling a couple of hours later. It would be dawn soon and the chance of sleep would be gone. Creaking floorboards outside his room made him jump. He lay still, instantly tense. The doorknob turned and the door slowly opened, just a few inches. Royal peeked around the edge of the door. Joel could barely see him in the dark, but he would recognize that shape anywhere. Even Royal's silhouette was athletic and hot; like a sexy shadow ghost.

'Joel,' Royal whispered, 'are you awake?'

It took Joel a second to reply. His heart was pounding and his throat suddenly very dry.

'Yes.'

Royal stepped into the room. Even in the dark Joel could see that he was only wearing underwear. He looked like a Prada model, perfect and gorgeous. Joel hated himself for thinking that. He had to stop having those kinds of thoughts about Royal – naughty, horny thoughts. Royal had a girlfriend, and had just been through the trauma of witnessing his roommate get kidnapped. Joel closed his eyes to cut off all temptation, and pulled the sheet up to cover himself.

'I can't sleep,' Royal said. 'Can we talk?'

'Um … okay … sure.' He heard Royal sit on the floor by the door, probably so that he wasn't looming over Joel and to give him as much space as possible. For some reason it irritated Joel that Royal was so thoughtful and considerate. Super-hot boys had no business being thoughtful as well as sexy as hell. It was seriously unfair.

'I'm not with her,' Royal said suddenly.

Joel was confused.

'What? Who?'

'Lana. I'm not with Lana.'

Joel didn't say anything. Now he was really confused. Everything he'd seen of Royal and Lana told him they were together. Every time Joel had been around them both, Lana's every action practically screamed "He's mine, mine, mine!"

'We *were* together,' Royal continued in a whisper, 'but now we're not. We've been on and off for about a year. We broke up again over the summer. She still thinks we're going to get back together, but we're not. That's what I was doing with Lana tonight – telling her that it's over for good. She was, ah, pretty enraged about it, really furious. I thought she might clock me at one point. Lana's, err, very, well, she's—'

'Mean as a viper on a diet of nothin' but pure caffeine and refined sugar,' Joel said, repeating what T.J. had told him about Lana. There was a long pause. Joel wondered if he'd overstepped.

'That's accurate, to be honest,' Royal whispered. 'And she's really jealous, like, crazy jealous. That's why, when she saw us in the quad, after the squirrel thing, I said we weren't friends. I didn't want her to suspect anything, to set her mind against you because she was jealous. She can be very mean. I didn't want her to be mean to you. I wanted to explain all this to you earlier, when we were in the kitchen here, before I went to the party, but you didn't give me the chance. You just walked out.'

So that explained why Royal was weird when Lana was around. He didn't want to trigger her crazy jealousy. Joel wondered what Royal didn't want Lana to suspect about him and Joel, there was nothing between them back then, but rather than ask about that, he went to the main point.

'So, Lana is not your girlfriend?'

'No, she's not my girlfriend. I wouldn't have … err … tried to kiss you if I was with someone else. I'm not like that. I don't cheat.'

Joel thought it best he just remain silent. Royal settled into his position on the floor and continued.

'I never really liked Lana, but her parents and my parents are friends, and we've known each other since kindergarten. Everyone expected us to go out, especially Lana, so I guess I just caved and dated her to keep everyone happy … but I was never happy. When I met you, I realized what I'd been missing, the feelings I'd been missing out on, things I never felt when I was with Lana, things I'd never felt for anyone before.'

Royal sighed deeply, sounding relieved, as though he'd been wanting to say all of that for a long time. Joel's heart was now trying to burst out of his chest, *Alien* style. He took a slow, deep breath and put his hand on his pounding chest to try to calm it down.

'I didn't know,' Royal continued, 'what I was feeling, what I was feeling for *you*, until tonight. I really,

really, like you, Joel. Squirrels and odd outbursts and pizza sauce and all.'

A flush of warmth passed over Joel's whole body, like a wave of sunshine. Royal liked him, *really* liked him.

'You must think I'm the worst person,' Royal said then.

'Why?' Joel asked.

'For, like, talking about my feelings when Carter is … When he's probably …'

'You're not a bad person,' Joel said firmly. 'It's not bad to have feelings or to want to talk about them, no matter what else is going on.' Joel's therapist had said this to him many times, but he didn't tell Royal that. He didn't want to discuss all of that with Royal, not yet. 'Life keeps happening, and good things can happen even when bad things are happening as well.'

'I guess,' Royal said, not sounding convinced. Joel considered what to say next. He wanted to say the perfect, right thing, something that would reassure Royal and bring them together, not the kind of clumsy, awkward thing he normally said. After a long while he couldn't come up with anything, and the break in conversation was becoming tense for Joel, so he blurted out:

'So, you're bisexual? Are all the hot guys around here bisexual? T.J. is bi too.'

A heavy, uncomfortable silence descended on the room. Joel could have kicked himself. Why did he always say exactly the wrong thing?

'T.J.?' Royal finally said, sounding hurt. 'Do you like him?'

'Well, I, well …' Joel didn't want to lie and say he didn't like T.J., because he did, but as a friend. He couldn't get that out.

'Is that why you were with him the other day, when I saw you at Lana's place? Because you think he's hot?'

'Err, no, err, that's not …' Joel didn't want to lie and say he didn't think T.J. was hot, because he did, but purely objectively, the way he knew young Brad Pitt was hot, or young Elvis, or the way he knew Lana was very pretty, but he didn't have any feelings for Lana and didn't want to date her. Just like he didn't want to date T.J. or Brad Pitt or Elvis. He couldn't get that out either.

'It's okay, Joel. T.J.'s a good guy, and he rides a dirt bike and has that whole bad boy thing going on. I get why you like him. Lots of the girls in my class do as well.' He stood to leave. Joel sat up, gestured for him to stay.

'Wait, let me explain,' Joel said.

'You don't owe me an explanation,' Royal said. 'Who you like is your business.' He paused, clearly deciding if he should say something more. 'Look, Joel, I'm, like, just a few hours into being bi. I had no idea I was bi before I met you, to be honest, but, I'm not new to gay people, because of my dads. I know that young gay guys hook up a lot. I'm, ah, not into that. I'm not looking to just hook up. You can hook up with T.J. and whoever else you want, but I don't want to be just another hook up on your list.'

Joel was so outraged he jumped out of bed and paced straight over to Royal, fuming. Although Royal towered over him, the fierce look in Joel's eyes made Royal back up until he bumped into the chair by the window. With nowhere else to go, and Joel still advancing on him, Royal dropped down into the chair, so that Joel was now towering over him.

'What you just said was 100 kinds of homophobic! And don't tell me you can't be homophobic because you've got two dads and you're bi. Unless you're gay yourself you can still be homophobic.'

'Sorry,' Royal said immediately, clearly meaning it.

'You should be! I don't have some list of hot guys I'm working my way through. Have you actually met me? I've never even kissed a guy let alone hooked up with one. Even if I wasn't a totally awkward, un-kissed virgin, I would not be only after hook ups! I'd want a proper boyfriend!' About then Joel realized he'd just called himself a totally awkward, un-kissed virgin and shut his mouth.

'Sorry,' Royal repeated. 'I'm really sorry.'

'Apology accepted,' Joel said, 'and I'm sorry I got all up in your face.'

'Apology accepted,' Royal echoed. 'You know what, you're scary when you're riled.'

'Thank you,' Joel said.

'You're welcome. Just for the record, I meant what I said. T.J. is a good guy.'

'I wouldn't really know,' Joel said. 'I've only hung out with him once, that day we were at Lana's place.'

'So, you're not, like, dating him?'

'No. I don't like him like that.'

'So, you're *available*,' Royal said, smiling. He took Joel's hand and wove their fingers together. Joel let it happen, distracted by a jolt of tingling energy racing up his spine.

'I am,' Joel choked.

'And you've really never even kissed a guy before?'

'No, but neither have you, I'm guessing, so no need to be uppity about it.'

'That's true,' Royal said, chuckling. 'So, when it comes to guys, we're both un-kissed virgins.'

'Totally awkward, un-kissed virgins.'

'Shall we, err, do something about that? The un-kissed part I mean.'

Joel froze. Royal felt it immediately and gently unwrapped their fingers, once more giving Joel the physical space he needed.

'Sorry,' he said, again, those blue eyes full of concern for Joel.

While Joel stared down at Royal, frozen, the sun started to come up. Golden light streamed in the window, bathing Royal in a warm glow; revealing him in all his underwear model glory. Sitting there in nothing but his briefs, Royal was the embodiment of teen gayboy desire. The dawn light brought out the luster in his olive skin, and made the muscles of his chest, arms and abdomen appear even more defined than they were. Joel's throat went dry, yet again. He'd never been in the presence of someone so beautiful that the experience was overwhelming, literally breathtaking. For a second, Joel thought he might never take another breath, that he'd just asphyxiate from the sight of Royal's perfect Creole hotness. He forced himself to speak.

'I … I do want to kiss you,' he said, 'I really do. So, so much. I just, I just have some big hang-ups, really big hang-ups. I don't even know how to explain—'

'You don't have to explain. You don't owe me anything. I'm not, like, entitled to kiss you. No-one is entitled to kiss you. If you never want to kiss, that's fine.'

'I want to, though,' Joel said, 'I just can't right now.' He took a deep breath. 'This is all too much,' he said, making a gesture that encompassed Royal's face, bare chest and underwear. 'Really hot, but too much for me right now.'

'I'm not going anywhere, Joel. I really like you. Take all the time you need. If you want to, if you think it'd help, you could talk to me about it. I'm a good listener. My gay dad taught me well.'

Joel nodded, relieved Royal was being so thoughtful, but also disappointed. He really wanted his first kiss. He really wanted that kiss to be with Royal. Would he ever get over his hang-ups and be able to kiss him? Royal was unbelievably hot. If he couldn't kiss *him*, what hope was there that he'd ever be able to kiss anyone? Would he still be an awkward, un-kissed virgin when he was forty years old?

He was suddenly very angry at Patrick, and at what Patrick and those other boys had done to him. This was their fault. They'd made him this way. The anger swelled up and burned in his gut. It was the first time he'd been anything other than sad and depressed about what had happened. It was good to feel something different. It was like a fire had been lit in a dark cave. Maybe this was a step toward healing? He hoped so.

'I will talk to you about it,' Joel said. 'Soon, I promise.' He took Royal's hand again, wove their fingers together, squeezed. Royal squeezed back gently.

The sound of Aunt Penn stirring in her room immediately changed the mood. Royal and Joel mutually dropped each other's hands and jumped apart. Royal got up and dashed out of the room, only to come dashing back in mere seconds later.

'Just me again,' he whispered. 'Can I very gently give you one little kiss on the cheek? With no pressure for anything else to happen?'

Joel blinked, taken aback, then nodded, yes. Royal leaned in and very gently kissed him on the cheek, then took a slow step back, making sure not to make any sudden moves that might spook Joel, and quietly left the room again.

Joel lay back down on the bed, sort of stunned, sort of deliriously happy. Not much more than a minute later, Aunt Penn's bedroom door opened and the sound of her slipper-adorned feet padded down the hall to the bathroom. They'd been so close to getting caught – standing hand in hand in the dawn light. Joel smiled from ear to ear. Then he remembered Carter.

CRYPT DREAM

Mist slithered low across a field of crooked tombstones, coiling like smoke through the narrow alleys of an old cemetery. Joel stood beneath the rusted metal entrance gate. He tried to read the sign but the fog was just too thick. The only word he could make out was "cemetery". At first he thought he was in St Louis Cemetery Number 1, in New Orleans, but then saw in the distance the Acadiaville water tower. This cemetery, with so many above ground burial crypts, looked a lot like those in New Orleans, but much shabbier, as though no-one had cared for any of these graves for a hundred years. Joel walked down an avenue lined with gnarled live-oaks, so covered in Spanish moss that the boughs seemed weighed down by it, nearly touching the ground. Crumbling crypts rose on either side of Joel like forgotten sentinels, their surfaces cracked, the names of the dead half-eaten by time and lichen. Somewhere behind him, water quietly lapped at the earth. The swamp was close, close enough that the night air smelled of rot and rain.

The moon hung pale above, half-veiled by clouds, casting just enough light to reveal the outline of a tomb ahead, larger than the others, and older too. It was topped by a large iron cross, rusted and leaning. The name on the crypt was worn down to almost nothing, but Joel could still work it out – DAVIS. The crypt's iron door hung on rusted hinges, and stood wide open. Of course it did.

Inside, the air turned colder, denser. It pressed against Joel's skin like swamp water. The tile floor was damp, the scent of mildew and old candles clung to the brick walls. There were no windows, no light, but at the back of the tomb stood a marble angel wielding a sword, its stone so white it almost glowed in the dark. On the floor in front of the angel lay a single coffin. It struck Joel as very strange. It wasn't made of wood, but of sheets of metal riveted together. Battered, heavy, clamped tight with rusted chains as thick as a man's wrist, and bolted down at the edges, it looked like it contained something too dangerous to bury.

A sound, faint at first, echoed through the crypt. A dull thud. Then another. Joel's breath caught. Then: *Boom.* It sounded like a fist striking the inside of the coffin lid. *Boom.* More urgent now. *Boom-boom-boom.* The chains rattled, trembled. Dust rose from the floor.

Joel stepped back, but his feet felt rooted to the damp floor. His heart beat louder than the pounding. He stared at the coffin and a thought came unbidden to his mind, which he spoke aloud:

'Carter? Carter, is that you?'

Another thump and boom. Then silence. Then the lid exploded open. Shrapnel from the rusted chains flew everywhere. Something surged upward out of the coffin, shadowy and very fast, a blur of movement accompanied by a strange rasping sound. Joel woke, heart racing, the sheets tangled around him like chains, the echo of that last thunderous boom still ringing in his ears.

BAD DREAMS COMING TRUE

Joel dressed for school with trembling fingers. It seemed as if overnight he had stepped into a whole new life. Some wonderful things had happened. He'd learnt that Royal was bisexual. Royal had confessed to Joel that he liked him, and they had held hands. Some really awful things had happened too. Carter had been abducted in the night. It had become clear that Joel's creepy dreams were not just ordinary dreams, they were strange visions of the future. To make matters worse, in the short time he'd slept after Royal had left his bedroom, maybe just half an hour, he'd had another dream. Thankfully, there hadn't been any zombies in this dream; but there had been a creepy cemetery, a chained-up iron coffin, and something escaping those chains. So, yeah, no zombies but still not great. He was just grateful he hadn't been sleepwalking again.

When Joel entered the kitchen he found Starr, Penn and Royal already seated at the table. Penn and Starr were dressed for school. Penn neat, tidy and professional as usual. Starr in her school uniform. Starr's eyes were worried and her face drawn. Clearly, Penn had filled her in about Carter's kidnapping. Sitting next to her, Royal looked equally glum, though he smiled warmly when Joel sat on the other side of him.

Joel did a double take at what Royal was wearing. He still had on his red board shorts, but was also wearing one of Aunt Penn's sleep shirts – the white one with a picture of a feisty kitten on the front with a caption that read "You Gotta Be Kitten Me!" On Penn it was almost like a nightgown, baggy and nunnish. On Royal it was snug and weirdly sexy. Before Joel could comment on it, Penn put a bowl in front of him and filled it with cereal.

'Eat up, Joel, we're in a hurry. We have to get Royal to school so he has enough time to change into his uniform before his first class.'

'Oh, I think he looks fine as he is,' Joel said, smirking.

'Luckily you're not in charge of Royal's wardrobe,' Penn snapped, with more irritation in her voice than Joel had ever heard from her before. 'Royal cannot be seen dressed like that on a day like this. Carter's parents will be at the school! What kind of message do you think that kitty t-shirt would send to them?'

'Sorry, I didn't think,' Joel said quickly, feeling truly bad.

Penn paused, took a breath. 'No, I'm sorry, Joel. I shouldn't have snapped. I'm just sick with worry about Carter.'

The rest of breakfast was a sad and rushed affair. Once they were done, Penn ushered them out to the car. Joel and Royal sat in the back, Starr in the front. As they were pulling out of the drive the sheriff turned up. Penn got out of the car to speak to him. He'd come to update Penn on the overnight search. They hadn't found anything. Just like the other disappearances. There some evidence that Carter had been dragged away, footprints, broken branches, that kind of thing, but no body, and nothing to suggest that Carter was still alive either.

Royal slid his hand toward Joel and Joel took it and held it tight. Royal leant toward him and whispered:

'Last night, err … there was something about last night that I didn't tell the sheriff.'

'What?' Joel whispered back.

Joel could tell that Starr was listening even before she glanced back at him in the rear view mirror.

'Everyone will think I'm crazy,' Royal said.

'I won't,' Joel said. 'I promise you I won't.'

Royal paused, swallowed hard, then continued.

'There was a smell, like old road kill, like something dead, and the … the one who took Carter … I couldn't really see, the mist off the swamp was super thick, but I … I think it was a girl.'

Joel's stomach tightened.

'A girl?'

'Yeah, I know that sounds crazy, Carter was strong, and solid, but this, this girl, she just dragged him off like he weighed nothing.'

Starr was still watching them in the mirror, her lips had paled. Joel's dreams of dead girls were flashing through his mind. He didn't want to say anything. He didn't want to seem crazy either, but he had to speak up. If the dreams were true, then maybe they could help to find Carter.

'What did she look like, the girl?' he asked.

Royal paused, glanced toward the sheriff and Penn to make sure they couldn't hear.

'Like a cheerleader from years ago,' he said, 'like from the nineteen-fifties or something. I know that sounds crazy. I feel crazy just saying it.'

'You're not crazy,' Joel said, his voice trembling. 'Unless I'm crazy too.'

'What do you mean?' Starr asked from the front seat, her voice thin.

'I've dreamt about that cheerleader,' Joel said, barely able to sound out the words. 'I've dreamt about her more than once. But in my dreams, there's more than one girl, and they're all zombies.'

*** ***

'Zombie cheerleaders?' Tashi said, looking from Joel to Starr and back again, her eyes wide and her face pale. They were at their spot, under the live-oak in the quad. It was just Tashi, Starr and Joel. Penn had taken Royal to his dorm room. He'd promised Joel he'd meet them in the quad once he was suitably dressed in his school uniform.

'You're telling me zombie cheerleaders are behind all these disappearances? You're telling me that zombie cheerleaders took Carter?' Tashi's voice broke on Carter's name. She'd been on the edge of tears ever since Starr had broken the news about what had happened overnight. Tashi's massive crush on Carter had turned instantly into an equally massive grief and worry.

'Well,' Starr said, glancing quickly at Joel, 'not exactly. We're just saying that Joel has had a number of dreams that seem to have come true, and that seem to resemble what Royal saw when Carter was taken, but Royal admits he couldn't see much last night, there was no moon and it was really foggy, so—'

'So what?' Tashi demanded.

Both Joel and Starr shrugged. They didn't know what to say. It was all so unbelievable and nuts.

Tashi lowered her voice and glanced around to make sure no-one else was listening. 'Let's look at this logically,' she began. 'We have three options. Option one: Joel and Royal are both delusional lunatics and hallucinated the whole thing. Option two: Joel and Royal are both fabricating this story about zombie cheerleaders for some completely incomprehensible reason. Option three: Joel's dreams are real and Carter actually witnessed a zombie cheerleader taking Carter.' Her voice broke on Carter's name again. She turned to Starr. 'Which option do you feel is true, deep in your gut?'

Starr blinked and thought a moment. 'I don't think Joel and Royal are crazy. And I don't think they are making this up.'

'I totally agree,' Tashi said. 'Option three it is then – there are actually zombie cheerleaders snatching people in Acadiaville.'

Starr blinked again. Her eyes were glassy with surprise and her lips paled almost to white, something of a feat given she was wearing pink lip gloss.

'I don't know why I'm so shocked,' Starr said. 'I've lived in the backwoods of Louisiana my whole life. Everyone around here believes in supernatural creatures, zombies, werewolves, vampires, ghosts, the whole lot. My gran is a very modern woman, but even she paints the doors and windowsills "haint blue", to stop ghosts and evil spirits getting into the house.'

'I'm Tibetan,' Tashi said, 'and we believe in *everything*.'

'What do you mean, everything?' Joel asked.

'I mean, *everything* – zombies, vampires, ghosts, mountain gods, nature spirits, demons, magic. We Tibetans believe in *all* of that. We just have different names for them.'

'So, I'm the only one who can't believe this is real?' Joel thought his brain might actually explode. There was a tight pressure building in his skull. 'I have a brain pain,' he said.

'Are you going to faint?' Starr asked. Joel shook his head, no. It wasn't the same feeling he got when he was about to faint. Starr and Tashi watched him sympathetically for a minute, then pulled him into a hug. When they broke apart Royal was crossing the quad toward them, perfectly and handsomely attired in his school uniform. Tashi spotted him coming and looked quizzically at Joel.

'Oh,' Joel said, 'I forgot to tell you! The other thing that happened last night was that Royal told me that he *likes* me and we held hands, like very romantically held hands.'

'I knew it!' Starr said triumphantly.

'You *romantically* held hands?' Tashi asked, eyebrows raised.

'Yes, we held hands more romantically than anyone has ever held hands before, in the entire history of hand-holding, but shush, he's coming.'

When Royal reached them he shyly said hi to Starr and Tashi, and sidled up beside Joel, standing quite close and smiling down at him like a cat at his freshly caught mouse dinner. Joel blushed. Starr and Tashi rolled their eyes, amused.

'You okay, Joel?' Royal asked. 'You're a bit red.'

'Just hot,' Joel muttered.

'Someone certainly thinks so,' Starr said, smirking.

Then it was Royal's turn to blush. And he did seriously blush, but he also smiled; a big, unashamed smile. He stepped even closer to Joel and took his hand. Starr's comment seemed to have emboldened him. Joel felt that he could stay there in the shade of the live-oak holding Royal's hand forever, but he knew he had to spoil the vibe by coming clean about his most recent dream. The crypt dream with the chained-up coffin, that was possibly where Carter was being held hostage. By zombies. For lord knows what mad reason.

What. Had. His. Life. Become.

'So, guys,' he began, 'I had another weird dream last night, well, actually, this morning.' They all looked at him apprehensively. 'It was about a cemetery, and a crypt, and a coffin chained shut, and someone in the coffin, who maybe was Carter. I don't know which cemetery it was, but it had lots of above-ground crypts, and was somewhere here in Acadiaville.' He waited for them all to call him crazy. He looked up at Royal, expecting to see a look of disbelief or even disgust. What must Royal think of him now? A fainty boy who has creepy supernatural dreams that apparently come true. But Royal wasn't looking back with disbelief or anything negative. He looked positively impressed, and was smiling at Joel with what seemed like pride.

'So, you're like a dream oracle, a seer?' he said warmly.

'A what?'

'A seer, someone who sees future events, through visions or dreams.'

'No, I … I don't know. Wait, you believe in all this stuff?"

'I'm Creole, Joel, of course I do. Also, my dad, the gay one not the bisexual one, he's a professor of folklore and he totally believes in this stuff. He was reading me bedtime stories about *loup garou*, that's Creole French for werewolves, since I was two. It's just stuff everyone here believes.'

'Where have I ended up?' Joel muttered to himself.

'In the Land of Voodoo, Joel,' Royal said. 'Voodoo and werewolves and vampires and—'

'Zombies,' Joel said faintly.

'Yeah,' Royal said, his tone solemn. 'Voodoo and zombies go hand in hand.' Carter's name hung in the air between them all but none of them spoke it.

'So,' Tashi said, bringing their minds back onto the task at hand, 'we have to find out which cemetery Joel saw. And then we have to find Carter.'

'No, we don't,' Starr said. 'We have to tell the sheriff. It's his job to find Carter. He's trained for this sort of thing.'

'The Acadiaville sheriff is trained to deal with zombie kidnappings?' Joel asked, doubtfully.

'Better trained than we are! We don't have any training that would be useful in this situation. I'm a teen costume designer for goodness sakes! What do I know about zombies?'

'I'm a culinary arts major,' Tashi said, admitting she didn't have the necessary zombie training either.

'The sheriff won't go searching cemeteries based on Joel's dream,' Royal said. They all looked up at him. 'On the way to my dorm I told Principal Stacey about what I saw last night. After telling Joel about it I felt like I could tell her. I don't think she believed me but she called the sheriff and told him anyway.'

'What did the sheriff say?' Joel asked.

'He told Principal Stacey to stop wasting his time, and if I said any more nonsense he'd have me drug tested.'

They all stared, three sets of mouths agog.

'He threatened to have you drug tested for telling the truth? ' Starr asked, her voice full of alarm.

'Yep. So, if we tell him about Joel's dreams he'll probably drag us all off to be tested, and when the tests come back clear of drugs he'll decide we're crazy and have us all committed.'

'So we can't tell the sheriff,' Joel said. Of all of them he was the one most likely to get locked up as a crazy person. He was the one who was having the weird sleepwalking dreams. He was the one who fainted all over the place. He was the one who couldn't interact in public without waving his hands around and shouting about squirrels.

'Okay, so it's up to us,' Tashi said. 'We have to find the right cemetery. We find the right cemetery, we find Carter.' A full minute passed before they all nodded agreement, Starr being the last. Royal squeezed Joel's hand as if to say "It's okay, I'll protect you". Then he dropped Joel's hand like it was a cold, slimy fish.

Lana Beaux and a few other senior girls walked over, all teary-eyed. Joel's face flushed and burned. Okay, so Royal didn't want Lana to see him holding Joel's hand. Lana's arrival silenced their discussion of finding and saving Carter. And set Joel's teeth on edge.

'Royal, there you are,' Lana said. 'I've been looking for you everywhere. Isn't it awful about Carter?'

Royal muttered a yes, looking and sounding uncomfortable. Lana stepped between Royal and Joel and took Royal's arm. 'We're going to the chapel to pray for Carter before first class. Surely you want to come?' Royal's shoulders slumped a little. After a beat he said, 'Sure, baby, let's go,' then he froze. He looked anxiously at Joel, clearly alarmed at having been caught calling Lana "baby". Lana noticed the look pass between them. Royal went to say something but Joel stormed off towards his first class, refusing to look back as Lana steered Royal away.

Joel felt gutted and ashamed. He'd believed Royal really liked him, but everything he said must have been a lie, especially the bit about breaking up with Lana for good. How could Joel have let himself fall for another guy who didn't truly like him? What was wrong with him? Just before he walked into the Creative Writing studio he remembered that Lana would be in this class with him. He couldn't face her. He turned around and didn't stop walking until he found himself by the bridge, the bridge over Little Bayou River where Carter was taken. He stopped in his tracks. Another wave of shame rolled over him. Here he was storming off in a huff because a boy didn't like him when Carter had been snatched by zombies and was, if the dream was true, trapped in a metal coffin.

What. Is. Wrong. With. You.

He slumped down on the grass at the bayou's edge and took a few calming breaths. A bird far off in the swamp started singing that strange joyful song. The shame he was feeling ebbed away, to be replaced with hope. Carter might not be dead. They might find him. They might be able to free him. It might all be okay. He took a few more breaths. So what if stupidly hot Royal Dumaine had lied to him? It wasn't the end of the world. Then his phone beeped. A text from T.J.

Hey cutie Care Bear boy, you want to go fer a ride in my boat after school today? Got my fingers and toes crossed. Very uncomfortable. Please say yes quickly so I can let my toesies loose.

It felt like a sign. Joel thumped out a speedy reply: *Yes please! But can we go RIGHT NOW?*

Sure thing. I approve of playing hooky! Meet me in 30 at the jetty behind the academy chapel. My fingers and toes thank you for the fast reply! Can't wait to see you!

*** ***

It was an unusually warm day for the time of year. Warm days were common in Louisiana right up until December. Joel perspired a little as he made his way to the chapel, weaving in-between and behind buildings so that no-one spotted him.

The jetty was a rickety thing jutting out into the swampy water in the middle of a grove of live-oaks and swamp Cyprus trees just beyond the chapel. The jetty didn't look like it got much use. Joel hid behind one of the oaks while he waited for T.J. The last thing he needed was to be spotted by people leaving the chapel on their way to class. As he hid there he felt quite naughty and rebellious. Though not rebellious enough that he wanted Aunt Penn ever to find out about him ditching school. Naughty and rebellious, yes. Have a death wish, no.

Twenty minutes later the sound of a motor boat drew Joel out from behind the tree. He was at the end of the jetty when T.J. came into view, in a boat that had seen much better days. T.J. pulled up to the jetty, tied the boat off., and helped Joel "come aboard". Joel wasn't sure if "come aboard" was the right phrase for getting into such a shabby looking boat. He wasn't a boat person at all.

'You look good enough to eat,' T.J. said in that thick Cajun accent once Joel had taken a seat. He looked Joel up and down in his school uniform. Joel blushed from head to toes. For the second time that morning. 'But ain't you just a bit warm?' he asked.

Joel admitted he was pretty warm so rolled up his sleeves and took off his tie. T.J. was wearing a white t-shirt and blue jeans. In the spirit of joining in as Joel loosened his tie, T.J. promptly took his t-shirt off and tucked it into the waist band of his jeans. Joel didn't know what to do with his eyes. T.J. noticed him averting his eyes, but also kind of peeking, and smiled ear to ear. He knew he was hot. Goddammit, Joel thought. Goddamn hot boys and their goddamn irresistible pectorals and abs and their irritating, but also equally hot, self-confidence!

T.J. steered them away from the jetty and then turned up the throttle, heading the boat into deeper waters. Joel smiled with delight, the wind was so cool and the air so fresh. He looked back at the chapel as they turned into one of the many waterways that crisscrossed the bayou and his smile died instantly.

His heart sank into his stomach, which was becoming a very familiar feeling. On the shore by the chapel stood an instantly recognizable figure – Royal Dumaine. He was looking right at them, watching as the boat disappeared around the bend.

ZOMBIE CHEERLEADERS AND OTHER TRUE THINGS

Part of Joel went straight to worrying about Royal's feelings. Another, more spiteful part enjoyed that Royal had seen him with T.J. That would teach Royal not to lie, and not to mess with Joel's feelings. Another part, the largest part, just felt overwhelmed. How was he supposed to deal with crushes on teenage boys and zombie cheerleaders all at once? The way he felt right now he would much rather be facing zombies than dealing with his feelings for Royal. He thought back over the previous night, looking for evidence of Royal's dishonesty, for signs that everything he said was false. Then he realized that T.J. was speaking to him.

Oh, right, he was on a date. With T.J., not with Royal. He focused on T.J., forcing his eyes to stay on the handsome Cajun boy's face, and not drop down to his bare chest, and caught the tail end of a question.

'—you move to Louisiana?'

Joel guessed he was being asked why he left Australia. As he answered he really hoped he was giving the right response.

'I needed a new start,' he said. 'Some bad stuff happened at my old school. I couldn't stay there. So I came half way across the world. As you do.'

'As you do. And I'm glad you did,' T.J. said with a wink. Just then they passed under a tall, iron bridge and out of the waterway they'd been in onto an open stretch of water. T.J. cut the engine, letting them drift. Joel gasped. In the middle of the bayou was an island with a cemetery, and behind the cemetery, a half-sunk church.

'Where are we?' Joel asked, though he thought he knew.

'The old Wytchwood cemetery and church,' T.J. said. 'Your school is built where the Wytchwood plantation was. This was their local church and graveyard. 'It ain't been used since the 1950s.'

'So there are two cemeteries around here?' Joel was wondering where the one with the tomb and the metal coffin was, the one he'd seen in his dream.

'Nope, five. There's this old one, Wytchwood, then there's Acadiaville Cemetery in town, Saint Augustine's Catholic Cemetery right next door to that, the Jewish cemetery on the other side of town, and then there's the Acadiaville colored cemetery out in the backwoods.' T.J. looked a bit uncomfortable. 'Segregation may be gone but people still like to get buried with their own folks.' He looked at Joel apologetically. 'Welcome to the South.'

'Do you know if there's a crypt at any of these cemeteries with the name Davis on it?'

'Yeah, there's probably more than one, that's a common name around here. There's definitely one in the colored cemetery. All Starr's relatives are buried there.'

'Starr Davis? My Starr?' Joel hadn't connected the name on the crypt with Starr, though he knew her surname was Davis. He felt foolish about that.

'There's only one Starr Davis,' T.J. said. 'And a damn shame too. Could use a few more of her around here.'

Joel was pleased T.J. was saying nice things about his friend, but the existence of multiple Davis crypts complicated matters. How would he know which cemetery he'd dreamed about? Without knowing that, Joel had no idea where to start their search for Carter.

'Why you asking about Davis tombs?' T.J. asked.

'Err, no reason, just curious.'

T.J. accepted that and came over to sit next to Joel. It was a small bench so their legs touched. T.J. was very warm. Joel liked the sense of heat. T.J. leant back and stretched out, putting one arm over Joel's shoulder. Joel froze. He didn't feel as freaked out as he did when he was close to Royal, but he had no idea what was about to happen, or if he was expected to do anything. This was his very first date. What did one do on a date in a boat floating on a bayou by a disused cemetery? Talk about movies? Recite poetry?

'So, Joel,' T.J. said, 'you're gay, right?'

'Err, yes.'

'Totally gay?'

'Totally. Absolutely.'

'Have you been with many guys?'

'Been with?'

'Yeah, how many dudes have you dated?'

'Dated?' Joel didn't think holding Royal's hand counted as dating.

'I feel like you don't want to answer. That either means you've dated *a lot* of guys or—'

'None.' Joel's temper was rising. What was it with these hot Louisiana boys implying that he was dating a trillion guys at once? How. Rude. Seriously.

'None? You've never—'

'Never.'

T.J. removed his arm from over Joel's shoulder.

'That's surprised me, Joel,' he said.

'Why?'

'You look—'

'What? I look like I've been with a million guys?' Joel thought steam may have actually been coming out of his ears.

'Don't get your boxers in a bunch. I was gonna say, with the way you look, so damn cute an' all, you must've had a lot of dudes ask you out.'

Joel blushed. Third time in a single morning. His ears burned.

'Err, no, actually.'

'Australian dudes must be dumb or blind, or something.' He sounded genuinely shocked.

'Or something,' Joel squeaked.

A long silence followed. Joel couldn't tell if it was a comfortable silence, if T.J. was just happy to drift there in the sun, or if it was an uncomfortable silence. It was certainly uncomfortable for Joel. He didn't know if he should fill the silence or just wait for T.J. to start speaking again. He still hadn't decided when T.J. put his arm back over Joel's shoulder.

'Do you scare easy, Joel?'

''Yes, I do,' Joel said, without hesitation and in full honesty.

'Are you the type that likes to snuggle when you're scared?'

'Well, if I don't faint, sure, but to tell the truth I've never had anyone who wanted to snuggle with me, scared or not.'

'That's not true anymore.'

Joel swallowed hard. What. Was. Happening? Was he being wooed? Was some old-fashioned wooing about to happen?

'I heard you faint sometimes,' T.J. said, 'that must suck.'

Joel nodded, too tense to do or say anything else.

'I'm gonna tell you a true, scary story, Joel, but if you feel dizzy or like you'll faint you tell me and I'll stop.'

Joel nodded.

'This here part of the bayou, this is called Lake Saint Adjutor. Everyone 'round here says this lake is haunted. Not by one ghost, but by dozens. A whole team of cheerleaders met their deaths here, back in the 1956, on April 30. That'just happens to be Saint Adjutor's feast day.'

Joel's heart pounded. His throat went dry, so dry he couldn't speak. T.J. continued:

'The cheerleaders were on a bus that careened off that bridge there and sank. They all drowned and were buried in that cemetery there, Wytchwood. The weird coincidence of it all is Saint Adjutor is the patron saint of drowning victims. Those cheerleaders, they all drowned on his saint's day. Now, the real scary thing is that on dark, moonless nights those cheerleaders crawl out of their graves as zombies, or so the folks around here say. The real spooky part of the story is that they've been turned to zombies by an evil priest named Père Cassamir. He's like a really evil necromancer, twisted by dark magic. It's said he lives in that cemetery there. Père Cassamir commands them zombies to hunt the swamp for innocent souls. Each poor soul they take, eventually joins them zombies in those broken down tombs, and becomes another slave of Père Cassamir.'

Joel had seen a priest in his dreams, a cassock-wearing, red-eyed priest. Had Carter been taken by these zombies under the command of some monster priest?

'Is this actually true?' Joel asked, sounding more terrified than he should be from merely hearing a spooky story.

T.J sat forward and looked straight in Joel's eyes with a worried recognition.

'Some say it is true,' he said. 'What have you *seen*, Joel?'

'Not seen. Dreamed.'

'I knew you were different,' he said. 'The minute I saw you, I knew. I'm different too. We're like two peas in a pod.'

'Do you have dreams that come true as well?'

'No, but I can cast spells, to charge up protective amulets and stuff, spells to heal people, stuff like that. My mom can too, and she really can tell the future with those tarot cards of hers.'

Joel's mind spun. He had that throbbing pain under his skull again. And for some reason Joel completely believed T.J. This was all true!

'Are you, like, a wizard?'

T.J. laughed that warm, very sexy laugh of his.

'Nope, I ain't a wizard, but I do practice voodoo.'

'Voodoo.'

'Yep. Voodoo is just a way of workin' with magic. I'm good at it too, not to brag. Well, I suppose that was a brag, but it were only a little one.'

'Are vampires and ghosts and all that stuff real then?'

'Some say so, so maybe, yeah.'

Joel thought a moment. If anyone would believe him about the zombies taking Carter, and possibly know what to do, it was T.J.

'I'm sorry,' Joel began, 'but I have to ruin our date.'

'You *have* to ruin it?'

'Yes. I have to tell you something, because I really need your help.'

And so Joel told T.J. everything. He described every dream he'd had, and how some things in the dreams had come true. Finally, he told him about Carter, about the dream he'd had before Carter went missing and the one with the metal coffin. Then he told him what Royal had seen, and smelt, when Carter was taken. After Joel was finished, T.J. just sat there silent for a while. Finally, he put his t-shirt back on, signaling the date was over, and said:

'I got to take you to talk to my mamma.'

***   ***

T.J.'s house was deep in the swamp. It sat on stilts overhanging the water. Made of timber boards, greyed and crazed over decades, it was adorned with nearly as much Spanish moss as the trees around it, like a Southern Gothic treehouse. T.J's dirt bike and an old, but recently painted bright pink, four-door pickup were parked in the yard; where at least a dozen chickens scratched about under the watchful eye of a very fat ginger tomcat. It was like something out of a movie. It appealed to Joel's graphic-novel-influenced sensibilities.

Joel climbed out of the boat and stood at the edge of the bayou, where the reeds swayed and the water reflected the washed-out sky like a tarnished mirror. A half-sunken houseboat listed crookedly against the opposite bank about a hundred yards or so downstream from T.J.'s house. Its paint had long since peeled away, its broken windows were smeared with algae and grime, and its timbers were being slowly pulled apart by honeysuckle vines. Joel had seen its like before, another wreck rotting in the shallows, but this one was different. A figure stood on the deck. An old man, hunched and still, one hand resting on the cracked railing. He wore a wide-brimmed hat, his eyes shadowed beneath the brim. Joel froze, the hum of cicadas falling away into silence.

The man wasn't moving. Didn't blink. Didn't even seem to breathe. Even so, Joel could feel his presence as surely as the sun on his back. A strange cold crept into his bones. Joel took a cautious step forward, squinting to see more clearly. The man's outline shimmered, faintly translucent against the greying wood. Through his form, Joel could just make out the wheelhouse door, cracked and hanging by one hinge. A heartbeat passed, then another; and then the old boatman slowly turned his head. A slow and deliberate move that brought him around to face Joel directly. Their eyes met across the water. Yet again, a feeling of sorrow passed over Joel, and then the old man just faded away. Just like the black man in the swamp, and the boy by the bridge, the old boatman just dissolved, like a lump of sugar dropped into warm water. That was the only way Joel could describe it each time it happened. Only the leaning houseboat remained, creaking softly in the breeze and refusing to sink. After his recent chat with T.J. about zombies and the like being real, Joel had to admit that the boatman was a real live ghost, or rather a real dead ghost. The same must be true for the black man in the swamp, the boy by the bridge, and the bespectacled teacher on the porch of Rosedawn house. Joel wondered what was happening when they locked eyes, when the ghosts seemed to just disappear. He hoped he wasn't hurting or killing them. Not that you could really kill a ghost, they were already dead by definition. He hoped he was helping them somehow, and that's what his gut told him. That something about Joel was helping them to "move on". Whatever that meant.

T.J. clapped Joel on the shoulder, making him jump like a Meer cat startled by a leopard.

'Come on', he said and led Joel onto the porch. He paused at the front door. 'It's not much,' he said shyly, 'but it's good enough for my mom an' me. We don't need nothin' fancy.'

'It's really cool,' Joel said, very distracted by what had just happened, but completely sincerely. T.J. beamed.

'I told ya,' he said, 'we're like two peas in a pod.'

The inside of the house couldn't have been more different from the outside. Joel recognized T.J.'s mother's hand in the decorations. The place resembled the fortune-teller's parlor behind the carwash. Rose-Marie's preference for orange, purple and pink was evident here too. There were lots of glass bead curtains, candles, throw rugs, and velvet cushions. It looked like a rainbow had exploded in the house and left its multi-colored remains everywhere. The place smelt familiar too, the same warm, sandalwood scent of the tarot-reading room.

'Mama,' T.J. called. 'We got a visitor.'

Rose-Marie came out of the kitchen with a tray of cookies.

'I had a feeling I'd be seeing you today, Joel.' She turned to T.J. and asked him to get iced-tea from the refrigerator. T.J. disappeared into the kitchen and Rose-Marie ushered Joel onto the pink velvet sofa. She gestured for him to open his hands for a cookie and then tipped the tray over so that warm cookies piled up until he couldn't hold anymore. Joel suddenly loved Rose-Marie Thibodaux very much.

When T.J. came back with the iced-tea, he sat next to Joel and poured them all a glass. The glasses were Disney themed, each featuring a classic animated character – Maleficent, Sleeping Beauty, and Aladdin. T.J. gave Joel the Sleeping Beauty one and kept Aladdin for himself. His mother got Maleficent. Joel suspected there was a message here but couldn't work it out. His brain was still pounding.

'Mamma,' T.J. said, 'Joel needs some help. He's been having dreams.'

Rose-Marie nodded knowingly.

'Dreams that come true?' she asked.

In-between nibbling on warm chocolate chip cookies, Joel told Rose-Marie what he'd told T.J. The dreams he'd been having, the zombies, Carter's disappearance. He also told her about the ghosts, which made her and T.J. blink in unison. Apparently seeing ghosts and helping them "move on" by dissolving them with your eyes was not a common skill.

Rose-Marie's reaction to Joel's story was very similar to T.J.'s. She sat quietly for a long moment, determinedly eating a cookie. When she finished she took a sip of iced-tea, then collected the few cookie crumbs that had fallen into her lap and deposited them on the tray. Joel was practically bursting out of his skin.

'Joel,' she said at last. 'You have a very special gift. *Un visionnaire* – you are a visionary, a true clairvoyant. A gift like that is one in a million. You can do a great deal of good with such a gift.' She smiled warmly at him, but Joel noticed her hands were shaking a little.

'So, can you help me? Can you help us find Carter?' Joel felt hope for the first time since Carter went missing.

'No.'

'Mamma! Why not?' T.J. frowned at his mother, confused.

'Because you are children. There are things in this world, monstrous things, that no child should ever have to face. Children should not, *can* not, deal with such things.'

'But, the sheriff doesn't believe us,' Joel said desperately. 'They have no idea where Carter is, or what is really behind these disappearances.'

'Listen to me, both of you,' she said. 'You are to stay out of this. It would take very powerful Voodoo to fight a whole pack of zombies, a power I don't have, and you don't have. No-one has that kind of power, no human anyway.'

'But Carter—'

Rose-Marie cut Joel off:

'Is already dead. Your own dream told you that, Joel.'

'But, no—'

'The motorcycle dream. In the motorcycle dream you saw Carter dead. I'm sorry, Joel, but you are hell-bent on saving someone who is already dead.' Her eyes were glassy, she was truly sorry. But that didn't matter to Joel.

'So, what, we just let the zombies keep taking people?'

'You leave it to the police. You put it out of your mind. You are sixteen years old. Your biggest concern should be high school and homework.'

'But—'

'No! This is beyond you, Joel. This is beyond all of us. Leave it be. That is what we do. We cast protective spells to keep our homes safe at night. We stay off the bayou after dark. We lay low, we don't poke our noses into places where they might get cut off. That is what we do, because it is all we can do, and it's what we've *always* done.'

'Has this happened before? Have people been taken before?' Joel's head was now properly pounding.

'I'm sorry to be rude, Joel, puddin', but this conversation is over. T.J., take Joel home, and then come straight back.' She got up and walked out, mask-faced, but still shaking a little.

*** ***

They sped along the live-oak lined road on T.J.'s red dirt bike, swamp on both sides of them. Joel was seated behind T.J., his arms wrapped tightly around the other boy's waist. Once again, T.J. had smirked and said "safety first" when Joel had hopped on the bike. Once again, he had taken hold of Joel's hands and drawn them closer together, until Joel's chest was pressed hard against T.J.s muscled back. The contact comforted Joel somehow. And he needed comfort right now.

Neither of them had said much after Rose-Marie had refused to help them. T.J. was more surprised by his mother's refusal than Joel, because he had never seen her so spooked before, which he'd mentioned twice as they were leaving, as though trying to digest what that meant. When they got to the bridge over to the academy, T.J. pulled over and turned off the engine. He took off his helmet so that he could speak to Joel.

'You still got that gris-gris bag I left at your place?'

'Yes.'

'Good. It's a protective amulet. It has to be inside the house to work. You can hang it on the front door.'

'Yeah, Starr did that already.'

'Great. Something you need to know with zombies running around at night – they can't cross over moving water. In the still, shallow parts of the bayou, they can move around, but they can't cross this bridge, because the water under this bridge is moving. It's moving so slow you cain't really see it, but Little Bayou River is definitely moving. The academy is on an island, surrounded by moving water on all sides. No zombies can get on campus.'

'Okay, so …'

'Don't leave campus at night. Promise me you won't.'

'Okay.'

'No, Joel, make me a proper promise.'

'I promise I won't leave Acadia Academy campus at night.' He was finding it hard to concentrate because his brain was doing the tango in his skull.

'Okay, let's get you home. You look a bit pale.'

'Pale and fainty is my natural complexion,' Joel said, not really joking.

Joel hung on extra tight for the remainder of the trip, not so much for the comfort of T.J's presence anymore but for fear of falling off the back of the bike. His head was really hurting now. When they pulled into the yard of Oakshade Cottage, Joel wished they'd stayed in the swamp with the zombies. Aunt Penn, flanked on either side by Starr and Tashi, was waiting for him on the porch. All three of them had their arms crossed over their chests, like three furious kindergarten teachers. They glared down at him; their faces showing a mixture of relief at seeing him alive and fury that he hadn't in fact been abducted but had snuck off to spend the day with T.J.

Joel fought the wave of guilt that hit him and dismounted the bike more awkwardly than usual and called to them.

'It's okay, I'm alright.' He turned to T.J., head pounding. 'Thanks for the ride, T.J., you'd better go.'

'Yeah, I'm readin' the room. I'm gonna take off.' he said. He dropped his voice and whispered. 'I don't think it's wise for me to give you an end of date kiss right now. I'll have to owe you one.' He winked, revved the accelerator of his bike and took off, just as Aunt Penn, Starr and Tashi descended the steps and advanced on him.

'Joel River,' Penn said in a hiss. 'I thought you'd been taken! What were you thinking!'

'I'm sorry. I just got overwhelmed and couldn't face classes.' He didn't say he couldn't face Lana Beaux. He thought that would sound pathetic and trivial. His head throbbed worse than it had been. His vision blurred. He staggered, reached out to Penn but couldn't see her anymore.

'Joel!' Aunt Penn's alarmed voice.

His head throbbed again. Suddenly, his mind was filled with a vision of somewhere else. All around him was a soft golden glow. It wasn't sunlight. It was flickering lamplight and candlelight. He was still in the yard at Oaksahde, but he could see, as if it was an image superimposed over his sight, an old shack on a bit of high ground in the middle of a swamp. All kinds of strange things hung in the trees around the shack: bones and feathers, shells and river stones, dozens of blue bottles and jars, flickering lamps and candles.

'Joel, can you walk?' Aunt Penn asked in an alarmed voice. He could see her there, and hear her, but through her was the shack and the swamp. The door to the shack slowly opened. An elderly African-American woman came outside. Her hair was coiled into thick, glistening dreadlocks like snakes. Each dreadlock was bound with red and gold thread. She wore a robe that shimmered like oil on water. Her vibrant eyes—not brown or black as you'd expect, but luminous blue—were fixed on Joel. He recognized her. It was the woman who'd appeared in the yard on Halloween, with all the birds.

'Welcome, bébé,' she said, as if he she knew him. '*Un visionnaire*, child of power!' Her voice was honey wrapped in thunder, smooth and ancient. Joel was so surprised by the sound of her voice that he lurched backwards, and then it was all gone and he was just looking at Aunt Penn, who was helping to steady him on his wobbly legs.

What. Was. That. A hallucination? A vision? What was happening to him?

THE WINTER

THE MEANING OF BIRD SONG

The weeks blurred by like a movie montage: misty mornings giving way to grey afternoons, autumn leaves dissolving into bare branches, Halloween decorations sagging in the rain and disappearing one by one. The nights turned cold and the mornings colder. As the weeks rolled by, Joel kept trudging to Starr's kendo practice and Tashi's archery training, shivering in his jacket while they moved with the effortless sharpness of winter wind—sleek, precise, and deadly—while he felt more like a half-frozen sloth clinging to a branch over a raging river, just trying to stay above water.

Much of their spare time had been spent scouring parish burial records to locate Davis tombs, which hadn't helped much as there was a Davis tomb in four of the five local cemeteries. So they'd resorted to visiting the graveyards one by one to see if Joel recognized them. The problem was, all of the local cemeteries looked much the same – above-ground crypts, live-oak trees, and a general vibe of neglect and decay. Even so, they had ruled out three of them during those visits, which narrowed it down to just two, Saint Augustine's Catholic Cemetery and the old Wytchwood Cemetery, which they were planning to visit as soon as Aunt Penn let Joel out of her sight. Joel really hoped it wasn't Wytchwood. That place gave him the proper creeps.

By early December, Joel was battling near-constant stress headaches, the kind that made his vision blur and his temples throb. He blamed the headaches on what had happened with Royal, on dread about what had happened to Carter and the whole Zombie thing, on the shock of realizing that he could see ghosts, and the ongoing situation with T.J. He hadn't seen T.J. since their first date; not because he didn't want to exactly, but because between swim practice, costume design studio, and creative writing deadlines, he could barely keep his head above water. And if he was being honest, he was also terribly confused, more confused than he wanted to admit. They'd been texting back and forth, but Joel was much slower to reply than T.J., who had raised the idea of them going on a second date a number of times. Joel couldn't keep putting T.J. off, but something inside him just couldn't bring him to make plans for another date.

Things with Royal had become fully horrible. They'd taken to pretending each other didn't exist, maintaining silence except for occasional tight-lipped sentences when they had to communicate during costume design classes, and looking anywhere but at each other during swim training. This was really very difficult for Joel, whose eyes betrayed him and sought out Royal at every opportunity, especially when he was in those red speedos. Somehow, not speaking about what had happened, about the hurt that had caused Joel to go on a date with T.J., and fervently ignoring each other, hurt even worse than out and out fighting would have done.

The only thing going well for Joel was his schoolwork. He'd submitted his poetry assignment early. His grade was better than all of the seniors except Lana, who he tied with. Miss Dill told him quietly that his grade was a big achievement for a junior, and put him in the running for the school's *Alice Dunbar Nelson Poetry Prize*. Starr and Tashi were killing it in school as well. Starr's costume designs, which she'd done with very little help from Joel and Royal, had been selected for the Christmas showcase, and Tashi was getting the top grades for her year in both the Film major and Culinary Arts. They all got As in English for their assignments on *The Color Purple*. On the outside, they were three high-achieving teens. On the inside, not so much.

It was Monday, which meant swim practice and pool boy duty, so Joel said goodbye to Starr and Tashi after their last class and headed off to the Dumaine Athletics Building. During training he stuck to his routine of the last weeks, performing his tasks while steadfastly ignoring Royal's existence, and trying to stop his eyes from wandering to wherever Royal happened to be. He kept his head and eyes down for the whole practice. When training was finally over, Joel stayed out by the pool, as usual, to wind in the lane dividers so that the team would be showered and back into their uniforms before he went into the locker room. After an appropriate amount of time had passed, he went into the locker room and did his usual tidy up. Once the team had all gone and the locker room was quiet, he went to the showers to make sure nothing was needed in there. He turned the corner into the shower room and spotted Royal, who was only *just* wrapping a towel around his waist.

Oh no, no, no, no! Not *again*!

Royal was literally, practically naked, not even wearing those skimpy red Speedos. What Joel wouldn't do for those speedos right now! Joel should have quietly backed out of the room but shock had him rooted to the spot. Royal turned toward the door and stopped still when he spotted Joel. Neither of them said anything. Joel's heart was pounding an irregular rhythm in his chest.

God. He. Is. So. Hot.

Joel made an immediate amendment to the Royal Dumaine Statute. Not only should guys as hot as Royal Dumaine be banned from wearing skimpy swimsuits, especially red Speedos. They should also be banned from being practically naked in public. Towel-wearing in public for hot guys was henceforth prohibited.

Joel averted his eyes by staring at his rainbow Chuck Taylors. 'Sorry,' he mumbled, 'I didn't know you were in here.' He glanced up at Royal, took in that wall of smooth, tanned skin, and, as had become his reflex, quickly looked away again.

'We should stop meeting like this,' he stuttered.

Oh. God. No. Stupid. Mouth. Again!

Royal's blue eyes were steely and his face flushed with either embarrassment or anger. Joel looked to the corner of Royal's mouth to see of if one of those trademark smirks was forming there. Nothing.

'Royal, can we—'

Royal silently stepped around Joel and walked briskly out of the shower room. So, they were not going to talk then. Joel waited for him to dress and leave. When he was sure he was alone Joel slumped onto a bench in the locker room and cried his eyes out. Once he was all cried out and properly exhausted, he finished tidying up the locker room and headed home. Half-way there he got a text from Aunt Penn:

You are 20 minutes late! This is unacceptable. Get home right now or you are GROUNDED!

After what happened to Carter, and Joel's disappearance from school to go out on T.J.'s boat, Penn had warned Joel that one more slip-up would get him grounded. She'd made him promise to be where he was supposed to be at all times, and to never come home late. He picked up his pace. He was just walking into the yard when his tension headache ramped up to a whole other level. A burst of pain seared through him. His vision blurred. He staggered. A strange bird was singing somewhere nearby. He lurched forward, fell on his knees. He called out to his aunt. She came running out onto the porch. Starr and Tashi followed close behind her.

'Joel!' Penn shouted when she saw him on his knees. She raced down the stairs toward him. 'Joel!'

The pain seared through him again. He slumped onto the ground. The bird was singing loudly now. And then everything went black.

*** ***

Joel knew before he opened his eyes that he wasn't in the yard of Oakshade Cottage anymore. He doubted he was even in his body anymore. The throbbing pain in his skull was gone. All bodily sensation was gone. Once again, all around him was the soft golden glow of flickering lamplight and candlelight. The shadows it threw stretched and danced along the warped wooden walls of the swamp shack he'd seen in the previous vision. The rafters were strung with bones and feathers, shells and river stones, bundles of herbs tied in red twine, and blue bottles filled with luminous liquid. Something, no, *someone*, was humming. Low and sweet, it reminded Joel of the sound of bees singing to flowers, a kind of lullaby.

He stood up slowly. Was he dreaming? This didn't feel the same as the other dreams. This one was heavier somehow. More real. The walls pulsed with light, as if moonbeams had soaked into the boards. Across from him, in a high-backed wicker chair, sat the same elderly African-American woman he'd seen in that first vision.

Her hair coiled into those thick, glistening dreadlocks bound with red and gold thread. Her robe shimmered like oil on water. Her luminous blue eyes were fixed on Joel.

'Make yourself at home, bébé,' she said. Her voice lilted in that same lyrical accent like honey and thunder, smooth and ancient. Joel opened his mouth to speak, but the words caught behind his teeth.

'I been waitin' on you,' she said, lifting a gnarled hand toward her heart. 'My name's Mama Estelle. Some call me a priestess, some call me a spirit, a ghost, some call me an angel, but I been called worse. You can call me Mama.'

Joel swallowed. 'Is this … are you, are you real?'

Mama Estelle chuckled, her laugh rolling like distant thunder.

'What is real, child, ain't your worry right now. I brung you here for a reason. It was the bringing that made your head hurt so bad, an' for that I'm frightful sorry. I brung you here to answer your questions.'

'What questions?'

'You're wondering if that boy Carter Herrera still got breath in him. You're wondering if he gone to the shadows, or if there's still a thread left to pull him back. You're wondering how to keep your friends and your aunt safe.'

Joel nodded slowly.

'There's hope,' she said, her eyes glinting as if a bright star had risen behind them. 'But not without danger. You and your friends have brave hearts, and you, bébé, you got some power, sure enough. Maybe enough to hold back the dead, if you stay smart and stay close to your friends.'

She pointed a bony finger at the window. Reflected in the glass was a cemetery with rows of above-ground burial crypts. Like the cemetery he'd seen in his dream. He still couldn't tell which cemetery it was.

'You will find your friend Carter on burial ground. You know the place I mean. You have already seen it. You will need your friends to help you find him. And you will need powerful gris-gris as protection. This gris-gris must be made right, with three powerful ingredients: dust from red graveyard bricks, dried leaves from a resurrection fern, and a drop of blood from *un visionnaire*. Your naughty friend, Thierry Thibodaux, he knows how to make such things. If you take protection gris-gris made like that and wear them over your hearts, the walking dead cannot touch you, or even see you.'

'I was told not to do anything, to stay out of it, because it was too dangerous.'

'I already said there was danger, but doin' nothing ain't an option no more. If you don't act, more than one of your friends will die.'

Joel's knees nearly buckled beneath him. He couldn't let anything bad happen to his friends. But what could he do? He was just an awkward, fainty boy who didn't even believe in any of this stuff until he'd moved to Acadiaville.

'But, how do you fight something that is already dead?' he asked, noting his voice sounded terrified.

Mama Estelle leaned forward. Her breath smelled of flowers and bay leaves and the richness of the soil.

'Listen closely, bébé – together you and your friends have the power and the skills to send the undead back to their muddy graves, but you need to know the one weakness of zombies. The dark curse that makes the dead walk again can be undone with blessed water.'

'Holy water? That's all?'

'That's all. A drop of blessed water to the heart, that will break the curse that makes them walk.'

Joel's mind boggled trying to figure out how to get holy water into a zombie's heart. He remembered what Royal had said about the smell of them and how fast they were. He shuddered and felt himself go pale. Mama Estelle somehow read his mind, or simply noticed him trembling like a hamster suddenly coming face-to-face with a lion.

'Don't underestimate yourself,' she said. 'You got a magical gift. You can see future things, you can peak through the hourglass of time, and see the sand falling, a little at a time.'

Joel had no idea what that meant. He was still thinking about the zombies and how they were super strong, super-fast and stank of roadkill. The curse that brought them back from the dead must be super powerful. An image flashed in his mind – a hooded priest with red eyes and skin as white and lifeless as marble. A priest who controlled the zombies with a twitch of his cold fingers.

'Bébé, now you listen to me extra hard, if you ever go up against *him*, Père Cassamir,' she said, spitting on the ground, 'you gonna need more than hope and courage and a few gris-gris. That twisted priest has powerful dark magic, dark enough to make him immortal, dark enough that he can raise and control the dead.'

Joel felt a chill ripple through him at the priest's name. The image of him in Joel's mind got clearer – those red eyes, the hooded cassock, and the darkness that gathered around him like a black halo.

'You'd need some powerful voodoo to fight him,' she continued. 'Power you can only get from *the Blood Royale*.'

The shack seemed to lean in around them, to shield them in greater secrecy. Even the air held still.

'What is that?' Joel whispered.

Mama Estelle didn't answer right away. She reached into a pouch that hung around her neck and drew out a scrap of cloth. About the size of a stamp, the scrap had the shape of a rose drawn at its center in dried blood. She held it like it was alive.

'The Blood Royale is the power of inheritance,' she said. 'It holds the right to rule, both the day and the night. It holds the power to fight evil, shielded with light and love. This power is magic held in blood passed down from kings. When used in the right spells, it is immensely powerful. And it is made even more powerful by the blush of *first love*. If you use the Blood Royale, child, you might just beat the demon priest.'

The shadows started to thicken, curling at the corners of Joel's vision. The swamp shack was melting into mist, Mama Estelle's voice thinning and sounding hollow.

'To use the Blood Royale,' she called, already distant, 'you must unlock its fullest power. It is made more powerful by the blush of first love! Do not face the twisted priest without it!'

Then the world of the swamp shack cracked, splintering like glass struck with a bullet, and Joel was falling backward, flickering stars streaming past his face. Then Mama Estelle's voice was in his mind, as if she were whispering to him from within his own heart.

'Bébé, I live in the song of birds. In the song of birds you will always find me.'

He woke with a gasp, drenched in sweat, Mama Estelle's voice vibrating in his bones. He was in his bed, in his bedroom. Aunt Penn was in a chair pulled alongside him. Her face was white with worry. She was holding his hand. As soon as she saw he was awake she hugged him tight.

'Oh, Joel, I was worried sick! I am so sorry I got angry with you! And I'm so sorry I sent that terrible text! I'll never yell at you again!'

COMING OUT ABOUT MARTIN

Joel, Starr, and Tashi were in his bedroom, a couple of hours after Joel woke from his vision of Mama Estelle. Outside the sun was beginning to set, the blood orange light of dusk making the bedroom window glow like stained glass.

'Way to never get in trouble with your aunt again,' Starr said, smirking.

'Yeah,' Tashi added, 'just faint the minute she raises her voice.'

'I know,' Joel said, 'if I wasn't such a nice human boy I'd use my NMH for evil and get whatever I wanted.'

Joel was still feeling weak after his blackout vision. To help perk him up, Penn had made them all soup. The three of them were stirring their bowls of soup cautiously, as though it might scream at them. One taste had made them all want to swear off the soup food group for the rest of their lives. Joel couldn't tell if it was meant to be French Onion, Mushroom, Miso, or something else. As far as Joel could tell, its closest relative was old dishwater. Why was Penn so bad at making eatable human foodstuffs?

Twice already Joel had tried to tell his friends about his vision of Mama Estelle and what she'd said. He hadn't been able to do it. He hardly believed it himself and was afraid that Starr and Tashi would think he'd finally lost his mind. Visions of ghosts, or spirits, or angels, or whatever Estelle was, were in a whole other realm of cuckoo. Sure, they'd accepted that zombies had taken Carter without much hesitation, but Joel was certain that was because Royal was the witness.

Steady, level-headed, and calm, Royal was the opposite of Joel. Where Joel was skittish, Royal was steady. Where Joel was muddle-brained, Royal was level-headed. Where Royal was calm, Joel was anxious and constantly embarrassing himself. Royal was the sort of person everyone believed without question, whereas Joel was the sort of person even squirrels distrusted. He absent-mindedly had another spoon of soup, and had to suppress the retch it triggered. He put the bowl down once and for all.

'Hey, guys,' he said, stealing himself to tell them about Mama Estelle for the third time. Third time's the charm, right? 'You know how I have dreams?'

They both nodded. They both put their soup aside.

'Well, I, err, also had a, well, a vision. When I fainted in the yard earlier.' And then he calmly told them everything he'd experienced, everything he'd seen and everything Mama Estelle had told him. All in precise detail. Strangely, when it came to his dreams and visions he could remember everything. If only he had that skill for exams, which he absolutely definitely did not.

It took a while to tell them everything. They didn't interrupt him once, just sat there on his bed quietly listening. When he recounted what Estelle had said about the undead harming his friends if he didn't do something, their faces paled and their bodies visibly tensed. Once he'd finished he waited for their response – waited for them to pass each other furtive glances that communicated that they thought he was nuts; waited for them to tell him his vision was just a fever dream, a hallucination, not anything real. But they didn't. They both had very similar expressions on their faces, which Joel couldn't quite read. Quiet disbelief? Stoic alarm? Resolved determination? Maybe all of that. Tashi was the first to break the silence.

'We should go to the last two cemeteries tonight then,' she said. 'We have to find Carter soon, and we're all here in the one place. Besides, I don't like the thought of leaving Carter with those zombie skanks any longer. Who knows what they'll do to him?'

Joel blinked. Then he blinked again. He couldn't believe that they believed him, but they obviously did. He hadn't told them about the ghosts yet, but he felt sure they'd react to that with the same acceptance. His whole body relaxed, releasing tension he'd been holding for months.

'Okay,' Starr said, sounding less determined than Tashi about more visits to cemeteries, but still willing. 'But we need help making those gris-gris.' She turned to Joel. 'Do you think Rose-Marie will—'

'No, she won't help us,' Joel said firmly. 'But I think T.J. will. He's some kind of magic voodoo dude.'

'Magic voodoo dude?' Starr and Tashi echoed, smirking, gently teasing him.

'Yeah, he can make protective amulets and stuff. He told me when we were on our date. The date I ruined. And Mama Estelle said so too.'

'I still can't believe you went on a date with T.J.,' Starr said. 'The same morning you found out Zombies are real and after Royal told you he liked you?' She looked half amused, half perplexed.

'Yeah. After Royal called Lana "baby", something in me snapped. I have to put him out of my mind.'

'So *that's* why you went on a date with T.J.?' Tashi this time, definitely sounding more perplexed than amused.

'It wasn't my proudest moment,' Joel said, 'but T.J. texted me right after I saw Lana in the quad and Royal called her "baby", and I thought it was a sign, so I went with it.'

'You should probably know,' Starr began, 'all of Lana's family, and her closest friends, call her "Baby". It's her nickname, because her mother's name is Lana too. They didn't want to call her Lana Junior, so they called her "Baby Lana", and then just "Baby". I know this for a fact because Lana and I went to the same kindergarten, and were in grade school together.'

'Everyone calls her Baby?' Joel asked, feeling sick.

'Yes. And she and Royal have known each other since they were little, their parents are old friends, so he's probably always called her Baby as well.' Starr patted him on the knee. A small gesture of comfort.

Despite the kindness Joel felt even sicker and felt the need to express it.

'I feel really sick,' he moaned, flopping down in the bed. 'Really, really sick.'

'Just be grateful Royal doesn't know you went on a date with T.J.,' Tashi said. 'You can fix this. It's going to be messy but it's fixable.'

'Oh, it's not fixable,' Joel said. 'Royal saw us!' He hadn't told them this before now. Partly because he hadn't wanted to talk about it, but partly because he was ashamed.

'What?' Starr and Tashi said in perfect synch.

'Royal saw T.J. pick me up in the boat!'

'What!' Starr and Tashi said in perfect synch, again.

'And T.J. had his shirt off!'

'What!' They said in perfect synch, yet again.

'I know! It was terrible!'

'All this time,' Starr began, 'we thought you were ignoring Royal because he called Lana "baby" that *one* time.'

'Which we really thought was not smart of you, Joel,' Tashi said. 'And should we ask why T.J. had his shirt off?'

'Because he's super-hot looking and it was a warm day and that's what super-hot looking boys do when it's a warm day.'

Starr and Tashi glanced at each other and then broke out in peels of giggles.

'It's not funny!' Joel fumed at them, literally puffing air out of his nostrils at them like he was firing invisible nose darts. They giggled even more. Then Joel started to giggle. It was either laugh, cry, or crawl under the bed and die.

'I have ruined everything!' he moaned.

'You haven't ruined anything,' Starr said, patting his knee some more. 'How many people can deal with dates with super-swol boys and jealous ex-girlfriends named Baby, and zombie cheerleaders, all at the same time? I think you're doing just fine, all things considered.'

Joel forced a smile but still felt awful. What must Royal have thought seeing him zoom off in a boat with a shirtless T.J.? He'd nearly fallen apart just because Royal had called Lana "baby"! He'd have fully melted down if he'd seen Royal in a boat with her, especially if she'd been wearing that satanic pink bikini of hers. How was he going to fix this when Royal wouldn't even speak to him? He supposed he just had to be honest with both Royal and T.J. and tell Royal everything before he had a chance to walk away from him again. He'd have to talk incredibly fast, but that was not really an obstacle because talking incredibly fast was one of Joel's superpowers.

Being honest with hot boys at high speed was not going to be fun. Ick. Ick. Ick.

'My bow and arrows!' Tashi suddenly said, making both Joel and Starr jump. 'I can dip my arrows in holy water! That should work really well against Zombies, right?'

'Definitely,' Star said, 'and I can bathe my sword in holy water too. Those zombies won't know what hit 'em.'

'We'll be like Deep South ninjas,' Tashi joked.

Joel looked from Starr to Tashi, his heart welling up with love for them. Not only did they believe him, but they were going to help. He wasn't alone in this. They were incredible friends, courageous and brave, just as Mama Estelle had said. Then he was struck with a stab of worry.

'Look,' he said, 'this is very dangerous. I don't want you to get hurt, or worse. Maybe I should find Carter on my own.'

'And what martial arts training do you bring to the table, pool boy?' Starr asked, teasing.

'Well, I, err,' Joel stuttered, 'well, I wield a mean stink eye.'

'You're gonna stop a pack of zombies with a stink eye?' Tashi asked, chuckling.

'I've been told my glare is withering,' Joel said.

'I think you have more than a mean stink eye,' Starr said. 'What was it Mama Estelle said? You can peak through the hour glass a little sand at a time? That means you can see into the future, maybe a few hours at a time. That would really help us. We'd know what the zombies were going to do before they did it.'

'But I have no idea how to do that,' Joel said, feeling a bit useless.

'Maybe I do,' Tashi said, before pulling an old-looking book from her bag. 'I found this in the library.

The only book on voodoo in the whole school. It has a chapter about clairvoyants. It says clairvoyants can see the future more clearly by using what's called a "focus".'

'What's a focus?' Joel asked.

Tashi flipped through the book to the right page and read a little bit before answering.

'It's an object that helps the clairvoyant to calm their mind and concentrate on what they're trying to see, but it's more about relaxing into the visions than trying to control them.' She closed the book. 'Is there an object that helps you feel relaxed?'

Joel shook his head, no, but instantly thought of something that did help him to relax. His most valued, most secret possession. But he couldn't tell them about that. No, never, that was his own special secret.

'Joel,' Starr said gently, 'you *do* have something, I know you do.'

'No, I don't,' Joel said, doing his best to sound as though he wasn't lying through his teeth.

'Yes, you do,' Starr insisted. She turned to Tashi. 'He does, he's just too embarrassed to admit it.'

'Embarrassed about what?' Tashi asked, intrigued.

'Nothing,' Joel said, his face a little red and hot. 'Starr doesn't know what she's talking about.'

'Joel, I know all about your little *precious*.' She said "precious" in a very convincing Gollum voice. Somehow that made this situation much worse.

'How? How do you know?'

'The day of the thunder storm, the day you were stuck on the library porch with Royal and he saw your, err—'

'Nipples. The day Royal saw my wet nipples.'

'Yeah, that day. Penn asked me to close your bedroom window so that the rain wouldn't come in. So, when I was in here closing the window, I saw his little feet sticking out from under your pillows.'

Joel groaned, grabbed a pillow and buried his face in it trying to hide.

'Little feet?' Tashi whispered. 'What on earth is it?'

Joel kept his face covered, but felt around blind until his hand found the other pillow. He reached under it and pulled out the object of his shame – a Care Bear, bright pink and velvety soft with a rainbow on his little chest. His most valuable, most secret possession.

'OMG, he's so cute!' Tashi squealed.

Joel dropped the pillow. There was no point hiding now.

'He's not *cute*,' he said indignantly. 'His name is Martin, and he's a very dignified fellow. He's my most valued and most secret possession.'

'Oh, yes, very dignified,' Tashi said. 'Can I hold him?'

Joel pulled Martin protectively to his chest.

'No. No you cannot.'

'Joel!' Starr chided, 'weren't you ever taught to share your toys?'

'Martin is not a toy. Martin is my emotional support bear.' He hugged the bear closer to his chest.

'It's okay,' Tashi said. 'I don't have to hold him. It's just nice being in his presence. He's the same pink as my hair! I think Martin will be a perfect focus.'

'So,' Joel began, pretending not to be mortally embarrassed about having just come out about Martin, 'what am I supposed to do to peak through the hourglass of time or whatever?'

Tashi looked in the book again.

'It says to hold the focus in your dominant hand, relax, be present with your breathing, think about what you want to know, and just allow a vision to come.'

Joel held Martin in his right hand, allowed himself to relax and silently asked: 'Show me what will happen when we're searching the cemeteries tonight.' He didn't have to wait long for a vision to come.

He saw mist coiling like smoke through the narrow alleys of an old cemetery. He saw the rusted entrance gate. This time he could read it: "Saint Augustine's Catholic Cemetery". Then he saw an avenue of gnarled live-oaks, heavily covered in Spanish moss. He saw a crypt with the faded name DAVIS. He saw a battered coffin made of metal, clamped tight with rusted chains. He saw something lurch upward out of the coffin in a blur. The he saw zombies! Lots of them, chasing Joel and his friends through shadowy woods, some dropping with arrows in their chest, never to rise again, some sliced through with a gleaming sword. Then he saw Carter running with Tashi, holding her hand. He was pale, battered, but running so fast, running for his life. Then he saw himself and his friends on the bridge, crossing the Little Bayou River to the school, with the zombie cheerleaders stopped in their tracks on the other side, unable to cross the flowing water. The visions faded and then he was just looking at his closed eyelids. He opened his eyes. Starr and Tashi were watching him anxiously.

'You know what,' he said, 'I think we're going to be able to do this. I saw which cemetery it was! Saint Augustine's! And I saw Carter. We rescued him! I mean, we *will* rescue him. And we'll get back here safely. But you two definitely need to bring your weapons! There's going to be lots of zombies!'

'So,' Starr said, her voice breaking a little, 'it's settled. We go tonight.'

THE BAYOU CREW

Joel had watched from the porch, with Martin the Care Bear stuffed under his arm, as Starr and Tashi strode back into the yard like two Southern ninjas on their way to war. The moon had been high in the sky, its silver light twinkling on the water of the bayou. After Penn had retired to bed, Starr and Tashi had gone to retrieve their weapons from where they were safely stored in weapons lockers at school. Joel couldn't believe they had weapons lockers at their school, but this was America, and the Deep South to boot, so he guessed it was par for the course. While the girls were gone, he had texted T.J., asking for his help with the gris-gris bags. T.J. had texted straight back and said he'd be over as soon as they were done.

Now Tashi was sitting below Joel on the porch steps, stringing her bow, her small hands deft and precise, while Starr practiced sword strokes in the shadowy yard. Joel's breath caught in his throat. They looked like something out of an action movie—half superhero, half comic book star, all deadly. Tashi with her bubble-gum-pink ponytail, pulling arrows from her old duffel one by one and whispering what he guessed were Buddhist blessings over them. Starr, with her smoky eyeliner and purple combat boots, was moving through her sword exercises so deftly and with such strength that Joel was surprised he hadn't realized what an athlete she was before now.

They were doing this. *For him.* For Carter. For all of them. Joel felt his eyes sting, overwhelmed by a rush of affection and awe.

'You two,' he said quietly, 'are the coolest people I've ever met. I can't believe you're my friends.'

Tashi grinned. 'Yes, we are cool, and you are very lucky to have us.'

Starr glanced over her shoulder, smirking. 'You're just saying that because I look so much like Blade, vampire-hunter, right now. The one from the comics not the movies.'

'I mean,' Joel said, 'I wasn't *not* thinking that, but I was more thinking how awesome you both are.'

Before either could respond, a car engine cut through the evening quiet, followed shortly after by bright headlights. A moment later a *very* bright pink pickup truck pulled up outside the yard, somehow glittering in the moonlight.

'OMG, it's like a Pepto-Bismol fever dream on wheels,' Tashi said.

Joel didn't even have to guess. Only one person in Acadiaville owned a bright pink, four-door pickup, and only T.J. would roll up to a zombie hunt in a vehicle that looked like it was owned by Barbie's redneck cousin. Joel's instant reflex was to hide Martin the Care Bear, but Tashi intervened as he went to chuck Martin under a cushion on the porch swing.

'Hey, don't treat Martin like that! And don't be ashamed of him!'

'Yeah,' Starr said, 'so you have an emotional support bear, so what. Anyone who has a problem with that is a jerk.'

'Agreed,' Tashi said. 'Besides, you need Martin as your focus. If you can't see into the future, we lose our advantage. So, it's not just you who needs Martin, we all do.'

Joel beamed, his heart warm with affection for his kick-ass friends who understood a broken human boy's need for emotional support bears. So Joel held onto Martin and prepared for the ridicule he'd cop when T.J. saw him holding onto a bright pink plush toy.

T.J. hopped out of the truck, all swagger and smiles, his arms loaded with four big Coke bottles of what could only be holy water, and a backpack slung over one shoulder.

'I come bearing gifts,' he announced. 'Holy water, courtesy of the totally unlocked catholic church, and gris-gris bags freshly made by yours truly.'

Joel tried not to notice how handsome T.J. looked in his Orville Peck tank top, tight jeans, and cowboy boots. He failed. It's okay to think you're friends are hot, right? It's not totally inappropriate, just a little bit inappropriate, right?

T.J. strolled up to him, eyes sparkling in the moonlight. 'Hey, Joel,' he said, voice low and just flirty enough to make Joel's knees feel weak. The he spotted Martin. 'What's with the bear,' he said, looking askance at Martin's rainbow chest badge. Joel stuttered, trying to explain. Starr stepped in.

'That's Joel's *focus*. It helps him to see the future. Without the bear, we've got no chance against the zombies.'

'Cool,' T.J. said, giving Martin a patronizing pat on the head. Clearly uncomfortable, he changed the subject. 'You ready to go save your jock schoolmate sort-of-friend from a gaggle of undead mean girls, dreamboy?'

Joel flushed at being called dreamboy. That was new, and sort of appropriate.

'Um, yes?'

'You don't sound too sure,' T.J. said, stepping closer. 'Should I give you a confidence boost? Maybe a pep talk? Or a kiss for luck?'

Joel squeaked. Starr snorted. Tashi grinned.

'Okay, okay,' T.J. laughed, raising his hands. 'No pressure. But if we make it through this alive, I'm calling dibs on a victory kiss. Fair warning.'

This was all very awkward. Joel wanted to tell T.J. that there wasn't going to be a second date, that there wasn't going to be a victory kiss, or any kind of kiss for that matter, because of, well, because of Royal. He was just about to pull T.J. aside to explain this when he was distracted by the sound of crunching gravel – footsteps coming down the driveway. It was Royal. He walked towards them slowly, as composed and unreadable as always, his hoodie pulled up and his jaw clenched tight. His eyes were fixed on T.J.

'Oh, Royal,' Joel said, realizing he should have texted or called Royal about the fact that they were mounting a rescue of his roommate and friend. How addle-brained could he be? 'Hi.'

'Hey,' Royal said, nodding once. 'By the sound of your voice you weren't expecting me. I thought we were going to find Carter together?' His eyes scanned the little war party, pausing a moment too long on T.J., who was still standing very close to Joel. T.J. didn't move. If anything, he moved closer.

'How did you know we were going tonight?' Joel asked.

'I texted him,' Tashi said. 'We need all the help we can get, and he's Carter's friend.'

Joel nodded, totally getting it but still feeling side-swiped.

'So, are we doing this?' Royal asked.

Joel cleared his throat. 'Err, yeah. We are. Of course we are. I'm sorry I didn't text you myself.'

Royal gave him a tight smile, the kind that didn't quite reach his eyes, and said nothing.

Starr sensed it first. The shift in the air. The brittle tension. She sidled up beside Joel and spoke into the awkward silence.

'Okay,' she said, her tone light but commanding, 'so now that the gang's all here, shall we go fight an undead cheer squad?'

'Zombie cheerleaders,' Tashi said, shaking her head. 'I still can't believe it.'

'Yeah, it's kind of wild that zombie cheerleaders are an actual thing,' Joel said, almost reverently. 'This is my life now.'

'It's all our lives now,' Starr said, clapping a hand on his shoulder.

Joel glanced between the five of them, all standing in the yard under the heavy hush of a Louisiana night, weapons and weird magic gear in hand. It struck him, suddenly and with overwhelming clarity, that they were about to march into a cemetery together to fight actual, reanimated cheerleaders. This was happening. And something about it—the whole ragtag, supernatural, Scooby-Doo-but-make-it-Southern vibe—made him pause.

'We need a name,' he said abruptly.

Tashi blinked at him. 'A name?'

'Yeah, like a team name,' Joel said, enthusiastically. 'We're going to fight evil. We need branding.'

Starr cocked an eyebrow. 'You want us to have a logo too?'

'I mean, I wouldn't say no,' Joel muttered. 'But seriously, we can't just be "those kids with the pink truck and the emotional support bear. We need something iconic.'

Tashi tapped her chin thoughtfully. 'What about *The Louisiana Ninjas*?'

'Oh, no,' Starr said, 'too red-state-pride-ish. What about *The Undead Obliterators*?'

Joel made a face. 'Sounds like a failed Netflix pilot. What about … *The Human League*?'

'That's a band from the eighties,' Tashi deadpanned.

'I *know*, but it suits. Humans V. Zombies, get it? No? Okay, how about, wait for it, *Joy Division*?'

'Also a band,' Royal said, not even looking away from glaring at T.J.

'Okay, fine, how about *Culture Club*?' Joel said.

Starr groaned. 'Joel. No.'

'You're gonna say no to *New Order* as well, aren't you?'

'Are you just listing bands from your mom's old cassette collection?' T.J. asked, grinning.

'How rude!' Joel exclaimed, with mock offence. 'My mother is nowhere near cool enough to know any of these bands.'

T.J looked perplexed. 'Sorry,' he said. 'They just sound kind of 1980s.' T.J. grimaced, as if tasting something gross.

'You didn't just use "1980s" like it's a bad thing?' Joel felt personally attacked.

'He did,' Starr and Tashi said together, shaking their heads disapprovingly at T.J.

'Wow. Just, wow,' Joel said. 'Look,' he continued, dramatically flailing one hand around, 'I'm just trying to find something with the right *vibe*.'

T.J. stepped even closer to Joel. 'What about just *The Vibe*?' He said it way too sexily. Joel nearly died on the spot. Like, literally not figuratively died.

'We are *not* calling ourselves *The Vibe*,' Royal muttered with more irritation than T.J's suggestion deserved.

'Okay, okay,' Joel said, defusing the situation. 'What about … *Bayou Crew*?'

The words settled in the air like the calm created by an Enya song. Everyone was quiet a moment.

'Actually,' Starr said slowly, 'I kind of love that.'

Tashi nodded her agreement. 'Mysterious, scrappy, slightly unhinged. Like us.'

'Yeah,' T.J. said, 'It works.'

Royal finally met Joel's eyes. 'Bayou Crew,' he repeated. 'Not bad.'

Joel beamed, weirdly proud. 'Okay then. It's official. From this night forward, we are the Bayou Crew.'

They all nodded, something unspoken and real passing between them like a pact.

'Should we make, like, a blood oath or something?' Tashi asked. 'Isn't that what's done in these situations?'

'No thanks,' Joel said, 'blood makes me all fainty.'

'Speaking of blood,' T.J. said ominously, turning to Joel. 'I need some of yours for the gris-gris.'

'What?'

'Yeah, you said in your dream you were told that the anti-zombie gris-gris bags have to be made with three powerful ingredients: dust from red graveyard bricks, dried leaves from a resurrection fern, and a drop of blood from *un visionnaire*. I already added the brick dust and the fern leaves, but I still need to add the drop of blood from *un visionnaire*. That's you, you're un visionnaire, a clairvoyant.'

'What? You want my blood?'

'Just a drop, from a needle prick to your thumb.' T.J. pulled a needle out of his backpack. Joel imagined it glinted sharply in the moonlight. 'Just a tiny drop,' T.J. repeated, gently taking Joel's hand. Joel winced as the needle pricked his thumb, a single bead of blood welling up like a ruby. T.J. caught it carefully on small scraps of cloth, then tucked one into each gris-gris bag with a practiced, almost reverent motion. 'Blood is a powerful ingredient in voodoo,' he murmured, knotting the final bag shut. 'Now those zombies won't be able to touch or see anyone wearing one of these.'

Then Joel realized something. 'There's only five bags.'

T.J. looked around them, understanding that, because of Royal's arrival, there were now five of them in the Bayou Crew. 'Oh, crap,' he muttered.

'I don't get it. There are five of us,' Starr said.

'What about Carter?' Joel said. 'He'll need one, once we find him.'

'Oh, crap,' Starr and Tashi echoed.

'I'll go without,' Royal said immediately. He didn't sound in the slightest bit reluctant or scared. Joel felt a twinge of desire in his belly that was completely inappropriate for the moment. He pushed it down.

'No,' Joel said flatly with a bit too much force. He thought he saw the corner of Royal's lips tweak in a small smile.

T.J. jumped in. 'He'd only be without one *after* we find Carter,' he said. 'Royal can wear one until we find Carter, then hand it over for him to wear. By then we should have already dealt with the zombies anyway.'

Joel didn't want to agree but the others were already moving on. T.J. pulled brightly-colored water pistols out of his bag, handing one each to Royal and Joel. A pink one to Royal and a green one to Joel.

'They're loaded with holy water,' T.J said. 'Aim at the zombies hearts and squirt.' He took his own orange water pistol and liberally sprayed Starr's sword and Tashi's arrow heads. 'I don't have another pistol for Carter, so we'll all have to cover him.' They all nodded.

Royal reached out and took the green pistol from Joel and swapped it with the pink one.

'Matches the bear,' he said gruffly, quickly looking away and testing his pistol's squirt range. Royal had no idea why Joel had the bear, and clearly didn't think it was odd or strange at all. Joel's face flushed. There was that totally inappropriate desire again. He tested his own pistol to distract himself from Royal Dumain's super Cajun hotness.

Then Starr said, 'Okay, Bayou Crew, let's go make some zombies regret ever joining the pep squad.'

They loaded into the truck with all the coordination of a newly-formed band on the first leg of its first tour. And just like that, the Bayou Crew rolled out.

T.J. was at the wheel, naturally, his arm slung across the back of the seat, grazing Joel's shoulders with suspicious regularity. Tashi sat by the passenger window, radiating focus and calm. Royal slouched in the backseat, brooding, saying nothing, while Starr hummed the tune to "Born on the Bayou" by Creedence Clearwater Revival, a song Joel had heard on the local radio many, many times since he'd arrived in Acadiaville.

The pickup rattled down the road, the sky above them a star-pierced indigo, dark and cloudless. Ahead loomed Saint Augustine's Cemetery, its rusted iron gates crooked and creepy. Somewhere beyond those gates was Carter. Somewhere beyond those gates, the walking dead were lurking. Joel shivered. T.J. put his hand on his knee to comfort him. It just made him feel worse.

Joel closed his eyes, listening for the sound of birdsong without much hope of hearing any. After a long moment he caught the distant sound of a Barred Owl, a hoot that sounded like a lonely person calling: *Who cooks for you? Who cooks for you all?* He immediately felt the presence of Mama Estelle and whispered, 'Please, let us get out of this alive.'

Beside him, T.J. leaned in and squeezed his knee. 'We will. I got you, dreamboy.'

In the rear-view mirror, Royal's eyes met Joel's. Royal looked so downcast, so hurt. Something deep and painful cracked open in Joel's chest. He wanted to climb over the seat between them and fold against Royal's strong body. He wanted Royal's arms to wrap around him and hold him tight. He wanted to apologize for skipping school to go on a date with T.J. He wanted to explain that, no matter how it looked, he didn't like T.J., except as a friend. He wanted to explain that he'd been unjustly jealous of Lana, and that's why he'd gone with T.J. in the first place. Then he felt ashamed of himself, yet again, for thinking about his romantic dramas when Carter was going through who knew what and they were all about to risk their lives.

And then the moment was gone. Royal turned to stare out the window, his face a mask of pain. As if an ominous omen, the pickup was suddenly swallowed by the shadows of giant swamp cypress trees, and they all headed silently toward the fight of their lives.

THE CRYPT AND THE CREEPER

Mist slithered low around rows of crooked tombstones, coiling like smoke through the narrow alleys of Saint Augustine's Cemetery. The Bayou Crew stood just inside the rusted gate, silent, breathing in the damp rot of old stone and much older bones. The moon, veiled by thin clouds, turned every shadow into a threat and every movement of the wind into a heart-jolting omen of doom. Joel clutched Martin tight beneath his jacket. He could feel the bear's soft head pressing against his ribs like a talisman. The gris-gris bag that T.J. made, an actual magical talisman, hung around his neck. They'd all donned them before getting out of the pink pickup. His heartbeat thrummed loud in his ears.

'Down this way,' he whispered, leading them down the avenue of live-oaks, the trees drooping under the weight of centuries and heavy drifts of Spanish moss. They moved quietly, boots crunching on gravel, the only other sound the wind blowing softly through the branches of the live-oaks. Even the crickets were quiet.

'I don't like this,' Tashi muttered, her pink ponytail glowing faintly in the moonlight. She nocked an arrow, its holy-water-drenched tip glinting.

'We're not supposed to like it,' Starr whispered back, her fingers tightening around the hilt of her blade. 'We're just supposed to survive it.'

At the end of the moss-dark alley, the crypt Joel had seen in his visions loomed, with the name DAVIS barely legible in worn letters. Starr stopped in her tracks.

'Davis,' she whispered.

'I forgot to tell you about this,' Joel whispered back. 'In my defense, I've had a lot going on … I think it's your ancestors' crypt.'

The crypts iron cross looked exactly as it had in Joel's dream. Rusted and leaning, as if in shame. The door, naturally, stood wide open.

'Joel,' Royal said quietly. 'Is this it?'

Joel nodded, swallowing hard. 'Yeah. The vision … it all starts here.'

They stepped inside. The air thickened. The damp chill curled around their limbs like a second skin. The marble angel in the back of the crypt gleamed bone-white, a sword clutched in its hand as though it were warning them, or judging them. And there it was, the coffin. Metal. Riveted. Shackled in thick, rust-pocked chains. It sat in the center of the crypt like a curse sealed in steel.

'Oh, crap,' T.J. almost moaned. 'You think Carter's locked in there?'

'I think so,' Joel whispered, a tremble in his voice. 'This is exactly what I saw.'

Royal moved ahead of them, examining the chains holding the casket closed. He found a padlock, also rusty, and tugged. It didn't budge. He looked around for something to pry it open. T.J. pulled a crow bar out of his backpack.

'I thought we might need this,' he said.

'Thanks,' Royal muttered gruffly. He set to working on the padlock. His biceps bulged at the effort. Joel would never have admitted it, this being a life or death situation and all, but he rather enjoyed the view as Royal's biceps strained and bulged.

What. Is. Wrong. With. Me. Focus! Zombies!

Then a link on the rusted chain snapped. Royal smiled and went to break the padlock loose.

Boom. A sudden sound from *inside* the coffin. They all jumped. Royal stood and stepped back, eyeing the casket warily. Tashi pulled her bowstring taught. Starr brandished her sword. Joel dropped his pink water pistol, swore under his breath, and scrambled to pick it up.

Boom. Another sound from inside the coffin. Then a dull, rhythmic pounding. Boom. Boom. Boom. Then the chains rattled. First softly, making a metal sigh that echoed in the crypt, then violently. T.J. raised his holy water-filled pistol in one hand, his other hand shaking ever so slightly.

Boom. Boom. BOOM.

'Back up,' Royal ordered, his voice low and commanding. 'Everyone back—'

The coffin exploded. Chains snapped. Metal shrieked. Shards flew like shrapnel. Royal shoved Joel behind him, shielding him with his body. What happened next unfolded so fast none of them had time to react. Something shot out of the coffin. A blur of shadow. A shadow that had a human shape. A man. A man dressed in rotting clothes that Joel recognized from Starr's fashion books as being from the 1700s. The man was gaunt and as pale as the angel statue, so pale he couldn't have been human. His lips were drawn back in a grimace, baring razor sharp fangs as white as alabaster. The word "vampire" roared in Joel's mind. With incredible speed the vampire slammed into T.J., pinning him to the wall.

'T.J.!' Joel shrieked.

The vampire's grabbed T.J. by the throat, holding him still, and sank those terrible fangs into the side of T.J.'s neck. T.J. gasped, eyes wide, skin paling as he was drained.

'Get away from him you creep!' Joel shouted, aiming his pink water pistol and firing, doing little more than dampening the tomb floor. And then Starr was there, her blade a streak of silver. She slammed it into the vampire's side. Holy water sizzled on contact. Smoke curled from the vampire's flesh. The vampire shrieked, throwing T.J. aside like a broken doll, and shoving Starr so hard she flew through the air and out of the crypt. Her sword rattled on the pavement outside as she thudded into the ground. She sat up, dazed, gasping for breath and holding her chest, winded. Tashi loosed an arrow. It would have struck true but the vampire was just too fast. It caught the arrow and threw it away, barely flinching. It turned toward her.

Royal moved like a bolt of lightning. He shoved Joel toward the crypt door, then lunged and grabbed T.J.'s limp body and Tashi's bow arm and pulled them both out of the crypt, bulldozing Joel ahead of him as he went. Joel struggled to keep up and stay upright, his mind still shrieking the word "vampire". When they got outside, Starr was staggering to her feet. Joel and Tashi helped get her up.

The vampire arrived at the crypt door mere seconds later. His face had a much more human appearance now, the pale alabaster skin flushed with T.J.'s blood. Dark-haired and dark eyed, he was strikingly handsome, in a kind of effeminate way. He smiled at them and readjusted his moldy jacket, as though he'd just arrived at a party.

'Well, that was … fun,' he said with a thick French accent. 'I do like a little to-and-fro over dinner. Sebastian Allard, at your service.' He did a pretentious little bow as he introduced himself. 'And you are? I do prefer to know with whom I am dining.' He bared his fangs, still dripping with T.J.'s blood.

'Run!' Royal shouted. 'Now!' He heaved T.J. over his shoulder, grabbed Joel's hand and bolted. They sped down the avenue of live-oaks, through the misty graveyard and out onto the gravel where the pickup was parked. The vampire didn't pursue them. Joel heard him laugh behind them, and then the sound of flapping, like wings, but actually the rags that were the vampire's clothes. Joel looked over his shoulder and saw Sebastian Allard the vampire speed in a blur in the other direction. Joel's heart thumped in his ears. Vampires! Goddamn vampires are real too! He squeezed Martin, pressed against his chest like a life vest, and tried to breathe. He felt like he hadn't taken a proper breath since they entered the tomb. He only managed to get one long breath in before the first zombie appeared.

She stepped out from behind a tree like a prom queen from hell – head cocked unnaturally, mouth wide with rot, blonde curls crusted with swamp muck, her old weedy pom-poms still clutched in her hands. It would have been funny if it wasn't terrifying. Her milky eyes were fixed on Joel. He instinctively felt for the gris-gris bag around his neck. It wasn't there. He looked around and spotted it snagged on the jagged edge of the crypt door, hanging there by its broken cord. Then another zombie staggered out of the shadows. And another. Dozens of them. All with their bulbous eyes fixed on Joel.

'They can see me,' he muttered.

'Oh, shit,' Royal said, looking to Joel's neck and seeing that the protective amulet was gone. 'They can see Joel!' he shouted to the others.

'Bayou Crew, *fight!*' Starr bellowed.

Tashi loosed another arrow. The cheerleader it struck collapsed instantly, unmoving. Starr waded into the fray, blade gleaming. The sword arced once, twice, and two more cheerleaders fell to the ground, their flesh sizzling from the holy water.

Joel squirted holy water from his pink pistol like he was in a Super Soaker war from hell. One zombie staggered backward, shrieking as the water burned through her chest to her heart. Then she dropped like a stone. Another reached for him. Joel froze in fear. Royal stepped between them and blasted the zombie with his own pistol. It was coming so fast it impaled itself on Royal's pistol. Royal hammered the trigger. The zombie shrieked and dropped. Royal shook the zombie gore from his pistol with a grimace.

'Yikes, gross,' he muttered.

Joel stared, breathless. Zombie-fighting Royal was even hotter than everyday Royal. Royal noticed him staring and half blushed, giving him a sharp look.

'Focus, *dreamboy.*' His use of the word dreamboy was a targeted stab about T.J., which Joel didn't appreciate, not at all, but this was not the time to fume about that.

'Right, yes,' Joel muttered to himself. 'Focus. Zombies now, relationship drama later.'

A zombie landed right in front of Joel, dropping out of the live-oak canopy above. Joel raised his pink pistol and squirted it full in the face. The creature howled and staggered back, and was then taken out by Starr. The five of them fought their way to the pickup, inching forward so slowly Joel thought they'd never make it, but for every zombie that came at them, two fell. Tashi's arrows were flying one after the other, Starr was a blur of fury and grace. Royal's speed and precision with his water pistol was nothing short of amazing. When they finally got to the truck, Royal deposited T.J. in the backseat. The jolt roused him. He opened his eyes and pressed a shaking hand to his throat.

'You're not dead!' Joel said.

'Not dead,' T.J. wheezed, feeling the wound at his neck. 'Ow, that crypt creeper fully bit me.'

Joel winced in sympathy and then winced all over again because Royal was bodily tumbling him into the front seat and buckling him in. He removed his own protection amulet and put it around Joel's neck.

'Everyone in!' he roared to the others, kicking away a zombie that lunged at him seemingly out of nowhere. They could see him now. He waited until Starr had climbed in beside T.J. and Tashi was safely next to Joel before getting into the driver's seat himself. He turned the key, pumped the accelerator and they were off, hurtling away from the graveyard with a handful of zombies chasing after them. Scarily, the zombies were keeping up with the speed of the truck.

'These zombies are fast!' Royal swore. 'I thought zombies shuffled about at a walking pace.'

'And what are you basing that assessment on?' Starr asked from the backseat, watching the zombies racing after them.

'Movies and stuff,' Royal answered.

'Clearly,' Joel said, 'Hollywood has lied to us yet again.'

They plunged forward on the narrow dirt road cutting through the woods, the pickup's tires throwing up a cloud of dust and stones. Spanish moss dangled from the trees overhead like skeletal fingers reaching out for them. The fog thickened the deeper into the woods they went, swallowing the view behind them, but not swallowing the deathly moans of the pack of undead cheerleaders that followed at pace.

Joel's heart pounded. His stomach roiled. Then, ahead of them, by the side of the road in a grove of Cyprus trees, a hint of movement in the shadows. Something was there. Was it more zombies?

'Carter!' Tashi screamed.

She was right. He was there – bloody, pale, wild-eyed, shirt practically torn off, and running like the devil was at his heels. He saw the pink pickup and veered toward them. Right behind him were three more zombies.

'Run!' Tashi shouted. 'Carter, run!' She climbed half out the window of the speeding truck and hung there, notching an arrow as she went.

'Tashi! Are you crazy!' Joel shouted, terrified she'd fall. He grabbed her waist and held her firmly in place. 'This is a clear driving safety violation!'

She laughed and loosed an arrow, it missed, she loosed another and a zombie went down. Then another, then the final zombie hit the dirt with a thud just as Royal screeched to a halt. Starr threw open the passenger door and Carter dove headfirst into the truck, accidentally shoving Starr into T.J.

'Ow,' T.J. moaned. 'Still not dead here, take care please.'

Carter slammed the door behind him and Royal hit the accelerator and took off, mere seconds before the pack of zombies behind them caught up. The zombies were close now. Too close. Joel watched them in the rearview mirror. The closest cheerleader suddenly leapt forward, reaching for the tailgate. Joel gasped, but luckily the zombie missed and fell in the dirt. It didn't stop it though, it lurched to its feet and raced after them again without missing a beat.

Then the bridge came into view. Wooden, rickety, spanning the midnight black water of the Little Bayou River like a lifeline.

'Floor it!' Starr screamed, her eyes on the zombies right behind them.

Royal didn't need to be told twice. They reached the bridge with only inches separating them and the zombies' outstretched arms. The cheerleaders stopped dead in their tracks as if hitting an impenetrable glass wall. They teetered at the bridge's edge, unable, or unwilling, to get any closer. One moaned like a ghostly fiend denied its dinner. Another clawed at the air. But not one of them touched foot on the bridge. The running water beneath it made it impossible for them to cross.

Out of nowhere Carter freaked out, screaming as if in agony and thrashing about, desperately clawing at the door to get out. Both Starr and T.J. had to hold him back to stop him from jumping out of the speeding truck. Despite being restrained, he pounded on the window so hard Joel was sure it would smash. Despite all the ruckus, Royal kept up the speed until they were on the other side of the river and then pulled up. Finally, Carter calmed down. He sat slumped in his seat panting from exhaustion.

The zombie pack was still on the other side of the river, not even attempting to come after them. The crew erupted in cheers and relieved laughter, Joel the loudest. Once the laughter died out, they stared back at the pack of zombies trapped on the other side of the bridge. Joel knew what they were all thinking – because it was what he was thinking. They needed to be certain they weren't going to be followed. The moon shone down, unbroken by cloud, casting silvery light across the bridge like a protective blessing. They stayed there for ten, maybe twenty minutes, to make sure nothing was coming after them, as one by one the zombies gave up and trudged back toward the cemetery.

Carter moaned from the back seat. 'Is … is it over?'

'For now,' Joel said. 'Yeah.'

Joel glanced over at Royal, so glad that he'd been with them tonight. He had literally saved Joel's life multiple times in one night. Royal smiled back at him, and Joel took that as an invitation to lean shoulder to shoulder with him. Just for a minute. Just to show how grateful he felt. Royal tensed a little at the contact but didn't say anything. Joel could only assume he was still upset about the thing with T.J. A moment later, Royal started the engine and steered the pickup towards Oakshade Cottage.

UNCOMFORTABLE CONVERSATIONS

Royal cut the engine and the headlights and let the pickup coast into Aunt Penn's yard. Joel was surprised Penn hadn't noticed them missing. She must be in a deep sleep after the taxing events of the last weeks. They got inside as quietly as they could, which wasn't easy with T.J. staggering about. In the end, Royal had to support him through the doorway. Tashi supported Carter who, despite his ordeal and his beat-up appearance, was more or less moving under his own steam. He seemed confused more than anything. Once inside, Joel gestured down the hallway towards his bedroom and whispered to Royal:

'Let's get T.J. to my bed.'

'The couch is fine,' Royal said, immediately depositing T.J. on the sofa. T.J. groaned when his head hit the back of the couch. Joel glared at Royal. Royal shrugged unapologetically and took a seat in the armchair in the corner. Tashi eased Carter much more gently into the other armchair. Starr tiptoed to the bathroom and brought back a First Aid kit. She squirted some antiseptic onto a bunch of cotton balls and handed half to Tashi, before dabbing the bite marks on T.J.'s neck herself. He winced but didn't complain. The antiseptic made the wound look a lot better, but did nothing about the massive bruise blooming on his throat like a very angry hickey. Starr finished her ministrations by sticking a small round Band-Aid on each puncture. She then went to help Tashi, who had checked Carter's face, arms and chest and found, other than a lot of dirt, just a few scratches to sanitize. Starr got a wet washer from the bathroom so that Tashi could clean him up. Carter watched Tashi throughout all this with a look of adoration on his face.

'You saved me,' he finally said, taking Tashi's hand. 'You saved me from those dead skanks with your arrows.'

'We all helped rescue you,' Tashi said, her voice breaking. 'And don't say "skanks". It's anti-feminist, even when you're talking about zombies.'

'Sorry, Tashi,' Carter said. 'I won't use that anti-feminist word again.'

Tashi smiled at him like a teacher at her favorite preschooler. She gathered up the dirty cotton balls, the washcloth, and Carter's shredded t-shirt and discreetly gestured for Joel and Starr to follow her into the kitchen. She put the swabs in the bin and rinsed the washcloth in the sink, and then waited for them to join her in a huddle at the kitchen table.

'Carter is very cold,' she whispered, looking toward the door to make sure Carter hadn't followed her in.

'I'll get him one of my hoodies,' Joel said automatically.

'I don't think a hoodie will help,' Tashi said, her tone grim.

'A blanket then?' Starr suggested.

'That won't help either. He's like, *unnaturally* cold.'

'What are you trying to say?' Joel asked.

'A hoodie or a blanket won't help because … because I think Carter is dead.'

Starr blinked, confused. Joel mirrored her.

'Did you take a blow to the head?' he asked, sincerely concerned. 'Carter isn't dead. I mean, he's walking and talking.'

Tashi ignored Joel's head injury comment and pressed on. 'We've seen a lot of things walking and talking tonight that aren't alive.'

Those words struck Joel like a blow. Tashi was right. The zombies could walk, run, groan and shriek. And the vampire, Sebastian Allard, the crypt creeper, he certainly walked and talked. And bowed like a pretentious bozo as well.

'So you think Carter's been turned into a vampire?' he asked.

'No, I don't.'

'Then what?' Starr asked.

'Follow me. I'll show you.'

'Wait,' Joel whispered, 'shouldn't we get weapons?'

'If he wanted to hurt us, he could have well before now. I don't think he's violent.'

Joel didn't think Tashi had enough evidence to make that statement but decided to trust her. He hoped she wasn't wrong. Tashi led them back to the living room. T.J. still looked spaced out, but a lot of the color had returned to his face. Royal was glaring at him from the corner armchair. Tashi pulled a footstool in front of Carter, sat down, and smiled at him.

'Hi, Tashi,' he said, 'I'm so glad you're back.'

'Carter,' Tashi said gently, 'take off your pants.'

Joel wasn't expecting that. He exchanged a curious glance with Starr.

'But … but, Tashi,' Carter whispered sheepishly, 'we're not *alone*!' He gestured with his eyes at everyone else in the room.

'Not for that!' Tashi said quickly. 'I want to see if you're hurt on your legs.'

Carter beamed. 'You're so nice, Tashi,' he said as he undid his jeans and wiggled out of them until he was naked except for his sky blue boxers.

Everyone in the room except Carter gasped. On Carter's upper thigh was a discernible bite mark. A human bite mark, not the puncture wounds a vampire would make, but a perfect impression of human teeth. It was bloody and swollen. Around the edges it was a foul-looking green color.

Tashi looked over at Joel and Starr, her face showing them that this bite mark was exactly what she'd expected to find.

'How did you get that wound?' T.J. asked, sounding alarmed though still weak.

'One of those nasty ska—' He stopped mid-word, looking at Tashi apologetically. 'Sorry, one of those *dead ladies* bit me.'

A wave of alarm went around the room.

'It hurt a lot,' Carter continued sulkily, 'and then everything went dark, I was really scared in the dark, but then I think I passed out. I think I was blacked out a really long time. When I woke up tonight the weather was colder and the moon was in a whole other spot in the sky. I was really confused, so I ran away. And then I saw you guys in that pink truck.'

Tashi wiped a tear away from her eye. Joel's mind was blank. He couldn't comprehend what was happening. No-one spoke for a good while.

'He freaked out when we crossed the bridge,' Starr said. 'Then he was fine again when we were back on solid ground.'

They all realized what this meant. Zombies can't cross running water.

'Carter,' T.J. said, 'have you … eaten … anything … since you woke up tonight?'

'Who cares if he's eaten?' Royal interrupted. 'He's been bitten by a zombie!'

'We have to know what he's eaten,' T.J. said. 'It's very important.' He turned to Carter. 'Have you eaten anything?'

Carter thought long and hard. 'No. I didn't eat.' He covered his mouth and whispered conspiratorially to Tashi: 'I was too scared. And too busy running away from those dead ladies.'

Tashi took his hand and squeezed. 'That's okay,' she said.

'If he hasn't eaten,' T.J. said, 'he hasn't fully turned.'

'Turned into what?' Royal asked, alarmed.

'A zombie.' T.J. hauled himself upright in his seat and took off the gris-gris bag around his neck. He tossed it to Carter. 'Put that on, buddy.' Carter put it on. 'There's a good boy,' T.J. said. Carter beamed proudly.

'T.J., can you explain what's happening?' Starr asked.

'Sure,' T.J. said. 'One,' he raised a finger, 'Carter has been bitten by a zombie. Two,' he raised another finger, 'zombie bites are fatal. Judging by the look of that wound, Carter died ages ago.'

Carter moaned. 'I knew it,' he said. Tears welled in his eyes. Tashi held his hand tighter.

T.J. raised another finger. 'Three, zombies don't fully turn until they start eating. The more they eat, the less human they become, and the more they rot.' He put up a fourth finger. 'Four, that gris-gris bag works against zombies. My guess is it'll stop his hunger. If he don't eat, he'll stay more or less as he is now. Forever. He won't age. He won't change. He won't rot. He's not alive. He's not dead. He's undead, a half-zombie to be precise.'

'Half-dead,' Carter moaned. He fell into Tashi's arms and stayed there trembling like a baby for the longest time.

Joel suddenly remembered what T.J.'s mother had said about Carter being dead already: *In the motorcycle dream you saw Carter dead. I'm sorry, Joel, but you are hell-bent on saving someone who is already dead.*

While Tashi comforted their sort-of-dead, half-zombie friend, Joel quietly asked T.J. what he thought was a very important question.

'What exactly do zombies eat?'

'Brains,' T.J. said flatly. 'Human brains, from the living. Dead brains are no good for them. They need 'em fresh.'

Joel half gagged, half choked. Brains! What. On. Earth.

'Don't worry,' T.J. added, 'if he keeps that gris-gris on, he'll never be hungry.'

'Tie it on *tighter*,' Starr said to Tashi, who obeyed immediately.

*** ***

It took them all a while to process what had happened to Carter. They sat around in the living room, silent for the most part. About an hour later Royal stood and, adopting the same "no sudden movements" attitude he had used with Joel, slowly approached Carter, who was sitting quietly in the armchair while Tashi held his hand.

'We need to get back to our dorm, Carter. Are you okay to come with me?'

Carter looked to Tashi, who nodded reassuringly.

'I'll come along with you until you're settled,' she said.

It took him a while but he agreed to go, but pointedly held on to Tashi's hand. Joel walked them out onto the porch. He knew there were more important things going on, but he needed to clear the air with Royal. He needed clear air more than anything he'd needed before. He waited for Tashi and Carter to go down the stairs and into the yard.

'Royal,' he said in a tiny squeak. He had to cough to get his voice to work properly. 'Err, sorry, Royal, can we … can we talk?'

'Wouldn't you rather be inside with T.J.?'

That hurt. And made Joel angry. And flustered.

'You … no, actually … no, I would not!' His arms started to flail about. He tried to control them by jamming them in his pockets. 'You, well, you … I like you a hell of a lot … but you … Lana! Baby! And so I … I went boat!

Oh. Dear. Lord.

Royal smirked down at him. 'You went boat?'

Joel shrugged, afraid to say anything else because he would come across as completely unhinged. But he stuffed the fear down and kept speaking anyway.

'Yeah … but … but only because you … you know … Baby!'

'Let me translate,' Royal said, smirking more. 'You got jealous because I called Lana "Baby", even though that's what everyone calls her, because it's her *life-long* nickname—'

'Well I—'

'Don't interrupt, Joel, I'm still translating. Then, even though you apparently like me, *a hell of a lot*, you went into a jealous fit and got in a boat with a nearly naked guy, who definitely was not me. Is that what you're trying to say?'

Joel felt that was a fairly accurate translation, except for the "nearly naked" part. What was with Royal and the nearly naked thing? He was weirdly prudish for a sixteen year old boy.

'Well—'

'Hold on, Joel,' Royal said, 'I'm not finished. I want to make something clear to you. Seeing you in that boat with *him* gutted me, really gutted me. I really like you. I told you I did. So if you kissed him or … or anything else … well, to be honest, I wouldn't handle that well, so, so just don't tell me, okay.'

'Oh! Nope. I didn't. Not even a little bit. Never would. Nope!' Joel hoped that was clear.

The relief washing over Royal's face was palpable. Joel rushed on.

'I'm, like, very, very sorry. I really am. I've never liked someone as much as I like you. And when you called Lana "Baby", I just, I just … fully freaked out. Do you forgive me?'

Royal nodded. 'I shouldn't, but I do.' He slowly leaned in and gave Joel a gentle peck on the cheek. 'See you at school tomorrow,' he said.

Joel was too busy blushing from head to toe to say anything so he just nodded.

Royal loped down the front stairs and caught up with Tashi and Carter, who were well outside the yard now. He turned and waved at Joel before he disappeared into the shadow of the live-oaks encircling the playing fields. Joel waved back, took a breath, stealing himself, and went inside to have the second uncomfortable conversation of the evening – with T.J.

*** ***

When Joel got back inside he was surprised at what he found. T.J. and Starr were both sitting cross-legged on the floor with a bunch of Aunt Penn's mason jars, which she used for making the vilest mayhaw jam Joel had ever tasted. Actually, he'd only ever tasted Aunt Penn's mayhaw jam. Maybe it was all vile? And what the hell was a mayhaw anyway? He put these questions aside.

'What you guys doing?'

'Making spell jars to keep that crypt creeper out of your yard,' T.J. said.

'What?' Joel said, a little stunned. 'You don't think he'll come here?'

'Probably not,' Starr answered, 'but T.J. thinks it's better to be safe than sorry.'

T.J. was pulling all kinds of weird looking things out of his backpack – roots, powders, dried leaves, animal bones, shiny pennies, and what looked like dirt. Joel knew it was probably grave dirt.

'Joel sat on the floor next to them. 'Feeling better, then?' he asked T.J.

'Much, thanks for asking.'

Joel took a breath, stealing himself again. 'Look, T.J., can we talk, like alone?'

'No need, Joel. I heard you talking to Royal. These timber cottages are not very sound proof.'

'Oh, T.J., I'm so sorry. You shouldn't have found out that way. I was going to tell you myself, I want you to know—'

'That you value me as a friend, that it's not me, it's you, that it's because you like Royal. I don't blame you. He's hot. Not my type, but hot.'

'I feel really bad.' Joel said.

'Don't. I'll get over it, in time.' His voice cracked, just a little. He was putting on a brave face but it wasn't very convincing. Starr looked like she wanted to sink into the floor and disappear. Instead, she hopped up and quietly exited the room.

'T.J.,' Joel said, 'I am so sorry. I should never have led you on. You're so, so great, it's just that, well, I—'

'You're in love with Royal.'

Joel balked at the love word, using that word was a really big deal, but he chose not to quibble.

'I like him a lot, yes.'

T.J. nodded his understanding. He started stuffing ingredients into the mason jars.

'Are you okay?' Joel asked.

'Not really. I'm hurt and broken hearted. But I'll recover.'

'I'm so sorry,' Joel repeated.

T.J. nodded, his eyes fixed on the mason jars. 'Give me a hand, will you?'

'Sure,' Joel said.

'A handful of each ingredient in each jar.'

Joel nodded he understood and started helping. 'What are these for?'

'They're spell jars, for protection. We'll bury them on the edge of your yard, one in each direction. So, one in the north, one in the south, one in the east, one in the west, making a kind of boundary. Once they're in place, nothing supernatural can come inside the boundary. No vampires, no zombies, nothing.'

'That's a huge relief. Thanks so much for doing this for us.'

'It's cool. We've had them at my place, and at mom's fortune parlor, since before I was born. I'll bury some around the school too. The river keeps out the zombies, but not vampires. Vampires have to be invited in to get inside the house, but I don't want that Sebastian creeping around your yard, or the school.'

'No, me neither.'

Starr peeped her head in the door to see if it was okay to come back. Joel motioned her to come in. She sat down on the floor and helped fill the spell jars.

"I still can't believe we fought a troop of zombies and survived,' she said. 'And saved Carter, who is now a half-zombie. What is our life like?'

'Crazy,' Joel said. 'I can't believe I didn't faint like a dozen times tonight. And I'm still hoping I'm dreaming it all.'

'You're not dreaming,' Starr said. 'And it's pretty obvious zombies and vampires are not fainting triggers for you.'

Joe let that sink in. Zombies and vampires are not fainting triggers, but hot boys he likes are? What kind of cruel condition has he got?

'We did good,' T.J. said. 'You especially, dreamboy. Without you, we wouldn't have stood a chance.'

Joel let the dreamboy thing pass. He had something else on his mind.

'I nearly got us all killed,' Joel said. 'My dreams were all wrong. I didn't dream about the vampire at all. I didn't even dream that we went to the cemetery in a pink pickup truck. That's a pretty big detail! It all went wrong because of me. Because of me that vampire got loose.' He turned to T.J. 'It's all my fault you got *vampired*, T.J. I'm so sorry.'

Starr giggled. '*Vampired* is not a real word,' she said, 'and definitely not a verb.'

'Well, I didn't want to say T.J. got sucked on by a vampire. That sounds indecent.'

'You could have said T.J. was *fed on* by a vampire.' Starr suggested.

'That's too many words,' Joel said. 'I'm sticking with vampired.'

'I like vampired,' T.J. said. 'It's got a certain ring to it. And don't worry, Joel, I'm fine.'

'No thanks to me,' Joel said. 'If it weren't for me that vampire would still be chained up. It can't be good he's out. Somebody chained that coffin up really tight. They wouldn't have done that if he was a nice vampire, would they?'

'Are there nice vampires?' Starr asked.

'Not that I know of,' T.J. said. 'But I didn't truly believe they were real until that crypt creeper was sucking on my neck like I was a big ol' blood popsicle.'

'Eww,' Joel said. 'Don't say *blood popsicle.*'

T.J. chuckled. Then Starr changed the topic.

'Hey, guys, I didn't have time to tell you this until now,' she said, 'what with the zombies and the vampire and Carter being bitten an' all, but that vampire was in a Davis crypt, and his name, Allard, is a name in my family. I have cousins named Allard.'

'White cousins?' Joel asked, realizing after he did that it might not be the most sensitive thing to ask, but the vampire was white. Really white.

'No, they're not white. But my gran is big on family history, and she told me that we got the name Davis from the plantation owners who owned our ancestors, who were all slaves on the Wytchwood Plantation. The founder of the plantation, Whitmore Davis, is my four times great grandfather, or maybe five times, I'm not sure. He had an affair with one of his house slaves, my four or five times great grandmother. Her name was Samantha *Allard.* She had a slave mother but a white father, a French aristocrat, whose surname was—'

'Allard,' T.J. said.

Joel knew that many African-Americans were descended from slaves, and some from slave-owners who had abused their female slaves, but hearing Starr say it so matter-of-factly shook him. It was another wake up moment – he was living in the Deep South, and this was the dark history of the place. Then he realized the other implication of what Starr was saying.

'So, you think that Sebastian Allard is one of your ancestors, that you're related to that vampire?'

Starr nodded, looking grim. Joel understood why. That was one seriously scary ancestor.

'Do you remember the story my grandma told, about the ghost protector, the one that has shadowed my family for centuries? What if it wasn't a ghost, what if it's a—'

'Vampire,' Joel said, thinking Starr was probably onto something.

'So,' T.J. said, 'let me get this straight. Your four or five times great-granddaddy on one side is a blood-sucking crypt creeper?'

Starr nodded again, her face paling.

'Great!' T.J. said.

'What?' Joel and Starr said in unison.

'According to vampire lore, there are some unbreakable rules. Vampires cannot go into the sun, it kills them. They can also be killed by a wooden stake to the heart or beheading. They cannot enter a home without the invitation of someone who lives there. Holy water burns them, and so does silver. The garlic and the crucifix things however are just myths. All vampires have super strength and speed. The older ones can fly, and some can mesmerize humans and compel them to do whatever they want, etcetera, we've all seen the movies. There is one thing that not many people know about vampires, that's never in the movies – they cannot harm their blood descendants.'

'What?' Starr said, perking up.

'If Sebastian Allard is your ancestor, he can't harm you, or your grandma. But there's some other things that are just as good. Vampires are bound to obey their living blood.'

'What does "bound to obey their living blood" mean?' Joel asked.

'It means they have to obey any orders their descendants give them,' T.J. explained. 'Oh! I nearly forgot! Vampires can't harm anyone carrying a lock of hair from one of their living descendants!'

'Wow,' Starr said, 'that's all really, really good to know. I feel *so* much better about all this now. Thanks, T.J.'

'You're welcome.'

Joel got up and went to the kitchen. When he came back he was brandishing a pair of scissors.

'Okay, Starr, time to take one for the team.' He waved the scissors in her direction in a mock menacing fashion.

'You are not cutting my braids off!' She backed away from Joel as though he were the vampire.

'We just need a little, just the split ends,' T.J. said.

'Split ends! How dare you!'

Joel chuckled. 'You seem more put out by the idea of having split ends than having a vampire four times great-grandfather.'

'You better believe I am,' Starr said, but then carefully examined her braids and offered a few up. 'Just the tips!' she warned, 'Or so help me, I'll sic my four times great granddaddy vampire on you!'

Joel very carefully snipped off just the very ends of the offered braids.

'Excellent,' T.J. said. 'Share a little with the whole crew and tell them to put it in the gris-gris bags I made them, or in a locket or something.'

Joel nodded and handed a little to T.J., who carefully placed it in his pocket.

The three of them finished filling the spell jars just before dawn. By the time the sun had cast the horizon a pale orange, the three of them were out in the yard, moving with quiet purpose. Joel and Starr each carried one of the jars, still warm from their hands, and T.J. had the other two. They buried them at the four corners of the yard: north under the rustling camellia bush, east beneath the leaning fence post, south by the massive live-oak that bore Aunt Penn's wind chimes, and west in the shadows of a pair of younger oaks. Joel felt oddly reverent with each jar they placed in the soil, whispering a quick hope into the dirt that the boundary would hold. When it was done, they stood in a loose triangle near the porch, not quite ready to part ways. T.J. shifted from foot to foot, eyes flicking toward the driveway.

'I should go,' he said, his voice flat, too casual. Joel nodded, then stepped forward, unsure of whether to hug or high five or just say thanks. In the end, he did none of those things.

'Hey, uh, T.J., thanks. For the jars. For everything.'

T.J. gave a half-smile, sheepish and sad. 'Yeah. See you soon, dreamboy.'

Joel opened his mouth to respond but stopped when Starr stepped forward and gave T.J. a quick, fierce hug that said what Joel couldn't. T.J. climbed into the pink truck and drove off, literally driving into the rising sun. Joel wasn't sure if he was imagining it, but he thought he heard the spell jars' magic humming faintly around them when the pickup crossed the invisible boundary. He and Starr traipsed to bed, exhausted. Joel for one was desperate to close his eyes. He was so tired he pulled off his dirty shirt and jeans and didn't bother to put on his sleep clothes. He just fell into bed in his underwear, hugging Martin to his chest. He was asleep before he had time to take another breath.

PRIEST DREAM

Joel was barefoot and shivering in the moonlight, dressed only in boxer briefs printed with tiny flamingos. He stood in the middle of Wytchwood Cemetery, the cracked stone path beneath him slick with moss and lichen. He looked up at a nearly full moon, shining as brightly as a lamp. All around him loomed the crypts, those old New Orleans-style tombs, coffins stacked in rows inside like forgotten drawers in a dead man's dresser. The air smelled thick and sour, like wet earth and wilted flowers. Spanish moss hung from the cypress trees like torn lace, swaying even though the air was almost still.

He didn't remember walking here. One second he was in bed, and the next, he was here, the humid air touching his chest like damp fingers. The cemetery faced Lake Saint Adjutor, with the drowned husk of Wytchwood Church behind it, half-sunk in the mud and water. Its steeple had tilted long ago, now slanting like a crooked finger toward heaven. Its doors were gaping open, choked with vines. Joel looked around, getting his bearings, until something moved.

A ripple spread across the surface of the shallow water in the entrance to the church. With a low, squelching sound, a figure rose from the muddy water. First the cowl of a sodden black robe, then a pale, skull-like face framed by dripping hair. The evil priest, Père Cassamir. Joel's heart froze. He tried to back away, but the cemetery path seemed to hold him, the weeds among the cracked stones wrapping around his ankles like cold hands.

The priest stood tall and terrible, his cassock clinging to him like rotten flesh. One bony arm lifted, pointing a jagged finger straight at Joel, and from the thing's mouth erupted a howl; raw, ragged, and full of hatred.

'You dare,' the priest hissed, voice booming across the shallow water, 'to defy my children?'

Joel stumbled back, breath catching in his throat. His legs felt like straw. Behind the priest, something else began to stir in the church's black doorway. One figure emerged, then another. A steady stream of the dead, clawing their way into the night. Not just cheerleaders this time—men in ragged overalls, old women with empty eyes, a long-dead high school jock still in his football uniform. And in the middle of them, barefoot and pale as milk, was Liz-Anne Landry. Her yellow sundress hung in tatters, her blonde hair still woven into the long braid she wore the last time Joel had seen her. In that dream of the town square. The dream where she was taken.

Joel's mouth went dry. His body screamed at him to run, but he couldn't move. The priest turned slowly and pointed toward the distant lights of Acadiaville Academy. The undead began to shuffle in that direction, quickly gaining speed, moaning with horrible purpose.

'Your friends will all die,' the priest said, a grin carving across his too-white face. 'They will all come here to serve me forever … as my undead children.' Père Cassamir gestured to a spot on the wet ground and two forms appeared there, two motionless bodies. Royal and

T.J. Their bodies were bruised and broken, their clothes torn, their eyes wide and unseeing. They were dead. 'I will be especially pleased to have these two, your handsome beaus.' He laughed, it was a cruel and high-pitched sound.

Joel staggered back. The priest's laugh echoed through the trees. The moss above Joel's head shuddered away from it. Joel turned and ran, barefoot and half-naked, heart pounding like a drum. Tombs blurred past. The trees seemed to lean in, whispering his name in brittle voices. He didn't care. He had to warn his friends. He had to—

'Joel!'

The voice came from everywhere and nowhere. A familiar voice. Was that T.J.?

'Joel, wake up!'

Something shook him hard, and the dream broke beneath him like rotted floorboards. The cemetery, the priest, the moaning undead, it all fell away.

Joel woke, soaked in sweat, heart slamming against his ribs. Morning light made what was in front of him seem even stranger. T.J. was right there, holding onto his arms, shaking him. As soon as he saw Joel's eyes open he stopped.

His face was tight with concern. 'Are you okay?'

Joel stared at him for a moment, dazed, shivering, then realized where they were. They were in the quad at school, just outside Rosedawn House, the girl's dormitory. He was still barefoot, still just wearing his flamingo boxer briefs. He'd been sleepwalking again.

'Let's get you covered,' T.J. said, noticing Joel's unease at being nearly naked in public. He took off his Orville Peck tank top and handed it to Joel. Joel's hands were shaking too much to put it on.

A window slid open nearby. Faces were appearing at the upstairs windows of the girl's dorm. Beginning with two girls at a window on the first floor, then another two on the third floor, then more. Soon a dozen girls were staring down at Joel and T.J, gasping and whispering to each other.

'Are they undressing?'

'They're getting naked right there in the quad!'

T.J. grabbed Joel's hand and led him away, heading at a brisk pace to the parking area in front of the admin building, Acadiaville House, where the pink pickup sat like a bright beacon.

'They're coming,' Joel said, stopping and forcing T.J. to stop as well. 'They're coming for us all.'

'The zombies?' T.J. asked. 'You had another dream?'

Joel nodded. Over T.J.'s shoulder a thin sliver of moon, paling in the morning light hung low on the horizon. In his dream the moon had been nearly full. That meant they had a little time.

'They can't cross the bridge, remember,' T.J. said. 'You're safe on school grounds.'

'Tashi lives in town, and Starr's grandma, and we can't stay on campus forever. The priest is after us now.'

'Père Cassamir knows about us?' T.J. asked.

'Yeah,' Joel said. 'He spoke to me in my dream. He threatened us all. The zombies will be coming for us before the next full moon. I have to do something, I have to—'

'You can't do anything right now. And you don't have to do anything alone. We'll get the crew together and work out a plan. But first, you need some sleep, you're exhausted. I'll take you home, and after you've had some rest you can text me and we can all make a plan together.'

Joel nodded. That made sense. He was coming to his senses, getting his bearings, then he wondered how T.J. came to be in the quad.

'What are you doing here?' he asked.

'I just planted spell jars at the four corners of the school to keep out anything supernatural.'

'Oh, thanks, T.J. And thanks for waking me up. If you hadn't been here, I might still be sleepwalking in front of the whole school.'

'That's okay. I'm glad I was here too. Now I'm taking you to bed—'

He stopped dead in his tracks, glanced at Joel's bare chest and flamingo underwear and then turned bright red. Joel blushed as well, then started to laugh. T.J. joined him. They were laughing together like friends, their relationship drama put aside for the moment. They were still laughing when they climbed into the pickup and headed back to Oakshade Cottage.

ANOTHER AWFUL THING

Aunt Penn left for school two hours early. She practically skipped out of the house after receiving a call informing her that Carter had turned up safe and well. She allowed Joel and Starr to get to school by themselves on the condition that they stuck together, went straight there, and didn't step foot off campus. After the events of the night before, Joel found it surreal that he and Starr were sitting in the kitchen in their school uniforms doing something as normal as eating cereal.

How did you go on with your daily routine after fighting zombies, meeting a vampire, and seeing first-hand that voodoo was real and magic worked? Was that what becoming an adult was really about – learning how to deal with supernatural creatures without interrupting your daily routine? Somehow Joel doubted that most adults knew anything about stuff like zombies and voodoo. If they did, the world would be very different. No-one would go out after dark for one. They'd rush home from their jobs as insurance assessors, Walmart greeters, and real estate agents and lock themselves securely in their homes by dusk, and then tremble in their slippers until dawn.

On the way across the playing fields to school, Joel filled in Starr about the dream he'd had with Père

Cassamir, and about the imminent zombie attack. She looked appropriately flabbergasted and immediately texted Tashi to tell her they needed to talk.

'I can't tell her about an imminent zombie attack by text,' she said. 'I don't think that's good Southern manners.'

Joel chuckled. Starr made even the most terrible things feel bearable. As the wooden bridge crossing Little Bayou River came into view Joel wondered aloud what would happen when the bodies of the fallen zombies were found. There were at least a dozen of them scattered between the graveyard and the school.

'I expect they'll cover it up,' Starr said. 'They must've been covering it up for years. Otherwise, everyone would know that there are zombies in Acadiaville Parish. Last I checked, that wasn't mentioned on the parish website.'

Joel nodded his agreement. He wasn't much for conspiracy theories, but Starr was right. The police and local authorities must be involved in a massive cover-up, there was no other explanation. By the time they reached the quad, Joel already felt like the day had lasted a week. He'd barely slept for days, and the efforts of the night before had drained him of every last drop of energy. The sunlight seemed too bright, the air too clean. Everything normal was beginning to feel suspicious. As they stepped onto the stone path toward the quad, Joel noticed students staring at him, some clearly whispering about him. Here and there were muffled gasps, and sputtered giggles, as people whispered about him. What were they saying? What was happening? He looked to Starr, who had also noticed it. She shrugged, as if to say she didn't know what was happening either. When they reached the quad a group of sophomores gathered there stopped talking so quickly that they emitted a damp sound as their mouths all comically clamped shut at the same time. That strange behavior could only mean one thing: gossip. Then a freshman girl skipped up to him and asked loud enough for the whole quad to hear:

'Did you really have sex with that Thibodeaux boy right here in the quad last night?'

What. The. Actual. Hellish. Nightmare.

'No, he did not,' Starr said, her voice angry, 'You should be ashamed to spread lies like that!'

A wave of hot nausea and dizziness hit Joel and his knees went weak. The faint sound of birdsong echoed in his ears. He began the breathing exercise his therapist taught him to cope with anxiety. He couldn't panic. Not here. Not in the middle of the quad in front of everyone. He couldn't pass out. He had to stay on his feet. He breathed in slowly through his nose, then more slowly out through his mouth, trying to keep it together, but his head was spinning. Starr took his arm and steered him to their tree in the corner of the quad.

It was clear on the way there that the rumor had spread like moss on the old stone walls. Joel and T.J. caught together. Joel and T.J. naked in the quad. Joel and T.J. *doing it*. Joel knew all too well that this kind of gossip takes on a life of its own. There's no coming back from it. It defines you forever. This was exactly what happened after what Patrick and the other boys from his old school had done to him. Even though, eventually, people had learned that those rumors weren't true, the mud had stuck. The sordid pictures had been posted online. Everyone had seen them. The terrible nickname, the mocking laughs in the hallway, the constant bullying, none of it stopped.

Tashi was under the tree waiting for them, her face grim. She had obviously heard the rumors too.

'I am so sorry, Joel,' she said too.

Why were they sorry? They hadn't done anything. He had sleepwalked in his underwear into the quad. T.J. had woken him and taken off his shirt for him, because he'd been shivering. And they had been seen by half of Rosedawn House. Joel should have expected this to happen. Why hadn't he been expecting this to happen? Oh, right, the zombies. He'd been preoccupied with the imminent zombie attack and the demon priest who was hell bent on killing his friends and resurrecting them as undead minions. The fact of the zombies should have deepened his panic, but it didn't, it helped him focus on what was important. He was deeply humiliated by the gossip, yes, but his friends' lives mattered a lot more. His breathing exercise started to work. The dizziness eased. He started to feel better. Once he was feeling okay, Starr and Tashi walked him to his creative writing class.

Then they turned a corner and came face-to-face with Royal. His expression hit Joel like a slap: jaw clenched, brow furrowed, lips a tight, angry line. The heat behind his eyes wasn't just anger. It was hurt. Betrayal. And worse, Royal didn't stop to say anything. He just walked straight past as if Joel didn't exist. It knocked the breath from Joel's lungs. His stomach dropped like he was on a ride going too fast.

'It's not true,' Joel said to Royal's back as he disappeared into a classroom.

Starr muttered, 'He can't believe it's true.'

But Joel knew he did, and that she knew too. Royal wouldn't have behaved that way if he didn't believe that he'd hooked up with T.J.

The girls dropped him off at the door to the writing studio. They enfolded him in a massive hug and held him there, to reassure him that he was going to be okay. Before they left, Starr looked him straight in the eye and said:

'You got this. You're not alone this time. We are your friends forever.'

Tashi nodded in fervent agreement, patting him on the shoulder.

Joel trudged into Creative Writing Studio, his shoes feeling like bricks. The classroom was warm and full of the smell of perfume and printer ink. Lana Beaux was already there, perched like a queen on the windowsill, surrounded by a gaggle of girls and a couple of the junior theater boys. Her voice rang clear across the room.

'I'm just saying,' Lana cooed, twirling her necklace around her fingers, 'you don't take your clothes off in front of the girl's dorm unless you're *begging* for attention.'

Joel flushed red. The group snickered. One of the theater boys spotted him and alerted the others to his presence. Lana Beaux stared right at him as if to say, *I will say whatever I want about you and you can't stop me.*

Joel went to his regular seat in the back row. Lana went to hers, right in front, her eyes on Joel the whole time, smirking. Joel gritted his teeth so hard his jaw ached. Then Miss Dill walked in, a red scarf flapping around her neck like a battle flag. She clapped her hands, instantly silencing the class.

'Alright, class, settle down. I have an exciting announcement to make this morning.'

The room collectively perked up. Miss Dill beamed.

'It is my great pleasure to announce the winner of the *Alice Dunbar Nelson Poetry Prize*. Our winner is …' she looked straight at Joel, '… Joel River.'

The silence was pointed. Joel could feel the disbelief passing over the room in hurtful waves. That oh too familiar buzz started up in his ears. Miss Dill clapped enthusiastically, encouraging the rest of the class to join in.

'Joel's poem, *The Heart Remembers,* will be set to music and performed at the Christmas Showcase by our talented music and theater departments.'

A low gasp rippled through the class. Lana went pale, then purple. She spluttered, 'That has to be a joke!'

'It is not a joke,' Miss Dill said firmly. 'Manage your disappointment, please, Lana. Now, another announcement – this year the Christmas Showcase will be held at the majestic Saenger Theater in New Orleans, on December 20th, which Principal Stacey told me this morning is Joel's birthday?'

Joel nodded dumbly. He couldn't speak.

'Perfect,' Miss Dill said. 'A star is born.'

When the bell rang, ending class, Joel practically fled the room, the sound of Lana's fury as she complained to her gaggle of friends buzzing behind him like a mosquito. He rounded the corner at an unsafe pace and—bam—Royal again. Joel bounced off Royal's hard chest and stuttered for a moment before he got over the surprise.

'Royal, please, can we …' Joel began.

Royal didn't even stop. For the second time he just walked past like Joel didn't exist. Joel stood frozen, one hand outstretched reaching for Royal but Royal had already gone. In American History, Starr waved him over. Tashi and Carter were already there. Joel slumped into the seat next to Starr.

'Hey Joel!' Carter said cheerfully, his eyes wide and happy. 'I'm a zombie now! Isn't that weird? But I'm not a bad zombie. I'm a *good* one!'

Joel blinked. 'Um, okay, yeah, I'm aware.'

Tashi smiled warmly at Carter. 'That was his opener to Starr as well. I tried to explain there are less startling ways to greet people, but …' She gestured at Carter helplessly.

Tashi noticed the glum look on Joel's face.

'What's up, Joel?' she asked.

'Royal hates me,' Joel said flatly. 'I ran into him again.'

'Oh, no,' Tashi muttered. 'So he really believes the rumors? I thought he was smarter than that.'

Before Joel could respond, their teacher walked in.

'Ready for a pop quiz?' Mr. Johnson asked, smiling at their answering groans. 'Just kidding. As we're at the end of the semester, it's movie day! *Gone With the Wind*, yet again.'

As the lights dimmed, Joel and the others huddled. Starr had filled in Tashi and Carter about the dream he'd had with Père Cassamir. The one that warned of an imminent zombie attack.

'We have to do something, and soon,' Starr whispered. 'Père Cassamir knows who we are and he's sending a horde of zombies after us.'

'I'm a zombie,' Carter whispered, 'and I'm not after you.'

'We know,' Tashi said gently, 'but the bad zombies *are* after us.'

'I hate bad zombies,' Carter hissed. 'They bite!' He absent-mindedly rubbed his leg.

After a moment Tashi's face lit up. 'I may have a plan,' she whispered. 'But I need a little time. And research. And some voodoo stuff.'

"What kind of voodoo stuff?' Joel asked.

'Stuff that T.J. will probably have to steal from Saint Augustine's Catholic Church.'

'I'm sure he'll do it,' Starr said. 'He's been amazing so far.'

The film played on. Scarlett O'Hara flounced through plantation drama while the Bayou Crew plotted a supernatural showdown. Joel's eyes darted to the screen, then back to his friends.

When the bell rang, they all rose slowly. Joel thought he should tell them what happened in creative writing so he mumbled:

'I won the poetry prize.'

Three pairs of eyes lit up.

'What?!' Tashi exclaimed

'You genius!' Starr said.

'That's so brilliant, Joel' Tashi cried, throwing her arms around him. Starr joined her. After they released him, Carter pulled him into a bear hug and took a big, exaggerated sniff of his hair.

'No wonder you won the prize,' he said. 'Your brain smells *delicious.* That must be why you write so well.'

Joel squeaked, 'Don't sniff my brain!'

Carter grinned. 'Just sayin', but don't worry, I'll never snack on you.'

Tashi yanked Carter toward the door.

'Zombie boy, no eating your friends!' she said with an apologetic grin in Joel's direction.

Left behind, Joel and Starr stood in the emptied classroom. Joel blinked.

'Did Carter just compliment my poetry and threaten to eat me in the same breath?'

'Yup,' Starr said. 'We're living a very weird life.'

Joel nodded. 'A very weird life,' he said.

*** ***

At the end of the week Tashi texted Joel and Starr summoning them to the library. The chaos of the last week—gossip, side-eyes, Lana's days-long tantrum about Joel beating her to the poetry prize—had finally dimmed to dull background noise. By the time Joel and Starr stepped through the arched double doors of the library it was late afternoon. The library at Acadia Academy was a quiet, cavernous refuge. Long windows filtered in dusk-tinged light, dust motes dancing in golden shafts. They found Tashi hunched at the back of the reference section, surrounded by towers of open books. Her pink hair was pulled into a topknot, dark circles shadowed her eyes, and a half-empty bottle of Coke sat next to her notebook.

'You look like you haven't slept,' Joel said, pulling up a chair. 'I know that vibe well.'

'I haven't slept much this week,' Tashi replied. 'But I found things. Old things. Bad things.' She flipped open her notebook and pushed it toward them. Inside were diagrams, timelines, and clipped newspaper articles that looked like they'd been printed on dot-matrix paper.

'The disappearances in Acadiaville go back to the 1780s. Always the same story – people just disappear into the night. There are folk stories about the demon priest that go back almost as far.' She pointed at a photocopy of a yellowed document:

> *The children who vanished near the church did not scream. The priest walked among them. His eyes like lamps in the dark.'*

Joel shivered. Starr's eyes were wide.

'That's from the diary of a local plantation owner. This priest,' Tashi continued, 'he's been seen many times. Sometimes they name him, Père Cassamir, but they always describe him: robes, pale face, eyes like fire. He's always with the undead. And the undead are always under his control.'

Joel sat back. 'So he's been raising zombies since 1780? He's been a busy boy.'

'A very busy boy,' Tashi echoed. 'And get this, the disappearances stopped suddenly in 1890. There's one folk story that says that a voodoo priestess defeated the priest in a sort of magical duel and trapped him in

Wytchwood church with some kind of spell. Guess what her name was?'

Joel thought a minute, then realized who it must be.

'Mama Estelle.'

'That's right. The story says she trapped the priest in the old church in 1890. His magic can't work beyond the boundary of the cemetery island. While she was alive, no-one disappeared. Since she died, around 1925, the priest has gotten stronger, until he was able to start raising the dead again in the 1950s, starting with that busload of drowned cheerleaders. He's still trapped in the church, but he can send the undead out to do his dirty work.' She flipped to another page. 'This is from an oral folklore collection. It says the priest was bound to Wytchwood church with a magical substance only found in those with royal bloodlines. Something called the *Blood Royale*.'

Joel blinked. 'Mama Estelle told me about that. She had some. She said it's the only thing powerful enough to defeat him.'

'She'd know, she used it to trap him in the church and contain his magic to that island.'

Starr whispered a question: 'But why does Père Cassamir want all these zombies? What's the point?'

'My guess,' Tashi said, 'is he's sending them out to find someone descended from a royal bloodline, so he can use the Blood Royale to free himself. It's just speculation but—'

Joel heard bird song. He looked around the library, but there were no birds. Starr and Tashi didn't appear to be hearing anything. The birdsong was only in his ears.

'I think that's right,' Joel said, the sound of birds in his ears telling him that Tashi was right. 'It makes sense.'

Starr whistled. 'He can't leave Wytchwood Cemetery. But the zombies can. So he's using zombies to find the Blood Royale so he can break free.'

Joel's throat went dry. 'And he thinks Royal or T.J. has it.'

'What?' Starr asked.

'In my dream, he was very focused on Royal and T.J.'

'He must think they're descended from a royal bloodline,' Tashi said.

'Maybe they are?' Starr said. 'It would fit with Joel's tarot reading.'

'And we can use that fact,' Tashi added.

Joel thought about the tarot reading Rose-Marie gave, about the two princes. Surely that couldn't be true? This was Louisiana. How many people were walking around who were descended from kings? Surely not many, and surely the odds were against the guys who Joel happened to be in a messy love triangle with being two of them. Joel gagged at the words "love triangle" and put those thoughts out of his mind. T.J. and Royal were just ordinary guys. Hot, but ordinary.

Joel leaned forward. 'So, do you have a plan?'

Tashi grinned, the kind of grin that meant trouble for someone. 'We lure the zombies to the old Sphinx Theater downtown. It's already falling apart, so no one goes there. We bait them in, seal the exits, and then—'

'Sprinklers,' Starr finished. 'Set up to rain down holy water.'

'Exactly,' Tashi nodded. 'T.J. said he can swipe enough holy water from Saint Augustine's. He's probably already done it.'

Joel felt his heart race. 'And if it works?'

'Then the curse on the zombies is broken. They all go back to being just plain dead. Their link to the priest will be severed. And Père Cassamir is stuck alone on his cemetery island with no way to reach us, or anyone else.'

Starr tapped her chin. 'What about Carter? This plan would be very dangerous for him.'

That's why he doesn't come along,' Tashi said. 'He'll stay here at school.'

Joel blinked. 'You thought of everything.'

Tashi stood, stretching. 'One last thing. If we make mistakes on the night, we don't get do-overs. This is a one shot thing.'

'Then we better not mess it up,' Joel said.

As they left the library, a hush fell over them; not fear, but awe. They had a really good plan. It may just work. But if it failed, they wouldn't live to see Christmas. No pressure then.

No. Pressure. At. All.

THE SPHINX THEATER SUPER SOAKER

The Bayou Crew huddled under a full moon outside the abandoned Sphinx Theater; their breath fogging in the pre-dawn chill. It was an unnaturally cold morning, even for that the time of year. Joel wondered if it was part of Père Cassamir's dark magic. The theater sat on one corner of the Acadiaville town square. The scent of pine and pavement was thick in the air. A low mist curled across the empty square opposite, like cigarette smoke in a dive bar. The marquee above the boarded-up theater entrance still read *I Know What You Did Last Summer – Midnight Screening*. No one had changed it since 1997.

They had all arrived separately. Aunt Penn had dropped Joel and Starr at Tashi's place on the other side of the square, thinking they were having a movie night. Then the three of them snuck out after Tashi's parents went to bed. Royal came in the car his parents had given him for his seventeenth birthday – the cherry-red Mustang. Carter stayed back at school. It'd taken both Tashi and Royal to convince him not to come. He'd really wanted to help them fight the zombie cheerleaders who had bitten and turned him, but as their plan was deadly dangerous to zombies, he needed to stay away. T.J. arrived last, on his dirt bike. When he hopped off his bike he pulled a massive super soaker out of his backpack.

'Let's kick some zombie butt,' he said, pumping the super soaker to arm it.

Royal rolled his eyes. Starr huddled them closer to share Tashi's plan with the others.

'This is where we make our stand,' she said.

'In this broken down theater?' Royal asked.

Starr calmly explained the plan. She explained that The Sphinx was the only building in town with sprinklers, that they would lure the zombies into the theater and switch the sprinklers on, which would pour down consecrated holy water. Tashi pointed to a pile of empty soda bottles sticking out of the nearest trashcan.

'They were all full of consecrated water,' she said. 'I filled the theater's sprinkler tank with them last night.'

Then Starr explained they'd lure the zombies in through the front, through the foyer and into the main theater. After she'd finished laying out their plan, Royal and T.J. were in unusual agreement.

'That's a good plan,' T.J. said.

'Yeah, good plan,' Royal added.

Joel hoped it was a plan that worked. He checked that Martin the Care Bear was still safely in his backpack and took a deep breath. 'This has to work. We'll only have the one chance.'

'It will work,' Tashi replied.

Royal then asked the question Joel hoped he never would.

'You sure they'll follow us here?'

Joel looked at him, nodded. 'They're after us. More specifically, after you and T.J.'

'What?' T.J. blinked.

'I saw it in my dream. Père Cassamir, the demon priest, you and Royal are his special targets. Believe me, I wish you weren't, but you are. I'll explain it when we get through this.'

311

Royal swore under his breath.

'Let's give them what they want,' T.J. said with a shrug. 'Bait the trap.' He took of his protective gris-gris and handed it to Joel. 'Now they'll be able to find us easy.'

Royal took off his gris-gris and gave it to Starr. It was stupid, but Joel felt a bit hurt by that. Royal hated him so much he couldn't even trust him to hold on to his protection amulet. They went in through the foyer door, which Tashi had unchained the night before. Inside, the theater was musty and cavernous, its crimson velvet curtains moth-eaten and drooping like shrouds. Broken seats lined the aisles, and the old projector loomed like a sentinel in a booth in back of the balcony. Joel climbed up to the projectionist's room. From there, he could see almost the whole theater, and more importantly, the sprinkler panel. Starr joined him, crouching at his side.

'We wait till they're all in,' she whispered, 'then you hit the red switch. Easy.'

'Easy,' Joel muttered, trying not to hyperventilate. His heart fluttered like a moth trapped in a jar. Starr gave him a reassuring pat on the shoulder before returning to the main floor with the others. They set the trap: Royal climbed up onto the stage in front of the dusty curtain. T.J. stood dead center of the main aisle, beneath a cobwebbed chandelier. Tashi and Starr crouched in the wings, weapons ready. The flickering emergency lights cast them all in eerie shadows.

And then they came. First it was just a noise, a low moan, like wind through a grove of ancient trees. Then the doors creaked open, and in shuffled the dead. Dozens of them of all shapes and sizes. Cheerleaders, mechanics, band geeks, even a set of creepy blonde triplets all wearing identical, blood-stained white dresses. Liz-Anne Landry lurked in their midst, her sundress stained and limp, her eyes milky and hollow. Joel's heart sank to see her like that.

'Showtime,' T.J. muttered.

Joel's hand hovered over the switch. Not yet.

The zombies locked their blank stares on Royal and T.J.

'Come on,' Joel whispered. 'Just a little closer …'

Then a zombie cheerleader stepped out from behind the velvet curtain right behind Royal, her head cocked unnaturally, mouth stretched in a rotten grin, her dusty afro matted with something slick and dark, and her rotting pom-poms twitching in each hand. Under the ghostlight her filthy uniform shimmered in a way that made Joel's skin crawl. Her milky eyes were locked on Royal, who turned and saw her leering at him.

'Okay, yeah, they can definitely see me,' he shouted to the others, aiming his water pistol. He sprayed the cheerleader enough that she staggered back behind the curtain, but Joel expected her to return any minute. Then another zombie dragged itself out of the shadows of the orchestra pit. And another.

'They're coming from the back of the theater as well!' Royal shouted, 'We're surrounded!'

Zombies were everywhere, streaming down the aisles from the foyer, emerging from every shadow at the back of the theater, crawling over torn seats and decades-old spilled popcorn like ants out of a broken nest. Every one of them was zeroed in on Royal and T.J.

In an echo of their battle in Saint Augustine's Cemetery, Starr shouted: 'Bayou Crew, *fight!*'

Tashi fired. An arrow flew through the air, clean and fast, pinning the zombie cheerleader as she lunged back through the velvet drapes. She sagged without a sound. Starr launched herself over the row of seats like she'd done it a hundred times before, her sword gleaming in the flickering stage lights. With two swift arcs, two zombies went down, holy water hissing as it seared their flesh.

Joel leaned over the balcony, aimed his pink water pistol down onto the zombies below and fired, drenching a zombie bus driver's face. He let out a horrible yell as smoke rose from his skin, and then dropped to his knees, and collapsed. Joel felt a bit bad about it. Public transport workers got a raw deal at the best of times. But the next wave of undead were already streaming in from the foyer, eyes wide and milky, so Joel had to focus.

A zombie landed right in front of Royal, leaping up from the orchestra pit like some deranged undead ninja. Royal roared and sprayed it in the face and heart. It screamed and reeled, falling back into the pit, where it lay still. Joel's arms ached from firing. Tashi's arrows zipped over the theater chairs, hitting target after target with terrifying precision. Starr was unstoppable, her blade a silver blur. T.J. was all speed and sharp reflexes, dropping zombie after zombie with his Super Soaker.

The remaining zombies surged forward. They were in the dead center of the theater, right where Joel wanted them to be. He dashed to the wall and slammed the switch. The old pipes groaned. For a long heartbeat, nothing happened. Were the pipes blocked? Or so old and rusted out that the holy water was leaking into the walls and ceiling before it could make it to the sprinklers? Another long heartbeat, still nothing happened. Joel held his breath, closed his eyes and wished with all his might that the sprinklers would work. A strange electrical feeling pulsed over his body. The air around him felt alive. There was a smell that reminded him of dust burning on an old heater that hadn't been used for a while. He shivered. Then, suddenly, WHOOSH, the sprinkler system erupted. Joel blinked. Had he made that happen? Just by wishing it? He discounted that idea and looked out over the theater. The sprinklers rained down a fine mist of consecrated holy water. The effect was instant. Zombies screamed, their skin steaming, bones blackening. Cheerleaders collapsed mid-sprint. A terrifying toothless old grandpa zombie let out a terrifying shriek and dropped like a stone, utterly still.

On the stage, Royal stood tall as the mist hit, and was soon drenched. Joel pushed down the sudden rush of feelings about how supremely hot Royal looked all wet in his white t-shirt, and averted his eyes when Royal looked up in his direction.

One by one, the last of the undead dropped. Their bodies sagged and stilled with a sigh, as if released from something old and cruel. Steam coiled up from the ruined corpses. The stench of burnt flesh mixed with the old popcorn and mildew of the theater. It turned Joel's stomach. When it was over, the theater fell into a strangely peaceful silence. Joel watched from above, numb with relief, giving Martin a quick squeeze in celebration.

'Hallelujah!' T.J. yelled from the middle aisle.

Joel clambered down the steps, knees shaking. Starr met him at the bottom, her sword dripping holy water.

'That actually worked,' she said.

'It actually did,' Joel breathed, catching his breath. He couldn't quite believe it. Breaking the curse meant that Père Cassamir had lost his minions, his only way of escaping his imprisonment in Wytchwood Cemetery. That felt really good. 'Now that they're free from the curse, I hope they can, like, go on.'

'Go on to what?' came a drawling voice from the shadows, 'Surely you don't believe in heaven and other ridiculous happy-ever-afters?'

Sebastian Allard entered the theater from the lobby, looking very different to how he'd looked when they'd last seen him in the cemetery. He must have been turned into a vampire when he was no more than eighteen or nineteen years old. Though young in appearance, he stood with an effortless kind of confidence, a natural ease sharpened by the crispness of his look. His hair was thick, dark, and slightly tousled, styled in a way that suggested he hadn't tried too hard, and yet every strand fell perfectly into place. He wore a pair of perfectly fitting jeans, and a crisp white long-sleeve shirt, which was half-unbuttoned, revealing pale, un-warmed skin. His deep, almost black eyes sparkled with mischief, and something darker, like hunger.

Joel and his crew all jumped to attention. Tashi and Starr wielded their weapons. T.J. aimed his Super Soaker. Royal moved protectively in front of Joel.

'Sebastian Allard,' Starr shouted, 'I am your living descendent. You cannot harm me and I command you to never hurt any of my friends.'

The vampire looked amused more than angry or thwarted.

'Do not worry, my dear,' he said. 'I'm not here to hurt anyone. I only came because I do enjoy a good show, especially a matinee massacre.' He turned to T.J., whose Super Soaker was shaking a little. 'Hello again, sweetheart, what a tasty treat you were last we met, so much so after I had starved for hundreds of years.'

'You got one lick,' T.J. muttered, not sounding quite as brave as he'd probably hoped. 'You won't get another.'

Sebastian smirked. 'Relax. I'm here to help. That was a bold little plan you all pulled off. Very messy, but effective. As a gesture of good will, I'll take care of the cleanup.' He indicated the pile of corpses.

Starr narrowed her eyes. 'Why?'

'Because, my dear,' he said with a wink, 'as you so boldly declared yourself, you are of my blood, my descendant. What is family for if not to clean up these little messes? And also because we can't have the local authorities catching on to the existence of zombies, or other supernatural beings.'

'Supernatural beings like yourself?' Starr asked.

'Indeed,' he said. 'I do not wish the local authorities to catch wind of my existence. That's why I disposed of the last lot of corpses you left littered across the parish like so much, how do you say these days, *roadkill*.'

Joel forced himself to speak. He needed an answer to what he'd seen in his vision of the priest that had led to their plan for the theater. Royal and T.J., wide-eyed and motionless, and the demon priest shrieking with glee over their dead bodies.

'Err, Mr. Vampire, why is the priest, err, Père Cassamir, after Royal and T.J.?'

His voice came out thin and cracked. Mister Vampire? Good. Lord. How embarrassing!

'Ah, *un visionaire*,' the vampire said, looking Joel over. 'The reason we are all here. Your arrival has set many things in motion.'

'What things?' Joel asked.

'Oh, for one, you have awoken the *Blood Royale*, which is powerful in its own right, but when ignited by first love, that most fundamental of powers, it becomes exponentially more magical.'

'The Blood Royale?' Joel's throat tightened. Was it true? 'What's that got to do with Royal and T.J.?' he asked, already suspecting the answer.

The vampire smirked, as if he knew something that Joel should have worked out by now.

'These two,' he said, gesturing with his pale hand towards Royal and T.J. 'They are distant cousins. And they are the last male descendants of Louis Phillipe, the last king of France.'

'The two princes,' Starr said, 'from the tarot reading.'

'Exactly,' Sebastian crowed, smiling proudly at Starr. 'They carry the Blood Royale, which the demon priest seeks to free himself, and does not want used against him, and which Joel has made much more magically powerful by seducing these two princes into loving him.'

'Seducing! I did not … seduce … both … never!' Joel fumed. The words "love triangle" flashed gaudily in his mind, as if that were the most important thing the vampire had said, and not that Royal and T.J. had magical blood that could be used to defeat the demon priest.

'I could watch you bluster all night,' Sebastian said, 'it's terribly amusing, but you have made rather a mess here which I need to clean up before dawn.' He sashayed down the aisle, toward the largest pile of zombie corpses, but paused beside T.J. He trailed a pale finger along T.J.'s collarbone. T.J.'s whole body tensed. 'I can smell the heartbreak on you,' he said, sniffing T.J.'s skin and glancing at Joel. 'Such a shame, you are such a beautiful young man. I like a fellow who can fight and flirt in equal measure. I would not have discarded you so callously.'

T.J. turned his head away from Sebastian's piercing gaze, and accidentally locked eyes with Joel. He looked away almost immediately, fixing his gaze on the dusty chandelier hanging overhead instead. Sebastian saw all this and chuckled knowingly, then walked toward the pile of corpses. Joel took that as his cue to lead his friends out of the theater.

*** ***

Outside, the sky was just beginning to lighten. Dawn was just a couple of hours away. They stood in a loose circle on the cracked pavement. No one spoke for a long time. Eventually, Royal pulled out the keys to his new car, which was parked on the square like a gorgeous red sculpture. 'Let's go,' he said without looking at Joel. 'I promised Starr a lift back.' T.J. waved goodbye and headed towards his dirt bike parked on the corner. Tashi hugged everyone and then crossed the square to her place. Starr slid into the back seat of Royal's new car and Joel got into the front passenger seat. The new car smell was a big change to the smell of dust, mold, and rotting corpses in the theater. Joel breathed it in.

Royal didn't look at him the whole ride back to school; his jaw clenched, knuckles white on the steering wheel. The tension in the car was heavier than the fog outside. Once they'd crossed the little bridge that marked the magical boundary surrounding Acadia Academy, Royal pulled over without a word.

'Thanks for the ride,' Starr said, hopping out.

Joel hesitated. 'Royal—'

'Good night, Joel.'

Joel knew when to give up. He got out and watched as Royal steered the car toward the student parking lot and disappeared. Starr walked with him in silence through the field toward Oakshade Cottage. The first dawn birdsong drifted from the trees, bright and out of placc.

'You okay?' she asked.

Joel shrugged. 'Not really. I don't think I can patch this up with Royal. It's so unfair, it's like what happened to me back home, all the gossip and stuff.'

Starr bumped his shoulder gently. 'Give it time. Boys are like zombies sometimes. Hard to read, always groaning.'

Joel smiled despite himself. Then he saw it. Over the trees, curling dark and thick against the pre-dawn sky, like swirling black clouds.

'Smoke,' he said, pointing.

Starr turned to look where he'd gestured. Somewhere deep in the swamp the smoke billowed, and the light of flames glowed in the gaps between the trees. A huge bonfire on the banks of the bayou.

'He's burning the bodies,' Starr said. 'Sebastian.'

Joel nodded slowly. 'Yeah.'

'I don't know how to feel about him,' Starr said. 'He helped us, and he's my ancestor, but, he *is* a vampire.'

'A dirty, flirty vampire,' Joel said, thinking of how Sebastian had acted toward T.J.

'Yeah, he was very flirty with T.J.' Starr said. 'You're not jealous, are you?'

'Absolutely, totally, and completely not,' Joel said. He'd never been surer of anything in his life. He didn't have those feelings for T.J. He only had them for Royal. And that was the cruel irony of it all.

They stood there a long while, watching the smoke rise. Neither said anything, both were lost in their thoughts. When the sun finally began to rise, Starr hooked her arm in Joel's and they wandered back toward home in silence.

Joel's mind was on a lot of things. On Royal and the injustice of being falsely accused of sleeping with T.J. On the zombies and Starr's vampire relative. And on what had happened with the sprinklers in the theater – how he had closed his eyes and wished with all his might that the sprinklers would work and then they had. Had he made the sprinklers work just by wishing it? He remembered the strange electrical feeling that had pulsed over his body and shivered again. Whatever had happened, he decided not to think about it. Too much weird stuff was going on in his life. He didn't need yet another thing to worry about. He held onto Starr a little tighter and felt so glad that he had a friends like her and Tashi. Friendship was a normal, wonderful thing. He needed less of the paranormal stuff and more of the normal wonderful things right now.

THUNDER AND LIGHTNING AND HAIL

The walk into Acadiaville was even longer than Joel remembered. Maybe it was the heavy clouds bruising the sky that made everything feel slower, thicker, like he was wading through invisible molasses. He was on his way to do some Christmas shopping. Aunt Penn deserved a Christmas present that wasn't made of macaroni and glitter, and he was determined to find something good in one of the artsy stores on the town square. She'd been the one steady thing in his life for a while now, and he wanted her to have something special. He was especially grateful for her after all the blood and gore of the fight at the Sphinx Theater the week before. Somehow family and normal things mattered more after you'd been in a battle with a horde of zombie cheerleaders.

He kicked at a loose stone on the road, sending it skittering into the swamp that bordered both sides of the road, and winced. His muscles were still sore after the strenuous "exercise" in the theater. Joel chuckled to himself. Some people did Zumba. Joel and his friends did zombie-boxing. The wind tugged at his jacket, and the first low rumble of thunder vibrated through the swamp Cyprus trees. Joel glanced over his shoulder at the horizon. The clouds back there were darker than slate, greenish, roiling and heading steadily in his direction.

Joel picked up his pace, his Chuck Taylors crunching in the gravel, but he was still half a mile out from town when he reached the old Acadiaville Diner. The diner had been abandoned for decades, sitting hunched at the edge of town like a shipwreck stranded on a dry sea. Its windows were filmed with grime, its silver trim rusted and peeling like old skin. The awning that covered two rusty old gas pumps was on a bit of a lean and had clumps of Spanish moss dangling from its corners.

Joel hesitated, adjusting his backpack on his shoulder. Back toward school he could see the rain already falling, a dark gray curtain sweeping across the fields, racing toward him. He bit his lip, weighing his options. Try to outrun it? Or take shelter? A cold drop struck the back of his neck, sending an icy shiver down his spine. Another plopped on his forehead. Decision made.

He jogged up to the diner's door and gave it a shove. It creaked open just enough for him to slip inside. Joel pulled the door shut behind him and leaned against it, breathing in the thick, musty air. It smelled of old grease, dust, and something faintly yeasty, maybe mold. As soon as Joel's eyes adjusted to the dark interior of the diner, he saw that he wasn't alone.

A pretty young woman, in her early twenties, was in there with him. Dressed in a waitress uniform, she was slowly moving from table to table, wiping them over with a cloth, and neatly re-arranging bottles of long-rotten ketchup and mustard. Her long hair was in a pony-tail, tied with a ribbon in a delicate bow. So delicate that Joel could see right through it. In fact, he could see straight through the waitress to the grime smeared wall behind her. Another ghost. She didn't look up at Joel at all, her mind was on her task. Once she'd wiped down all the tables, she stared out the window for a few moments, looking lost and lonely, and then went back to the tables and started wiping them all over again. Joel felt so sad that this was the poor woman's existence, doomed to the eternal task of wiping down tables in a greasy diner forever.

The rain outside began to hammer down in earnest, drumming a furious tattoo against the metal roof. Joel pulled his hood up and moved deeper into the diner, sidestepping the ghost waitress and a puddle of water that had leaked in through the broken windows. He peered out through a shattered pane. A few sharp taps sounded, something falling on the roof, and then a small hailstone shattered on the ground outside. Then another. Joel flinched as one ricocheted off the ground and hit the window with a thwack. The waitress didn't even notice.

A low engine growl cut through the noise of the storm. Joel stiffened, heart leaping into his throat. Out of the curtain of rain came a cherry-red Mustang. It slid under the diner's battered awning, its headlights slicing through the downpour. Joel stiffened, his heart leaping into his throat.

'Please, not him,' Joel muttered, ducking instinctively behind the counter. But of course it would have to be him. How many red Mustangs could there be in Acadiaville?

He dared a glance over the dusty counter top. His stomach twisted into a sick knot. Royal stepped out of his car, looking hot as usual in a black duffel coat, dark blue jeans, and that easy confidence he carried like a second skin. Joel crouched lower, heart hammering against his ribs. What was it with storms throwing him and Royal together? Why was Mother Nature being such a total hassle?

He remembered the tarot reading – the priestess card that meant that Mother Nature was playing match-maker, pushing Joel and one of the princes together. The prince Joel was meant to be with. He scoffed. Even a supernatural match-maker wasn't going to get Royal to forgive Joel. Not that Joel had done anything wrong. Sleepwalking in your flamingo-print boxers was not a crime. Joel was the one who'd been wronged, who everyone was gossiping about.

The hail intensified, drumming loudly against the diner's battered shell. The door banged open and Royal stomped inside, shaking rain from his jacket so vigorously it unsettled the dust. A particularly large hail stone shattered one of the side windows, sending shards of glass scattering across the floor. Joel yelped and crouched lower behind the counter. He could hear Royal moving cautiously forward, his sneakers squeaking against the wet floor. A moment later his handsome face peered over the counter and spotted Joel.

'Joel?' His voice was low, and cold.

Joel squeezed his eyes shut for a second, willing himself to become invisible. When that didn't work, he stood up slowly, trying not to look as pathetic as he felt.

'Hey,' he said, voice cracking slightly.

Royal raised an eyebrow, crossing his arms. The storm raged louder, the walls trembling under the assault of hail and wind. Royal glanced toward the broken windows, then back at Joel.

'You taking shelter from the hail, or hiding from me?'

Joel flushed to the roots of his hair. 'I ... I didn't know it was you.'

Royal didn't believe him for a second. Thunder boomed, shaking the windows. A hail stone broke through a second window. Joel crouched back down for shelter. Without another word, Royal vaulted over the counter and slid down to hunker opposite Joel as the storm shrieked around them.

They sat there in an awkward silence, the only sounds the cacophony of the storm and the pounding of Joel's heart. Joel fiddled with the frayed edge of his sleeve, stealing glances at Royal from the corner of his eye. The tension between them was thick enough to chew.

Finally, Joel swallowed hard and said, 'About ... about what people are saying.'

Royal didn't look at him. He just kept his eyes fixed on the far wall, his jaw working like he was grinding down words he didn't want to say.

'About me and T.J., I mean. It's not true. We went on one date. One. And we didn't ... we didn't sleep together.'

Royal stared straight ahead, hands clenched into fists on his knees. 'The whole of Rosedawn House saw you, Joel. Saw the two of you.'

'No, they didn't ... well, they did, but they didn't see what they thought they saw! I was sleepwalking ... and T.J. was, was just there ... planting jars! And then I woke up and everyone was gawking and gawking ... and I ... I ... flamingo underwear!'

Royal's eyebrows twisted into a frown. Joel couldn't tell if he was getting angry or just processing the nonsensical stuff Joel had said. After a long minute his brows unknotted.

'Twice you've hurt me. Why should I believe you?' he asked.

Joel winced, the words slicing deeper than he expected. 'I know I've screwed up. Maybe you have every reason not to believe me. But I'm telling the truth, I swear.'

Royal closed his eyes for a second, then opened them again, blinking hard like he was clearing away a thought he didn't want to have. Joel could see it, the part of Royal that wanted to believe him, that was fighting the hurt and the doubt lodged deep in his chest.

Outside, the hail slowed, then tapered off into a soft, misty rain. The worst of the storm had passed, but Joel wasn't sure the same could be said of the storm between them. Royal let out a slow breath and stood up, brushing dust off the seat of his jeans.

'Come on,' he said gruffly. 'I'll drive you the rest of the way into town.'

Joel blinked up at him. 'You don't have to—'

Royal was already walking toward the door. 'I know.'

Joel followed, stopping briefly at one of the tables where the waitress was re-arranging a broken ketchup bottle. He stood right in front of her, so that she'd see him. She looked up at him, surprised that someone else was there with her, and Joel deliberately looked into her eyes. A feeling of sorrow passed over him, and then the waitress faded into the shadows, dissolving like a lump of sugar dropped into warm water. Just like the black man in the swamp, the boy by the bridge, and the old boatman. Joel hoped this meant she was finally free.

Royal and Joel climbed into the Mustang, the leather seats slick and cold from the damp air. Joel didn't say anything about the waitress. He wasn't ready to share his ghost-seeing ability with Royal yet. He pressed his damp hands between his knees, sneaking glances at Royal as they drove into town. The windshield wipers made a kind of rhythmic song that kept Joel focused and calm, while the headlights cast ghostly reflections off the rain-slick streets.

Joel wanted to say something, anything, to fix the aching distance between them, but the words that would fix this situation just wouldn't come. Maybe some things couldn't be fixed with words? When Royal pulled up at the curb by the town square, Joel hesitated, hand on the door handle.

'Thanks for the ride,' he said, voice unsure.

Royal shrugged, eyes not meeting his. 'See you around, Joel.'

Joel slid out into the misty air, the door thunking shut behind him. He stood on the wet sidewalk, watching as the Mustang's taillights disappeared in the distance. Christmas lights blinked dully all around him, casting broken reflections in the puddles at Joel's feet. But he barely saw them. He just stood there, heart heavy, unsure if Royal believed him. Unsure where they stood at all.

*** ***

Joel gently placed the wrapped present he'd bought for Aunt Penn in his backpack. He was pretty confident she'd like it. He walked around to Tashi's place, earbuds in, humming along to a synth-heavy 80s playlist. Acadiaville looked like a movie set strung with lights and adorned with garlands. He texted Tashi that he was nearby and she sent back: *Come up. Be warned. It's ... a bit weird.*

Intrigued, Joel opened the door leading up to Tashi's family's apartment and climbed the stairs. When he got to the landing Tashi called out and he followed her voice into the peaceful room with the Buddha statues, where he saw a sight that explained Tashi's text.

Carter Herrera was sitting cross-legged on a bright pink meditation cushion, wearing a "Buddha Is My Homeboy" hoodie and a serene, slightly spaced-out smile. His skin was still pale as uncooked pastry dough and he moved a bit oddly, but he didn't look dead. Not in a scary way, anyway.

'Hey Joel!' Carter said cheerfully, his eyes wide. 'Happy pre-Christmas! Did you know Jesus came back from the dead, and so did I? That means Jesus and I are, like, buds. Zombie buds! Isn't that cool!'

Joel blinked. 'Um, yeah, that's cool, happy pre-Christmas to you too.'

Tashi was beside Carter, smiling warmly at him. 'That's been his topic of interest all morning. I tried to move him on to something else but …' She gestured at Carter helplessly.

'I love thinking about Jesus. I love lots of other things too, lots more things than I used to love,' Carter beamed. 'Tashi says I'm like a flower. Like, being a zombie peeled away my outer layers and now my real self can bloom. Isn't that beautiful?'

'I was trying to explain why Carter's whole personality has changed. That was the one bit he remembered,' Tashi said.

'My remembering gets stuck sometimes,' Carter said. 'Makes school hard.'

'Wait,' Joel started, 'how are you here, Carter? How'd you cross the bridge from school?'

He pulled a gris-gris bag out from under his shirt. 'T.J. put some things in this for me. It means I can cross the bridge, and cross the magic boundary around the school. T.J. is very nice, and pretty handsome. It's a shame you broke his heart.'

'Carter!' Tashi exclaimed.

'It's okay,' Joel said, because it was true. It *was* a shame that Joel had broken T.J's heart. Joel regretted it deeply. He sat down on the nearest cushion. 'So, Carter, you've gone from actor jock to zombie to… Buddhist flower child?'

'Exactly!' Carter said. 'I feel … peaceful. Like, soft. Like I don't need to prove anything anymore. It's like I can finally breathe. Even though I don't *technically* need to breathe.'

'He's become very interested in everything I'm into,' Tashi said, a little flustered. 'Which is flattering, I guess. But also strange. Because he used to act like I was invisible. Now he wants to talk about the Four Noble Truths and his attachment issues.'

'I'm working through my karma,' Carter added solemnly.

Joel suppressed a laugh, not wanting to hurt Carter's zombie feelings. 'You guys … are so great.'

'Want to join our meditation session?' Tashi offered. 'Carter was just learning calm abiding. I think he's ready to level up from just *abiding* to, you know, *calmly* abiding.'

Joel hesitated, then nodded. 'Honestly, I could use some calm. My brain's been running like a raccoon on Red Bull.'

'Great,' said Tashi. 'So, calm abiding, or Shiné in Tibetan, is a basic Buddhist meditation where you rest your attention on the breath. No big deal if your mind wanders. Just notice, and bring it back gently. No judgment. It's like training a puppy, you have to be gentle and kind, you can't get cranky at a cute little puppy. Our minds are like puppies, all over the place but not to blame, because they haven't been trained yet.'

Carter nodded like a solemn monk. 'Tashi says the goal is to get less tangled in thoughts. I think that's like becoming as still as an alpine lake.'

Joel thought that sounded very appealing. 'Sounds great, Carter,' he said.

'Since I died and came back with *feelings,* I'm really good at saying things,' Carter said, not at all ironically.

'Okay,' Tashi said, 'close your eyes and gently pay attention to your breathing.'

Joel closed his eyes and tried to focus on the rhythm of his breath. In, out. In, out. He let himself soften around the edges, let go of the urge to fix or do or understand. The warmth of the room, the scent of the incense, and the strange safety of being with people who didn't mind that he was weird or scared or complicated helped him to settle and relax. It all worked better than he expected. Five minutes passed in relative peace. Then Carter sighed, deeply and dramatically. 'Am I enlightened yet?' he asked, not at all ironically.

Tashi snorted. 'Not quite.'

Carter groaned. 'This enlightenment thing is taking *so long!*'

'Try not to get distracted,' Tashi said, trying to keep a straight face. 'Just relax.'

'It's *very* hard to relax,' Carter said, eyes still closed, 'when I can smell Joel's brain from here. Joel has a *very* tasty-smelling brain.'

Joel squeaked and opened his eyes.

'This again with my brain, Carter!'

'Don't worry,' Carter added quickly, 'See?' He pulled the gris-gris from under his hoodie like it was a VIP pass. 'Still wearing it. It's working great.'

'I am very glad of that,' Joel said, still a little squeaky.

They finished the meditation, if not exactly in a state of divine clarity, then at least more relaxed than they started. Tashi stacked the cushions in the corner and turned to Joel.

'Hey, can you take Carter back to school and do a handover with Royal? We're kind of … co-parenting Carter right now, while he adapts to life as a zombie.'

He really didn't want to see Royal again today, and seem like a stalker, but he also knew he couldn't say no. Tashi needed him. Carter needed him.

'Co-parenting?' Joel asked.

'Yeah, I don't know what else to call it. It's a little weird,' Tashi admitted, 'mostly because I have a massive crush on Carter and think he's totally hot. Can you co-parent someone you think is hot?'

'Do you really think I'm hot, Tashi?' Carter asked, perking up.

'Yes,' Tashi said without missing a beat.

Carter lit up like a Christmas tree. 'Thanks, Tashi! You're so nice! I think you're hot too! Isn't that great, Joel? She thinks I'm hot, I think she's hot, it's perfect!' Then, without warning, he pulled off his hoodie and shirt. 'You wanna touch my pecs, Tashi? Because I *really* wanna touch your boo—'

'Not in front of company, Carter,' Tashi interrupted. 'Remember how I explained that to you?'

'Oh, right, yeah.' Carter said bashfully. 'That's our special private thing.' He started putting his clothes back on again.

'Yes. It is,' Tashi said. '*Very* private.'

Joel wiggled his eyebrows at Tashi and whispered, 'Second base with a hot zombie, you go girl.'

Tashi blushed so that her hair and face were nearly the same shade of pink. 'Shush, you,' she said, 'or I'll heckle you while you're getting your award at the showcase. Now go!' She ushered them toward the door. Joel laughed all the way down the stairs. He laughed even more at the innocent and confused look on Carter's face.

*** ***

The walk back to Acadia Academy was mellow. The sun was low and golden. The air was cold but not biting, and scented with something faintly swampy but also of pine and cypress. Carter walked with a light spring in his step, looking at everything like it was brand new.

'Isn't Spanish moss *beautiful?*' he said, stopping to stroke a drift of moss hanging low in a swamp Cyprus tree. 'It's like, so nice.'

Joel snorted. 'I can't imagine you stopped to stroke the moss before you—' Joel stopped mid-sentence, not wanting to be insensitive.

'Before I died? No, I wouldn't have. I was such a bro.' Carter sighed. 'I'm so sorry. To everyone. For everything.'

Joel shot him a side-eye. 'Even for that time you called me "fainting boy" in front of the swim team?'

'Oh. Yeah. Especially for that. Royal gave me a proper scolding about that. He didn't want anyone to tease you. He's really nice, and also very good looking. It's a shame you broke his heart too.'

Joel stopped in his tracks. Carter smirked at him. He was joking. Great, Joel thought, now I am the butt of jokes from half-turned zombies. They came around a bend and the bridge and the school gates came into view. Royal was leaning against a live-oak just the other side of the bridge, scrolling through his phone, looking annoyingly cool in his duffel coat and jeans.

Joel sighed. 'Guess this is your handover point, Carter. Your other co-parent is here.'

Carter waved. 'Hi, Royal!'

Royal looked up and saw Carter and smiled, then saw Joel and the smile died on his lips. 'Hey, Carter,' he said a bit stiffly.

Clearly no "hey" was coming for Joel. Nothing Joel had said to Royal in the diner had made any difference. Joel sighed and said goodbye to Carter, then crossed the bridge and headed towards Oakshade Cottage with his head down.

THE CHRISTMAS SHOWCASE

Aunt Penn's old white sedan rumbled over the Atchafalaya Basin Bridge like it was held together with duct tape and good intentions. Joel sat in the front passenger seat, Starr and Tashi were in the back, while the trunk rattled with bags full of costumes for the Christmas Showcase.

'Okay, kids,' Penn said, flipping down her sun visor to check her lipstick, 'here's the plan. We'll check in at the Hotel Monteleone, have an early birthday dinner for Joel at the Carousel Bar, and maybe get inspired by the ghosts of famous writers who stayed there.'

'Which writers?' Joel asked.

"Oh, sugarplum, only the best: Ernest Hemingway, William Faulkner, Eudora Welty, Truman Capote, and Anne Rice.'

Joel loved a bunch of them –Truman Capote, Eudora Welty, Anne Rice. But he didn't love being called *sugarplum*.

Starr leaned forward between the seats. 'Truman Capote stayed at the same hotel where we're staying?'

'Lived there part-time,' Penn said. 'Swore he was born in the hotel, but the facts say otherwise. Still, the man had style, and was a literary genius.'

'I just hope they have enough vegetarian options at the restaurant,' Tashi muttered. 'Getting vegetarian food in New Orleans is hard.'

'They have vegetarian options,' Penn said. 'I checked. As if I'd take three avid vegetarians to an all-meat restarant.'

'*Two* avid vegetarians and one avid vegan,' Tashi interjected from the back seat.

'*Two* avid vegetarians and one avid vegan,' Penn echoed. 'I also checked for vegan options, which they have.'

Joel let their chatter fade into the hum of the car, his gaze drifting out the window. The highway stretched ahead like a ribbon unwinding into the winter haze. He found himself thinking of Royal again. How his eyes had burned when he said, *Twice you've hurt me. Why should I believe you?*' That sting hadn't gone away. Joel had explained and apologized by text—a bunch of texts actually, all of which went unanswered—but the distance between them now felt too wide to cross, like the Mississippi in flood. Did Royal hate him? He acted like he did. But sometimes Joel caught him looking; softly, with something like yearning. Maybe it was all in Joel's head. Maybe Royal just looked at everyone like that and Joel had mistaken it for something else. Or maybe, heartbreakingly, Royal *wanted* to forgive him but couldn't yet, or never would.

'Penny for your thoughts?' Penn asked.

Joel shrugged. 'Just wondering if a carousel bar can spin me back in time to fix all my dumb mistakes.'

'The problem with time travel,' Starr said from the backseat, 'is by trying to fix one problem you might cause a bunch of others.'

Tashi chimed in: 'Yeah, you might fix your relationship dramas with Royal and T.J., but cause a nuclear Armageddon.'

'My relationship dramas *are* an Armageddon.'

Penn gave him a glance that said "Oh, you poor thing" and patted him on the knee.

They arrived in New Orleans just as the sun was dipping behind wrought-iron balconies and mistletoe-decked lamp posts. The Hotel Monteleone glowed gold and warm in the twilight, like something out of a Southern Gothic fairytale. Bellhops in red jackets helped unload their bags. Inside, the carousel bar turned slowly under a domed ceiling, its lights twinkling like Christmas stars. They took a table near the rotating bar and ordered drinks. Penn had a Pink Fizz, the girls had Arnold Palmers and Joel had a Shirley Temple. He was just despondent enough not to care what anyone thought about his drink choices. His super-sweet mocktail came with a little paper umbrella. That made him smile.

'To Joel!' Penn toasted. 'For his birthday, and for being the sweetest and most-deserving winner of the *Alice Dunbar Nelson Poetry Prize*!'

Joel blushed. 'Thanks, Aunt Penn. And thanks for the trip. Really.'

'No need for thanks,'' she said, her voice cracking on the last word. She was tearing up. 'I am so proud of you.'

Dinner was delicious and a lot of fun. They ate and talked about Capote, about *In Cold Blood* and *Breakfast at Tiffany's*, and how wild it was that the same person had written both. Then, inevitably, the conversation turned to boys.

'So, Tashi,' Starr said with a wicked smile, 'how's your *boyfriend*?'

Tashi laughed. 'We're not using labels like boyfriend and girlfriend, *yet*. He's doing surprisingly well. We meditate together. He's ... sweet. Which is weird because before he ...' she cast a furtive glance at Penn, ' ... went missing and got, err, that virus, he was kind of a lovable jerk. Now he's just lovable.'

'Now he's just *lovable*?' Starr teased. 'Does that mean you *love* him?'

Tashi blushed but didn't answer.

Joel poked at his dinner. 'Maybe I should get that virus. Sounds like it'd be an improvement for me, real personal growth.'

Penn raised an eyebrow. 'Let's avoid deliberately getting viruses. That sounds decidedly unsafe.'

'And what about you, Joel?' Starr asked. 'What are you going to do about Royal?'

Penn's ears almost twitched as she focused her full attention on Joel while pretending to watch the carousel bar spin.

Joel made a face. 'Wallow in despair. That's about all I can do. He hates me now.'

'He doesn't hate you,' Tashi said. 'He's just ... confused.'

'He doesn't believe me about what happened, and he can't even look at me.'

'You've got to give him time,' Tashi said gently. 'He's a lot more sensitive than he looks. He was really upset when he thought you'd got with T.J.'

'That makes two of us,' Penn said as she sipped her Pink Fizz.

'I just don't know how to feel about it,' Joel said. 'I mean, if he truly liked me, he should believe me, and stick up for me. I'm the one everyone's gossiping about.'

'He wouldn't be upset if he didn't have feelings for you,' Starr added. 'But you're right, he should believe you. But boys are dumb.'

Joel shrugged. He was pretty sure the feelings Royal had for Joel were disgust and loathing. Once they'd all finished their main meals, they decided not to get desert at the Carousel bar. The deserts sounded amazing but Joel felt like a simple ice cream cone. He also wanted to check out a bit of the French Quarter. Tashi did a quick Google search and found an Ice Cream parlor a few blocks down Royal Street from their hotel that had vegan gelato. Because it was his birthday, Aunt Penn agreed to let them go. She handed over their hotel room swipe-card with only a little trepidation. Penn was staying in the Eudora Welty Suite by herself, while Joel and the girls were staying in the two bedroom William Faulkner Suite.

'You've got one hour to go get ice cream. Stay together. Do not talk to any strangers. Go straight there and come straight back again, no deviations off Royal Street. Be back here by nine. Knock on my door to let me know you're back.'

"Yes, Aunt Penn," Joel said, saluting.

The French Quarter at night was alive with music, crowds, fairy lights and garbled Christmas carols. Joel, Starr, and Tashi ambled down Royal Street, peeking into windows and debating what flavour of ice cream or gelato was superior.

'Vegan chocolate gelato is elite,' Tashi declared.

'Yeah,' said Starr, 'but Peanut Butter flavor is just as good.'

Joel was about to vote for Belgian Chocolate when a neon sign in rainbow colors caught his eye. A gay bar. Loud techno music pulsed from inside, and a crowd of people milled about on the pavement. Standing right out front, looking very much like a Calvin Klein model, was T.J., wearing a muscle shirt and jeans, the kind of outfit that said "I lift weights" and "I know you're looking."

'Hey, T.J!' Joel said, surprised.

T.J. turned. His face twitched, like he wasn't sure whether to smile or run. 'Joel … err, hi.'

"Hi T.J!" Starr and Tashi said brightly.

'What are you three doing here?' T.J. asked, looking over his shoulder in a suspicious way.

'It's Joel's birthday tomorrow,' Starr said. 'We just had dinner at the Carousel Bar. And we have our school showcase tomorrow.'

'Cool,' T.J. said. 'Happy birthday, Joel.' He shifted awkwardly.

Joel was about to make a dumb joke about T.J.'s overly snug muscle shirt when he noticed a Band-Aid on his neck, a rainbow-colored Band-Aid. Not one of the ones Starr had used to cover the bite marks Sebastian Allard had made. This was new. Before he could speak, Sebastian himself sauntered up behind T.J. He looked like the perfect twink, beautiful and stylish, wearing black slacks and a white silk shirt unbuttoned just enough to show a teasing amount of chest. His lips curled in a lazy, satisfied smile.

'Sweethearts,' he purred. 'What fun to run into you here.'

His arm slinked around T.J.'s waist. T.J. tensed a little, looking at Joel and the girls, then just leaned into it. Joel's jaw dropped. Tashi's too. Starr straight-up gasped.

Sebastian grinned wider. 'Oh, don't look so shocked. It was inevitable that T.J. here and I became … friends. He is so deliciously open-minded. To find such a warm and welcoming new friend is such a delight, especially after I had spent such a long time out of action.'

'What is going on?' Starr snapped. "I *ordered* you not to hurt any of my friends. That includes T.J.'

Sebastian tutted. 'I haven't hurt him. Quite the opposite, I've opened his eyes. Introduced him to ... new pleasures.'

T.J. gave a weak, slightly embarrassed smile.

Joel's heart twisted. 'T.J., are you okay?'

Sebastian kissed T.J.'s cheek. 'He's divine. Aren't you?'

'Yeah,' T.J. said. 'I guess. Super divine.' He looked at Joel defiantly, as if to say, "This is none of your business."

Joel's temper flared. He glared at Sebastian. 'So, what, you followed T.J. home after we saw you at the theater and you mesmerized him or whatever and compelled him to let you—'

'I have not compelled anyone. In fact, it was T.J. who sought me out.'

Joel's mouth fell open. 'What?' He looked to T.J. for some kind of explanation.

'Not that it's any of your business, Joel, but yeah, I went looking for Sebastian in the graveyard. Ever since that first night at the Davis crypt, I couldn't stop thinking about him.'

'Why?' Joel couldn't believe his ears.

T.J. adopted that cocky attitude that Joel knew all too well. 'Look at him, Joel. You have to admit he's hot as hell.'

Sebastian beamed. Joel was flabbergasted and couldn't speak.

'He's a vampire,' Starr said, and in those three words she'd said everything she needed to.

'And Joel's a psychic, and I'm a voodoo priest, so what? It seems like almost everybody's got something supernatural goin' on.' T.J.'s cockiness had turned stubborn and defiant.

'Yeah, but most of them have a heartbeat,' Tashi said with a scoff.

'He drank from you,' Starr added. 'That first night. It can't be a coincidence that after you were bitten you couldn't stop thinking about him.'

A small flash of understanding crossed T.J.'s face, but he squashed it down. 'I don't have to explain myself to any of you,' he said.

Sebastian gave them a facetious wave and steered T.J. inside the bar before anyone could protest. The bouncer shot the teens a look that said "No minors allowed", and the door shut behind them with a hollow thud.

Starr stood there, fists clenched. 'He's feeding on him. I *know* it.'

'He is,' Joel said. 'There was a fresh Band-Aid on his neck. This is all my fault. It's my fault Sebastian got out of that crypt—'

'Joel,' Tashi interrupted softly, 'none of this is your fault. 'Besides, it looks like T.J. was like, *with* Sebastian. And with him willingly.'

But Joel barely heard her. His vision blurred. The sidewalk swayed. For a second he thought he might faint right there in front of the trio of drag queens sitting in the bar window sipping fruity-looking cocktails.

'This is all my fault,' he moaned again. 'T.J. is getting *vampired* because of me.'

'Not to be pedantic in this high-stakes moment,' Starr said, 'but *vampired* is not a verb.'

Joel's head spun. He staggered and had to steady himself against a lamppost.

'Okay,' Starr said, gripping his arm. 'We're going back to the hotel. Now.'

They didn't get ice cream. They didn't even speak much on the walk back. The streets felt colder, the city less magical. The carousel bar had stopped spinning when they passed it. Joel felt the same, like something had wound down inside him. When they got back to Penn's suite, she opened the door in her over-large kitty night shirt. 'How was the ice cream?'

'It was fine,' Tashi muttered, 'but we're all so tired, we're going straight to bed.'

Penn raised an eyebrow but didn't press. When they got to the Faulkner Suite, Joel collapsed on his bed and stared at the ceiling, his heart still hammering. The showcase was tomorrow. His birthday was tomorrow, and it was promising to be the worst birthday yet. Carter was a zombie. T.J. was allowing himself to be a meal on wheels for the twinkiest vampire who ever walked the night. A demonic priest was out to get Joel and his friends. Royal hated him. And it was all Joel's fault. Starr and Tashi came in and lay down either side of him, to cuddle and try to make him feel better. Starr pulled Martin out of Joel's backpack and tucked him under Joel's arm. He was glad he wasn't alone. But no amount of cuddling would ease his guilt.

*** ***

The Saenger Theater looked like something out of a dream—a dream soaked in velvet and gold leaf and ghost light. Joel had struggled with his guilt over Sebastian getting his fangs into T.J. all day, but had to obey when Aunt Penn ordered him to get ready for the showcase. It was a big night for him after all. They walked to the theater from their hotel, Joel marveling at the architecture and people and noise of the French Quarter. Strains of jazz music seemed to come out of every building.

When they got to the theater on Canal Street, Joel stared up at the glittering marquee, blinking at the twinkle of fairy lights wound around the old façade. The marquee read *The Acadia Academy Christmas Showcase!* People bustled through the broad doors, wrapped in scarves and evening coats. Inside, everything gleamed under the massive, star-speckled ceiling painted like a night sky. Joel felt underdressed in his vintage, blue velvet jacket and black jeans, but Tashi looked like a riot of punk glam in a tartan blazer over a gold mini-dress, and Starr, ever radiant, wore a long black velvet dress she'd sewn herself, with large star-shaped earrings that reflected the lights.

In the grand foyer, the visual arts students had transformed the space into a pop-up art gallery. Joel wandered among the displays: paintings, digital art, sculptures, even a glowing, wall-sized photo collage lit with fairy lights. He paused in front of a brooding portrait of a boy staring at a dark bayou. The luminous almost see-through brushwork reminded him of his dreams, his visions.

Starr noticed Joel's interest. 'It looks like one of your dreams, huh?' she said.

Joel nodded. 'It kinda does.'

The ushers herded them into the theater proper. Joel still couldn't believe how opulent it was; curtains of crimson velvet, gold-trimmed balconies, and an enormous chandelier. They found seats in the fourth row, close enough to see the smudges on the footlights. The lights dimmed.

First up was a one-act play written by Lana beaux and performed by the theater students. The main character was a moody grunge musician, played by Carter, who was grappling with his desire to reinvent himself as a Hollywood star without losing his credibility as a punk rocker.

'Okay, that set is killer,' whispered Starr, clearly thrilled by her own costuming contributions. And they were good. Plaid flannel shirts with beading in paisley patterns, combat boots painted luminous pink, orange and green, leather jackets with biker designs in rhinestones, all perfectly made and sparkling with glam-punk attitude. Joel found himself oddly pulled in by the play. The plot was predictable, sure, but Carter's ghostly performance made sense. It was as if he *was* a washed-up junkie rocker. Being a zombie must give one special insight into that lifestyle.

Tashi leaned in during the third scene and muttered, 'This is surprisingly good, right? For something written by Lana Beaux, I mean'

Joel grinned. 'Yeah. It's eating me up inside. But Carter is amazing.'

Starr elbowed them both. 'Shut up. My costumes are doing amazing work.'

After the final dramatic scene in which Carter died like a champ and the stage lights blacked out, applause filled the theater. The stagehands cleared the set, and Aunt Penn, in her guise as Principal Stacey, stepped up with Miss Dill and another teacher for the awards portion. Joel's name was the first one called. He froze for a second, palms sweating, then began walking stiffly toward the stairs up to the stage. That's when he saw him—in the wings, mostly hidden behind the curtain, but unmistakably Royal, holding a guitar and watching Joel with unreadable eyes. Joel stumbled slightly. Get it together, he told himself. It's just a high school prize. Just walk.

Penn handed him a slim envelope and a certificate with the words *Winner Alice Dunbar Nelson Poetry Prize* in big Gothic font. The applause felt far away. Joel forced a smile, ducked his head, and scurried back to his seat before he dissolved into an anxious, sweaty mess. The music students were already setting up.

The brief set was eclectic. Some moody jazz, a piece with hand percussion and flute, and then a riotous, punk rendition of "Santa Baby", the song originally sung by Eartha Kitt in the 1950s. The whole audience clapped along. Royal was at stage right, playing guitar with an easy grace, his fingers confident and smooth. Joel wasn't surprised that he was a really gifted guitarist. Royal was excellent at everything. He caught Joel's eye again, and this time, something passed between them. Joel couldn't name it. Then came the final number. A music teacher stepped forward and announced that it was a special collaboration, a song based on Joel's poem. Joel's heart stopped. He knew this was coming but hadn't understood how completely anxious it would make him. Things were made even worse when Royal stepped to the mic, his guitar slung low. He adjusted the stand, looked out over the crowd, then down at his guitar. The soft, aching chords began.

'The heart always remembers what the mind tries so hard to forget,' he sang. His voice was low and haunting. Nothing like the clipped, half-joking drawl Joel usually heard from him in the halls or locker room. It was velvet made into a heart-piercing blade. Joel felt his entire body react, his skin coming alive with goosebumps.

> The heart always remembers what the mind tries so hard to forget.
> A glance in the hall like a ghost lost in the light,
> You smiled at someone else, and I vanished from sight.
> I coded my feelings in notebook lines,
> Pressed like wildflowers, all lost to time.

Every word Royal sang made Joel feel like he had been turned inside out, like his heart was outside his chest. When Joel wrote that song, he hadn't imagined it being sung and sounding like that. It was like the voice of his heart was coming out of Royal's mouth.

> Your name is a song I don't dare to hum,
> It echoes too loudly when the day is all done.
> I dream of a love that never began,
> Like rain that never fell or a bird that never sang.
> But truth sits quietly where hope once slept,
> A secret too heavy for all the tears I've wept.
> The heart always remembers what the mind tries so hard to forget.

The song climbed, aching toward something delicious and impossible. Then, during the final line, a repeat of the first, just when Joel thought he couldn't bear to hear any more, Royal's voice cracked. Just a little. But enough. Then he stopped singing. The silence was heavy. Royal looked out over the crowd for one long second, then slowly shook his head.

'I can't sing any more of this,' he said, 'it's gutting me.' He walked off the stage, guitar still in hand. A hush fell. Then the bass player—a wiry girl with electric blue hair—stepped up and picked up the final verse. She sang it differently to Royal, but still beautifully. The song ended with a soft flourish of piano. The applause came slowly. Then all at once. But Joel wasn't clapping. He was already on his feet.

'Where are you going?' Starr hissed, but he didn't answer.

He dashed backstage. He asked a senior tech kid, 'Where's Royal?'

The kid shrugged. 'He just ... left.'

Joel didn't wait. He darted out the backstage door into the cold New Orleans night. Down the street, two blocks away, he spotted a familiar silhouette. Royal, walking fast, guitar case bumping his leg with every step. He was heading toward the streetcar stop. Joel ran.

'Royal!' he shouted. No response.

The streetcar was already pulling up. Joel watched helplessly as Royal stepped on. The car clanged and started away, heading toward the Garden District. Joel stuck his hand in the air, flailing like a madman until a cab skidded to a stop.

'Follow that streetcar!' he yelled, scrambling into the back seat. It felt ridiculous. It felt perfect. They rolled down St. Charles Avenue, past live-oak trees wrapped in Spanish moss and houses lit up with fairy lights. When Royal finally stepped off the streetcar near an old mansion that looked like something out of *Gone with the Wind*, with a jasmine-draped wrought-iron fence, Joel shouted at the driver.

'Stop here!'

He jumped out, barely remembered to throw a few crumpled bills at the driver, and sprinted down the sidewalk. Royal didn't go into the mansion where the streetcar had stopped, but turned down a side street. Joel chased after him, glancing at the street sign as he went so that he could find his way back. First Street. That should be easy enough to remember, Joel thought.

A freezing wind was blowing straight down First Street, hitting Joel full in the face, whipping his hair around. Oh, great, he thought, when I finally catch up to Royal my nose will be red and drippy and my hair will look like a long-haired cat that's been caught in a rain storm. He stopped and stamped his feet in pure tantrum mode. And the wind stopped. The night air was suddenly silent and totally still, but with a hint of an electrical smell.

What. The. Fricken. Heck.

The strange smell sparked a visceral memory of what had happened with the sprinkler system in the Sphinx Theater. How it'd not been working and he'd wished with all his might that it would and then, whoosh, holy water had rained down, accompanied by that same electrical smell. He'd deliberately put that experience out of his mind, but now, standing on the pavement in the Garden District with the night air having apparently gone still at the stomp of his foot, he had to admit there might be something to the idea that he could wish things into being, or make things happen with his mind. A passing car threw him in its headlights and then moved down the street to illuminate Royal as he reached another corner. Joel hurried on, putting the possibility that he could make things happen with his mind aside for now. He had a more important issue to deal with – boy trouble!

Royal strode ahead of him for two whole blocks, then went into the yard of another impressive mansion on the corner of Coliseum Street. He had just mounted its steps when Joel caught up to him.

'Wait!' Joel gasped.

Royal turned, key poised at the door. 'Joel, what are you—'

Joel didn't stop to think. 'I have to explain. Please. Just let me explain.'

Royal's eyes narrowed, but he didn't interrupt. Joel stammered and waved his arms around. He desperately needed to explain, about the rumors and about why he was such a freak, why he was the way he was with guys. The terror he felt when he was alone with a boy he "like" liked.

'Royal, there's something … something about me you need to know. Back home, there was this, this awful thing that happened. This guy, Patrick, who I liked and I thought liked me but, he … he … he did something terrible to me.'

And then Joel explained the awful thing that had nearly broken him. The spiked drink. The pictures spread all over the internet. The gossip. The bullying. Royal's face went from cold and unmoving to pale and horrified. His eyes glistened with sympathy. But still he didn't speak. The thing with T.J. was still standing between them, so Joel did his best to explain that. He told him about the dream with the priest, about how he'd been sleepwalking, and how T.J. had only taken off his shirt to be kind, because Joel was shivering. Then, without taking a breath, Joel charged on and tried to explain his feelings for the guy standing before him – for Royal, his Louisiana prince.

'I told you I like you, like, a hell of a lot, and I meant it but, well, actually … I think I don't just *like* you. I think I *love* you. I think I've always loved you, from that first day when I screamed "alligators" at you in your parents' limousine. And I think, like, nature or voodoo ghosts or something is pushing us together, because we're actually seriously *meant* to be together. And I know you hate me and probably will never forgive me but I just had to say all of that.'

It had taken so long for him to work his feelings out, not the least because of the zombies, vampires, and werewolves and such. Everything that had happened since he'd arrived in Louisiana had been overwhelming and unbelievable and crazy—but magical and wonderful too. He had only truly worked out his feelings when listening to Royal sing his song.

'I wish we'd met when there weren't zombies running all over the place and kidnapping people, and mad priests up to no good. If we could've just had a moment to, like, connect with each other without all that—'

'If you love me,' Royal interrupted, 'then why did you write that poem about T.J.? It's a really beautiful poem, you must love him to write that. Singing that was the most painful thing I've ever done, to be honest. It totally gutted me.'

Joel blinked. Royal thought the poem was about T.J.?

'No!' he shouted. 'That poem is about *you*, stupid!'

'About me?'

'Yes, about you, stupid!'

'Stop calling me stupid!'

'Sorry I didn't mean to—'

Before Joel could say any more, explain any further, he had arms around him. Royal's strong arms held him firmly but also carefully, gently. Joel thought of the first time those arms had held him that way, when Royal had carried him to the boy's dorm after he'd fainted. He felt the same rush of helplessness now, but this time the wave of emotion that hit him was not scary but thrilling, though it still left him as limp as it had that first time.

He leaned into that feeling, and the memory of that embarrassing first day faded to nothing, replaced by the intensity of this new moment. Royal held Joel still and leaned down to kiss him. He asked for permission with his eyes. Joel nodded his consent. Their lips met suddenly, so softly at first, then more urgently. The delight of it made Joel dizzy; a delicious light-headedness. He clung to Royal's arms, fearful of falling. The kiss was sending tremors through his whole body, lighting up nerve endings Joel didn't know he had. It was as if a fire had been lit inside him.

He was kissing his Louisiana prince with his whole being. It's what he'd hoped for – for so, so long. His first kiss with a boy. His first kiss ever. His first kiss with the guy who had so completely stolen his heart from the first moment they'd met, on that dusty road in the middle of the swamp. His heart swelled. He felt so completely alive and so completely happy.

SNOWFALL AND OMEN SONG

Royal took Joel by the hand and led him over to a porch swing. They sat down and started swinging to and fro. The air had the scent of the coming of snow. Joel knew snow was rare in New Orleans, so decided that might just be how New Orleans smells at Christmas time.

'It's probably way too early for this talk,' Royal said, 'but with all the ups and downs we've had this year, I think we need to define things.'

'Define things?'

'Yeah, define our relationship.'

'Oh, right,' Joel said, nervous all of a sudden though he didn't know why. 'Sure.'

'I told you already I'm not into hookups. If it's cool with you, I'd prefer that you didn't hook up with anyone else either.'

The idea that Joel had the confidence to hook up with anyone, or that anyone would be interested in him, was crazy to Joel. Then he remembered T.J., who had liked Joel a lot. The gut-wrenching guilt that Joel felt about T.J. being fed on by that crypt-creeper Sebastian rose in full force. As it did every time he thought about T.J. now. He pushed that aside and focused on Royal. This talk about hookups must be about T.J., about their date, and Royal thinking there might be something between them.

'Yes, that is good,' Joel said, realizing immediately that he hadn't used the right words. 'I mean,' he explained, 'I don't want to hook up with anyone else, and won't, not ever, not with anyone.'

Royal visibly relaxed. 'Great,' he said. 'And we know how we feel about each other so should we, err … put a label on it—'

Joel interrupted. 'Actually, you know how I feel, because I told you just now, but I don't know for sure how you feel. You didn't say anything back.'

'Sure I did.'

'No, you didn't,' Joel said. 'I think I'd remember it.'

'I did,' Royal said. 'I told you I loved you, like this …'

He leaned in and kissed Joel again, sending those tremors through his whole body once more, tingling along nerve endings in waves of bliss. Joel went as weak as jelly. He was so wobbly he nearly slid out of the porch swing.

'Oh,' Joel stuttered, 'is that what that means?'

'Yes, that's what that means.'

'It wouldn't hurt you to use your words though,' Joel said, smirking.

'Okay, sure. I love you, Joel River.'

The words sent a shiver of delight through Joel's brain and pulsed all the way down his limbs to his fingers and toes. Every inch of his skin erupted in goosebumps. Completely disarmed he said:

'I love the way your voice works on my body.'

'And I love your body, Joel River.'

Joel's body responded to that statement by tingling all over.

'Now, about the label thing?' Royal said.

'Label?'

'Yeah, like … boyfriends. Should we define our relationship as a boyfriend thing?'

Joel's heart did a happy somersault. 'Yes, absolutely! Let's do that!'

Royal beamed. 'Great, that's a huge relief, to be honest. So, to put it in legal-type language, we are exclusive boyfriends, like dating each other exclusively.'

'I accept those terms,' Joel said. 'Do I need to sign a contract or anything to make it official?' Joel *really* wanted to make it official.

'A verbal agreement is sufficient,' Royal said, smiling.

Joel leaned into Royal's warm body and drank up the heat. He nestled there a while, happy beyond words. He was settled enough now to notice his surroundings. The air was sharp with wood smoke, and there was a hush all around, velvety and reverent. The shadowed porch looked out over a beautiful garden. Moonlight spilled over two tall crepe myrtles either side of a paved path, and in an out of the way corner of the yard a bare wisteria vine clung to a small wrought-iron gazebo, which looked more like a very big birdcage than a proper gazebo. The neighborhood was hushed but luminous, bathed in the soft glow of streetlights that illuminated the row of trees that lined each side of the street.

A faint movement in the garden caught his eye. In the shadow of the little iron gazebo were two moon-silver eyes. Joel peered in that direction without letting on to Royal that he'd seen something. A car went by and in the passing glare of its headlights a face was revealed. A young girl, perhaps thirteen years old, her hair in Shirley Temple curls. The white of her dress sparkled for a moment in the light, and then went dim again once the car had passed by. Joel thought she looked like a child from an old painting he once saw in a thrift shop; a little girl of the old South before the Civil War. Her dress had a full, hooped skirt, and its collar was elaborate lace. She was staring intently at the house, or perhaps at Royal. She didn't appear to see Joel, or was choosing not to acknowledge his presence. He kept watching her, wanting to help her "move on", but she never even glanced in his direction, so he turned his attention back to Royal, snuggling into his chest.

Long minutes later, when Joel looked back towards the gazebo, the girl was gone. He looked around, but couldn't find her. He did however notice the house for the first time. It stood taller than all the houses around it and was really a mansion, not a simple house. Joel had done a bit of reading about New Orleans architecture in prep for this trip, so he knew this was an Italianate house of stuccoed brick, probably built around the 1860s. It had a two-story cast-iron gallery, or veranda, across the whole front of the house, and smaller, romantic-looking Juliette-style galleries on each side. Joel thought it was truly beautiful.

'Royal, are you, like, really, really rich?'

'My parents are rich. I only have $139 in my account.'

'That's 109 more dollars than I have. I'm just a poor human boy. A very poor human boy.'

'That's so cute,' Royal said.

'You did not just say that my being poor was cute?'

'Oh, I did, sorry. In my defense, I think everything about you is cute.' He leaned in again and kissed Joel until his mind went blank and he forgot what they'd been talking about, and even where he was. He was brought back to reality by his phone beeping; once, twice, three times in quick succession. Beep, beep, beep.

Joel came up for air and checked his phone. One text from Tashi and two from Starr.

Form Tashi: *Where are you? The showcase is over now!*

From Starr: *Joel, where did you go? The show is over.* And then: *Any minute now your aunt is going to realize you're not here!*

'Shit,' Joel said. 'I'm in big trouble if I don't get back to the theater right now.'

'There's no point going back to the theater now. Just text your aunt, tell her you're with me and that I'm driving you back to your hotel.'

'She will *murder* me, like literally not figuratively, murder me.'

'Tell her I was really upset and ran out of the theater and you chased after me to make sure I was okay. All technically true. Just leave all the kissing out of it.'

'Okay, but you're probably about to be a widower, or whatever they call people whose brand new boyfriends have just been murdered by their aunts.'

'Let's just face the music. What else can we do?'

Joel knew Royal was right, but he still hesitated for a long moment before hitting send on the text. He sent it to Penn, Starr and Tashi all at once.

Penn texted back in mere seconds, telling Joel to come back IMMEDIATELY and that he was GROUNDED and that Christmas would be CANCELLED if he didn't get back IMMEDIATELY, and that she was VERY DISAPPOINTED in Joel and, one last time for emphasis, to get back to the hotel IMMEDIATELY. That was three all caps "immediatelys" in one short text. A few seconds later the phone beeped again. Another text from Aunt Penn: *I hope Royal is okay. Tell him thanks for driving you back.* Joel showed Royal the text.

'Tell her I'm fine, and that we're leaving now.'

Royal's cherry-red Mustang was parked in the drive. When Joel slid into the passenger seat this time it felt very different, like he belonged. He could finally enjoy the drive. He glanced one last time towards the gazebo, but it was still empty, no girl. He realized he was getting so used to seeing ghosts that he barely reacted to them anymore. Seeing ghosts had become almost routine. His life was weird.

As Royal pulled the Mustang out onto the street, he put on a song, an 80s track that Joel knew well – Depeche Mode's "Never Let You Down Again". The first lines burst out of the speakers: *I'm taking a ride with my best friend / I hope he never lets me down again*. Joel got the message. He looked at Royal, who was suppressing a smirk.

'Well played, Mr. Dumaine, well played.'

Royal took his hand, and held onto it unless he needed it to steer or change gears. The trip only took a few minutes, and by some miracle Royal found an empty parking space on the street pretty close to the Hotel Monteleone. Joel thought they'd say their goodbyes in the car, but Royal got out and opened the door for Joel like a proper gentleman would for a proper lady, only Joel wasn't a lady, just a human boy with a proper boyfriend.

Finally. Thank. Heavens.

Royal walked him all the way to the hotel, then through the swanky lobby and into the elevator. When they got off on their floor, Joel took the lead, heading straight to Aunt Penn's door. It felt a bit like a death march. He was in a lot of trouble. Penn opened the door after a single knock. Her eyes were vivid, furious. Starr and Tashi lurked behind her, looking anxious on Joel's behalf. Penn opened her mouth to let Joel have it but then saw Royal and stopped.

'Hi, Principal Stacey,' Royal began quickly, 'I'm sorry you were so worried about Joel tonight. I was very upset and ran right out of the theater. Joel came after me to make sure I was okay. And I am, now, thanks to him. Joel is a very good and kind person. He really helped me out tonight. I hope you know that whenever Joel is with me, I'll make sure that he's safe. And you have my word that nothing like this will ever happen again.'

'Well, it better not,' Penn said, the heat in her voice ebbing away.

'I promise it won't,' Royal said.

Wow, Joel thought, Royal is really good with adult humans. Aunts, principals, and parents are all under his sway. Joel couldn't help but beam up at him. Royal smiled back.

'I'll see you at school,' he said, 'after the holidays.' He leaned in and gave Joel a gentle kiss, totally aunt appropriate. His had went involuntarily to rest on Joel's waist, which everyone noticed, especially Joel himself, who felt all wobbly again.

When they pulled apart and Royal was about to leave, Starr pointed to the window with a gasp.

'Look, it's snowing out there,' she said.

Everyone turned to look. Flurries of white powder were falling gently from the sky, bringing with them a soft light and a hushed silence that only came with snowfall. The soft call of a bird sang in Joel's mind.

'It's a sign,' he said. 'A really good omen.'

Royal smiled and gave him a kiss on the cheek. 'See you soon,' he said, and then he was gone.

And the snow was falling. And Joel felt that nothing could ruin this feeling. Not an evil priest, not a twinky vampirc, not a horde of zombies. This feeling was bigger and beyond all of that. He went to the window and pressed his forehead against the glass, to feel the radiance of cold coming from the snow outside. Starr and Tashi joined him there, linking their arms in his. They looked out over the French Quarter, with all its twinkling lights, watching quietly as the snowfall thickened. The street down below was empty, or at least it seemed so until Joel spotted a figure lurking in the shadows of a building opposite. She was so translucent that the swirling snow almost made her invisible. Joel recognized her instantly – the girl from Royal's garden. She was staring up at the window, directly at Joel. They locked eyes. Joel expected a wave of sorrow to pass over him, but nothing happened. The girl just kept staring at him. No, not staring, glaring. She seemed furious, livid. Suddenly, she turned away and walked down the empty street and disappeared into a flurry of snow. Ghosts are weird, Joel thought to himself. He realized then that he still hadn't told Star and Tashi that he could see ghosts. He decided to save it for a special surprise on Christmas morning.

The room spun, and suddenly Joel was in another vivid flashback of Royal holding Joel still and leaning down to kiss him. The memory of that kiss sent tremors through his whole body, lighting up nerve endings Joel didn't know he had. It was as if a fire had been lit inside him. The room spun again and Joel was back in the hotel room with Starr, Tashi and Aunt Penn. He understood, finally, that these flashbacks were part of his gift, his prophetic dreams and his ability to see the future. This was his gift looking backwards to show him something important. Royal was important. Royal was everything.

He cast his eyes out over the beautiful sight of the French Quarter being dusted by heavy snow, and the Mississippi River beyond. The bird in his mind sang even louder now, so joyfully. His whole body relaxed with it. He audibly sighed with delight. Starr and Tashi hugged him tighter, echoing his contentment with their own happy sighs. He leaned into the hug. For the first time in more than a year, since the awful thing happened, Joel felt that he might not be permanently broken after all.

Hey y'all! If you read *Joel River and the Zombie Cheerleaders* and loved it, please consider leaving a review at online places where such things are kept – Amazon, Goodreads, StoryGraph, etcetera. It doesn't have to be a long review, just fabulous. Reviews are a huge help to authors like me for some very real reasons:

1. They boost the book's visibility so new readers can find it.
2. They help bookstores and libraries decide what to stock.
3. They help readers to get a clear picture of what the book is like.

Also, here are three extremely serious (and slightly ridiculous) personal reasons I need your review:

1. Every time someone reviews the book, a new Care Bear is born.
2. I'm powered entirely by validation and black coffee, and guess which one I'm out of?
3. Your review may be the only thing stopping me from rereading my own book for the 50th time while muttering, 'Is this part any good? Is all this hard work worth it?'

Thanks for reading—and reviewing! 📚

ABOUT THE AUTHOR

Ash Manning writes paranormal romance, fantasy, and more to-do lists than could ever reasonably be completed in one mortal lifetime. Fueled by cookies (any kind, no discrimination) and the lingering synthesizer magic of eighties music, Ash spends most days surrounded by cats who refuse to respect personal space and sloths who don't actually live with Ash, but who Ash deeply understands on a SPIRITUAL level.

When not inventing swoon-worthy supernatural heartthrobs or magical realms full of danger and destiny, Ash can be found dancing awkwardly in the kitchen to Culture Club, Joy Division, Human League, Eurythmics, The Cure, Bronski Beat, and even Tears for Fears; all the while pretending that making a list totally counts as getting something done.

Despite the chaotic energy of half-finished notebooks and suspicious cookie crumbs in the keyboard, Ash somehow manages to deliver stories packed with steamy romance, saucy humor, and just enough fantasy to make you question whether that weird noise in the attic might actually be a vampire.

Ash lives in a perfectly haunted little nook of the world, where the cats run the show, the cookies vanish mysteriously, and every full moon is a writing deadline. Probably.

Visit Ash here: ashmanningbooks.com